Duilleog

COPPER PENNY
PUBLISHING

Titles by Donald D. Allan

The New Druids Series

DONALD D. ALLAN

Duilleog

**A New Druids Novel
Volume One**

DUILLEOG: A New Druids Novel, Volume One
Donald D. Allan

All inquiries should be addressed to:

Copper Penny Publishing
E-Mail: donalddallan@gmail.com
Web page: donalddallan.com

National Library of Canada Cataloguing in Publication Data

ISBN-13: 978-0-9947956-1-8

Cover Design — JD&J Book Cover Design. http://www.jdandj.com
Cover Credits — Images and art purchased from http://www.123rf.com/profile_designwest, http://www.123rf.com/profile_1enchik, and http://www.123rf.com/profile_epantha. Use of the triskelion within this novel from http://en.wikipedia.org/wiki/File:Triskel_type_Amfreville.svg. The image is licensed under the Creative Commons Attribution 3.0 Unported license and is attributed to the author Cétautomatix (artéfact), Ec.Domnowall. Part One title page art: http://www.123rf.com/profile_odina222. Part Two Title page art: Copyright: http://www.123rf.com/profile_martm
Map Credit — Stephen Chase

For my loving wife, Marilyn,
And our beautiful children, James and Katherine.

YOU FLY ME TO THE MOON.

Duilleog

A New Druids Novel

Volume One

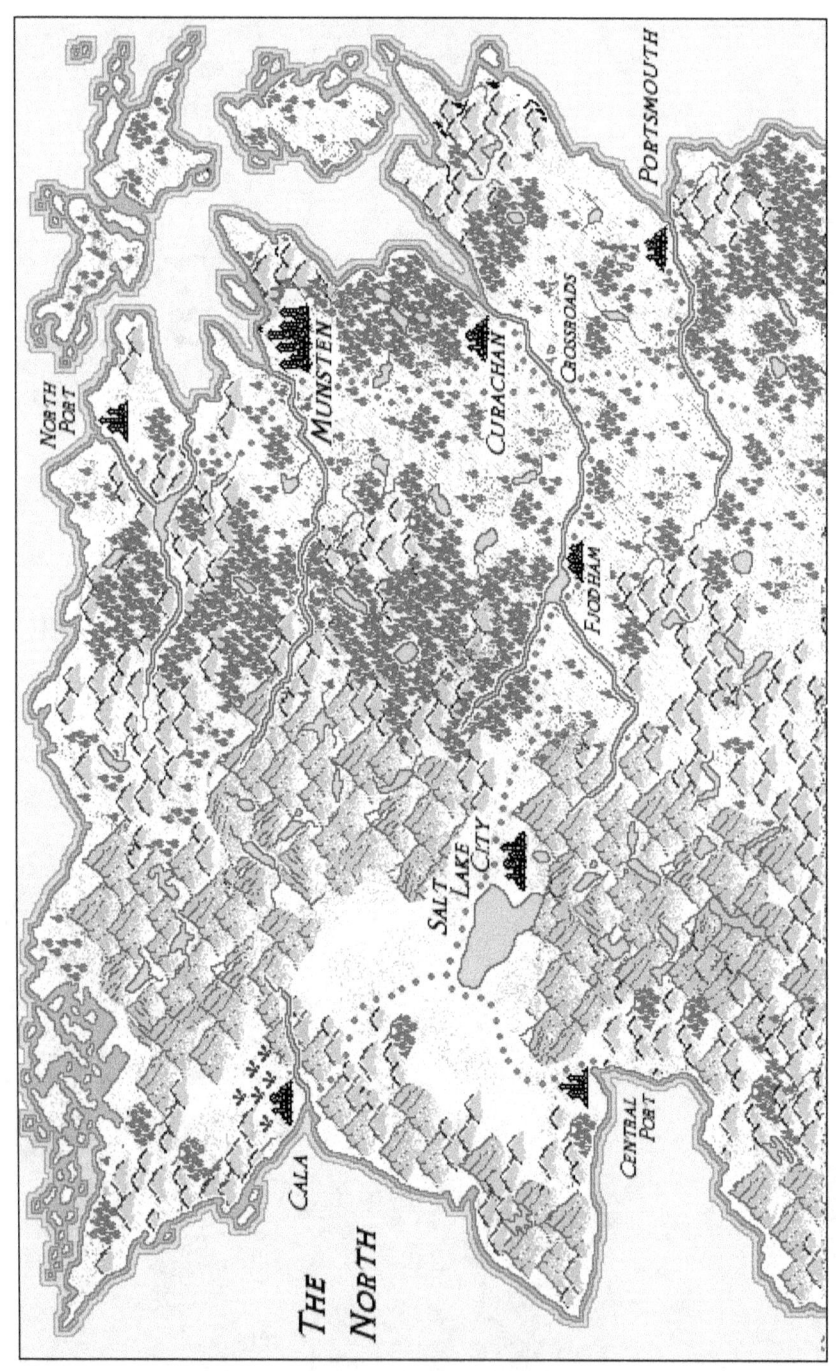

Map of North Belkin: Munsten and Cala Counties

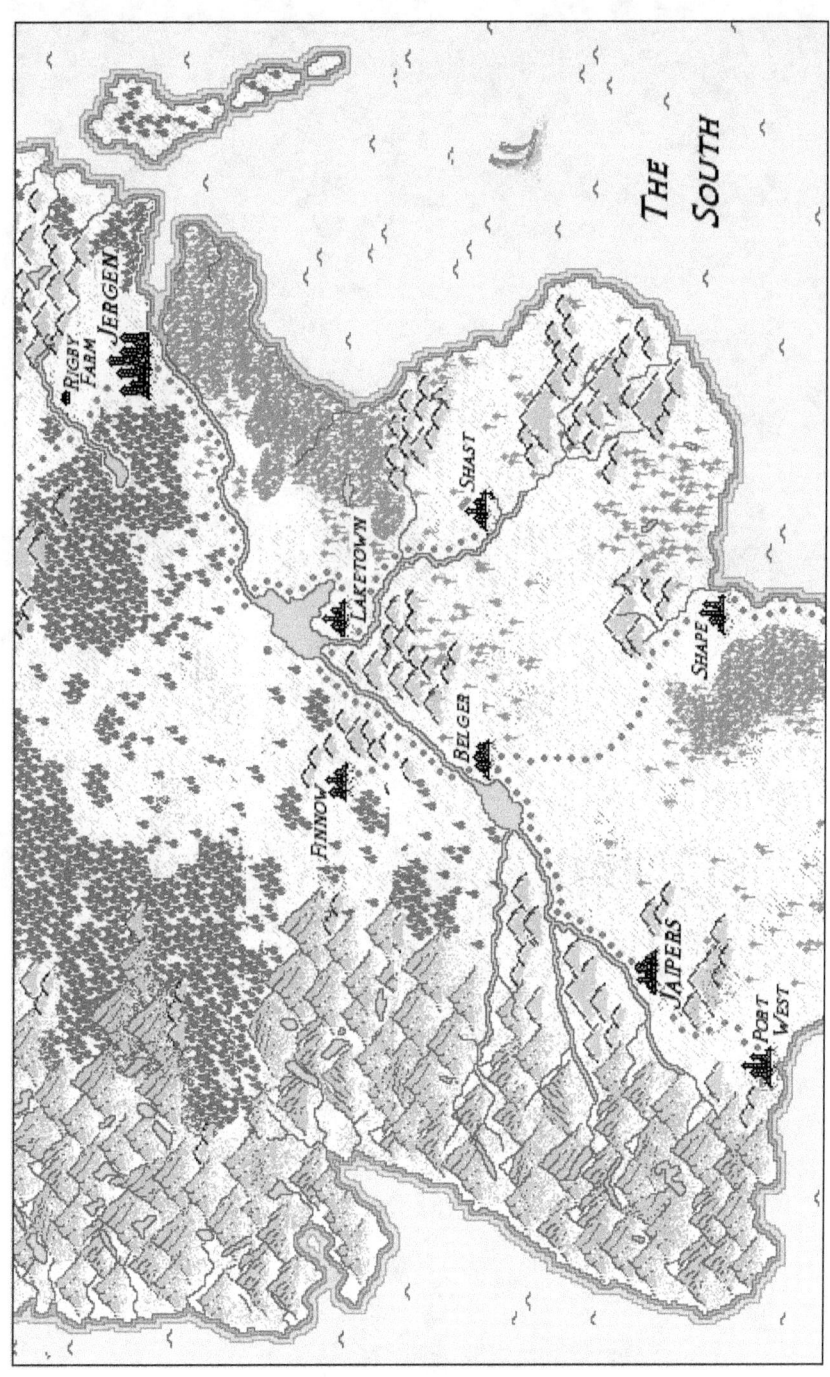

Map of South Belkin: Turgany County

Part One: Beginnings

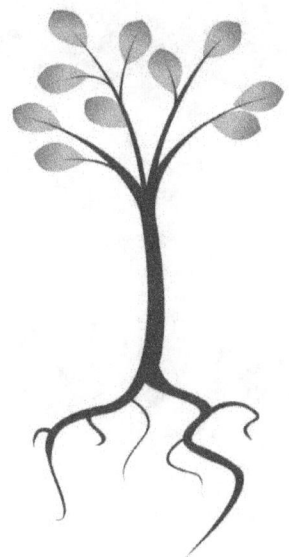

Duilleog

One

South of Jaipers, 900 A.C.

THE HARD, SHARP edge of the iron knife pressed against my neck froze the blood in my veins. I went as still as I could, held my breath and waited to feel the blade slice across my flesh in a fiery line. Every nerve in my body screamed for me to fight and flee but he held me from behind in a vice-like grip I couldn't hope to break. His breath, foul and rotten, washed over me in waves, and I could feel his chest rapidly expanding against my back. I knew he had been running before he snatched me, still asleep, from the ground. He towered over me and his arms held me with a strength beyond my own. Despite my struggles, I knew with a certainty that there was no escape. Time seemed to slow to a crawl.

The man had the fingers of his right hand painfully entwined into my hair, forcing my head back and exposing my throat. As a result, my mouth was forced open and now it was as dry as an old bone. He held me tilted back against him and where he moved; I was forced to follow. The knife in his left hand moved slightly and dragged across my neck and I felt coldness from the blade's caress. Immediately, pain shot through me and I cried out in shock. Panic gripped me.

Here it comes! Not now! I can't die!

My eyes darted over my small camp—still dimly lit against the night by a small fire—to search for anything that could help me. My meagre fire warmed a beaten tin pot suspended by a hook from three branches draped over the flames. The pot contained a soothing tea made from herbs I had gathered the day before as the sun had just started to set. A small, dented and scratched tin drinking mug sat on one of the rocks that surrounded the fire. A couple of feet away, my pack lay next to my sleeping roll, but it contained nothing more than some extra clothing, some food and the herbs I had carefully bundled and sorted in the way I had taught myself over the years. I couldn't forget my other possession; which was the small, sharp and pitted iron knife that was now pressed against my own neck.

I was on foot with rags wrapped around my feet and I wore pieces of crude cloth hand sewn into a functional, patchwork tunic with matching pants I had tied to my waist with a cord. There was nothing that could help me escape and I had nothing I could trade with this man that could purchase my freedom. The cold and fear seeped into my flesh and I shivered uncontrollably. I was ashamed to hear a whimper escape my lips.

My single valued possession was buried in the soft dirt directly under my sleeping roll and I knew this man couldn't possibly have knowledge of it. He could not have seen me with it or using it—I was far too careful for that to have happened. I knew it was safe, at least for now. It was worth more than my life and I would never exchange it. I immediately dismissed it as an option. My mind raced in circles as I tried to figure out what he wanted from me. Here I was: destitute and barely scraping a living from the woods and hills that surrounded the nearby town of Jaipers. I had nothing to offer him for my escape. And so I waited. I waited to feel the knife open my throat from ear to ear. I waited for him to say anything—anything at all—to break the fear and apprehension that mounted within me for every laborious second that passed.

I was quickly losing my efforts not to cry out and I could feel tears streaming freely down my cheeks. My heart pounded painfully in my chest and loud in my ears. I was only sixteen years old and too young to die. It wasn't fair. I rolled my dry tongue in my parched mouth, looking for any moisture that would free my speech and let me reason with him. I felt the knife press deeper in response before I could get a word out.

"Shut yer mouth, boy!" rasped the man in my ear. He whirled around, dragging me with him, to stare out into the darkness that surrounded my camp and I stifled a scream at the sudden movement. I could feel him turning his head above mine to look out into the dark.

With the moon obscured by dense clouds, it was a much darker night than normal. The light from my fire flickered and pulsed unevenly, reaching, at best, a short distance of ten feet into the surrounding area. My meagre camp was centred in a small clearing within a copse of maybe twenty trees. I was not far from the road that led into the town of Jaipers located three miles away to the north. I found the site to be perfect for my gathering needs as the trees and bushes were sufficiently thick enough to hide the light of my fire from the road. A small stream flowed a few yards away and had the clean and cold water from the nearby mountains feeding it. It also contained small brook trout in the deeper shaded spots.

Some of my best herbs were found along the stream's edge where the trees shaded them. I came here often to rest before striking into town to sell or trade my plants at the local open market. Gathering herbs was the one thing I could do well, and it benefited me by allowing me to trade for those items I could not forage or make myself. The town folk knew me by sight and a few knew me by name; at least those who thought to ask. I had regular customers like Dempster, the cook at the town's inn, and my good friend Daukyns. Daukyns was a Wordsmith and led a small congregation in the Word from the town common hall and partnered with me with the salves and unguents I made from my gatherings. Most of the town folk had added my plants to their food or traded for my pots of unguents; especially the healing ones. I had worked the area surrounding the town for close to four years and it was starting to feel like home despite my normal reluctance to be anywhere near other people or confined within the town walls. Food was my usual choice for trade, but once, every few months or so, I would indulge myself and trade for a hot bath at the inn. As needed, I would trade for used cloth or shirts and pants to replace those of mine that were beyond repair. My discarded clothes I would turn into a coarse thread to help make new ones. It was a routine I was happy with and it was better than my life from before.

I preferred the solitary life away from people. I had lived in the woods for a long time now and through trial and error, I had found a way to co-exist with the wilderness. I now felt at peace surrounded by trees, plants and grass. The small animals in the area knew me and seldom ran from my approach. I sensed a deep empathy with the outdoors. I knew where to find my plants and recognised the benefits of plants intuitively. I tended the herbs where they grew and took only what I needed to trade for goods that would keep my scant possessions in good condition and my belly full. One day would blur into another and the seasons would pass as they were meant to pass: without my trying to mark them. The summers were hot and the winters wet and chill. Yet I persevered through the years. I was trim, fit and healthy. I wanted for nothing except peace and solitude.

Yet here I was, at the mercy of this madman. I tried to calm myself so I could think. After a time, I was successful, and I finally took notice of the absolute silence in the air. The crickets and frogs had gone still at the disturbance in their nightly ritual. The clearing and the surrounding area seemed to be holding its breath waiting for something. I sensed a feeling of dread from outside the firelight. It frightened me and added to my distress.

I looked into the darkness and observed that our combined shadow from the fire stretched out and melded with the dark. The night waited in silence and I waited for any sign from this man that could tell me what he wanted. With a grunt, he swung me around to stare across the fire into the dark. My night vision was long since shattered with the light from the fire and I could make out nothing.

"Where are you, you Godless bastard?" he muttered under his breath and I realised with an intake of breath that this man was afraid of someone pursuing him and probably wanted nothing from me. I was merely a convenient hostage, I concluded. With this thought, I felt the first stirring of hope rise within me.

He swung me around again to stare into the night.

His breathing continued hard and fast. The smell of alcohol and stale, stinking sweat were strong in my nostrils and yet I could smell something else above all this. It was a scent that touched the back of my mouth and left a faint metallic taste: the unmistakable smell of blood. My fear doubled. This man had blood on him! A lot of blood or I wouldn't be able to smell it so clearly. He had killed already and could easily do so again.

A twig snapped behind us, startling me with the sharp and loud explosive sound in the silence. The man whirled quickly to face the direction it had come from and somehow managed to press the knife further into my neck. My flesh felt like it would split across the edge of the blade and I would soon see my blood fountain into the night air. I was now having trouble breathing, and I obscurely wondered when I had started to breathe again. I peered into the night through the fire, desperate to see anyone who could help me but, the light was too bright. The flames crackled. A spark shot high into the air and my eyes followed it, wishing I could join it until it disappeared from view.

"Come out into the light so I can see you!" yelled the man, his voice loud and abrasive in my ear. His accent was strange, and I wondered where he was from. More importantly, I was sure I heard a note of fear in his voice and felt a glimmer of hope rise again within me. Someone out there made this man afraid.

We both strained to hear a reply from the darkness but there was none. The silence stretched until my assailant became increasingly agitated.

"I'll open this boy's throat if you don't come out into the light so I can see you!" he yelled again and tightened his painful grip on my hair. My ear was now ringing.

"I don't think you'll do that," came a quiet voice from somewhere beyond the fire. I recognised the voice at once. The voice belonged to the Reeve of Jaipers, a good man called Comlin. He had spoken to me many times in town and had been kind to me. "You wouldn't have anything to hide behind then, now would you? You do realise that you have a young man there who means pretty much nothing to me or anyone else around these parts. I'm not so sure you've thought this out too clearly."

As the magistrate for Jaipers, when I had first entered the town, Comlin had approached me wanting to know where I was from, how long I was staying in the area, and later, once I had traded my wares, where I had learned to gather herbs. He always wanted to know everything he could about me. And I had told him the truth—well, mostly. I hid from him the painful truths—stuff he hadn't needed to know. I wasn't going to open my past up to anyone. I had promised my mother to stay hidden and safe and I hadn't broken that vow. Thankfully, after the initial scrutiny, Comlin had pretty much left me alone but would often stop by to talk to me when I came to town. He would want to know if I had seen anyone suspicious in the area. It was easy to see he took his job of defending the people of Jaipers quite seriously. Unexpectedly, I became his eyes and ears in the area surrounding the town and surprised myself by finding the role exciting in a small way. I enjoyed our arrangement if you could call it that. I also looked forward to seeing him in town and I had long ago noted his genuine concern for my wellbeing.

I was relieved to see him here and now. I trusted this man and knew he would save me; although I honestly knew not how as I stood there in the madman's clutches.

"Blessed Father," muttered my captor. He raised his voice and called out to Comlin.

"Yer nuttin' but a small town Reeve. You've nary an idea wut yer up against. You need to go back to your town and forget all about this. Be smart, not stupid. This boy is only moments away from spilling his blood all over this ground and it will be your fault."

"Well, that's an interesting concept," answered the Reeve in a slow, drawn out way, as if he was thinking it over as he said it. "I should just turn around and walk away while you hold that boy with a knife to his throat? Tell me something why'd you kill Bill and what did you take from his house? Answer me that."

The man growled in frustration.

"That business is my business," answered the man. "He wasn't supposed to come home when he did. This would have been a lot cleaner if he had stayed drinking at the inn. Not my fault and what's done is done. Why do you care about some old man?"

Silence was the only reply from the darkness. I waited, straining to hear anything that would show me where the Reeve stood.

"Bill was a good man," came the soft reply. "You broke into his house to rob him. You killed him and then stole from him while his corpse cooled at your feet."

I heard the regret in the Reeve's voice. Silence followed. Then I heard a soft sound, like something being stretched, and wondered what it could be.

"You come out into the light, you bastard!" hissed the man, his spit spraying into the night air with his rage. "You have no idea what you are messing with. This is bigger than you can imagine."

A sharp thrum filled the air, and I felt, rather than heard, a hard, wet crunching sound explode next to my head. The man went rigid, and I felt him exhale in one long sigh against my cheek. Then he simply crumpled to the ground and his hand, still tangled in my hair, pulled me down with him. I was forced to spin around and bend over to release him, only to find myself staring down at the feathered end of an arrow, plunged deep into his right eye. His remaining eye was half closed and sightless.

The arrow had pierced his head straight through and now the point was forcing his chin to his chest. I reached up and fumbling, freed his hand from my hair. It dropped with a heavy thud to lie limply beside his head in the dirt. I scrambled backwards away from the body and around to the other side of the fire. My eyes remained locked to the still form, waiting for him to rise. The man seemed to writhe on the ground through the flames of the campfire.

I could see that he was dressed in dark leathers and that the front glistened with what appeared to be drying blood. His face was rough and unshaven. His eyebrows were long and thick and shaded his eyes. I kept my eyes locked on the body, looking for any sign of movement as the Reeve emerged behind me into the light, patted my shoulder and approached the body. He carried a short bow in one hand and I could see he carried a small leather quiver across his back with the fletching of his arrows sticking out the top. I had never been happier to see the Reeve Comlin.

He glanced back at me briefly. "You okay, Will?" he asked.

When I nodded, he crouched down beside the body.

My hand crept up to my throat to feel for blood and came away with only a drop or two. I could feel a burning where the knife had scratched me. I was alive and unhurt; I realised with a start and suddenly began shaking. I drew my knees to my chest and tried to stop them from trembling. Suddenly, the warmth of the fire seemed distant, cold and remote.

The Reeve smiled grimly at me and turned his attention to the body. He looked it over quickly and reached out, removing a leather purse that was tucked under the belt tied around the man's waist. He hefted it in his palm and I could hear metal clink. The Reeve untied the purse's drawstring, opened it and spilt the contents into his hand. I watched as his palm filled with a couple of silver groat and several copper pence coins. With a clink, a small red gem landed on top of the pile and the Reeve grunted in surprise.

"Not what I thought," he said.

I opened my mouth to ask him what he meant but my teeth chattered so I clamped my lips shut. He held the gem up to the fire and it flashed in the light. It had an odd shape I couldn't quite make out. He shook his head and poured the coins back into the purse, dropping the gem on top. He cinched the purse closed and tucked it under his own waist belt. "This goes into the town treasury until we can sort out what to do with it." This time the Reeve looked at me, his gaze had a hard edge, as if he was, appraising me.

"You'll be alright, Will," he said. "The shakes will pass. You did good, and you held still and let me take that shot." The Reeve glanced at the arrow protruding from the man's face and shook his head. "I lost that arrow, though, and it was my best one, too."

He grabbed the flight of the arrow and lifted the dead man's head to reach behind it. I heard a loud snap and watched as he held up a steel arrowhead covered in blood and something else that I didn't want to think about.

"This is worth keeping," he muttered and quickly wiped it on a nearby patch of grass. He reached over his shoulder and I watched as the arrowhead disappeared into his quiver with a dull thud. He pried my knife from the dead man's hand, recognised it as my own, and tossed it over to land near my bedroll. I glared at it glinting in the firelight, the handle nothing more than tightly wrapped rags, the steel pitted and stained, and I was no longer sure I trusted my own knife.

The Reeve looked the man up and down and started examining his leathers. He untied the waist belt and then opened the straps that held his tunic closed. The Reeve grimaced at the blood now on his hands. He felt around inside the tunic and extracted a folded piece of parchment, opening it carefully to avoid getting blood on it. His eyes quickly scanned over whatever was on it and then he folded the parchment back up and stuffed it into his own leather tunic. He checked the waist and trousers and then he reached the man's feet, where he wore a pair of black, soft-soled, leather boots. They were laced up with a strange leather strap that wound up around his calves. The Reeve removed them with strong tugs and, once he had them off, he tossed them over the fire to have them land next to me. I glanced at them, confused.

He looked meaningful at my rag-wrapped feet. "Yours. You earned them."

He roughly removed all the man's clothing until he lay naked, and without much dignity, on his back in the dirt. I found my eyes returning to stare at the man's sightless eye. It haunted me. I watched as the Reeve squatted and bundled up the clothes; he tied the trousers legs around them to hold them together.

He stood up and stretched out his back, groaning a bit before he whistled once, softly, into the dark. The sound startled me and I blinked. The Reeve looked down at me and stared for a bit, with an unreadable expression on his face, until I started feeling uncomfortable under his scrutiny.

"I didn't mean it," he said cryptically. I had no idea what he meant, and I just looked blankly back up at him.

He chuckled a bit, and the sound startled me. He shook his head and smiled. "I lied to him to throw him off guard. You do mean something to the people around these parts. You have a gift with those herbs of yours. A rare gift, Will. The town appreciates your skills."

Out of the darkness emerged a large shadow that coalesced into a piebald horse I recognised as the Reeve's. It had responded to the Reeve's whistle. The horse looked down at me and startled me by seeming to duck its head for a moment. I had seen the Reeve with his horse numerous times before in Jaipers. I always had a strong bond with animals and this one was no exception. He was proud to be the Reeve's horse. His dark brown and white patches were distinctive and I could tell that he was well cared for. The horse stood proudly in the firelight and continued to watch me. I forced a smile at him and he finally looked away.

The Reeve walked over to the saddle and removed a hemp rope that hung from the saddle horn. He measured a short length, cut it off and quickly secured the trussed up clothes next to his saddle bag. He returned to the dead body and expertly tied the feet together with one end of the rope and secured the other end to a metal ring hanging from the back of the saddle. The Reeve checked the girdle of the horse and stroked its nose with affection before clucking at it and turning it so it was facing away from the fire and the dead body. I could sense that the horse was dreading what it seemed to know was about to happen and I didn't think it was looking forward to the effort.

The Reeve put his left foot in a stirrup and swung himself up onto the horse with practised ease before he looked back at me. Still sitting on the ground with my arms wrapped around my knees, I now had to crane my neck to look up at him. It hurt, but at least the shaking in my legs had seemed to reduce somewhat.

"Come into town tomorrow," the Reeve said. "I'll want you to make a statement to the garrison officer on what happened out here. I'll arrange for you to get a hot bath at the inn as well. Fair enough?"

I nodded, not sure what else I could say. Time was starting and stopping and then rushing along. Nothing was making much sense. I wasn't at all sure what had just happened.

"These things happen, Will. You'll be fine now," said the Reeve as if reading my mind. "Take some time to work it all out in your head. You're a strong lad and you'll put this behind you. It had nothing to do with you—just remember that."

He clucked at his horse and it started to walk away, then he stopped it with a slight tug on the reins. He looked back at me again. His horse seemed to do the same. This time, staring into its mournful eyes, I was sure the horse was not happy about dragging the body back to Jaipers.

"One more thing, Will, one of the town folk has a high fever and could use your attention. She's not alone; many are sick." He waited until I nodded again.

My mind already started working on the problem. I had collected a few herbs that would knock a high temperature down. It wouldn't take me long to brew up a remedy.

I think the Reeve knew I was already thinking about the problem because a look of satisfaction settled on his face as he gave the horse its head.

The horse slowly started to walk into the darkness and down the deer path that led out of the clearing to the main road. The rope tied to the man slowly lifted from the ground until it hummed taut and unceremoniously, the dead man was pulled across the ground. The remaining shaft of the arrow sticking out the back of the head scraped a shallow furrow into the dirt and marked his passage. Appalled, I watched the head flop from side to side as he was dragged away; his arms trailing behind him until he was out of the light and into the darkness. I knew the image would stay with me forever. I wasn't sure how much of the man would be left by the time he arrived in town. Not much, I imagined and shuddered.

Eventually, the soft noise of the horse's hooves hitting the dirt quietly faded into the night and the sounds of the crickets and frogs returned to fill the air.

I was alone, and I was afraid.

Two

Outside Jaipers, 900 A.C.

FTER A WHILE, the shaking and fear subsided, and I felt I could move again. I had no idea how long I sat there unmoving. My eyes finally drifted over to the small pool of blood that marked where the dead man's head had lain on the ground. The dirt seemed to refuse to absorb it. Next to the blood, I saw something glistening pink and tan and I was horrified. I frantically grabbed handfuls of dirt and from where I sat tossed them over to the spot until, after several attempts, I managed to hide the evidence. Only then did I awkwardly struggle to my feet and start to walk around my camp to work out the aches in my legs formed from remaining still for too long. I rubbed the dried tears from my cheeks.

I found myself pacing around my campfire. I was consumed with anger: anger at the Reeve, at the dead man, at Bill—who I barely knew other than him being the only drunk at the inn with money—and even anger at the whole damn town for letting this happen. I stalked the clearing and tried desperately to find a way to vent my building rage. I kicked dirt over where the blood lay and even ground away the line the arrow had made in the ground as best as I could with my rag-covered feet.

After a time, my anger faded, and I found myself over by the stream scrubbing my hands, face, and neck with wet sand until they hurt. At one point

I started sobbing and I couldn't manage to stop myself and felt foolish the entire time. Then I couldn't get warm and ended up throwing all my gathered wood onto the fire until it roared skyward and I could feel welcomed heat sinking into my bones. I sat, shivering, as close to the fire as I could stand, my skin screaming with the heat. At one point, I'm embarrassed to admit, it occurred to me there might have been more men out there lurking and lying in wait for me, and they would now be drawn to the flames and me. Frightened, I knocked my fire apart in a frenzied haste before sanity returned to me and I managed to rebuild it.

What followed was a long and turbulent night and by morning I was surprised to awake lying in my wraps, on my sleeping roll, next to a burnt out fire. I had no memory of falling asleep or even going to bed. The sun was just clear of the horizon and I heard the birds singing loudly into the morning air as if nothing was wrong in the world. I lay there listening to their songs until my bladder forced me out of my warm wraps. Even in summer, the mornings could be cool in this region and today was no exception.

I relieved myself against a nearby tree and then grabbed my cooking pot and made my way to the stream to fetch water for my morning tea. I splashed my face with water. Now refreshed, I felt somewhat better. The memories of the night's events were starting to fade in intensity. I reached up and fingered the area where the knife had cut me and I was pleased to find the wound closed and almost gone. Sometime during the night, I had calmed down and remembered to apply my healing unguent to the small cut on my neck. My unguent had remarkable healing properties imbued in it through my craft. I rarely had the opportunity to apply it to myself and to be honest; I was proud and enjoyed the results.

I returned to the cold campfire after gathering some fuelwood and after finding some burning coals buried beneath the ash; I blew the fire back to life with some dry grass and kindling. I slowly built the fire back up to a good height that would boil the water in my tin pot in no time. Once bubbles formed in the water, I brought out some dried green tea leaves and added a generous pinch to the water along with a few dried chamomile flowers. I watched the leaves unfold in the water and I leaned over to breathe in the vapours, letting the scent fill me up as I exhaled in contentment. Soon I was sitting cross-legged with my eyes closed next to the fire, relaxing with my cup and trying to find my inner peace. My herbs were simply the best, I had to admit, and I chided myself for not having made this tea last night. I should have known better and I could have avoided the horrible evening lost in my fears.

I rested there for at least an hour, reaching out with my senses to the trees, the stream and the wildlife. They imbued me with their natural peace and serenity, and I embraced the calming effect. I quickly drained the last of the tea in my cup and determined it was probably time to head to town to fulfil my promise to the Reeve. I snorted at the thought—I was already heading to town with my backpack full of herbs when the incident happened. Now I had one more reason to leave the comfort of the woods. I took a last look around at my peaceful camp from where I sat and groaned as I rose to my feet to tear it down.

I washed out my pot and cup at the stream and refilled my water skin. I rolled up my sleeping roll and fastened it below my pack, tucking my pot and cup inside where they belonged. I took the time to gather fresh fuelwood and laid it out under the small shelter I had made for the purpose of keeping it dry until next time I returned. I had similar caches all over the region. I always found it wise to prepare for the future as best as you could and gathering fuelwood was one of the simplest preparations I could make. I hooked my water skin to the outside of the pack and then stood to look around to ensure no one was observing me.

I had discovered over the years it was always prudent to be attentive to your surroundings. *Not that any harm ever came to me.* This thought drew a snort from me as I remembered last night and recognised the lie this belief now was. Still, habits meant I always left my campsite cleared of any signs of recent use. Some signs were unavoidable, such as the remnants of the campfire, but nonetheless, I did the best I could. I was always on my own and relied only on my wits and power of observation to avoid trouble. I finished peering around and seeing no movement in the surrounding area and no one travelling on the nearby road, I simply closed my eyes to listen. After a time, hearing nothing but the wind through the trees and the birds calling to one another, I opened my eyes, certain no one was near.

I moved over to where my sleeping roll had lain the night before and dug up the loose soil where I buried my most prized possession. I soon unearthed my small leather pouch and scooped it up, shook the dirt from it, and then quickly filled in and smoothed over the hole in the ground. As I held the soft leather pouch, I could easily feel my possession. I took the time to tuck the pouch into a small pocket sewn inside the front of my tunic, placed up high near the left shoulder. It was the best hiding spot I could think of to conceal something on my body and felt it was an unlikely place to be searched; I was confident it would remain hidden from prying eyes or fingers. The object inside the pouch was far too important to me, and it was all that remained of my past and my mother.

I hoisted my backpack over one shoulder and glanced at the area where the blood had spilt on the ground and I was pleased to see I could now barely make it out. I gave the area a once over to make sure I left nothing behind and I was startled to see the black boots lying exactly where the Reeve tossed them last night. That they belonged to a dead man filled me with a small measure of revulsion and I simply couldn't bear the thought of wearing them. *Still*, I thought and glanced at my ragged feet and then back at the boots. *Perhaps it wouldn't hurt to try them on and see what it feels like to wear real boots.* I couldn't remember the last time I wore something solid on my feet. *I must have at some point when I was younger.* Images of running through a castle corridor teased my memories and faded just as quickly as they had come.

I slipped my pack off my shoulder, laid it on the ground and sat down next to the boots, grabbing one before I could change my mind. I turned it over in my hands and enjoyed how soft and supple the leather was against my green–stained, rough and calloused hands. The leather was dyed a rich, dark black and showed no wear. It seemed to absorb the light, and I found it hard to examine the boot closely. My eyes refused to stay focused on them and it was disconcerting. I could feel more than see the stitching was doubled, tight and expertly done. The sole was thick and showed no wear on the heel. The boots were meant to reach mid-calf and laced up the front. Strangely, the upper half of the boot held leather straps that wound up over the upper calf. It was an uncommon design, and I only knew how they were worn from having watched the Reeve remove them from the man. Inside the boot opening, I observed a small maker's mark stamped into the leather but knowing nothing of leather marks, I merely ignored it. I stored the detail for later, should I have a chance to inquire about it. I didn't know much about leatherwork but I knew one thing for certain: these boots had cost the owner quite a bit of coin.

My revulsion had faded and was replaced with curiosity. I untied my foot wraps, flipped the top laces out of the way and pulled the boot over my right foot. The boot was only a little large, so I wrapped the leather straps around my upper calf and tied it off, making it snug enough. I enjoyed the wonderful feeling of having leather protecting my foot and scrunched my toes inside. After years of wearing rags on my feet, the feeling of wearing real boots was amazing. *Odd*, I thought, *I had thought the boots a little large for me but they now seemed to fit remarkably well. Goodness, they feel good on my feet.* I eagerly reached out and pulled the other boot on.

Immediately, my big toe struck something inside. I pulled out my foot and peered into the boot but could not see anything. I tipped and shook the boot over an open hand but nothing fell out. I reached in and groped around until I felt the toe part of the foot lining peel back a little and grasped a small round and flat object with my fingers. I extracted my hand and saw with amazement I held a small gold coin. Right away the hairs on the back of my neck stood up, and I shivered despite the warmth of the day. My blood pounded in my ears and for just a moment I grew incredibly dizzy. I closed my eyes and shook my head. The dizziness fled as quickly as it had come. I opened my eyes, and all was normal again.

I looked closely at the coin and right away I could see it wasn't a typical round coin. It was elongated and stretched out like someone had pulled it slightly apart from opposite sides. It was only the size of the pad of one of my thumbs and it was smoothly worn down on one side as if someone had been rubbing it repeatedly for a long time. I turned the coin over and, even slightly distorted, I could make out an embossed symbol that looked like three swirls joined in the middle. I was sure I had never seen this symbol before but it was vaguely familiar somehow. I had never held a gold coin before, nor had I ever seen one this close, but I was sure the coin was made from real gold as it shone with a lustre I had rarely seen and then only from a distance as the richer merchants sold their wares inside their shops.

Once, some months ago, I had seen a rather fat merchant bite a gold coin and so I too bit my coin. It was hard and hurt my teeth. I looked at the coin and couldn't see if I had made a mark and so I wasn't sure if it had passed the test. I didn't care though; the coin felt so wonderful in my hand. It had such a surprising weight for something so small. I held it in my palm and flipped it over and over, staring in wonder. A brief flash of recognition went through me but I shrugged it off as yet another one of my annoying memories that would intrude at odd times.

I hadn't seen many coins in my life, except for the occasional pence, halfpence or farthing in trade for my herbs, but this did not seem to be a recently issued coin. The symbol on the back, for instance, was not on current coins. Older coins typically held the cameo of the king, but those went out of favour after the war when the Lord Protector took over. Today coins bore the country of Belkin's coat-of-arms. So whatever the symbol meant, it must have been from a long time ago; probably from well before the war. I wondered how long it would take to wear down and elongate the coin over repeated rubbing and I was sure it was a long, long time.

I doubted any merchant would accept the coin with it being so deformed, but it was still worth something by weight if I could find a gold buyer. A gold coin of this size was called a mark and was equal to nine silver groats and one groat was worth four copper pence. I had owned two groats once, payment for providing a significant amount of healing unguent to the Jaipers garrison captain last year. I was certain I could exchange this coin for a few groats.

Excitement at my new wealth raced through me. Images of what I could purchase swam before my eyes. I could obtain new clothes and get rid of these rags. My clothes were fine in the summer heat but come winter I would be wet and cold. It would be wonderful to be able to stay dry and warm. Maybe I could bargain for leathers like the Reeve wore. I could get a nice oilskin cloak to keep the rain off—that was a certain purchase. Or a large leather backpack instead of the one I had painstakingly stitched together with scraps of leather and pieces of cloth. I looked forlornly at my poor backpack on the ground and shook my head.

I soon added other items to my imaginary list and my head reeled with the possibilities. Then I imagined the Reeve finding out and looking at me with disappointment and my excitement came crashing down around me. I knew at once I should really return the coin to the Reeve. I would face too many questions if I suddenly showed up with gold in my hands after the murder. It wasn't mine, and people would naturally assume it was connected and not be wrong.

I tied the second boot to my calf and stood up to test them. My feet felt so protected and I imagined this must be what it would be like to walk on the clouds. I thought of my trip to Jaipers and realised, even though it was only about three miles to the south gate, with these boots on I would make good time on the rough and rocky road. Delighted, I threw my patchwork backpack over my shoulders and started the downhill journey north to town and squinted against the sun, now well above the horizon and in my eyes to the east.

By the time I reached Jaipers, the sun was well established in the sky, the heat already oppressive. The clouds had cleared during the night and now the sky was clear and blue. It was such a clear day I could easily see the snow-covered tops of the Turgany Mountains far to the west. My eyes followed the mountains down to the hills surrounding the large broad valley nestling the town of Jaipers. From where I walked on the road, I could now look down over the town of Jaipers and I watched it shimmer in the rising heat. Hoisted above the town was the Baron's flag but it lay sullen against the flagpole in the absence of any wind. With the sun now burning overhead, I had broken out into a sweat, my back was soaked against the backpack and I could feel sweat running down to the crack of my bum. It would be hot in town but at least it offered shade and the town well held cool water.

Jaipers, like all small towns in Turgany County, was fortified with a wall made of massive logs sunk into the ground and cut to rough points at the top. Not all the towns had walls, but they reduced the taxes the town was required to pay each quarter. Walls also rewarded the town with a small garrison of at least twelve men and one officer; all supplied by the Baron of Turgany, Andrew Windthrop, whose flag flew over the town. The garrison was provisioned, barracked and fed by the town, but the Baron paid the men. I did not know if the tax savings offset the cost of the maintaining of the wall and feeding the garrison or not and to be honest; I didn't care one way or another. I did know Jaipers was proud of its wall and its garrison but that was all foreign to me. My home was with nature and not within the town.

The town was round in shape and had been cleared of trees for a mile around to provide a clear line of sight in all directions, presumably for defence. Defence against what, I had no idea. The town had two gates: one to the north and one to the south. The north gate gave access to the river pier and to the road that travelled east to the next town downriver called Belger, located beside the lake from which it took its name. The gates were very sturdy structures and were double planked and reinforced with iron bands. Small wooden towers were built on either side of the gates and leaned out over the wall. The gates were closed at nightfall and guarded continuously by the garrison. Captain Gendred, the garrison officer, insisted on closing the gates each night at sunset notwithstanding the fact there hadn't been hostilities in the county since the war. He was a very stern and serious man but he was friendly to me. I had provided him with a few unguents that helped his men with aches and pains and this seemed to have warmed him to me. I grew to know his men as well, and I had no troubles with any of them.

Jaipers was not a large town. There were about four hundred people living within its walls. Another eight hundred to a thousand people lived near the town in small hamlets and farmsteads and they regularly came to town to trade and barter for goods and provisions. The nearby Potsman River had a working mill and a lone sawmill that provided valuable resources to the town and to the county. More importantly, the road I was now on led south-west to the western seaport, named, with little imagination, Port West.

Port West and this road allowed critical goods to travel from the west coast of Belkin to Jaipers and then over one hundred miles downriver by barge to Jergen, the port city on the east coast. From there, goods travelled north to the capital city of Munsten and then supposedly onward to the rest of the country. The market in Jaipers thrived on this trade route. The market was centrally located in the town and had a few semi-permanent structures for those merchants who could not yet afford to purchase a full store in the small commercial district.

Due to the walls constraining the town size, real estate within the walls was limited and expensive and it could take merchants many years of hard work to be able to afford a store and pay the additional taxes required through ownership to the Baron. As a result, many merchants set up shop outside the town walls between the river pier and the far north gate. These makeshift dwellings were supposedly illegal and the garrison could without warning demolish any structures found outside the walls, but no one could remember that happening in many years. Everyone knew, though, the best merchants would be found inside the town, but everyone also knew the merchants outside the wall typically specialised in those items that were hard to get or illegal to possess—such as weapons and armour. Since the war, no commoners were allowed to possess weapons or armour, other than small personal knives. The irony that it was the commoners who won the war was not lost on most people, but the law remained nonetheless and people obeyed, for the penalty was severe and often death was the judgement for violations.

Outside the north gate was where the large warehouses were built where the river, road and town all converged. Barges lined the nearby piers, with stables placed in proximity to provide shelter for the large, hairy workhorses ponderously pulling the barges up from down the river. Barges were a constant sight, coming and going from the piers, offloading and loading their steady stream of goods—the route downriver being the luxury route. Little of the goods stayed in Jaipers. Most were destined for the larger towns and the capital city of Munsten. A few merchants chose to use the road skirting the river, despite the risk of highwaymen, and often I sat and watched them line up their carts and rumble down the road, bristling with hired armed guards, and disappear over the horizon.

Sometimes I wished I could go with them but my promise to my mother kept my feet safe in the woods and out of sight. The town knew the Baron had men of the Army of the Realm policing the road but they couldn't be everywhere and every so often tales of highwaymen raiding caravans would trickle into town. I would listen to these tales and be glad I remained safe to the south in the woods and hills outside the valley. Most merchants preferred the barges: they could carry more, and they were safer on the water than on the road, but they cut into the profits and still required men to guard the goods when the barges moored for the night.

The road leading up to the south gate was deserted at this time of day. I approached the gate and was relieved to enter the shade below the wall and fully open my eyes. I blinked and rubbed my eyebrows; they were sore after squinting for so long. The sentry guard positioned outside the gate looked bored, hot and tired. He knew me well enough and greeted me pleasantly by name, nodding toward the open gate to let me know I could enter. As I passed through the gate, I smiled to myself as the town opened up in front of me.

The sounds and smells of civilisation always seemed to overwhelm my senses after so long by myself. The smell of so many people living in proximity was foul. Their noise was a loud drone obscuring any other sounds. People filled the areas where they lived with their presence. I always felt disconnected when I entered the town and today was no exception. *Except—perhaps today, after all that has happened—a little human companionship would be welcomed. And*, I admitted to myself with a smile, *coming into town meant I got to see my good friend, Daukyns.*

I could only stay in town for a few days before I knew I would find my feet taking me back outside to the peace and quiet in the woods and hills. But for now, I was happy to return and my stomach growled with hunger. I had not broken fast this morning, and I now regretted it. I also had a terrible thirst and the town well beckoned me.

I had a route I always liked to take in town: first to the inn, then to the common hall, and lastly to the merchant square to sell my herbs, potions and unguents. Afterwards, I would head back to the inn for a hot meal, a bath, and a warm soft bed. It was a comforting routine, and it allowed me to minimise my time around people.

Somehow, not long after I entered Jaipers, word would get around and I would find myself providing advice to those with ailments. They would seek me out and sometimes surround me. They suffered from ailments real and imagined but all of them would look for cures from me. I had a sense of illnesses; gained from long discussions with Daukyns and through my knowledge of herb lore. I dimly remembered that my mother, too, had a gift for healing and I seemed to have the same gift and that pleased me. And so I helped people. Daukyns would break it up when people grew too adamant with me. It was all strange and wonderful.

I tossed these thoughts aside and smiled as I cleared the gate and stepped back into the sunlight of the town. A few people nearby waved to me in recognition and carried on with their business. The town seemed almost deserted but I knew they were somewhere sheltered in shade from the oppressive heat of the day.

Thankfully, all three of my route destinations were centrally located in the town just past the garrison barracks and their stable. As I passed the barracks, I watched three new guardsmen being outfitted out front by the garrison Quartermaster. The Quartermaster waved at me and the three new men glanced at me without interest. I waved back and stopped at the nearby well.

The well was the only one in town and was fairly large with a roof structure built over the top. It was a marvel of engineering and the town was proud of their well. A thick rope with a pulley and handle mechanism lowered and raised an enormous bucket for when large quantities of water were required, but usually, people just threw down the smaller bucket on a rope. At night a large wooden cover was lowered and locked over the opening but during the day it lay propped up against one of the building's corner supports. As was typical, a few children were hanging around to pull up the smaller well bucket for people and looking for handouts in return. As I approached, they handed me the rope and said hello. They knew me well enough to know I had nothing to reward them with and therefore I could do the lifting myself. I dropped my backpack beside me in the shade offered by the well cover structure, grabbed hold of the knotted rope and hauled up the bucket. I pulled the bucket out of the well, rested it on the stone wall and grabbed one of the large tin ladles tied to the support beams, scooping out water and dousing myself with it. The cool water hit me like a balm and washed the dust and heat of the road from my body. I gulped a second ladle and then a third to slake my thirst and finally refreshed, handed the rope back to the waiting children who eagerly dropped the bucket back down into the well, looking for potential customers. I frowned at the faintly odd taste in my mouth but I shrugged it off and laughed as I wrung the water out of my hair, relishing the brief respite from the heat and taking the time to look around the town.

South of me was the gate I had just come through. West of the gate was the garrison barracks and the attached stable house for their horses. The quartermaster was still outside with the new recruits except now they were talking and looking over at me with interest. They were no doubt discussing my healing salves, and I hoped it would mean more business for me. They turned away when they saw me looking back at them and so I ignored them too. Across the road from the barracks was the small Reeve office with a tiny gaol inside. I hadn't seen the Reeve when I walked past and that was fine with me; I had more important errands to attend to before I could spend time with him. I also wasn't ready to discuss what had happened last night and the thought of answering questions from the garrison captain worried me.

The well was positioned southwest of the town's crossroad. North of me was the Woven Bail Inn, a tall three-story building that towered over the town; here would be my first stop today. Across the road from the inn was the town common hall. This would be my second stop and the one I looked forward to. The common hall also served as the home of my good friend, Daukyns, who ran the town's Word community. Down the road toward the north gate was the central open market and near that was the commerce area comprised of a half-dozen merchant stores. Near the stores were the town storehouse and the granary building; both were maintained and stocked by the garrison for times of conflict. They could be empty for all I knew but knowing the garrison captain as I did, they were probably meticulously maintained. West of the well, the road led to the housing area where the wealthy people in town lived; mostly the merchants and guild representatives. The Reeve told me about twenty families lived there, but I had never gone down the road to see.

Down the road to the east was where the remainder of the town's sixty or so families lived. Despite the separation of families by wealth, the children mixed and played and fought in the centre of town. It was a simple matter to tell the children apart from the quality of their clothes and by whether they wore shoes. I glanced at my boots and wondered what people would make of me now. I knew what my friend Daukyns would say: "All people are equal regardless of their wealth or success". I swear the Word had more quotes than the old religious church once had. I think both the rich and poor would consider me an upstart and glare at me.

I said farewell to the children at the well and wished them good fortune as I shouldered my backpack and headed over to the inn. They didn't even spare me a glance. One of the children started to cough as I walked away and I was surprised to hear how wet it sounded. Colds like that rarely occurred in the middle of summer. I made a mental note to look for him later once I was settled.

I turned my attention to The Woven Bail Inn ahead of me. It was the largest building in town, providing rooms mostly for the richer barge captains and the caravan leaders. Outside the town was a larger hostel housing the crews of the barges from out of town. It was a cheap imitation of The Woven Bail and I avoided it. The Woven Bail Inn was a towering three-story affair and held at least a dozen rooms of varying quality. It boasted a large common bar and a room with a bathtub. More importantly, it had a kitchen that the inn was famous for and this is where I headed. My business with the kitchen was what provided me with a free room when available and often a free bath, too.

The kitchen entrance was around back and as I approached, I called out and Dempster, the cook, opened the door and greeted me like an old friend which for a solitary person like me always seemed a strange thing. Dempster was a very tall and very fat man. He had little hair left on his head, his face was typically bright red, and the apron stretched across his girth was stained with all manner of food, grease and who knew what else. The owner of the inn was always telling him to stop eating the profits and Dempster would laugh his rumbling, deep, laugh and claim a fat cook meant a good cook and that he should be pleased. I secretly craved any of the food this man prepared. He cooked from the heart and you could taste it. He was the reason the Inn was famous, and the owner knew this. So did Dempster, and he always got what he wanted from the innkeeper. Sometimes it was hard to tell who ran the inn.

The smells from his kitchen wafted out into the still air around me and I smelled fresh bread. It was white bread, if I was not mistaken, not the tough whole grain kind most people ate. My mouth instantly watered. White bread was like clouds on my tongue. Soft, fluffy clouds.

Dempster hustled me into his kitchen and eagerly watched as I pulled out bundles of herbs from my backpack. He had requested some very specific herbs the last time I was in town and as I lovingly laid down the tidy bundles on his preparation table, I named them out loud: thyme, oregano, chives, green peppercorns and mint. When I say they were tidy bundles, I mean they were very tidy. The herbs I sold in town were always tied together gently with willow bark strips. Each plant was trimmed to the same length, and each leaf was healthy and bursting with life. The bundles marked by willow bark strips would last several days longer than most people expected. I cultivated them specifically this way, and it was what made people want my herbs over anyone else's. I was often asked to explain the high quality of my herbs and I would always just shrug and smile, explaining it was because they came from high up in the hills around Jaipers. Despite some doubtful looks, this explanation seemed to always satisfy the curious and kept my secret safe.

I watched, mildly amused, as Dempster quickly examined them for quality and tasted them. Satisfied, he exclaimed they were up to my excellent standard. He looked over the herbs once more and then glanced sideways at me, seeming a little dejected. I smiled and then watched his face light up as I pulled out a small bundle of mint and marjoram and laid them next to the other herbs. He laughed, pounded me on the back, then rubbed his hands in anticipation and said he had a special recipe that could make good use of the mint and thanked me. He placed a finger beside his rather large nose and pondered me for a moment, then rummaged in his pantry and brought forth packages containing oats, cornmeal, and a generous pound of salted pork. I was very pleased with the more than fair exchange.

As I packed away the goods, Dempster surprised me by pulling out a small sachet of coarse salt that could only have come directly from the salt mines across the river outside the town of Finnow. I could see the special package markings from the Finnow Salt Guild as he pressed it into my hand. Dempster had once decided to painstakingly educate me in the markings of food guilds and Finnow was easily recognisable with the small minnow symbol. Finnow had a sense of humour, apparently.

By its weight, the pouch must contain about an ounce of salt. He smiled at me as I opened it to peer inside. I gasped when I saw the deep purple colour of the salt and identified it as Life salt. If it weren't for the hue, the unmistakable faint lavender smell would have confirmed what it was. Life salt was the most prized salt of the Finnow mines. It was rare and provided more flavour than ordinary salt. My mouth salivated at the smell and I thought about the number of herbs I would need to gather to equal the cost of this ounce of salt: baskets and baskets of herbs. I couldn't believe he was giving me a whole ounce of Life salt—it was far too generous. I started to protest, but the cook grabbed and closed up the pouch, stuffing the salt into my pack. He tapped the side of his nose with a finger, gave me a knowing wink and then mentioned the Reeve had stopped by that morning and not to worry about it. All was square, he said.

A bit dazed, I found myself being gently pushed out the door and outside with a large heel of white crusty bread thrust into one hand, the melting butter leaking between my fingers, and my backpack held against my chest with the other. I stopped and stood outside the kitchen door as it closed and took a large bite of the still warm bread. It was so delicious. I chewed and swallowed the bread as quickly as I could and felt each bite land in my empty stomach. I yelled a quick thanks to Dempster, laughed at his 'ya ya' response, and started toward my next stop. As I shouldered my backpack, I groaned at the weight of it—it hadn't been this heavy for a long, long time. I felt giddy and rich.

The salt was a wonder although I couldn't help but question why the Reeve asked the cook to provide me with Life salt. I simply couldn't understand but decided I wouldn't argue it. With the salt, I could produce some amazing things.

My mind clicked with possibilities. Recipes I had never tried before came to mind. I would need nightshade, I knew at once. With the salt, I could extract a pure alkaloid essence. The process ran through my head without having to think about it. I could create a cure for the strongest poisons. A poison cure would help people so much! More recipes swam through my head as I made my way across the road and over to the common hall and my good friend, Daukyns.

The common hall was not much more than a rectangular building with rows of simple benches that could hold maybe a quarter of the town inside. It was used by the town mayor to provide the town with important news and it was used to debate issues. More importantly, the town held celebrations in the common hall and outside in the spacious grounds surrounding it. I always made a point of being here for the harvest time during *Mabon* and the harvest dance at *Samhain*. It was fun to sit back and watch people enjoying the bounty of nature and I felt more in common with them at that time than any other.

As I expected, Daukyns was sitting in the shade outside the entrance to the common hall. The town allowed my friend to conduct his Word services in the building. In the back, there was a small storage room Daukyns was allowed to use as his home. And it served, more importantly, as a workshop for our joint efforts. He always seemed to be the happiest person in town as far as I could tell. He spied me right away and stood and rushed over as I approached; his face flushed its usual red as he reached out to embrace me.

"Will!" he shouted, wrapping me up in his arms and squeezing the breath out of me. I muffled a hello into his chest and he finally released me. A few people walking nearby smiled as they passed. Our friendship was well known in town but what we produced, I think, was even more known and valued.

"How have you been, Will? It's been a few weeks, has it not?" he bellowed as much as his aged, reedy voice would allow. He held me at arm's length and looked me up and down to see if I was still whole and hale. I gave him a once over at the same time.

Daukyns was a strange looking fellow. He always wore the same light brown robes that dragged on the ground and with sleeves that were hemmed far too long for his arms. They covered his hands more often than nought, meaning he always had to hold his arms slightly raised so he could push the sleeves up to free his hands. His hair was bright white and gleamed in the sun except for the startling large bald spot on top. This bare dome of skin was always burnt to a deep red by the sun and many people in the town had said his brains were baked as a result. He was not a young man—most would consider him elderly. His eyes and mouth were heavily creased and wrinkled but his laugh lines were the more predominant.

He sported an overly large and bulbous nose that was as deep a red as his scalp often was. He was known for a fondness for wine and always found a way for the town people to keep him well supplied. The front of his robe certainly had seen its share of spilt wine and the purple stain seemed almost an intentional part of the design.

I couldn't help but notice how tired my friend seemed, and more so than usual. Dark circles hung under his eyes and his left hand trembled with a shake that seemed worse than normal. My friend was not as well as I would like and I feared age was catching up with him. I doubted he was taking the herbs I had provided him with. Knowing Daukyns, he had probably given them away to someone he felt more deserving. I would have to talk to him again about that and dreaded the conversation. The last time had frustrated me to no end. I turned these troubling thoughts aside and forced myself to smile up at Daukyns.

"I've been well, sir. I found a good supply this time out. Better than usual. The sun and weather seem perfect."

Daukyns laughed. "Good, good! Come on inside. Let me see. You look well but tired, Will. Come."

With that Daukyns brought me into the common hall and we walked to the back room where he slept. I glanced at him as we walked, noting the irony of his last statement. *He* was the one that looked like he hadn't slept in days. We entered the small room, and I paused to admire the supplies we used for our joint venture. Our materials were all neatly laid out on the small table pushed up against the wall nearest the door. It was covered with small clay jars, beeswax, clay tubs of lard, a stone and a wooden mortar and pestle, a sharp knife, a jar of expensive pressed and filtered olive oil and a series of small copper pots suspended over unlit candle burners.

I surveyed the table quickly with a knowing eye, looking for anything amiss, but everything seemed in order. Daukyns had restocked the jars and consumables and it all looked satisfactory. There was enough here now to make full use of my herbs. Little would remain afterwards but once I was finished, I would be able to purchase more supplies for my next visit. Satisfied, I dropped my backpack to the floor next to Daukyns' cot and started pulling out my special herbs and stacking them on the table. These bundles were wrapped with the fronds of the catkins. I had found only catkins would stay neutral with the herbs they touched and not diminish the potency I had imbued in the bundles. I carefully placed the herbs on the table and Daukyns moved over to examine them. I wasn't worried what he would think: these herbs would stay fresh for weeks—my cultivation technique assured that. Daukyns watched closely, gasping as each bundle was brought forth and lovingly laid down on the table.

"So much this time, young man!" he said as I laid the last bundle down on the table. "Is that what I think it is?"

He pointed at the poppy flowers. I nodded, secretly pleased he had noted my special find; I knew he would. They were a spectacular find. I had the location memorised and would return to harvest the site as often as I could. The poppy, I knew instinctively once I had found them and examined them, would produce one of the single most powerful pain reducing unguents I could create. Daukyns and I had discussed their potential the last time I passed through after he had heard some merchants speaking of it down at the pier. My latest outing was to specifically locate the flower. Daukyns had pointed me in a likely direction to look and, surprisingly, he had been right.

He had a knowledge of plants I could only dream of attaining. But together we made quite the team. It was through my friendship with Daukyns I had been able to fully grasp my talents and make good use of them. He was a mentor and more importantly, my friend. But on this last venture, he had steered me unerringly to where I would likely find a source for the flower. I watched as Daukyns picked up the poppies and examined and smelled them eagerly.

"They were right where you thought they might be, sir. You will need to tell me who your source was! He was so exact about the location. I mean, I pretty much just walked straight to them. How did he know a battle had been fought there?" I said. "The evidence was everywhere, I mean, everywhere I looked! I..." I stopped when I noticed Daukyns' face had darkened and he looked away. "What is it? What did I say?"

"Nothing, it's not you, my boy. The source for the poppy location was from Bill Burstone. He used it to treat the pain of his burn scars. He created some kind of pain reliever. But that's not what bothers me. Something terrible has happened to him and I am sorry to say that he was murdered—murdered!—just last night and right in his own home. Horrible, horrible business." Daukyns tutted and ran a hand over his bald pate. He reached out with his other hand and ran it over his copy of the Word lying on the table. "Killed over gold, they are saying. Gold of all things." He shook his head and moved to the doorway and peered out into the empty common room.

I stood frozen in thought at the words of my friend. I gripped the table to steady myself and tried not to think about what Daukyns was saying. He carried on talking not noticing I had grown quiet.

"The town was in quite the state last night until the Reeve dragged the murderer's corpse back just after midnight, at least according to the guards I've spoken to. All morning I have been trying to reach out to the humanity in people—bolster their courage with the Word! It was hot work and I've only just returned. You know, to get my strength back up. You'll hear about it all soon enough, Will. Everyone in the market has been gossiping about it. Can't get them to shut up, really. Oh, and the captain has locked up Bill's home and posted a guard..."

His voice trailed off as he turned away from the doorway to face me and realised I was staring at him with tears once again starting to slide unwelcome down my cheeks. I convinced myself that I had nothing to do with what happened last night—that I had just been an innocent bystander at the wrong place at the wrong time—but now? The events had come full circle and were entwined in my life: Bill Burstone had been the source of the poppies. The poppies I had gone out to find because of him and then I came face-to-face with his murderer and watched the man die. My peace was shattered.

"What is it, my boy? Your face just went as white as a spirit! Sit, sit!" and he steered me to his cot. Once I sat, he fetched me a cup of water from the bucket by his door, sloshing the contents in his haste. I took the cup and sipped the warm water as Daukyns continued to question me. I just needed a moment to centre myself.

"What happened, Will? What do you know about this?" he asked. Slowly at first, and then in a flood, I told him what had happened last night. I surprised myself by leaving out the part where I found the coin in the toe of the boot. I summoned the courage to speak of it when Daukyns distracted me.

Daukyns had been looking down at my boots. "So these are his boots? Lord Protector, have mercy!" He sat next to me, wrapping an arm around my shoulder and squeezing me against him. "What a horrible thing to witness, Will. And to think what must've been going through your mind when he held you with that knife, your very own knife, right to your throat!"

I looked around the small room serving as my personal apothecary as Daukyns continued to spout disbelief. Somehow, opening up to Daukyns had improved my mood and feelings about the whole event. The bundles of herbs lay quietly on the table looking as fresh as when I had harvested them. I never let them lie around too long, lest someone notice their durability and start questioning me about it. Daukyns had noticed their long life a while ago but I felt he deemed it better to leave it unspoken. I found I couldn't sit here any longer with my work beckoning me and so I struggled to my feet and handed the empty cup to Daukyns, commenting that he needed a fresh bucket of water. Daukyns ignored me and kept up his vitriol, now speaking in anger, questioning the sanity of the Reeve and how he could just leave me out there after all that had happened. I smiled and picked up the first bundle and started to untie the catkins holding it together.

"Well, I am fine now. Speaking of the Reeve, he wants me to see him today and talk to Captain Gendred so I best get started with this while the herbs are still fresh."

Daukyns stopped his rant and sat quietly behind me for a spell and then stood up and patted my back as we moved to the door. "Very well, my boy. Very well. I'll leave you to your work." Daukyns stopped in the door. "We'll talk about this later, Will. You need to get this all out. Things like that affect you in small ways you wouldn't expect. Trust me, I saw so much of that during the war. You can't keep it locked up inside."

Daukyns grew quiet for a moment as if considering telling me something more and I waited, looking at him with an eyebrow raised. When he said nothing further, I turned my attention back to the herbs. He watched me for a spell as I sorted out the herbs and then quietly he left and closed the door behind him.

No sooner had he left than I reached into my tunic and pulled out the small pouch, opened it and emptied the contents into my palm. The coin hit my palm first, followed right behind by my small sickle, which landed on the coin with a soft clink. The sickle was made from a black glass that seemed to gleam with an internal light. It was comprised completely out of a singular piece of glass— with a blade only two inches in diameter. The blade was sharper than anything I had ever seen and I had never been required to sharpen or hone it. It was also unbreakable, stronger than iron and harder than rock.

The sickle had always been with me. It was given to me by my mother, of that, I was sure, although I no longer had any memory of the exchange. I knew somehow she taught me how to use it and how to hide it. It had been hers and she had entrusted it to me when all the bad things happened—so very long ago I was no longer sure what I remembered correctly anymore. My mother's face was long forgotten in my mind—I only remembered the look of her closed eyes. I would sometimes see other women and wonder if they looked like my mother once did. That saddened me. My only memory of my father came down to one: I remembered his back as he walked down the tunnel away from me and my mother and back into the burning city. His last words to us were to follow the tunnel out to the sea and not look back. But I did. Once outside I saw the entire city in flames above the cliffs. I was six years old at the time. That was ten years ago.

I turned the sickle over in my hand. It was such a comfort to me. It fit my hand like no other instrument. It was small but more than adequate. Once I had cut myself with the blade. It had bit deep into my fingers and I felt it scrape across the bone. Shocked, I stuck the finger in my mouth and expected it to fill with the hot taste of my blood. When all I tasted were the herbs staining my skin, I drew my finger out and examined it in awe. Not a single mark showed to indicate the blade had cut through my flesh and touched the bone. My finger was untouched: whole and unblemished. It was a true moment of wonder to me.

Later, I experimented with the blade and tried to cut myself. I tried to nick my finger and when the blood immediately welled from the small cut I was stunned and I wasn't sure what to believe anymore.

Much later I had been harvesting a large amount of sweet mint and a wild dog barked in the woods nearby, startling me and a nye of pheasants. The sickle slipped and again I felt it pass through my flesh. This time it ran across a good portion of my left wrist. I cried out and dropped the sickle to grasp my wrist. I waited to see blood well through my fingers and when none appeared I let go and held up my arm and spied not a single mark on my wrist. The feeling and pain of the cut remained though and ran down my arm in waves until it finally faded away. I stared at that wrist forever until I decided it was best left as a mystery. Nonetheless, I was very careful with the blade afterwards.

I always kept it hidden. It meant everything to me. It linked me to my mother and brought back the feeling of being loved. I also felt more in commune with nature when I held and used it. During these moments the world would fade away and all that would remain were the plants and their nature. My mother was always foremost in my thoughts and it was during these times I missed her the most and oddly, felt closer to her.

It also concerned me it would be perceived as a weapon, and therefore illegal. If it was found on me I thought I would be likely arrested and the blade removed from me forever. I knew I wouldn't be able to bear it and so I kept it hidden at all costs.

I stared at the little sickle I held in my hand. The light coming through the cracks in the wallboards caused it to glint and as always its simplistic beauty stunned me. I then picked up the first bundle of herbs and started to work. The sickle gleamed and grew brighter as I focused my efforts and I soon lost myself in my work.

Three

Jaipers, 900 A.C.

ATE IN THE afternoon, I finally put down the small sickle and rubbed my tired eyes. The small room smelled pleasantly of beeswax and herbs, the mint being the most predominant. Daukyns always said he slept in this room better on these days than any other and that he always woke feeling renewed in spirit and body. I often asked him why he never took any of the herbs for his own use, but he would always just smile and give them all away or sell them for coin to use on the less fortunate people of Jaipers. I had stopped trying to change his mind about this some time ago and now I simply handed them over to him and enjoyed the pleased look on this face. And so, I stood there in the small room and breathed in the fragrances and a sense of tranquillity filled me; I cherished these moments. The work with the herbs was so soothing to my soul. Cutting the herbs in such precise ways that released their most potent strength was something that came so naturally to me it was easier than breathing. The herbs spoke to me, but not with words. I really couldn't explain how I did what I did or how the plants spoke to me—I just knew how to make use of them. In simple terms, and as best as I could explain, with the sickle I could release the strength of herbs and combine them with others to amplify their potency well beyond normal means. I had no idea how I did this, only that the sickle became a part of me and allowed me to extend my awareness into the herbs and let me create powerful medicines.

I laughed to myself. Daukyns knew something about what I did; I was sure of that. He called it the work of the Word and I have long since abandoned trying to change his mind about that. I picked up the sickle and placed it back in the pouch. Just then a glint from the table caught my eye, and I looked over to see the gold coin lay there, forgotten until now. I sucked in a breath when I saw an unmistakable soft yellow glow came from the coin. I glanced quickly over to the beams of sun streaming through the wallboards and saw they had moved to the back of the room and could not be the cause. Slowly, I reached down and poked the coin and when nothing happened; I picked it up and found it was warm to the touch. I held it between thumb and forefinger and noticed my right thumb fit the coin where I had assumed someone had been rubbing it. I gave it a quick rub, and the world *shifted*.

Between one blink and the next, the surrounding walls became transparent, still visible but like a faint mist. All around me lay the town with all the buildings and structures—everything—turned to mist. I felt so exposed and visible, almost as if I was standing naked in the middle of the town for all to see. A feeling of falling passed over me and I reached out and grasped the table for support as my head swam. I felt dizzy like I had been spinning myself around. I looked all around me at the wonder of it all and ignored the feeling of unease.

I couldn't help but notice the people of the town. Where the walls were watery mist, the people in town stood out like bright beacons of various colours. I could see where the people were walking around town they were leaving a faint and quickly fading coloured trail behind them to mark their passage. Then I noticed all the animals around town. The dogs, cats, birds, even the small insects that scurried about—they were all bright with colour and stood out like a bright fire in the dark night. This is what the coin allowed, I knew –it let me truly *see* people and life.

I looked to where Daukyns sat outside the common hall slumped in his chair. He had a colour to him too—a blue streaked with grey that pulsed with his breathing and I guessed this to mean he was asleep. Unbidden, a strong impression came to mind as I looked at Daukyns. As I watched him I suddenly knew he was ill with age. The knowledge came with a certainty I could not dispute, and I was filled with astonishment of being able to intimately know something so soundly when it should be impossible to know.

Yet as I examined Daukyns, it all was so clear to me. I could sense the worn effect his age had on his body and not just by his surrounding colour—which I now could see seemed faded or missing in places. I could sense how hard his heart worked to keep his blood pumping through his body. I could feel the pain in his joints and how hard his lungs worked to draw in air. But something else was wrong with him: his liver and kidneys were dying. With an intense shock, I knew he only had a few days left to live. I don't know how but I stumbled out of this strange vision and *shifted* back to normal.

I found myself feeling trapped within the suddenly confining walls of the small back room. I closed my eyes and sat heavily on Daukyns' cot. *What had I just observed? What had I just done and how?* I glanced down at the coin still held in my hand and knew it was the cause. *Any idiot could figure that out,* I thought. *But there's more to it than that. I feel drawn to this coin. But what had it just allowed me to do? It had allowed me to see through walls and I had just seen the effect of age on a human being in a way no one had ever seen before. It had allowed me to see;* I realised with increasing horror, *that my good friend Daukyns was going to die, and soon.*

I sat on the cot for a long time and wondered what I could possibly do with this ability and knowledge. It was not normal that anyone should know when another person was going to die. The knowledge weighed on me like several stones tied around my neck. I imagined myself trying to explain this to him and knew there was no way to prove it. I would have to think on this. Questions crowded my mind and with an effort I tore my gaze from the coin, distraught, and wondered what else I could sense with it. Before I could change my mind, I gave the coin a rub and *shifted* again.

As soon as I could once again look out into the whole town the claustrophobia evaporated. With relief, the dizziness did not return and this time I felt like I did when I first exited out of the town and back into the open country: free. I paused and looked at Daukyns, still asleep in his chair and unaware of all that was going wrong within him and wondered what I could do to help. I observed him for a little while and after a time came to a conclusion: the only thing I could do was to ease his pain with my herbs. For a moment I felt a strange urge to reach inside him, but I was horrified at the thought and I backed away and fled into the town.

I looked around, and I focused in on a merchant in the open market square closing a deal with a woman only a few years older than myself. I recognised both of them and knew them well enough from my times in town. She was quiet and worked down by the river repairing baskets used by the barges. She was friendly to me and once we had talked about the birds. She watched them all the time, she had said. The merchant was a man I avoided. He sold produce at the far edge of the market. His wares were worse than second-rate, but he always managed to sell to the less fortunate in town.

Watching them through the coin I could see more than I normally could. This time I knew and could sense this poor woman was starving. Before when I had seen her in the market she had looked no different from others in the town who were without money. She was thin and hungry. But seeing her through the coin, I could feel the hunger coming off her in waves; visually it flashed through the colours surrounding her in oranges and yellows.

I could sense her focus on the mealy potatoes the merchant hawked, and that she wanted to buy them without giving away her need to him. The sights and smells of the food in the market were making her head faint, and she struggled to maintain her composure. But the potatoes right in front of her were increasing her hunger, and I found myself sharing the same hunger. My mouth watered at the thought of sinking my teeth into the flesh of the roots. I could imagine tearing off chunks and swallowing them whole. I could almost savour the feeling of food hitting my empty stomach.

I forced myself to shake off the connection and studied the merchant to see what he could tell me. The merchant was smirking at her—a smirk hidden behind a practised smile. I sensed at once he knew she was starving and didn't care. He only knew he could take advantage of that and the sickly yellow of his avarice pulsed all around him. It was sickening, and bile rose in the back of my throat. His potatoes were the cheapest in the market, but he could sell to her for more than these old potatoes were worth. He knew she would pay despite her protests. Her plight meant nothing more to him than a chance to earn more coin.

I felt nauseous and unclean watching him like he was infecting me with his greed. Instinctively, my hand reached up to the sickle in my pouch and I grasped it through the leather. I tore my gaze away from the merchant and felt my sickness fade. Gasping with relief, I turned my attention elsewhere and stopped when I spotted the Reeve sitting in the inn, looking my way. I almost shouted in surprise then with a laugh, I realised it only *appeared* he was looking directly at me. He was watching a couple in the dining room, sitting between him and me. They were laughing at something and he looked almost wistful watching them.

The Reeve, I noticed with curiosity, had a deep blue colour surrounding him and it was tight and compact and looked solid. He wasn't the only man in town with such colours but his colour was the deepest blue. With the gift of the coin, I knew he was an anchor in a storm—and he would bring stability where it was needed. I knew he could be trusted, and that he was a good man. I smiled, thinking I didn't need the coin to know that, but it was good to have the proof right before me.

I watched as the innkeeper approached the Reeve and spoke, handing him a beer. The innkeeper's aura was a mix of colours. There was the dark green of greed there, I sensed, but stronger than that was that same blue colour I knew probably meant the innkeeper had an honest sincerity. The innkeeper was an honest man but only to a point. He warred with good intentions and the desire to do well at his business. I found it odd his desires should conflict so strongly within him and realised I knew nothing of such things. The Reeve smiled at the innkeeper and gave him a coin and waved off the change. Once the innkeeper moved away, the Reeve returned his attention to the couple and suddenly I felt like I was intruding.

I looked around town and marvelled at all the colours that surrounded people. I could have watched for hours when I suddenly became aware of a presence all around me. It was comforting, and it urged me to look elsewhere in town. I had felt this presence before, of that I was certain. It didn't frighten me. It reminded me of the peace of the woods and the smell of freshly fallen rain. Before I could think, the presence drew me to a strong pulsing green aura in a quiet eastern area of town and as soon as I saw the aura the presence faded.

I looked about where I was and recognised the shacks standing near the garrison wall in the eastern part of town. This was where the poorer people lived in ramshackle homes. They were barely tolerated by the garrison soldiers, but they were left to their own for the most part. Daukyns spent most of his time and effort here and knew the people intimately. Being rather poor myself, I did not pity them. I felt kinship more than anything, despite the fact they seldom spoke to me.

Now that I had seen the strange aura, it pulled at my curiosity and I felt as if I was being dragged across the town until I found myself standing inside a small shack. I felt strange and physically disconnected from my body. I knew with certainty I was still standing inside Daukyns' cramped room but I also knew I was standing inside this shack. Beside me lay a woman on straw simply piled up on the ground. On the other side of her, there was a small child asleep and exhausted next to her with one hand clasping hers. The woman's aura was thin and pulsated with a bright and sickly yellow-green colour. Her face was flushed with a very high fever and I knew a bad sickness racked her body.

I stared down at the woman and tried to understand what it was I was seeing. Her aura stretched from the woman and reached out to the child next to her and I realised to my horror the sickness in the woman had spread to the child. I focused on the green aura, setting the particular colour to memory, and looked around quickly, finding others in the area also showing the same colour. Whatever ailed her, it was spreading throughout the town! Shocked, I dropped the coin in the dirt and immediately found myself standing in the small room with the walls tight all around me. Whatever this sickness was it was spreading like a vile sludge across town.

A sense of falling overcame me and I had the sudden urge to vomit, sweat beading my brow, but I managed to fight it down. Nausea and the feeling of confinement in the small stuffy room combined to force me to crave the outdoors and open air. I had to get out the room.

I quickly placed the coin back in my pouch, securing it in my tunic and fighting off another urge to vomit. With my teeth clenched, I gathered up the pots of unguent, two dozen in all, all marked on the lid with symbols made from practised brush strokes. The symbols identified the contents—symbols my mother had taught me years ago. The small pots were sealed with beeswax and would stay potent for years. It was a labour of love but with the need to vomit growing stronger, I heedlessly threw my share of the pots into my backpack, left the others for Daukyns on the table, and blew out the candles. I gathered my remaining bundles as the sweat on my brow turned cold and then broke out all over my body. My stomach lurched once more, and I clamped my jaw shut with force to stop myself from spewing.

I ran my eyes over the table and snagged my precious pouch of Life salt and was pleased to see, despite the need to throw up, that half of it still remained. I threw this in my pack and looked at the remaining mess on the table. Daukyns always insisted on cleaning the worktable. He said it made him feel part of the process. His pots sat neatly stacked on the table. I knew he shared them with the people who needed the contents the most in town. In return, he got to stay and run his community Word services and they kept him stocked with food and more importantly to him, in wine.

Satisfied, I slung my backpack over my left shoulder and ran quickly out of the small room and through the adjoining common room. Once back outside in the open, I could no longer contain myself and I leaned over, violently ill next to the building. I had little in my stomach and dry heaves soon painfully overtook me. The remains of my breakfast of bread soured my mouth and I spit as clear as I could before wiping my lips clean. I sank to the ground, thankfully upwind from my vomit and lay exhausted. I felt so much better as I mopped the sweat from my brow and grabbed the sickle through my tunic.

The last time I remembered being this sick was the time Daukyns had taken me out to fish from a small boat on the river. He had to turn back soon after because I was ill then and felt much the same as I did now. Seasickness was what he called it. Whatever it was it was horrible. I closed my eyes and enjoyed the light breeze that had picked up while I had been working. The breeze drew the sweat from my skin and cooled me.

The coin was foremost in my thoughts. Somehow it was allowing me to see intimate details about the health of people. The colours surrounding them were clearly tied to them as well, and I had yet to figure that out, but it seemed intuitive. Green was clearly not good. The coin freed me to move about and observe without being seen. It allowed me to tap into the surrounding nature. I realised then the coin combined with my knowledge of herbs would be a uniquely powerful thing. With them, I could help cure people of sickness and ensure the correct herbs were administered. The thought of being able to help people so directly and so effectively was intoxicating to me. My very core yearned to reach out to people and help them.

The coin, I knew with a certainty, was a boon surely meant for someone like me. My sense of ownership grew threefold, and I knew I had to keep it and work more with it. I couldn't share the knowledge of the coin with anyone— including Daukyns or the Reeve. Like my sickle, I could not give it up. I knew I was torn but had until that moment felt I would be turning it over to the Reeve. Now I knew I never could. A certain amount of guilt consumed me. I remained lying up against the wall with my eyes closed and forced myself to relax.

Once I composed myself and my stomach seemed settled, I hurried over to where Daukyns sat, still slouched over and snoring peacefully. Without the coin I could no longer see his aura or sense his pain but looking closely at him, I could now make out the deep lines around his eyes and for the first time I saw just how old he really was, and I could see the ghost of the pain he felt by the set of his jaw. I never really noticed how he had aged before—or maybe I did but refused to admit it. I suddenly felt such sorrow for him and I wanted to ease his pain. I reached out to wake him and warn him when a hand clamped down on my shoulder, startling me and almost causing me to cry out.

"Let him rest, son," said the Reeve softly and with some warmth. "He needs it. Come with me. We need to talk." The Reeve walked slowly away toward the inn and didn't check to see if I would follow. I took a long look at Daukyns and watched a line of drool run down the corner of his mouth. *He was my only true friend in this whole town. I couldn't lose him.* I shook my head and looked around to find the Reeve already several feet away and still walking.

I caught up to him and he slowed his pace to accommodate my shorter stride. He glanced down at me once and grunted. I wasn't exactly sure what the grunt meant and decided to ignore it. My head only reached the midpoint of the Reeve's upper arm. At sixteen, I was likely as tall as I would get and I resigned myself to having to always look up at people. We walked in silence side–by–side for a few minutes and passed the inn where I had assumed we were destined. I said nothing but watched as the inn went by and decided to wait him out and felt more mature for it.

We started left down the residential road and paused as a couple of children rushed by, pushing a hoop with a stick and laughing with endless energy. I had never been one of those kids and felt a longing to join them despite knowing it was impossible to be a kid again. I watched them disappear around the corner and looked at where we were.

I had never ventured down this area of town before. I never had the need and was worried people would get suspicious. The people living here were wealthy. Their money fuelled the town, which in turn fuelled the barony. They had power and stature and didn't like anyone interfering with that power nor intruding into their private area of town. As I took in my surroundings, the occasional window dressings would shift ever so slightly, and I knew we were being watched. I suddenly felt very exposed and the dirt on my clothes seemed to stand out all the more. I was one of the poor and not tolerated in this part of town. The presence of the Reeve was likely the only reason I wasn't already asked to leave.

A river barge captain had once told me the houses were nothing special, but to me, they were homes with living rooms, kitchens, bedrooms and all the fine belongings that anyone could possibly want. They gave shelter from the wind and rain, warmth in winter and shade in the summer sun. The buildings were well tended, and some had been washed with coloured stains, making them bright and cheery. The windows had real glass, and the roofs were shingled with clay pieces. I wondered what it would be like to live under a dry roof instead of the stars and trees. I sighed. That life was not meant for me. Living outdoors was my world, and it called to me, but I strived to imagine living in a house until the Reeve broke me out of my reverie by starting to speak to me at last. I felt some measure of satisfaction when he broke the silence first and I grinned to myself.

"Bill fought in the revolution all those years ago. He made a real name for himself but not with the Baron. It was the Lord Protector himself that he impressed. Bet you didn't know that, did you?" He didn't wait for a response but kept talking, almost as if to himself. "I don't think anyone in this town knew. He kept that to himself. Very private. Sure, they all imagined that he must have done something of value once and they knew that he had money. He had his large home that he paid for in coin and he always had money for beer and wine at the inn. Did you know he was a knight in the King's Guard?"

This last question shocked me, and I looked up at the Reeve to see if he was joking. He seemed to be waiting for an answer, so I mumbled a no. I hadn't known that. He certainly didn't look like someone from the King's Guard—but a knight, too? The King's Guard was the elite in the land—except they were now called the Lord Protector's Guard. Knights were all allowed to wear armour and carry swords and had horses and squires and all that other stuff, didn't they? Bill, when I did chance to see him, was usually sitting slouched outside the inn drunk, smoking a pipe and watching people wander by. The burns on his face and hands were horrible to look at and people always kept clear of him. He yelled at people a lot, too. He was, everyone knew, a bitter man. Daukyns liked him though, and that thought kept my tongue quiet. Daukyns was an excellent judge of character.

"He was. Wait till you see his armour. The way he told it, he had been a very honourable Protector's guardsman of some stature. It took years of speaking with him to piece that together, but I did. After the war, he was given a knighthood, lands to go with it, people to work that land and a purse to keep it running. He tended his land and collected taxes for the Realm for years. He took a wife and had kids, too." The Reeve paused a moment before continuing. "I think he loved being a knight but ten years ago that all changed and he came here by himself to live. He moved into that home right over there." And the Reeve pointed to the house at the end of the road.

It was, no doubt, where we were headed. I took an appraising look as we approached. The house looked like all the others except it was a little better-taken care of, but it was hard to say why. The wood was a little better trimmed. The windows were framed a little straighter. The roof was a little more even and better shingled. Flowerpots adorned the porch and were obviously well watered based on how vibrant they were. I didn't truly understand the need for a house since it separated you from the earth. The flowers were held in little clay pots and I could sense they felt so constrained and frustrated. Their roots reached deep in the soil only to find themselves blocked by fire-hardened clay all around them.

As we closed the last few yards, I could make out a guard standing in the shadow of the porch beside the door. I knew him by sight but not by name. The poor man was in full garrison dress and he looked bored but alert. I pitied him and the heat he must have been suffering dressed in all that armour. He spied us as we walked toward him and seemed to stand up a little straighter. A quick glance to the Reeve confirmed to me that he didn't notice the respect the town garrison returned to him. He was oblivious to the guard and kept speaking to me. The guard gave me a tight smile and nodded once.

"He wouldn't say anything of his wife and kids," continued the Reeve. "I only knew he had them because he let it slip one day. But, mind you, he never mentioned them again and I suspect they no longer live or no longer care about him if they do still live. Something happened ten years ago that made him give up his knighthood, his lands, his people and to come to this small merchant town miles from anywhere of any importance. What could cause a man to do that, I wonder?"

I thought then of the burns marking Bill's face, neck and hands. They were bad but long healed, and I suspected they marked his body elsewhere. Daukyns had mentioned he used the poppy plant for the pain of the burns. The pain had never truly faded, he had explained at my look of surprise. If something had happened to his family in the past, I suspected a fire was involved. I didn't doubt Reeve Comlin thought so too. Little escaped his notice.

We reached the two steps leading up to his porch and front door. The Reeve paused, took out a cloth and wiped the sweat and dust from his face and then from the back of his neck. He placed one foot on the bottom step and leaned an elbow on the lower railing post beside the steps. He nodded at the guard who nodded back. The Reeve waved one arm in the direction of the other houses.

"These folks had no idea who lived here. Sure, they knew Bill. Knew he once owned land but not why and what happened to him. He had money. That's for sure. Paid his taxes and never traded for anything—he always paid good coin. That was enough for these people around here. They didn't need to- or want to—know more than that." The Reeve leaned down and spat on the ground.

"They also don't seem to care that he is now dead and murdered in his own house other than for the pleasure of gossiping about it. Already people in the town are jostling to buy the place. Captain Gendred closed down the housing office this morning in disgust. That was a respectable thing to do, I thought. Bill hasn't even been buried yet."

The Reeve looked over at me and at the guard and I nodded my agreement. The guard, suddenly thinking he was part of the conversation, nodded too. The

Reeve looked at me a little longer and I had to look away. Something was bothering the Reeve, and I had yet to figure out how I was involved in any of this other than almost being killed by the same man that had killed Bill. Here I stood outside his house and I had no idea why. For some reason, I felt guilty, and the hidden coin came immediately to my mind. I started to say something about it when again some part of me stopped my words. A sudden insane urge to run came to me but I held my ground and waited, opting to simply look down the street to the other houses.

"Follow me," he ordered, and he started up the stairs. The guard turned to the front door, pulled a key out from around his neck, and quickly unlocked and removed a shiny brass padlock from the door. The hasp was newly installed and stood out against the wood. The guard stepped aside to allow us passage. Clearly, the guard expected us, but he looked strangely at me. I suspected he was wondering why the Reeve would bring me into this home. *Much like I was wondering.*

The Reeve pushed open the door and walked into the house, waiting for me to follow him. I glanced at the guard, who was thankfully now ignoring me and walked through the door behind the Reeve. I stopped just inside to look around and I blinked repeatedly to clear the sun from my eyes in the sudden gloom.

Once my sight adjusted, my first impression was I had entered a place of meticulous order. This was my first time in a house and even not knowing what to expect, I could easily tell there was no clutter anywhere to see. The walls, floors and ceilings were all made of expensive and expertly joined wood planks. Trim covered the bottoms and tops of the walls. The furniture was of superb quality and precisely placed, gleaming with oils and immaculate. The walls and furniture were empty of any belongings or keepsakes. There were no items hinting of family life, or loved ones, or any personal possessions.

To my nose, the house smelled strange. It was hotter than outside despite the shade and the heat stung my nose when I breathed in deep. The smell told me the house had been locked up for a few days with no air to freshen it. With no movement of air, the sweat on my skin had nowhere to go, and I was soon dripping with it. From out front I heard the guard cough and watched as the Reeve turned his face to the noise with a frown. The cough was the same wet sound I had heard earlier, and I couldn't help but think of the sick woman with her child in that shack. The sickness was spreading.

From where I stood at the door, I saw the first floor contained a living room opening up to a small kitchen with a wood stove that vented through the back of the house to the outside. There was one small door in the kitchen and I surmised it opened to a small adjoining pantry much like in the kitchen in the inn. A dining area was beside the kitchen and contained a simple table with one chair pushed up tightly against it. From the dining room, a backdoor led behind the house to where a privy and wood store would likely be located. Beside me a narrow flight of stairs led upstairs but glancing up, I couldn't see what lay above us on the second floor. If it was like the inn, I expected to see a bedroom at least.

The Reeve called out a greeting and a rough reply from outside the back door was heard, confirming another guard was positioned behind the house. I hadn't expected that and wondered what would warrant two guards. Before I could ask, the Reeve clasped my shoulder briefly in a tight grip and then headed for the stairs. I followed after him and we made our way to the second floor until we stood in a narrow hallway. The heat upstairs was heavy and thick, and I wiped my sleeve across my brow and blinked when the sweat stung my eyes.

Two bedrooms and a study were the only rooms upstairs off the hallway. I imagined this house must be considered a large private home by Jaipers' standards. One bedroom was clearly the one Bill had used; the spread was still rumpled. The other bedroom was empty except for a narrow cot pushed up against the far wall. Both bedrooms were small compared to the study, which took up most of the upper floor. The Reeve led me directly into this windowless room. It contained a centrally positioned, beautifully ornate desk with a thick, padded leather chair glistening with oils. A large wooden chest sat on the floor behind the desk and pushed into the far-right corner. What caught my attention was that each wall was covered from floor to ceiling with shelves filled with books and scrolls of all shapes and sizes. I had never seen this much-written word in one location and marvelled at the wealth they represented. My eyes hovered for a moment over a hollow in the bookshelves behind the desk displaying an elaborate coat-of-arms I did not recognise. Then I noticed, as I made my way into the room and could peer into the corner once hidden from the hallway, that an armour tree stood proudly bearing a full set of plate armour. I had never seen anything like it before. It was made of solid metal and shone like a looking glass. Draped from the armour hung a large, two-handed sword, worn with use. I knew this sword was not ceremonial and was well used and cared for.

All this I noticed automatically but my eyes were drawn to the arc of blood that crossed the desk, over the coat-of-arms and the wall and rose up over the bookshelves. I looked up and saw the blood continue across the ceiling. At my feet, in front of the desk, lay a massive pool of blackened, dried blood. It was here Bill had bled out and died. There was so much blood it was still drying and looked sticky. Disturbed by our entry, swarms of flies rose and buzzed all over the place, and I was glad my stomach was empty. Anything I had in it would be gone by now and I resisted an urge to gag as the coppery smell of the blood reached my nose. I covered my mouth and nose with a hand and breathed through my fingers and mouth. Flashes of memories from my childhood of blood covering floors and walls overcame me, but they vanished as quickly as they had come and I blinked them away.

The desk had several scrolls and papers strewn over it and it was in such a state of disarray I knew Bill had never left it like this. It was uncharacteristic of the house and from what I could tell of Bill's obsession with neatness, with everything being in its proper place. The mess on the desk was out of place. The blood on the desk had been smeared in places and I knew the murderer must have been going through the papers when he had been found, killed Bill and then resumed his search. I glanced behind me at the study door that lay fully open and against the wall; no blood marked the outside of it. I pulled the door closed enough to examine the back and there I found blood. The murderer had hidden behind the door, swung it closed when Bill entered, no doubt focused on the disarray of his desk. He would have stepped forward and grabbed Bill from behind and opened his throat in one motion. It was the only thing that made sense from what I was seeing and I imagined the scene playing out in my head.

The Reeve was staring at me and so I told him what I thought happened and he nodded in agreement, seemingly pleased with my conclusion.

"The only thing the murderer touched was this desk," he said. "He went through the drawers and pulled out the papers. I believe Bill came home unexpectedly and came in here; most likely he heard something. He probably walked in and stopped when he saw the mess on his desk and knew that someone had been here. That's when the murderer stepped out from behind that door and opened Bill's throat with one cut. An expert cut, I might add, it's not a simple thing to cut a man's throat. He cut both veins and his voice in one cut. He knew what he was doing and had done it before. Bill bled out in seconds. He never had a chance." The Reeve's head and eyes followed the blood that had sprayed across the ceiling and over to the far wall.

"The murderer then took his time and finished looking for what he wanted and left. He was caught leaving by the back door by the neighbour in the house behind this one. He called over thinking it was Bill heading to the privy. When the man ran, he called out and was lucky to have the garrison patrol already out front to hear him. They saw the man run off and gave chase. One went inside the house and found Bill lying dead in his own blood. They chased the man to the wall and watched him disappear over it thanks to a knotted rope left for that purpose. I tracked him south and found him with you."

The Reeve looked at me and waited. I had no idea what he was waiting for and suddenly I felt uncomfortable and out of place. The events here had led to that man scooping me off the ground and then dying with an arrow through his eye. It was senseless. I glanced around the room looking for anything to explain why this had happened so I could break the silence with the discovery. Then a thought occurred to me—a little detail that didn't add up.

"Where is the knife he used?" I blurted out. At my camp, he had used my knife. I didn't remember seeing another one when the Reeve had looted his body.

The Reeve smiled at that. "Good question. I have no idea. I've looked all over for it and even questioned people in town. No one has seen it. Best I can figure is he lost it somewhere between here and where you were." The Reeve sniffed and pointed a boot at the chest in the corner. "Have a look in there."

I moved over to the chest, careful to step over the blood, and waved the flies away. As I stood over it, it was clear that this was an expensive chest and expertly made of the finest woods. Brass bands wrapped the chest and gave it strength and I figured it would probably take at least two strong men to lift it while empty. Leather handles were fashioned into the sides on metal rings. The domed lid was oiled and gleamed even in the dull light coming into the room from the hallway. The hasp of the chest was unlocked and so I reached out and pulled the lid up with surprisingly little effort.

I gasped when I saw the contents. Everywhere I looked I saw gold crown and half-crown coins. The inside of the chest was lined with inset drawers and held bags all bulging with more coins. It was a tremendous fortune; it contained more money than the entire town could earn in a lifetime. I had heard the expression "a king's ransom" and now I knew what one looked like. The light from the hallway glinted off the coins and flashed in my eyes. I couldn't take my eyes off it. Some coins were new but most were old, I thought, and certainly dating from before the war. The cameo of the king stood out on all the coins in the chest. I was reminded of my own stolen coin and felt the guilt descend on me again.

The Reeve came over and slowly closed the lid, looking down at me. "Now that is quite a sizeable fortune and more than a knight with simple lands could ever amass in twenty-five years, don't you think?"

I had no idea how much a knight made but certainly thought the Reeve must be right. Just how could Bill have that much gold?

"It-it-it's..." I stammered searching for the right word. "Amazing!" I finally got the word out, but it still didn't convey my complete sense of awe. "He has so much gold!" I still thought of my coin. My coin didn't have the King's image on it—it wasn't like these.

"Had," corrected the Reeve drily. "He *had* so much gold. Question is: why did the man who killed Bill not take any of it? His purse didn't contain a single gold mark."

I looked sharply at the Reeve to see if he suspected I had a gold coin on me. *I should tell him what I found in the boot*, I thought. *Now is the time*. I opened my mouth to confess, but I saw the Reeve was looking right through me at some memory. I could tell his mind was not on me, but the murder.

"He didn't come here to rob Bill, that's for sure. Even if he didn't come to steal why not take some of this gold? Nothing makes sense." The Reeve didn't seem to be speaking to me but was thinking out loud more than anything else. He was trying to make sense of the murder, to talk it through. The Reeve turned and moved over to stand behind the desk, careful not to disturb the blood. "The parchment in his tunic, you remember that?" This was directed at me and I nodded. I hadn't really thought about the parchment until now.

"It's a map of the town and it identified Bill's house. It also showed where the guards did their patrols. When I showed it to Captain Gendred he was furious, and rightly so. The map allowed the thief to pick when and how to get to Bill's house undetected. Someone drew that map, someone who knew the town. Gendred wants the head of whoever aided the assassin." The Reeve opened a desk drawer, looked inside and then just as quickly closed it. It was clear he had already gone through this room in detail. "The murderer was after something here and I'm not sure he found what he wanted. Even if he did take something, I am not convinced he had time to hand it off. He was on the run from the house all the way to the clearing where he stumbled across you and I was on his heels the entire time. He didn't drop it anywhere. There was no time. I'm convinced of that. I wonder who Bill was to warrant an assassination."

The Reeve looked thoughtfully at the armour on the tree and his eyebrows furrowed in thought. He slid some papers around on the desk, avoiding the blood. Then he looked up sharply at the armour once more, his eyes a little wider. I didn't really notice at the time though. Instead, I was focused on something the Reeve had just said and it confused and angered me.

"You were on his heels the entire time? From here to my camp? Why didn't you run him down before he got to the woods? Why didn't you stop him before he grabbed me!" My voice raised in pitch as my mind reeled. The Reeve looked at me, at first a little startled, as if drawn out of some deeper thought, but now he glared at me and the look stifled further protests.

"I was following him to see where he was headed. There may have been more of them out there and I am pretty sure there was. He had no supplies on him, remember? He was meeting with someone else. Someone who had his gear." This froze the anger in my blood as I remembered my fears that night, remembered kicking down my fire in the fright of being discovered. I felt my cheeks redden in embarrassment and hung my head a little, knowing the Reeve was right.

"Will," he continued a little softer seeing my reaction. "Somehow he knew I was following him. That man had skills in the outdoors. He left no trail that I could find and that was a first for me. I tracked him by other means." The Reeve grimaced before continuing and I wondered what he meant. "I honestly don't think anyone could have snuck up on that fellow. He moved like a shadow. It was uncanny. I have no doubt that he was a professional thief, maybe an assassin based on the murder, although it was sloppily done judging by all this blood." He gestured around at the room. "Either he was terrible at the actual killing part or he revelled in the act. I'm pretty sure I know the answer to that and I'm pretty sure he led me into those woods to ambush me and then when he found you lying there felt he had an edge on me. He probably thought having a hostage would lure me out to him for a direct confrontation. It was not a smart thing to do. I don't do direct confrontations very well." A hint of a smile ghosted across the Reeve's face and for a second I almost saw a different man looking back at me—a harder, crueller man. The thief had clearly underestimated the Reeve, and I thanked the Word silently.

"Will," he said after a moment's silence and I looked up to see him staring earnestly at me. "I didn't know you were there until I saw the light of your fire and saw him pick you up off the ground. Believe me, I was as surprised as you were."

When I nodded my understanding the Reeve looked around the room. "Good," he said simply and then changed the subject. "Bill didn't keep an inventory and I have no idea what he kept in here. Whatever he took he must've dropped as he ran or else he never found what he wanted. Bill's dead, and that man is dead—a tragedy all around. Senseless."

I almost told the Reeve about the coin at that moment. I had no doubt the coin was what the murderer was after and perhaps it would provide the Reeve with what he needed to understand the murder. But I was sorely torn. I only needed a few days with it, nothing more. I desperately needed to determine what made it work, how it let me see through walls, and more importantly, how it showed me what ailed a person just by looking at them. I sensed it would allow me to better treat people, and I argued with myself that the number of potential lives I could save outweighed the need to do the right thing. Plus I couldn't shake this feeling the coin somehow belonged with me. And so I warred with myself and stared meekly at the Reeve, waiting until he gathered his thoughts. He clamped a hand on my shoulder and squeezed it briefly in warmth.

"I wanted to show you this to give you some closure. To prove to you it had nothing to do with you. I owed you that after what you experienced last night. And you've got a keen eye, too, Will. You've confirmed my own conclusions here and I thank you for that."

I nodded, not sure how to respond. I didn't feel like this provided closure. The Reeve looked around the room one more time and beckoned toward the exit and the stairs.

"Enough. Let's go to Martha and see to her sickness. Let's see if we can't do something to help her and her son. There's been enough death around here."

With one last glance to the armour in the corner, he escorted me out of the house to the street.

Duilleog

Four

East Side of Jaipers, 900 A.C.

W E MADE OUR way back to the open market and carried on past it down the road to the east side of town. I recognised at once that this was the area where I had glimpsed the sick woman and her child through the coin. A few people stopped and stared openly at us as we walked down the dusty streets, most likely wondering what I had done to warrant the Reeve's attention. As we moved further east, the wealth of the people dropped rapidly. The people who lived on the east side were the poor of Jaipers. They patched together their clothes like me and they were covered in dirt with visible streaks of sweat lining their faces. These poor people could barely scrape a living from the town. I heard a shriek and moments later I watched three children, close to my age but acting so much younger, run past on bare feet thick with calluses and laughing, oblivious to the poverty that surrounded them.

In this area of town, the homes were nothing more than shacks made of twigs and branches combined, rolled and tied together into log-like shapes and then stacked and held together with hemp ropes, and the gaps filled with mud or clay from the river banks. The roofs were made from woven straw and barely served to keep the rain out. Typically, a small cooking fire lay out back, away from the house in a vain effort to reduce the chance of fire but mostly to try to keep the smoke clear of the inside.

The shacks were small. A man of my short stature might be able to stand up inside some of them, but most people would have to stoop. In summer, like now, the shacks provided some shelter from the sun and rains. In winter, the people froze unless they huddled together for warmth but at least they could stay dry and warm and that was half the battle. The town allowed the shacks to stand and even had laws on how many could be placed together and how far apart they needed to be. The garrison only made sure no shacks were built too close to the town wall. Fire was always the fear and the people who dwelled here knew and took precautions. They policed themselves.

I spied a lean dog panting in the shade of a nearby shack, his tongue lolling out of his mouth farther than I thought possible. He raised his head to stare at me rather directly and I moved to the other side of the Reeve to escape his notice. He kept his eager eyes locked on me as we passed, and it was unnerving. I felt sympathy for the poor animal, but his stare was far too aware for my comfort.

Thankfully, I was distracted by an elderly couple who nodded politely to the Reeve as we strolled past and he nodded back and smiled. I then noticed a young girl of maybe four years of age wearing only a roughly sewn patchwork pair of shorts and nothing else. She stood with one arm raised and holding the support beam of a porch awning with the thumb of her other hand stuck firmly in her mouth. Snot ran freely from her nose and she interrupted her thumb sucking to wipe it away before popping her thumb back into her mouth. Her skin was deeply tanned, but it was hard to tell with the layers of dirt that coated her from head to feet.

She stared unblinkingly at us as we slowly passed, and it was clear that she was ill with the sickness. *She is probably in the early stages*, I thought. Her eyes were darkened and sunk into her head. I could count her ribs and couldn't help but notice her distended belly. She was so hungry, and I felt her hunger, too. I felt an urge to do something for her—anything at all—and considered what few coins I possessed and knew it would not be enough. What could I do to help her short of emptying my own meagre pockets? Shame crept up my neck and red-faced, I walked faster to be clear of her gaze. In a moment I was a few paces ahead of the Reeve and heard a soft *tsk* escape his mouth. I glanced back at him, expecting to see him looking hard at me and judging me, and I was surprised to see him staring back at the poor girl. He must have felt me looking at him and quickly strode forward to join me, indicating the path ahead that led between two shacks.

I thought of Daukyns then and all the work he did in this area. It was here that he distributed the unguents and herbs I gathered. He took what little coin he could get his hands on and spread it here—equally to all—and spread the Word with it.

"The Word," he once told me, "was better understood by the poor."

When I had asked him why he merely smiled at me and said, "Those who have nothing appreciate the simpler things in life all the more." He laughed then and leaned into me as if sharing some great secret.

"The Church," he whispered theatrically loud, glancing about to see if anyone was listening in, which was ludicrous since we had been sitting alone outside his small room. "The Church would take from the poor. They always have, haven't they?" And then he had laughed as if it was some great joke. After a time, he calmed and drained the wine from his small cup in one swallow.

"The Word," he added then, "Would never *take* but *give* to those who need. Real charity work—not that save my soul for heaven crap. That was what the Word was always about." He hugged his empty cup to his chest. "The balance. It is all about the balance." Then he fell asleep.

I shook my head to return my thoughts back to the present, looking around at the shacks and seeing that many of the people were sitting inside the narrow strips of shade their shacks offered from the sun. The people did not look well, and I could hear many people coughing with a wracking, wet and deep sound. It was clear to me that the illness was spreading. I was surprised that Daukyns hadn't mentioned to me just how widespread the illness was and I wished he had better prepared me. Dull eyes followed us as we walked through the area and I felt such pity for them. A quick glance to the Reeve let me see he too was surprised at how many people were sick and a shadow of sorrow crossed his face. I realised then that Daukyns could not have known just how bad it now was.

Where was the Word in this side of town? I fumed. Where was the balance? Daukyns preached the Word in this town and spread the knowledge. Knowledge was the path for humanity, he always said. And people were supposed to treat one another equally. "Do unto others as you would have them do unto you", was one of Daukyns favourite borrowed passages from the Church. That way of thinking seemed distant here in Jaipers. If even small towns like this could not hold true to the Word, what hope then for a stronger, brighter future? *The war had changed nothing*, I thought glumly. The brighter, better future promised by the Revolution and the Word, where was it? The evidence all around me told me that it had failed but part of me yearned for a solution through the Word, a way to fulfil the promise and help these poor people. Daukyns had tried to make a difference every day here but never seemed to solve anything, and sadness filled me knowing that his solution would not, in the end, make a difference.

"This way," said the Reeve, interrupting my thoughts as he led the way between buildings.

I was glad he chose to lead. I would not have been able to explain how I already knew where the woman lay with her little boy. I hung back a little as we approached the woman's shack. I wasn't sure what the Reeve expected me to be able to do with her and apprehension filled me. I had always merely looked in on someone the Reeve wanted me to see. Almost always it was merely a simple fever or some minor infection from cuts and scrapes. I would brew some tea with my herbs or apply some of my healing unguents and be gone. I knew, admittedly with a certain pride, that my teas and unguents always worked. And very quickly, too. But as I stood there taking stock of the woman's shack, I felt far removed from what I felt was comfortable or appropriate. I was barely a man, untrained in healing and positive I would be caught as a fraud at any moment.

So, I stopped on the road and stared at the shack, trying to will myself to keep moving. Absently, I noticed this shack was not unlike all the others except that maybe it stood a little higher than those around it. Then I noticed that flowers had been planted lovingly alongside the front wall in an effort to brighten it. The plants were well tended and thriving. I sensed from them that they were happy here and felt how their roots dug deep into the soil. I knew that the woman in the shack doted on them. The sight of the flowers eased my discomfort somewhat. Based on the large pile of clothing that lay in a woven basket on her small porch I knew she probably mended clothes for a living. Next to the basket lay a large section of a log that served as a seat, a worn smooth section marking her favourite spot. There wasn't much of anything else and it was probably just her and her boy living here.

The Reeve arrived at the doorway and held back the piece of patch-worked cloth that served as a door and beckoned me in with a tilt of his head. Mustering my resolve, I dipped my head under the low doorframe and entered first, the Reeve following in behind me. As I entered, I stopped in the sudden absence of sunlight and waited for my eyes to adjust. The Reeve came in quietly behind me and announced who we were. As my eyes started to pierce the gloom and I could make out the legs of the woman huddled under a thin blanket and beside her was her son, his back turned to us and blocked the rest of her from my view. He was sitting on the dirt floor holding a small container of water. The smell of vomit, urine and faeces struck me with full force and I gagged despite my best effort not to.

"Martha, I've brought the young healer to see you," announced the Reeve in a quiet voice and he waited for a reply. Startled by his title for me, I looked first at the Reeve then back toward the woman and her child. Healer, I wondered. What a strange title for me. But I admitted to myself that I liked it and for an instant, I imagined my mother's approving smile and that gave me some strength.

The young boy, no more than eight, slowly turned his head to look at us and then turned back to his mother and gently shook her shoulder.

"Momma," he said, exhaustion plain in his voice. He shook her again. "Momma, please wake up." And the boy coughed a little. After a couple more attempts, I heard her murmur 'all right' and she stirred and tried to sit up.

The Reeve quickly closed the gap between them and squatted down and held her back down. "Shh," he said. "Lie back and relax, Martha. No need to fuss. The healer just needs to have a look and see what he can do for you."

The boy chose that moment to cough. The sound was from a thick, phlegm-filled hack and it took him like an attack and I noted that it was deep and wheezing. It drained the boy of any remaining strength and he swooned but was caught by the Reeve's quick hand. He held the boy steady until his senses returned and I remained at the door, unsure of where to begin.

The Reeve looked back at me with an expression that seemed to implore that I hurry up and do something. I blinked, shrugged my backpack off my shoulders onto the floor and moved over to the other side of the woman's litter so I could see her better. Her bed comprised of nothing more than old straw with two thin blankets placed on top with her lying between them. The stains and the smell told me she lay in her own filth. Her boy had no sense to clean her up, and she had no choice but to relieve herself where she was. Her right arm sat exposed outside the blanket beside me and by the frightening ease of which her bones could be made out, I knew she was wasting away; to such a large degree it was frightening. The illness was robbing her of the flesh of her body and it had already almost fully consumed her. I squatted down beside her and looked over the shape hidden by the blanket and did not know where to start. The Reeve had called me a healer, but in truth I was nothing more than a boy who created potions. I knew nothing of treating sick people; I had no right to call myself healer. Her boy deserved someone more knowledgeable to take care of his mum and I felt like a pretender.

The Reeve waited a moment and then quietly told me to lift back the blanket and have a look. I glanced to him and he held my nervous gaze. The eyes that looked back at me seemed to plead. Whatever doubt I felt about my abilities, it seemed the Reeve did not share them. I saw a glimmer of hope behind those eyes and it humbled me on the spot. I broke my eyes from that stare and lifted a hand to pull back the blanket. I looked over at the woman's face and was startled to find her staring right back at me with recessed eyes surrounded by black circles, radiating fear and sickness. The whites of her eyes were yellowed, and the lids were crusted all round. Dried dark-green snot clung thickly to her nostrils and her lips were pasty white and cracked, bleeding and swollen. The top of the blanket, pulled up to her neck, was sprayed with dark green phlegm and bright flecks of blood. She stared back at me and did not seem to blink. She just stared and stared, and I felt frozen in place by the anguish and fear I saw there. Whatever certainty I had left washed out of me and I believed she must have sensed this, for she startled me by touching my foot nearest her with her hand.

"P–p–please..." she said so softly that I could barely make out the word and for a moment I thought I saw hope spark in her eyes.

"Right," I said with an uncontrolled squeak. Red-faced and embarrassed, I cleared my throat and repeated myself. "Right, I'll just have a quick look. Is that alright?" I waited and after an almost imperceptible nod from her, I gently pulled back the blanket.

I am not sure what startled me the most. It was either her nakedness—I had never seen a woman undressed before—or it was the emaciation of her body. She was wasted away. Black and blue circular blotches surrounded by white, flaking, dead skin marred her skin. She looked like she had been severely beaten. Her ribs stood out like the bars of a cage and I thought back to the starved girl I had seen by the porch and thought now that the girl had looked fat compared to this poor woman. Her stomach appeared to be sucked in tight against her spine. *This woman should be dead*, I thought. No one could starve this much and not be dead. I had no idea how she clung to life. What skin she had—that was not covered in pustules—was yellow and looked like leather left out too long in the sun. I had no idea what I could do to help her. I almost turned away at that moment but an urge to do something rose up inside me and almost took my breath away with its intense ferocity. I felt the Reeve staring at me and when I looked briefly at him, his eyes pleaded.

The desire to help was so strong and yet I felt so helpless and tears stung my eyes in frustration. Then I remembered the coin and fumbling, I reached up to grasp my leather pouch through my tunic. The coin called out, and I knew I needed to hold it but I couldn't do that with the Reeve present. Inspiration struck, and I glanced at the boy and then asked the Reeve if he could remove the child for a moment. *The boy should not be in here in any case,* I thought to myself, *and so the request was not unreasonable.* The Reeve looked quizzically at me, grasping my tunic, and then nodded and lifted the boy up in his arms and carried him outside.

Alone with the woman, I saw that she had now fallen asleep or passed out—I didn't know which—but I was relieved that she would not witness what I was about to do. Her breathing was shallow, rasping and strained as she struggled for each breath. I quickly pulled the pouch out of my tunic and emptied the coin into my hand. My fingers shook with the need to hurry, and quickly I placed my thumb on the worn spot and rubbed it and immediately I *shifted* and the woman changed before my eyes.

She was surrounded by a sickly yellow-green colour that swirled and pulsed around her. Like before with the walls in Daukyns' room, the coin was making her flesh ghostly like fog and I could look inside her. It was repulsive and impressive all at the same time and part of me wondered in awe at all the moving parts of the human body. I was observing the beauty of life and I felt the need to understand how each part worked together. Her heart was pumping, and her blood moved through her veins. I followed those veins to her lungs and saw that both of them were full of a thick, dark fluid that stuck to the insides and robbed her of breath. I did not understand how she could breathe at all with what remained of her lungs. I intensified my gaze and noticed tiny flashes of yellow light and my eyes focused on a tiny particle that came floating out of her opened mouth when she exhaled. As I watched, it drifted lazily in the air and disappeared out of my sight. The mote was so small—smaller than a particle of dust, its light the only thing that alerted me to its presence. Intuitively, I *shifted* my gaze and saw, with horror, the very dust in the air light up with these same motes. They filled the shack, and I saw that I had been breathing them into myself from the moment I had entered. A wave of nausea struck me, and I had to fight back a sudden urge to vomit. Terror struck me as a cry escaped my mouth and I fought the desire to run from this shack and never stop. I heard the Reeve outside call in with a question of some kind, alarmed probably by my cry, but I bade him remain outside and thankfully he did.

With an effort, I forced myself to remain where I was and leaned forward to look closer at the woman and felt my vision draw closer and closer to her without me moving. What were these things? What harm were they doing? I had to know. She grew in my eyes until suddenly I was within her. I had to be— I was surrounded by her flesh but knew I was not physically there. I could feel myself still kneeling beside her but my vision, what my eyes saw- that was inside this poor woman. I was stunned.

My gaze had pierced her skin, and I rushed into her lungs and I now found myself moving and drawn to one of the tiny motes trapped in her lungs. My thoughts seemed to guide what I saw, and I moved closer and closer to the mote until it filled my vision. I knew right away that this was no mote of dust. It was alive and pulsed. Tiny hairs all around it swam and propelled it through her. I watched in increasing horror as this monstrous thing suddenly gripped another object inside this poor woman and attacked it. The hairs pulled the object in tight against it and I watched, repulsed, as it transferred part of itself into it. This part immediately started devouring the object from the inside. I knew, with sudden clarity, that this small portion of the woman was dying right in front of me. These motes were, one–by–one, attacking this woman from the inside and destroying her. They had laid siege to her body, and they were winning.

Trembling now, I pulled my vision back a little and watched more motes swim toward more parts of this poor woman and knew they wouldn't stop until she was completely dead. Hundreds and thousands of the motes, more than I could count, were invading this woman. They darted about and drove toward the healthier parts of her with such malevolent intent. The motes were a natural part of this world, I somehow knew, but they served no purpose. They invaded and killed, spread and destroyed, leaving a path of destruction behind them. They gave nothing back to the world. They took and took. At these thoughts I felt the presence again and knew that I had just discovered something important, something the presence wanted me to see. A moan from the woman broke this thought, and I turned my attention back to her illness.

I had no idea how to fight these invaders No army could hope to conquer something this small. I felt powerless and rage began to grow and simmer in me. I quickly ran through the healing my unguents and herbs could provide and knew that what little lore I possessed could do nothing to stop this invasion. A loud ringing noise started in my ears, startling me, and with it an urge rose quickly up within me, fuelling my mounting anger. A desire to heal this woman was now so strong that it was almost overwhelming me. I felt like a man drowning, looking upwards at the surface of the water and knowing he couldn't make it. Knowing that he would soon suck in a lungful of water with that last killing breath, and even knowing that it would be his last, unable to resist.

The Reeve had called me a healer, and I was determined now to do just that—whatever the cost. I focused my gaze on the motes and recognised them for what they were: an abomination of nature. The motes lived to destroy. They added nothing to the world except pain, misery and death. They upset the balance of nature. I struggled with my inner emotions, dizzy now with the effort; the ringing in my ears was so loud it hurt. I felt that my very being was trying to reach out to cure this woman, and I did not know how to do so. I was the drowning man, and the surface was so far away. The task seemed impossible and my anger and urge to heal grew without an outlet.

I focused on one mote and studied it. It was so ugly to my eyes. Never had I seen such an aberration. With my *vision*, it appeared larger than I was and it loomed over me. I did not understand how this coin allowed me to observe things as I did but I marvelled at the power it afforded me. I stared at the mote as it arrogantly destroyed yet another piece of this woman and felt an intense hatred for it join my anger. I had never felt such hatred. It matched my anger and made my mind come into sharper focus and I watched, repelled, as the mote started to move toward another part of the woman and intuitively I *reached* out and willed it to stop.

And it did.

I felt like I held it, squirming, in my hands. It struggled to swim away yet with no more effort than a thought I grasped it firm. Experimenting, I released it and it continued its path toward the object. Exulted, I grabbed it again and held it. My hatred and revulsion grew, and I imagined my hand closing on the mote, squeezing it, crushing it. To my delight and astonishment, the mote collapsed in on itself and ruptured. The hairs around the cell ceased their motion, and I released the mote. It floated there, unmoving and lifeless. I had destroyed it and felt elation soar through me. Like that drowning man, I suddenly burst free of the water and sucked in a lungful of glorious air! I knew what to do: I had killed the invader with nothing more than a thought! Eagerly, I *reached* out to another mote, grasped it and crushed it. I moved to another and repeated my attack. I went to another one and another one, gleefully killing them with my righteous anger. As I progressed from one mote to another, a thought finally occurred to me that this would take forever to accomplish. I *reached* out and grabbed two of the motes and crushed them. Then three, then four at a time, and then it seemed as there couldn't be a limit. I pulled back my vision and saw all the motes in the woman as one. They stood out like sparks of fire in the night sky. I grabbed them all at once and with a thought crushed them. Rapture filled me and I nearly toppled. My soul leaped in the knowledge that this unnatural enemy had been destroyed. As the feeling faded, the green colour that had pulsed over the woman ceased and withdrew and a wonderful soft blue slowly emerged to engulf her. I could sense that the balance of her health was restored, freed from the invaders, but I also sensed that I had more to do if she was to live. The ravages the motes left behind in her were extensive. I had killed her invaders, but their damage was still everywhere.

Her ragged, shallow breathing continued, and I turned my attention to the fluid that filled her lungs and I pushed at it and watched as it came up through her throat. Her eyes snapped open, wide with fear, and her hands shot to her throat. It was choking her, but I was resolved to finish this and so I pushed harder and was rewarded with a mass of phlegm, enormous in its volume, pouring from her mouth. She twisted violently onto her side and coughed and spat what she could out of her mouth. I kept pushing until her lungs were clear but saw then that I had collapsed them. Her throat convulsed, and her face grew a deep red with her effort to breathe. I pushed air into her lungs and as they inflated, she took over and she gasped in mouthfuls of air and collapsed on her litter exhausted, eyes closed in surrender to the joy of breathing freely once again. Colour returning to her face, she drew air deeply into her lungs. Her entire body suddenly relaxed, and I realised with relief she was unconscious from exhaustion.

She was no longer in any danger that I knew, but she was still so very weak. I worked my way through her skin and pushed dead cells out of her and urged her skin to heal those areas blackened and damaged by the motes. I do not know how I knew what to do but trusted in the power of the coin to guide me. In time, I knew I could do no more to the woman and that she would need nourishment for her body to replace what flesh she had lost to the illness. I had done it. I had saved this poor woman, and I felt such a strong feeling of gratitude to the power that permitted me to help her. The presence flickered again, and I felt a sense of amusement and then a nudge to remember the boy.

I pulled back my vision from the mother and turned it quickly to the boy, lying limp in the arms of the Reeve.

I repeated my actions against the motes within him and found it much easier this time, but it was accompanied by a feeling of weariness deep within me and my head started to pound. I ignored this, eager to keep healing, and *reached* into the boy's lungs and pushed the phlegm clear of his young lungs, watching as the Reeve suddenly put the boy down on the ground and pound him on the back. I heard the Reeve's cry of disgust as the thick, green phlegm poured clear of the boy's mouth. I heard him call my name for help, but I ignored him as I poured air into the lungs. The boy was clean and required nothing more from me.

I glanced at the Reeve and I crushed the motes inside his body. Another glance to the air surrounding me and another within myself and the area was clear. Each effort was now accompanied by a feeling of weariness that warred with the elation at defeating this invader. The pounding pain in my head and the weariness within me grew stronger with each effort but I pushed it away and ignored it. I was unstoppable and my eagerness to continue filled me and drove me. I was truly the healer now. The title the Reeve had given me was mine to keep. But I sensed it was something more. I wasn't just healing; I was restoring a balance to the world and felt the righteousness of it.

Inspired, I pulled back my vision until I could observe the entire village and saw that almost everyone was infected to one degree or another. It had spread throughout the town. But how was it spreading and how had it spread so quickly?

I opened my eyes and looked around the room I was in and was drawn to the small container of water the boy had used with his mother. I *shifted* and right away observed the bright yellow motes aggressively swimming in the water and I was revolted. Then, shocked, I knew the answer: the town well! By the Word, water was the source! It all came together for me then: everyone in town, from the rich to the poor, used the same well.

I travelled to the well with my vision and quickly entered it. And with a fright I spied a large family of rats living in a burrow where the water met the sides of the well and where the lining stones of one wall had fallen free. An elaborate series of tunnels led up from their nest to the surface near the open market. Motes swarmed all over the rats on the back of fleas and leapt from one rat to the next. All the water of the well was teaming with the motes and I saw the dead carcass of a rat lying half in the water and another one that floated, bloated with gas, on the surface. I felt bile burn and sour the back of my throat. This was the source that was infecting the village. The invaders had spread from person to person—inhaled and exhaled through the lungs and ingested in the water they drank every day. It had spread until it had consumed the entire village.

I remembered that I had drunk from that well that morning and recalled the funny taste of it and realised with a shock I had drunk water that had a rotting carcass of a dead rat in it. I clenched my teeth and willed myself not to throw up. My throat convulsed, and I fought with myself to quell my stomach. Without hesitating, I glared at the invaders in the well and crushed them with a thought. The rats, oblivious to my action, carried on. I thought briefly of killing the rats but no sooner had the thought occurred to me then a pain sharpened the pounding in my head and I quickly turned away from that idea. The motes were an abomination, but not the rats. I could not kill them.

I could do something about these motes, however, and my hatred of these invaders continued to consume me as I clenched my hands and jaw with determination. The wrongness of what they did stoked my rage and made me forget the growing pain in my head. I observed the entire village once again and saw the invaders light up brightly wherever they hid—in people, in water containers, on the fleas that covered the rats, cats and dogs. They even drifted freely in the air. Without hesitation, I reached up with my free hand; fingers curled and stretched upwards, and with a cry of exultation crushed my hand into a fist and smote the invaders wherever they lay.

My head and vision exploded with an agony beyond reckoning and I found myself lying on my side, immobile. I blinked against the white pain that clouded my sight and dimly made out the Reeve rushing into the shack with his arms outstretched toward me. I thought I heard him cry out my name as he reached my side and grabbed me. For an instant he became a woman who I at first thought was my mother, but it wasn't her, I knew at once with sadness. As I closed my eyes, I smelled the fresh scent of rain.

Blackness consumed me, and I embraced it.

Five

Jaipers, 900 A.C.

I WOKE IN a strange room and braced myself to feel the pain come crashing back into my head, but slowly, I realised with relief, it was gone. The pain had been excruciating and consumed my entire being; I would do anything to never feel it again. I trembled at the memory and lay for a spell, simply relishing the absence of pain. It was almost blissful. After an effort, I was able to crack my eyes open and a quick glance failed to provide me with any recognition of where I was. I shifted my eyes and took in my surroundings. I lay on the thick mattress of a real bed and I was covered with sheets—real sheets! They were pulled up to my chin and tucked under my sides, cocooning me in a feeling of security. A brief memory of my mother returned to me, but it eluded my attempt to hold on. Sunlight streamed in from a window somewhere to my left and highlighted the dust that danced in the air. I closed my eyes and thought back on what I could remember since the pain claimed me.

I had flashes of memory of being woken up a couple of times before. Something was pressed briefly to my lips. I remembered someone's hand in mine, gripping it tightly with rushed, frantic words telling me to stay. I had heard a grown man crying, and that frightened me. But the pain was always there, pounding in my skull and consuming me and I hid from it in the welcomed darkness.

I felt so very tired and knew it was no normal fatigue. This consumed me and robbed me of any movement. My arms and legs felt like they were tied down with enormous weights and I could barely manage to wiggle my toes. This frightened me a great deal, and I started to cry softly without meaning to and once I started I found I couldn't stop. I wasn't sure what I cried for—whether it was in relief or some sorrow. And yet sobs threatened to rack my body until the very act of crying sapped me of what little strength I had left and once again the blackness took me.

I dreamt.

I dreamt that the motes had not been killed, merely subdued for a time. I floated above the town and I watched as the motes, now man-sized, formed lines that surrounded the town to lay siege. I knew this to be ludicrous upon inspection, but in my dream, it was so very real. Outside the wall, the entire town's people stood armed with nothing more than sticks and hammers. I had no idea why they were outside the safety of the walls. Where was the garrison? And I spied them, there, inside the inn, sitting at tables and drinking and eating: all the soldiers of the garrison with their captain seated with them. They sat safely inside the walls, ignoring the siege and the army outside. I watched as they pulled roasted chickens apart and gorged on the meat and laughed when they sloshed the wine from their cups to the ground. I tried to call out to them, but they ignored me.

I turned from them and screamed at the people to run back inside the town gate, but no one heard me. Except there: one young woman. She stood facing away from the motes and instead stared at me without expression. She held a watering can in her hand, but it was tipped, and water spilt freely onto the dirt. Where the water hit the ground, the first shoots of plants erupted from the soil at impossible speeds. As one the motes took one step forward, and I tore my gaze from the strange woman. The motes changed into the figures of men: soldiers, armed and lethal. The villagers didn't stand a chance against them and I shouted at them. *You need swords*, I screamed. *You need me! I can help you! I can help you all!* I tried then to destroy the motes as I had before, but they remained strong. I could do nothing. But with my effort, they noticed me and in horror, I watched as the soldiers turned as one toward me and left the ground to fly and circle me faster than I could move. The villagers turned and watched impassively as the soldiers marched in the surrounding air. I screamed in fear and then they closed. One grasped me close and impaled me with a sword. I felt my flesh and bone split and tear, and the agony was excruciating. My mouth opened to cry out, but no sound emerged. I watched, horrified, as something travelled down inside the length of the blade, the metal bulging and stretching to accommodate it. I felt it enter me and then squirm inside me. Pain erupted throughout my body as it devoured me from the inside.

I woke screaming in the arms of none other than the Reeve. He held me in his arms like a child. I was sobbing uncontrollably into his shoulder and the horror of my dream replayed over and over again in my mind as he tightened his arms around me and patted my back. I cried for a long time and I did not know why, only that I had to. I couldn't seem to control my emotions and only managed to stop when my embarrassment overcame my need to cry. I pulled back my head and widened my eyes at the snot and tears that covered the Reeve's tunic at the shoulder. My shame consumed me. The Reeve grabbed me by the upper arms and gently pushed me back up against the pillow behind me. I stared at the large wet spot and Reeve glanced at it and chuckled.

"Yup, pretty gross," he said, and I surprised myself by laughing with him.

I realised that I had very little control over my own emotions. I sat inside my head listening to myself laugh with a kind of awe and tried to will myself to stop. Eventually, the laughter ran down and I lay there simply staring numbly up at the Reeve sitting on the side of my bed. I glanced around the room and finally recognised it as one of the expensive rooms in the inn. Candles lit the room, and it was night outside. A cool breeze entered the open window on my left and stirred the curtains. Outside the window, I could hear the chirping of crickets and the faint sound of frogs down by the river's edge.

The fatigue I had felt earlier was diminished somewhat but still overpowering. My arms and legs were not as heavy as before. I still needed much rest, and I knew I would be unable to leave this bed by my own power for some time. And this made me feel trapped for some strange reason. I could feel the forest pulling at me and I knew that I would feel better with the dirt beneath me—I just had to get there. This sudden longing filled me but I realised the futility of it and forced my attention back to the Reeve.

"W-who..." I started, but my voice cracked and faded before I could speak further, and I raised a hand to my throat. The Reeve reached out and grabbed a skin of water hooked on the nightstand beside my bed. He pulled the stopper with his teeth and handed it to me. I reached up with shaking hands and took it, the weight pulling my arms down to my chest as I struggled to raise it to my lips. As the opening touched my mouth, the memory of the dead rats in the well returned and I quickly turned my head to avoid the water and cried out. Water splashed on my cheek and ran down my neck.

"It's just water, son. Drink, you need it," soothed the Reeve as he tried to reposition the skin to my lips.

I clamped my mouth shut and shook my head weakly and when he stopped, I looked at him. "Where is the water from?" I asked, only able to achieve a dry whisper.

"The well," replied the Reeve and when I stared at him in horror, he chuckled and explained that at one point a few days ago I had cried out about the well water and at the urging of the Reeve, the captain ordered the garrison to investigate. They had been disgusted when they found the rat's nest and quickly cleared them out and replaced the missing stones on the inside of the well walls. The town had then formed a bucket line and drew hundreds and hundreds of buckets of water until it once again tasted clean. I nodded in gratitude, reaching for the skin as he raised it to my lips and I drank the clear, cool water. I felt the water hit my empty stomach and a terrible thirst took hold of me and I eagerly sucked on the opening of the skin like a new born calf on its mother's teat until the Reeve pulled the skin free.

"Easy now. Take it easy. Not too much!" he said. "You haven't eaten in a week."

"A week?" I spluttered in shock, spraying water. "A week? How is that possible?"

I looked frantically around the room trying to find some clue that the Reeve was lying. A week! It seemed so implausible.

"Yes, son," he replied quietly. "Well, six days anyway. Close enough. You've had little but what water we could force down you and some broth that the cook made up special for you."

"Daukyns? Where is he?" I demanded and watched as the Reeve looked quickly down and with a sinking feeling I knew that there was something more to be said about my friend. He paused as I looked at him in disbelief.

"Daukyns spent the first twenty-four hours with you. He stayed until he was sure you were going to be okay," he finally told me before looking away.

"W-wait, there's something else, isn't there? Is he alright?" I tried to push myself up in the bed. The fatigue was returning in waves and it was getting harder to stay focused, but I fought the urge to sleep.

The Reeve laid a hand on my chest and with very little effort pushed me back down until my head lay back down on my pillow. "No," he said. "He's not. But that can wait. You need to get stronger. Thought for sure you were dead, son, and that isn't an easy thing to come back from."

"Dead?" I shook my head at the absurdity and pleaded to the Reeve with my eyes. "Never mind that. What about Daukyns?" The illness I had seen in him was the forefront of my fears. *It must have taken hold*, I thought. *I needed to see him and help him with the coin.*

Remembering the coin froze my thoughts and panic struck me. Where was it? I had it in my hand when I passed out in the shack and I was suddenly certain that the Reeve must now have it. What must he be thinking? He would figure it out quickly and know where I found it and know that I hid it from him. My thoughts became jumbled and I could not focus on Daukyns. The coin and the fatigue rose up inside me and it was all I could do to fight it off and remain awake.

The Reeve looked at me for a long while. I was not sure whether he was seeing if I was going to stay awake or if he knew what he was going to say to me. I could only look up at him and wait for my energy to come back.

"I heard you cry out," he started slowly. "I was outside the shack helping the boy clear that junk from his mouth and then you yelled." He peered at me looking for some reaction and when I simply stared back he continued.

"It was a yell of anger and victory all mixed together—not one I expected to hear. I rushed in and you were on your side, staring right at me." He paused and took a breath. "You were glowing, son. A blue light was bursting out of you and as I watched it snuffed out like a candle flame and, and..." The Reeve paused longer this time. "I was pretty sure you had just died right in front of me. I've seen men die before and well, son, you looked like you just died. By the Word, one of your eyes was still open and the other half shut! I rushed over and couldn't find any life in you at all."

The Reeve stood up and turned away from me. He went over to the door and looked outside. Satisfied with something, he came back and sat down on the edge of the bed but kept his head toward the door, so I couldn't see his face. I was stunned. Was I glowing blue? Is that what I looked like when I used the coin?

He said nothing for a spell and then continued. He spoke so softly that I had to strain to hear him.

"Wasn't much I could do at that point. Then Martha woke up and her son crawled over to her. They were hugging each other and crying, and I was just sitting there with you dead in my arms. I covered you up and ran and got Daukyns. When I told him what had happened I don't think I've ever seen that man get so distressed in my life and I feared he wouldn't make it over to you.

Never seen a man's face get that red and not fall over." The Reeve grew quiet again. He shook his head.

"He put a glass to your mouth, and it fogged over and he said you were still breathing and after that, it got pretty hectic. I talked the innkeeper into putting you up here—the cook helped with that, you should know. He's pretty fond of you. You've been here ever since. Anyway, I've had so many questions going through my mind to ask you and when you are stronger, you and I need to have a talk."

With that, he turned his head toward me and I detected a hint of what looked like fear in his eyes, but that couldn't be. He didn't know what I had done, but he knew I had healed that woman and her boy. *Certainly, nothing to fear from me*, I pleaded to him with my thoughts. Perhaps he had no idea what to do about me and I wasn't sure how or if I could answer any of his questions. I had no idea what I had done or how.

With a shock, I remembered my sickle and my hand shot up to my shoulder. With a sinking feeling, I realised that I was naked under the blanket. My sickle had been found! My world crashed around me and I cried out. I struggled to rise, but the Reeve pushed me back into the bed. He put a hand into the open front of his tunic and my eyes locked onto my leather bag as he pulled it out and lifted it over his head. He had tied it to a leather lanyard. He pulled my head forward and put it around my neck, tucking it under the blanket. I reached up and grasped the bag and immediately felt the sickle and the coin inside. My relief was instantaneous, and I sank further into the bed and closed my eyes, unable to keep them open any longer.

"We'll talk about those when you get stronger, too." I heard him blow out the candles and the room darkened through my eyelids and I fell into a dreamless sleep.

Six

Jaipers, 900 A.C.

I WOKE IN the morning with the sound of the cook placing a trencher beside my bed. My eyes fluttered open and blinked at the bright sunshine that filled the room. The cook smiled down at me and clapped his hands.

"At last, you're awake! I've brought you something to eat, young Will. Hard cheese, fresh bread, milk, and whole oats. Sit up, sit up! I'll help you. You need to eat! Goodness you've wasted away to almost nothing!"

The cook continued a stream of dialogue, not waiting for an answer from me. The sight of the food filled my mouth with saliva and I wiggled my butt in the bed until the cook grabbed my armpits and lifted me until I could get my upper back against the headboard. The cook took a huge steaming slice of fresh warm bread and dropped it into the bowl on the trencher. It was filled with cooked oats and fresh cheese all soaking in warm milk.

"One second, young man," he said as the bread soaked up the liquid. He took a knife and cut the bread into small bites. He then took a spoon and, sitting on the edge of the bed, slowly started to feed me. "This will fatten you up in no time."

The first spoonful entered my mouth, and I knew that food had never tasted so good. I was ravenous, but less than halfway through the bowl I grew nauseous and had to ask the cook to stop. My stomach was betraying me.

"Hmm, the Reeve was right," he mumbled and nodded to himself as he stood up and looked carefully at me. "I'll leave the bowl here in your room, in case you want more later. Okay?"

I nodded, needing to focus on my churning stomach. Dempster stood there and seemed uncertain as what to do next. The innkeeper picked that moment to poke his head in and frown at the two of us before disappearing down the stairs muttering to himself but the words were lost with the sound of his stomping feet.

"Sorry, Will," he said, wringing his hands over his belly and glancing back the way the innkeeper had left. "I have to return to the kitchen."

Without waiting for a reply he hurried back down to his kitchen, his steps loud on the stairs.

The feeling of nausea slowly faded, and I sank back in bed and tested out my strength by lifting my arms and legs. I wasn't much stronger but I could feel the improvement. This weakness in my limbs was strange to me. It was a bone-deep weariness and not a strength issue; I felt drained from the inside and I simply couldn't do anything for very long. A sudden longing to escape to the woods came over me and I had to push it away. The pull to escape the town was getting stronger, but I assumed it merely came from my having spent more time in town than ever before. *Until I could walk to the jacks by myself*, I thought, *the woods would have to wait.*

I had also spent more time in a bed than ever before and I wondered for the first time how I was going to pay for all this. Then I wondered what the Reeve was going to do with me and if he knew what I had done and to what extent. I worried about my future and wanted to run and hide in the woods. I could smell the trees through the smoke from the village cooking fires— nothing could hide that from me. I felt their pull but trapped in this room by my own weakness, I could do nothing but wait and while I waited, I fell asleep again.

When I awoke it was stifling hot in the room and judging by the temperature, it had to be afternoon. I had thrown the sheets off my chest during my sleep and I was covered in sweat. Surely sweating was a good sign of my recovery. I opened my eyes to see the Reeve sitting on a small stool next to the bed.

"Ah!" I cried in shock without meaning to. This waking up and finding all sorts of people next to me was getting tiring. I was used to the outdoors and waking up to solitude. My nerves were rattled. I pushed myself up in bed and marvelled at the strength that was returning to my body. It felt good.

The Reeve reached out to the trencher, brushed some flies away and spooned the remains in the bowl around and glanced at me with questioning eyebrows. I nodded and held out my hands and he handed me the bowl. I quickly spooned some cold milk and oats into my eager mouth and swallowed blissfully. Within seconds I drained the bowl and was scraping at a bit of bread lodged on the bottom when the Reeve reached over, smiling, to gently remove it from me and placed it back on the trencher.

"I'll get the cook to send you up something more filling," he said. "I'll be right back." And with that, he grabbed the trencher and disappeared out the door. I listened to his boots thudding down the stairs and fade away as he moved through the common room toward the kitchen.

I lay back, listening to the quiet of my room, and worried about what the Reeve would do with me. What I had done was insane and unbelievable. He would have reported it to the captain and he would tell his superiors. My mother made me promise to remain hidden and with a sinking feeling, I knew that I had failed that promise. The only option left was honesty. I knew the Reeve was a man I could trust and trust him I must. He would help me; I only had to ask. My heart felt a little lighter with that decision made and I waited in silence for the Reeve to return.

A little while later, I heard the Reeve clomp back up the stairs. He knocked once on the door frame and entered the room, closed the door and sat back down on the stool. He looked over at me and spoke simply: "Food's on its way. So, tell me what happened."

It took about an hour, but eventually, I told the Reeve the whole truth—except where the sickle came from and what it did. Everything else, well, it just sort of poured out of me. The Reeve interrupted only a couple of times to ask me questions but for the most part, he just sat there and listened intently. When I finished, I lay back, drained, and he sat unspoken, not even looking at me. I waited in the uncomfortable silence and finally, he looked up.

"Well," he said, "ain't that something. Listen, we... "

The heavy steps of the cook on the stairs stopped him from continuing and he rose with a slight scowl to take the trencher from cook when he knocked quietly on the door. The Reeve thanked the cook who left with a beaming smile, and then he placed the trencher on the nightstand beside the bed within my reach. On it was a generous pile of sliced roast pork, with small red potatoes and roasted onions all smothered in a thick gravy. A sharp knife was jammed into the wood in the middle, and the Reeve grabbed it and started to cut up the meat into small pieces. I watched as he stole a piece of pork, popped it into his mouth and he chewed it thoughtfully.

"Mmm," he said around the mouthful, "tasty. That cook knows his business."

"Reeve Comlin," I started to say, determined to make him understand that I had done what I thought was right. I was sure he was disappointed in me and would punish me somehow.

"Yes, Will?" he replied, his attention focused on cutting the pork and potatoes.

"I–I'm sorry," I said.

Startled, the Reeve glanced over at me and seeing the look of distress on my face, dropped the knife, sat quickly beside me on the bed and grabbed my shoulders, forcing me to look into his face. I didn't know what to expect but what I saw there were embarrassment and disbelief. The Reeve searched my eyes.

"Sorry? You're sorry?" he exclaimed and I could hear the disbelief in his voice now, too. "Son, son, son," he said, lowering his head and shaking it as he let me go. I watched as the shoulders of the Reeve started bouncing and I realised he was laughing. Laughing! I watched him with growing disdain. How could he sit there and laugh at me?

Still chuckling, he looked up at me. Seeing the look on my face, he starting roaring in laughter. I was sure that the inn's common room could hear him. Probably most of the town could hear him, too. I crossed my arms and glared at him. This was not what I expected.

After what seemed like an eternity, he stopped and wiped his eyes dry. He grabbed the trencher and dropped it into my lap. I kept my arms crossed, determined to stay defiant but did glance down at the pork and gravy and quickly swallowed my saliva, hoping the Reeve didn't notice.

"Eat, eat!" he ordered when he saw me sitting there. "Lord Protector knows you deserve it!"

He sidled back over to the stool and waited until I finally gave in and attacked the food on the trencher. It was pure bliss. My mouth was soon filled with gobs of pork, potatoes and onions. The gravy was hot, rich and delicious. The crackling on the pork was succulent and crunchy. In less than a minute, I devoured the entire trencher and seriously considered licking the wood clean. The Reeve was looking on in wonder, however, and so I handed the trencher back to him and watched him place it on the nightstand.

"Obviously you think you did something wrong. Am I correct?" asked the Reeve when he saw that he had my attention.

I nodded, thinking only about the theft of the coin.

"Hmm. Interesting. What exactly did you do wrong?" he asked. When I started to answer he cut me off with a raised hand and I realised he was being rhetorical. He leaned toward me on the stool and forced me to look at him.

"You saved that poor woman and her son, then me by your account. Then you destroyed this 'thing' in the well. Then you removed it from the entire town and likely saved hundreds of people from this sickness. You did all this without any concern for your own well-being and with it now being—what—a week of near death almost to the point of killing yourself, you now think you did something wrong. Did I get that right?"

I nodded, numb. I couldn't get past that I had kept the coin hidden from the Reeve. Surely that theft was more important to him. *It involved Bill and the assassin and it was bigger than this town,* I thought. I waited for him to bring it up and laid back, still weak, but I could feel that I was getting stronger.

"Show me the coin," he demanded.

Meekly, I pulled out my pouch, drew open the drawstring, upended it and let the coin fall free to land on my open palm. It lay there unassumingly, the worn side up. I was fascinated by it and drawn to its mysteries. It was such a small and simple thing and yet it had allowed me to do so much good and I had no idea how I managed that. My entire life had been about healing: gathering herbs and making potions and unguents. My mother—and again I strained to remember her now forgotten face—she used to speak to me about healing and how important it was. Her words were now long forgotten but her intent and passion were now deeply embodied within me.

The Reeve leaned closer to get a better look at the coin, but I imagined that he already had ample opportunity to examine it—both the coin and my sickle—and I had a feeling of sinking dread. I had not yet figured out why the Reeve had returned both items to me. Surely he would want to turn them over to the garrison captain. I pushed the coin around on my palm with a finger.

"That was in your hand when you collapsed," stated the Reeve quietly. "You held it so tightly that there was an imprint of it on your palm and I had to pry your fingers loose." He reached up to scratch the whiskers on his neck and then sat upright and stared at the coin.

When I was lost in the *vision,* I had no real sense of time. All that existed was the *vision* and dealing with eradicating the motes. I could sense that the Reeve was waiting for me to explain the coin and how it worked. I wasn't sure what I should say or even if I *could* explain. There was so much I did not understand. I could only tell him again what it did.

"Where'd you get it?" asked the Reeve. My eyes darted to his and with a sudden clarity, I realised that he had not associated the coin with the thief and the murder of Bill Burstone. He thought this coin had always been in my possession. He thought it was mine. If I wanted I could lie, pretend it was mine, and be able to keep the coin. Or, I admitted to myself with guilt, I could admit where I had found the coin and clear my conscience and give it up. I was torn. I could feel greed and desire well up within me and the loudest voice was demanding that I claim the coin as my own. With an effort that felt almost physical, I pushed those feelings away, closed my fingers around the coin and held my hand out to the Reeve.

Confused, he reached out, and I dropped the coin into his hand.

"I found it in the boots you gave me from the killer," I said quietly, looking down at my lap in shame.

The Reeve opened his hand and looked closely at the coin. "This was in the boots?"

I nodded.

"And this is what you used to wipe out these 'dust motes'?"

"Yes."

"How does it work?"

"I have no idea," I replied slowly, unsure how to explain what I did know. "I kind of rubbed my thumb along the worn spot and things, well, things just *shifted*."

"Shifted? What do you mean?"

"I dunno, it's hard to explain. I see the world differently. I'm here but there too."

"And you just rubbed your thumb along the coin?" said the Reeve and I nodded. "Like this?" and I watched as he rubbed his thumb along the worn spot on the coin. I studied him closely to see if he changed or glowed with light as I had. I looked at the Reeve's eyes and he looked calmly back at me.

"Well?" I said.

"Nothing," he replied. "Nothing happened. It's just a coin." He looked at the coin, then at me, and tossed it into my lap on top of the covers. "Try it again," he ordered.

I picked up the coin and placed my thumb on the worn spot. I hesitated, worried that the pain would come back and my hand shook a little. I could feel the Reeve waiting patiently for me to demonstrate the *vision* and I took a deep breath and rubbed the coin. The world *shifted.* I braced myself for the pain and sighed with relief when I felt nothing.

I turned my gaze to the Reeve and the tight and bright colours that surrounded him. The first thing I looked for were traces of the motes and I confirmed they were no longer within him. I also checked myself and was happy to see that I too was clean. I looked past the startled expression on his face and took in the entire village with my sight. With a profound sense of relief, I could find no more signs of the motes. The village was clean.

I knew I should check on Daukyns and in a moment I was observing the town hall and found Daukyns lying on his pallet in his small room. To my horror, he was very close to death. Half his body no longer functioned and was senseless. The colours that I expected to see surrounding him were absent on the damaged side of his body. He looked like a man cut in half and all along that line his colours flashed with agony. His breathing was laboured, rapid and shallow, with only one lung that functioned. I looked inside him and found a large blockage in his brain that stopped the flow of blood like a dam. Beyond the blockage he was damaged beyond my ability to heal—that part of his brain was dead. The man I knew as Daukyns was gone and would never return and I knew that he would never wake from this sleep. My only friend was leaving this world and I could do nothing.

I pulled back. My vision and my grief came upon me suddenly and swiftly and despite my best attempt to control my emotions, I started to sob. I put my face in my hands and turned away from the Reeve.

"What is it?" demanded the Reeve, concern in his voice. "You glowed again—all over! I waved my hand in front of your face and you didn't even blink. What happened and why are you crying? Will!"

After a few minutes of ignoring the Reeve's continued demands for an explanation, I managed to calm myself down and explained what I had seen. The Reeve looked at me with a blank face. I had no idea what he thought of all this or why he was suddenly so still.

"No one told you what had happened with Daukyns?" he asked curtly. "Correct?"

I nodded and watched my last tears drop to my lap, quickly absorbed by the blanket and disappearing with only a small wet spot to mark the spot. I had to stop this crying all the time, I decided. I was always so damn emotional. With good reason this time, I argued with myself. Daukyns was dying.

The Reeve shook himself, seeming to realise that I was merely lying there with tears streaming down my face. He reached out, clasped my arm and squeezed it with sympathy.

"I'm sorry, Will. I wanted to keep this from you until you were stronger and out of that bed. And, well, I didn't know how to best tell you." He paused and took a deep breath before continuing. "Daukyns collapsed the day after he helped me bring you to the inn. One moment he was fine and then he started talking strange, his words were all mixed up, and then suddenly—bam!—he dropped like a stone to the ground, arched his back and then lay still. He hasn't moved since." The Reeve's words had come in a rush and now he just stood there, relieved to be free of the effort of telling me. He ran his fingers through his hair and looked at me.

"It was a massive stroke, we're pretty sure. We moved him to his room and we check on him routinely and feed him as best we can. We've seen it before. It doesn't look good for Daukyns. Not good at all. I'm so sorry, Will. I know you and he were close." The Reeve squeezed my arm again and let go. He sat back on the stool and hung his head.

We sat in silence for a spell. My thoughts on Daukyns and how much I owed the man for his support over the years. I had known he was not doing well, but I felt no small measure of guilt that my collapsing had sped up his decline. But some part of me knew that there was nothing I could do to fix that and so I lay in bed trying desperately to get control over my urge to keep crying. I finally managed and wiped my face clear of snot and tears. I looked over to the Reeve and saw grief there, too. I wondered what the Reeve thought of me crying all the time. He probably believed I was just a child, and I was embarrassed. *Then again*, I thought, *maybe he wanted to cry too.*

The Reeve pushed his hands against his knees, stood up and walked over to the door. He opened it a crack and looked outside to the corridor. Satisfied that no one was listening in, he softly closed the door and latched it, turned back to me, and sat down again. I watched him curiously, not knowing what was coming next.

"You need to keep your ability quiet, Will. You understand?" he demanded with a quiet voice but with urgency there that was unmistakably serious. His eyes bore into mine and it was all I could do not to flinch. "No one will understand all this. Hell, *I* don't understand all this. I don't get how you are able to do what you do! Certainly seems that only you can make that coin work." The Reeve scratched his neck again where there was redness, and I knew it was probably a bug bite and felt a sudden urge to fix it but resisted. *What the hell is wrong with me? I can't fix everything and I can't fix Daukyns.* The coin seemed like a useless thing to me and I clenched my fist around it.

"Yeah, I get it," I mumbled, looking away. "I just want to get out of here, back to the woods."

"Not anytime soon, son," said the Reeve, and I looked at him again, startled with him calling me son. "We need to figure this out first. One of the things that Daukyns said before, well, before... well, he said he might understand what you could do and what you did to the town. He confirmed to me that the coin was Bill's and insisted that you be allowed to keep it. He said he was positive that it was meant for you. Did he ever speak to you about this?"

"No. He didn't know I had the coin," I replied honestly. I was surprised Daukyns would say that. The Reeve must have figured out where I found the coin—or at least tied it to the assassin. "You knew where I had got the coin!" I blurted out.

"Yes, Will. I did," he said, merely looking back at me.

"You were testing me," I said meekly. "Weren't you?"

"Yes, I was."

I thought about that for a moment and realised that I had deserved the test and more importantly I knew I must have passed it. "So what did Daukyns say about it?" I asked.

"He never got a chance to say anything. All I found out was what he told me. That he had been looking into something with Bill. He meant to tell me more, I think, but then shortly after that, he collapsed. But don't worry, we'll figure this out somehow."

The Reeve sat back down on the stool and then pried open my hand and took the coin from where I still clenched it tightly. The Reeve raised an eyebrow at the sharp indentations in my hand and then he tried rubbing the coin again and again. After failing to get results, he handed it back to me.

"Yours for now," he said simply. Somewhat surprised, I took the coin from him and dropped it back into my pouch.

"Thanks," I said, "I didn't think you would return it to me."

"Well, I've had a long thought about it. Seems to me that it kinda belongs to you, you know?" He was looking up at the ceiling searching for his words. "You used it and I don't think anyone else could. Daukyns, when he told me it should stay with you, that decided it for me. I haven't even told the captain about what you did. Only you and I know, Will." He paused while I digested that. "You really glow all over when you use it, Will. You can't hide that. You'll have to be careful."

He grew quiet.

"Well," I said to break the silence. "Okay, I will."

The Reeve just looked at me and smiled.

"I–it kinda feels right," I stammered. "Right that I have it."

"Will. You healed this entire town despite it almost killing you, but you did it anyway. The coin allowed that to happen and so it seems to me that the town owes *you* that coin."

I wasn't sure if the logic was right and it made me feel uncomfortable. I was glad the Reeve had kept all this hidden from the public, especially the captain. I needed to stay hidden; my promise to my mother was very prominent in my thoughts. It looked like I was still holding onto my promise and I was glad.

"I think the coin was meant for me," I almost whispered. "And so it feels right that I have it. I can't explain that and I'm sorry I can't. I nearly didn't tell you about it at all. I wanted to, but I was afraid you would take it away."

"If you hadn't used it the way you did, I would have and turned it over to the captain."

"I understand, Reeve."

I sat a moment longer thinking about the coin and what could have led to it arriving into my hands. I shook my head to clear the thoughts away. Those 'what ifs' weren't helping. I didn't know what had happened to bring the coin to the attention of an assassin.

"What do you suppose Bill and Daukyns wanted with the coin?" I asked. "Do you think they knew what it could do?"

"I've no idea. He and Bill were looking into something. Somehow the coin entered into it. Brought the attention of that thief—and the others I'm sure are still out there. Did Daukyns ever hint at anything about this?"

"No," I said after a moment's thought. "Last time I was in town was over a month ago. Daukyns hadn't said a word. He was just being Daukyns, you know?"

"He's a smart man, by the Word. He wouldn't be wasting his time on just any whim. We'll have to ask him when he recovers." The Reeve glanced sideways at me, gauging my reaction. I was surprised and saddened. The Reeve had no idea that I knew just how bad Daukyns' condition was. I wondered if he truly knew.

"Yes, we will," I murmured and felt my eyes prick with tears. I wiped them hastily before they could fall. The Reeve rose from his stool and paced the room.

"Daukyns knew that Bill had owned the coin, so how did Bill obtain it and from where?" I sensed he wasn't looking for an answer and was merely talking out loud so I laid back and watched him go back and forth.

"He couldn't have had it for long. Bill lived here for years with no trouble. The coin shows up and wham, he's killed for it. Hmm... maybe. Maybe whatever they were looking into revealed that he had the coin and they came for it. Either way, the result was the same."

The Reeve stopped at the door and quickly looked out into the hallway. Seeing no one there, he resumed his pacing. He kept talking.

"So Bill Burstone had the coin. Someone knew about it. They came here and stole it from him, killing him in the process. That man was a professional. So someone of importance wanted that coin and wanted it badly enough to kill for it. Right?"

This last was directed at me and I answered with a quick yes, not really knowing the truth.

"There's more than one. That's certain. They haven't come after me so they must think the assassin didn't get his hands on it. They must think the coin is still in the house somewhere."

I had forgotten that somewhere in Jaipers there lurked associates of the assassin. I felt a chill. The map found on the thief had far too much detail of the guard movements. The Reeve had told me Captain Gendred was looking into it and trying to figure out who it possibly could be. From this, everyone would know my involvement. It didn't take me long to determine that I, too, could be a target and suddenly the coin felt very heavy around my neck. It must have shown on my face for the Reeve stopped pacing and asked what was wrong.

"They'll come after me, won't they?" I asked.

The Reeve laughed. "No, Will. It's me they'll come after. I was the one who took the thief down. Everyone in town saw me drag his body to the graveyard. But I suspect it's the coin they want. They'll think it's still in the house."

I nodded at this. That seemed to make sense, and I relaxed somewhat.

We continued to talk quietly until the sun touched the horizon. The light started to dim in the room and the Reeve said he had to be going.

"Tomorrow we'll talk about that glass sickle," he said as he started toward the door. He placed his hat on his head and looked at me for a moment. "There's more to you than either you or I understand, Will. There's a mystery here I mean to get to the bottom of. I need to talk to Captain Gendred. You understand that?" When I nodded he continued. "He already knows about the chest of gold coins and I'll let him know that there may be another attempt to recover it. He'll understand that. He told me that he's already sent word to the capital by pigeon asking for them to arrange transportation of the chest along with a contingent of armed capital guards.

"He already has a reply, and the chest is going directly to the Lord Protector, but it will be many weeks before we see the contingent arrive. Gendred isn't happy. Word of that gold will get out and all hell will break loose around here. This business with the coin changes things and he needs to increase his watch—but without knowing about the coin. Don't worry about that. I'm not convinced he needs to hear about that just yet. I can't explain it, Will. That coin belongs to you. I can feel it and I've long trusted my gut. Helps that Daukyns agreed to it before... well, before."

The Reeve paused at the door. "You should know that the captain has already placed a guard outside the inn at all times at my request. You're safe here, son." And with that, he disappeared out the door and down the stairs. I heard him greet the innkeeper and then all was silent except for the quiet murmuring and the clinking of drink glasses that rose from the guests in the common room as they enjoyed their meals. Soon the crowd would build and laughter and music would fill the night air. They were sounds I was not used to hearing but over the past few days, I had grown to like them. Perhaps I could one day be at ease with this many people at once, but for now, I was happy to remain hidden in my room, listening in with obscurity.

I went over everything the Reeve and I had discussed and could find no fault in it. It gave me comfort knowing I had a guard outside. Then I worried it might draw attention to me but managed to push those fears aside.

I sighed to myself and tuned the sounds from downstairs out of my thoughts. I knew what I had to do now about Daukyns. Sorrow threatened to overwhelm me and I waited until I could control my emotions again. I owed my friend this last mercy and so I blinked back my tears and pulled the coin from my purse, rubbed it, and *shifted*.

I watched Daukyns struggling to breathe and sorrowed at how little remained of the man I knew. Nonetheless, I took the time to confirm what I knew to be true: Daukyns would never recover from this. The damage was severe and now so little of who he was remained. I knew what I wanted to do but was unable. I wanted to ease his suffering completely. Complete his death and release him. I could do it so very easily and with barely any thought but it would be murder through and through and I felt a sharp pain tweak my head to confirm it. I could not take his life, even when I knew that there was nothing I could do to fix him and even when I knew he had no future left. So I did what I could. I found a way to block the pain in his body and watched his breathing ease somewhat. I soothed his body and calmed his heart. His face relaxed, and I felt his relief. I stayed with him and watched over him, remembering how he had helped me and gave me friendship when no one else even noticed me.

I watched as he stopped breathing and I held my breath with him.

I watched as his heart stopped and felt mine break with it.

I watched as his body relaxed and sank into his pallet and a sigh escaped both of us.

I watched patiently for his spirit to rise up and seek the heavens.

The Church says our souls rise and travel to heaven when we die. When I had asked Daukyns about this, he laughed and said that it was a fairy tale for children and used to hold people to the teachings of the Church. He then spoke lovingly of the stars and patiently explained to me how we all came from them. He often said that he wanted to return to them and when he died he would. And so I waited and watched to see if he would rise out of his body to the stars. But nothing happened and his body just lay there as if abandoned or forgotten.

I'm not sure how long I watched, but after a time I realised that nothing more would happen here. All that was my friend Daukyns was gone from this world and no spirit would rise to an afterlife in heaven or fly to the stars. I was deeply saddened. I lay in my bed and held off the tears that threatened to overwhelm me and debated with myself on whether Daukyns' disbelief in an afterlife had excluded him from finding one in the end, but, after a time, I came to the decision that this was unlikely. The simple truth was evident before my eyes: there wasn't a spirit or an afterlife. You have this life and that is it. You have to make the most of it.

My grief overwhelmed me and I pulled back my vision. I covered my head with the blankets and quietly cried for my friend until sleep thankfully took me in its embrace.

Duilleog

Seven

Jaipers, 900 A.C.

FIVE DAYS LATER, I was more or less recovered. I had eaten better over the last few days than I ever had during my life and I felt positively fat. My strength returned to my limbs, and I took walks around my room until I felt sure that I wouldn't fall down. I had been in great shape before I fell ill, and it appeared it hastened my recovery.

Two days ago, the garrison captain and the Reeve had stopped by my room to discuss the events I witnessed regarding the death of the assassin. The captain was only focused on what had happened to me and nodded when I described the arrow shot that ended the thief's life. He gave the Reeve an appraising look and then stood up and warmly patted my shoulder.

"Thank you, Will," he said. "That's what the Reeve told me. Glad to see you're doing better and recovering from that illness. Bad luck having that thief grab you and then coming down sick."

He looked around my room. I was certain he didn't know how to excuse himself politely and I had to stop myself from smiling. The Reeve had an eyebrow raised, staring at the captain.

"Well," he said after a moment, "I'm satisfied." And he turned to leave and then turned back. "Um, sorry to hear about Daukyns. He was a good man. Those creams you made with him were potent. I don't suppose you'll be...?" he drifted off looking meaningfully to me.

At first, I had no idea what he was hinting at then I realised he wanted to know if I would still be making the unguents. I struggled to find a response. His question caught me off guard and I wasn't sure what I wanted to do now. I hadn't given it any thought. The Reeve noticed my discomfort and jumped in to answer for me.

"Captain, young Will here will need a little more time to mourn his friend. The funeral's today. Ask him again in a few days, hmm?"

The captain looked embarrassed, mumbled an apology and lurched out the door. The Reeve and I listened to him descend the stairs, call out a greeting to the innkeeper and disappear out onto the street. I looked at the Reeve and he shook his head.

"Thank you for keeping the coin secret, Reeve Comlin."

He grunted, sat down on the stool and looked me over. "You're looking much better. How's the strength?"

"Much better, thanks. I made it down to the kitchen this morning and startled Dempster. Did you know he talks to his food?"

The Reeve chuckled. "I'm not surprised." He stood suddenly, said he had to go and left.

Yesterday the Reeve stopped by before the funeral and found me eating a meal in the common room. He joined me and had a beer and we talked about small things in the town. He updated me on Martha and her son: they were both doing well. Martha was still in bed but recovering her strength remarkably fast. I was glad for the news and was ashamed that I hadn't thought of them at all. The innkeeper stopped by the table and sat with us.

"Young Will," he said and nodded politely at me. "Reeve. How's the beer?"

"Fine, John," replied the Reeve as he took a sip. "As always, up to your high standard."

The innkeeper nodded, pleased with the compliment. He looked around, silent and then glanced over at me. "So," he said. "You're looking better."

"Yes, sir," I replied, feeling a strange tension in the air.

"That room comfortable enough?"

"Yes, sir."

"Good. Good."

The Reeve coughed, and the innkeeper looked over at him.

"I'm sure he'll be well enough to leave by tomorrow, John."

"Of course!" said the innkeeper. "No rush. No rush. You just get better, lad."

With that, the innkeeper rose, hurried over to another table, grabbing empty mugs and promising more beer to the couple seated there. He signalled the waitress then disappeared into the kitchen. The waitress hurried over, dropped two frothy mugs in front of the couple and with a swirl of her skirts, hustled over to another table. The man stared at her bottom and his wife, I assumed, smacked him on the arm and scowled at him.

I turned to look at the Reeve and found him staring at me in thought. "Any idea what you're going to do, Will?"

"I haven't given it much thought, actually. I have to leave soon. Get back to the woods. I can feel it pulling at me."

The Reeve frowned at me and grew quiet in thought. "Well, you can't stay here any longer. Dempster arranged that room for you but the innkeeper wants it back, I think."

"Right," I replied and looked around the inn. It was bustling with activity. The inn was popular with the barges and travelling merchants, and the rooms cost a premium. I was staying in one of the nicer rooms and likely the innkeeper wanted to earn his coin. I had to leave the inn and was startled to find that I was torn about that. One part of me wanted nothing more than to run out into the woods and never come back and the other part of me wanted the comfort and companionship.

"You'll stay with me tomorrow. Okay?"

I nodded and watched the innkeeper speaking with Dempster in the doorway to the kitchen. Dempster glanced over and his face reddened. I had overstayed my welcome.

The Reeve and I talked every evening. Almost always about the coin and what it could mean. His interest in me had raised my caution at first but after a time I warmed to his presence and looked forward to our talks; even when they uncomfortably seemed to focus almost solely on me and my past. We talked about the sickle and I surprised myself by telling him where it had come from and how my mother had given it to me shortly before she died. I found myself explaining how I used it to gather herbs and how it made my potions and unguents so much more powerful. The Reeve just shook his head and didn't press me for more information. It was all beyond his ability to understand, I think, and rather than press the issue he simply took note and let it go. I admired that in Reeve Comlin. He was a good man, and I trusted him. And he trusted me as well, it seemed. Before we knew it we had formed a friendship, and it came at a time when I needed it most.

The funeral ceremony for Daukyns that afternoon was a large event. I was pleased when most of the town came out to pay respects. Seeing their numbers reminded me of how many lives Daukyns had touched and how many families he had provided for when no other would or could. I noted with sadness that only a few of the more well-off people in town came to say goodbye and I am sorry to say I was not too surprised.

Daukyns had been the only Wordsmith in Jaipers and so Captain Gendred presided over the funeral and spoke a few kind words. We buried him outside of town in the graveyard and when my time came, I said words that I cannot recall with any clarity. I didn't cry though, and I was pleased with that. I was weary of crying and done with it. Tears were not helping me and they wouldn't help Daukyns, and truth be told, the tears only drained me in the end. I was finding it hard to relate this shrouded body to the man I had so admired. To me, we were burying a remnant, a tossed aside piece of clothing—not a man. *Certainly not my friend Daukyns*, I thought. Daukyns was that smiling, peaceful man who looked out for me and cared for me when I had no one else. That was the man I knew—not this canvass wrapped remnant.

The ceremony concluded. I watched in silence as he was placed in the grave and a couple of the garrison men shovelled dirt over him. I stayed and watched until the dirt was packed over his grave. A few people stopped by with a word or two for me before they wandered away, many not sure what they now should do. I thanked them and waited.

Once I was alone, I drew some seeds from my pocket and planted them on Daukyns' grave. The flowers that would grow here were those that he and Bill Burstone had sent me after—the poppies. I took out the coin and using it, I urged the seeds to grow quick and strong and I felt their acceptance and desire to obey. I knew within a few days they would sprout and reach for the sun. I felt some measure of joy in that before noticing a large number of fresh graves dug in the graveyard. There was at least a dozen. People killed by the sickness before I could cure them. One grave, I knew, contained the assassin and one contained Bill Burstone. I felt it wrong he be allowed to share the same ground as Bill Burstone and the kind people of Jaipers.

I crouched down by Daukyns' grave and reached out to the tree that grew beside it. *Please watch over my friend*, I whispered. I was sure I imagined it, but it felt like the tree lent me some of its strength. I felt a little more solid and the cobwebs that had clouded my thoughts seemed to vanish. An urge to lie on the ground rose within me, but I resisted it and looked instead over to Jaipers. I had to complete my business there and then I would need to go. I needed to get back to the woods and soon. I could no longer resist the pull. I would have to tell the Reeve that I wouldn't be staying with him tomorrow. The decision made, I almost felt relief and the pull from the woods reduced. I stood and looked down at the grave.

"Goodbye, my friend," I said to Daukyns. "I'll look to the stars for you."

My feet almost took me straight out of town and down the road away from Jaipers but I needed to get my backpack and say my farewells and so I trudged back to the inn. I spent a moment emptying and repacking my backpack. By the time I finished, I was completely drained and collapsed on my bed, sleeping straight through until morning. When I woke I felt more like my old self than I had in days.

I stopped to speak to Dempster and have a quick breakfast, then I moved out to the street. The Reeve picked me up as soon as I appeared outside the inn. I felt better with my backpack settled on my shoulders. Its weight was a comfort, and I was grateful to bear it once more. The Reeve scrutinised me.

"You're looking hale," he said.

"Mmm. Yes, much better, thanks."

"Are you up to going through Daukyns' belongings?" he asked. "I think you should take what you can. He would want that, I think."

I nodded, and we crossed over to the common hall and went into the back room to go through Daukyns' belongings. We gathered the items and laid them out on the table. They didn't amount to much. All that he owned were his small, leather-bound book of the Word, his wooden wine cup and what remained of the materials we used to make our potions and salves. So I packed away what remained of the candles, beeswax, two clay jars and a small burner plate the blacksmith had made for us. We buried Daukyns in his wine-stained robe and not surprisingly, it was the only clothing he possessed. I glanced around the tiny empty room and was saddened to see that nothing else remained of him. He had kept nothing for himself throughout his life. He was a frugal man and gave all that he had to anyone he felt more deserving—which was pretty much everyone.

I secured my backpack and hefted it onto my shoulders. It weighed more than it ever had before and I was glad that my weakness was mostly gone. I worried that my stitching wouldn't be able to handle the added strain. I stared at the wine-stained wooden cup where we found it on the small worktable.

My thoughts returned to my decision I had made yesterday to leave town and return to the solitude of the woods. I could no more fight the urge to leave than to force myself to stop breathing. I needed time to myself to sort out the jumble of my thoughts. I also had to think more about this healing process and try to come to terms with what it was and what it meant to me and my future. It was simply too much to take in and with all the distractions of the inn, I found I couldn't keep my mind straight on the problem.

My first thoughts about my healing ability had come to me when I still lay convalescing in the bed in the inn. My first excited reaction was that I should heal everyone I could. And then, unbidden, I remembered a conversation with Daukyns about equality we had one day not too long ago, maybe three months back in the early Spring.

Daukyns had often taught me from the Word. I remembered that he spoke to me about the word 'equality' and with it the concept that everyone was equal. As we spoke we strolled through town and I happened to observe two young and malnourished children being shooed away by an overweight, rich couple in the open market. It was a clear, bright and cloudless day: the husband, red-faced, and huffing and puffing to catch his breath, and his wife with one fat finger buried in her mouth tasting the merchant's sample, were buying a rather large bag of beet sugar—a rare luxury—from an equally overweight merchant. Children stopped to stare at the enormous bag of sugar and even from my distance the hunger and longing on their faces was there for everyone to see. The sight of the children so close to them and looking into their business drew the ire of this fat couple and they had turned on the children and chased them off, shouting after them. The woman had struck one child with her open hand. Equality: there was none. Just the haves and have-nots. The scene angered me and Daukyns picked up on it right away as he was wont to do with me.

"I sense your anger," he started quietly and when I saw that he was talking about the scene I had just witnessed I nodded, my lips pressed together. He continued speaking quietly for my ears only. "You are looking at this from the wrong perspective."

When I stared at him in disbelief, he continued his explanation, both of us walking side–by–side and aimlessly through the open market. Everywhere, children laughed and ran carefree through the throngs of people like rabbits, their squeals of laughter competing with the shouts from the merchants calling out their wares. To my ears, the noise was deafening but somehow Daukyns' words sounded in my ears as though we were sitting in a quiet glen.

"You see the starving children and the fat couple and think, 'There is no equality in the world' and you would be right." He laughed at my curt nod in agreement. "My work, the work of the Word, is to remove that inequality by little bites—not large ones! That was the work of the revolution twenty years ago. No, today, it is little bites."

We stopped at an apple merchant stall and Daukyns took a moment to ask for one of the more wrinkled, aged and mealy apples from last fall's harvest to be donated to him to hand out to the needy. They haggled for a bit but in the end, Daukyns always won out and a half–bushel was promised. Satisfied, we moved on with me carrying the bag of apples. Daukyns continued after he looked to see if I was still paying attention.

"That fat couple ask for me to include them in the Word, and I do, and for that, they donate a tuppence on a regular basis to further the work of the Word. I take that tuppence and provide it to the parents of those two starving children and with that coin, their parents buy food to fill their bellies. A small bite into inequality, do you see?"

I did. I understood it but hated it. What he described was not the way to equality. What he had described was the sacrifice of one to another. I did not see how it improved matters unless the obese couple was aware of how their coin was being spent and why. They had bought their way into the Word and I could not see how they were changed by this process Daukyns described. To me, they were happily ignorant of it all and I suspected that they would have been angered to find that their money was being spent on the urchins they had just callously shooed away from their presence. But this was just a simple example. In the grander scheme, equality could never mean that everyone had equal belongings. How could you reward the man who strove to do as little as possible equally with a man who worked his fingers down to the bone to feed his family? There had to be a solution. But I knew not what at the time and today I was far from wiser. I never spoke these thoughts out loud to Daukyns but now I wished I had.

The question of equality was important to my understanding of this healing gift. The more I thought about it the more I realised that the town was distracting me from the answers. I had to leave town and the sooner the better.

"Will, are you okay? You're just standing there," said the Reeve, and I found myself once again in Daukyns' small room with my backpack on my shoulders staring at the wine-stained, wooden cup on the table.

"I can't stay in town, Reeve. I feel trapped and need time under the stars again. Back in the woods," I explained in a burst.

"What are you talking about? You're coming to stay with me for a while," he replied. "We agreed yesterday." The Reeve looked unhappy.

"I know and I'm sorry. I need to get out of town—back out to the woods. The pull is too much."

"The pull? What do you mean, Will? Nothing is pulling you. You need to stay here, safe with me. I can't protect you out there."

"The pull is there. I feel it stronger than ever. It's like a thirst I need to quench," I said and felt the need to bolt for the woods rise up within me. I forced myself to calm and stilled my tapping foot. I had to get the Reeve to understand and quell his fears. "No one will know where I am, and I will be careful, I promise. I have to go. I've no choice. You just have to trust me. I promise this: any sign of trouble and I will run back here as quick as I can."

"Any sign of trouble and you won't be able to run back here!"

I didn't answer. I picked up the wooden cup, looked at it briefly and set it back down.

The nights and days convalescing in the inn had left me little to do but think about my future. I knew now that a part of me had already decided what I would do and the rest of me was just catching up. Fate, or whatever you called it, had led me to this path, and I had no hesitation in stepping boldly forward and accepting it. It had started with my mother and her passions and now that I knew I could heal people and make a real difference I would go forth into the world and heal people. The coin would allow me to do the impossible. I thought of all the people out there suffering right now and I wanted to get to them. What use was this gift if I could not use it on those who needed it?

I was concerned that people would react badly seeing me use my powers. After all the effort the Word had done following the revolution, I would hate to be used as proof of miracles by the Church. I was convinced I could cover my work with my unguents and potions and keep the coin hidden. I would be careful not to extend myself as I had with the motes. I couldn't afford to go through this restoration period again—especially on my own. It would kill me, and it was far too risky. I would be cautious and wary. I could do this.

I just had to sort out how I would do this. It is one thing to heal someone, and another to convince someone to let you, and another yet again to do it with a new-found power and not scare people.

"Will?" the Reeve probed as I stood there not answering him. I turned and looked at him to let him see the sincerity in my eyes.

"I have to do this, Reeve," I said, putting as much conviction into my voice as I could. "I have to go."

The Reeve blinked at me and then nodded. "Fine," he finally agreed. "But you tell me where you are going and when you expect to be back."

"I will. I'm going back to the same clearing." I didn't need to amplify that—he knew which one I meant.

I checked my straps on my backpack and hoisted it on my back. The Reeve gave it a look.

"I think you'll be needing a new backpack, son."

I craned my head to look. It bulged in weird places and despite my best efforts, it was unbalanced. "I know," I said. "It's on its last legs, I think. I'll try to be back in town in two weeks. I have a lot to think about."

The Reeve made a noise and then he clapped me on the back. "Fine," he said. "Just watch your back. Keep your fires small and watch the road."

I grasped his forearm with my own. "Thanks, Reeve. Thank you for everything." I felt uncomfortable and let go of his arm and moved out on to the street, turning toward the south gate. The Reeve came up behind me.

"Daukyns had a good friend in you, Will. He'll be missed more than these town folk realise just yet. He touched all their lives in small but significant ways. The families will go a little hungrier, their homes a little colder when winter arrives, and, perhaps, they will look back and realise just how much they owed Daukyns." He paused before adding, "And you, Will."

At my startled glance over at him, he chuckled and patted my shoulder. "Daukyns raised just about most of his money and goods by trading and selling the unguents you made with him. You knew that, right?" and when I nodded with a puzzled look on my face about where this was all going he ruffled my hair and continued. "And you never charged Daukyns a penny for any of that. All that he had to trade or barter with came directly from you. You were the source of Daukyns' goodwill." The Reeve looked surprised for a moment and then laughed. "Good Will! That's who you are, Good Will!" He clapped me on the backpack so hard that I stumbled off balance with the force. The Reeve grabbed my pack and held me upright with a quickly mumbled sorry.

"Will, the town doesn't know what you did for them, I'm sorry to say, except for the more observant of them—which isn't many people. I'm sorry you don't get the recognition you deserve." When I raised my eyebrows at him he hurried on. "For the healing. The healing! Even if you don't feel that you do deserve any. But, on behalf of the town, our thanks for our lives, Will." As he finished his speech, I felt him deposit something in my backpack and he gave me a gentle push toward the south gate.

I stumbled, this time keeping my balance and laughed. I looked back.

"You're welcome, Reeve!" I said as I waved farewell. The outdoors was only a few feet away, and I felt the pull stronger than before. The urge to run became as compelling as the need to breathe.

I exited the gate and nodded to the garrison guards posted there and they wished me safe travels.

"Where ya oft tae this time, Will?" asked one guard, a man I had seen many times in town but I had no idea what his name was. He knew mine, and it somehow annoyed me.

"I'm off to the hills again," I answered. "The garlic should be ready for harvest."

The guards shared a glance and then shook their heads and I laughed and waved farewell. As I started down the dusty road, I had to keep myself to a calm walk. It would seem strange to the guards to see me run off down the road and I wanted nothing to stick in their memories.

As I forced myself to walk down the road, I remembered my farewell that morning to Dempster. He was such a nice man, and he had spent what time he could find away from his kitchen to sit by my bedside and talk to me. He opened up to me about all his dreams and his past and I found I knew more about him than I probably should at one point. He helped me pass the time though and fed me well and for that I was grateful. He had also talked the innkeeper into giving up that room to me. I wasn't sure who ran the inn, now that I knew more about how it worked. If I could choose, I would have picked Dempster.

When we spoke during those quiet times, he would speak lovingly of his favourite recipes and the tricks of his trade, such as how to get his pastries light and flaky and how to reduce costs without sacrificing flavour. He had such a passion for cooking and after having eaten his wares for the past few days, I could eagerly agree that he was well talented. He told me that he used to cook in the capital city of Munsten for a rather rich family. When I asked why he left Munsten for Jaipers, he refused to explain but he did say that he was better off in Jaipers. Safer, he added, and I wondered how Jaipers could be safer than the capital city. Certainly, he would have been better paid and more revered in the capital city than out here in the remote outlying country. But he said he was content, and that was enough for me.

Often, he and I would discuss what I could forage in the wild and he made several suggestions and described numerous mushrooms and plants and how to properly skin and prepare a rabbit. At one point, he carried me down to the kitchen and we skinned a rabbit he had purchased that morning and I found I was quite adept at it. I knew intuitively where the joints and tendons were. It was easy.

At his suggestion, we even went so far as to review some of his recipes and I offered up advice on some specialised herbs and spices to spruce some of them up. Rather than take offence, he was genuinely pleased. My time with Dempster was a warm and comforting time and I owed him for his kindness. We also developed some simple meal ideas that I could prepare in the wild and I was excited to try some out. I liked simple food and recipes that required little preparation, but Dempster assured me that once I tried some of his recipes that I would never be able to look back and to be honest, after eating so much of Dempster's wonderful food, the new recipes beckoned me eagerly. The best meals, Dempster said once, were the simplest ones and his recipes for me were just that.

He did try to make me promise to find him a truly specialised herb one day: the threaded, bright red centre plucked from the centre of a purple crocus flower. I told him that I had never seen the flower he spoke of and he looked sad and wistful for a moment as if remembering a better time. He then patted my arm encouragingly and said now that I knew what to look for and he was sure I would be successful. He called it saffron and the look of longing in his face made me wonder what it would be like.

In the end, we compiled a large list of herbs and spices for me to gather and I promised him the next time I went out of town I would fill it for him.

I turned my attention back to the road, glad to have the sun behind me, and I lengthened my stride, eager to hurry back to nature and my inner peace.

Duilleog

Eight

South of Jaipers, 900 A.C.

I N TIME, I found myself back by the small copse of woods where the thief had grabbed me. I stood at the edge and surveyed the area. The site hadn't changed since I left, other than some small animal tracks. My eyes were pulled to the area where I knew the blood lay just under the dirt. The events that had transpired repeated in my memories and with an effort I pushed them aside. *The man is dead and buried. I'm alive and that's all that matters.*

Determined to leave the events behind me, I dropped my pack and took the time to gather up some additional fuelwood to augment what I had already previously gathered and found myself with a generous supply. The weather remained hot and dry and after settling in; I built a small fire and boiled water from the stream to make tea.

When I arrived and opened my backpack to get out my tea I had quickly found the small purse the Reeve had placed in my pack and when I opened it I found it held several pence and three silver groats. It was a large amount of money and I knew, without doubt, it came from the Reeve's own pocket. Perhaps I should have returned it, lest it diminish my efforts, but I was honest with myself and realised that I was grateful for the wealth. I was already thinking of ways to spend it that would ease my efforts and improve my conditions of life in the outdoors. I packed the coins away, buried my leather pouch and set my bedroll over it. Lovingly drawing out my tea supplies, I soon had a comforting cup, steaming in my hands.

It was only early afternoon but as I lay back by the fire, contentment settled in and I felt that the trees were comforting me. As I drank my tea and cleared my mind, I turned my thoughts to my healing powers. I had to reach an internal set of rules. Limits to what I could do and when. It had to feel right, I knew. I needed a method, a set of principles. I needed my own version of the Word.

And so I considered what rules I should apply to my art of healing. The first came to me right away: I should heal everyone that I could equally. With a sense of smugness, I congratulated myself, but then the idea started to nag at me and I pondered equality. Daukyns knew I had issues with this concept. I imagined myself sitting with Daukyns and decided to just talk to him as if he were truly there.

"Does everyone deserve to be healed? What about a murderer, hurt while dealing a mortal blow? Should that person be healed when they are destined to be hanged for their crimes?" I asked out loud.

"Why would they not?" questioned the ghost of Daukyns.

"It would be a waste of healing, that's why. They are going to die, anyway."

"Well, assuming they were truly guilty of the crime, why should they be made to suffer while waiting for that sentence to be completed?"

"Why are you answering my questions with questions?" I said a little louder. Daukyns ignored me. I thought for a moment about what he had asked. "Would that not be a waste of my skills when I could use them to heal other, more deserving people? While this man is suffering, so are others."

"What do you mean by 'deserving'?" was the returned question. I was expecting them now. "Who decides who deserves care?"

I sensed that there were two distinct problems. Those who needed to be healed, and those who deserved it over others. I soon found mulling over how to categorise whom I meant by more deserving and got lost in the myriad of possibilities. The ghost of Daukyns was forgotten and disappeared. I was getting more and more confused and more elaborate possibilities flooded my thoughts. There had to be a simpler way.

The more I tried to rationalise equality, the harder it became. I wondered at how I would respond to being asked to heal a murderer destined to die and asked myself how I could do nothing and allow him to suffer until his death. That seemed overly cruel to me. Perhaps like with Daukyns I should use my gift to ease that passage? This quieted my thoughts for a while and I brewed a new cup of tea.

Then I considered whom I thought I was that I could judge and pass sentence on what constituted a more deserving person. The problem weighed heavily on me again. It seemed almost spiritual in nature. Daukyns often spoke of the weak and the destitute and them being equal with the Word and I found myself drawn to Daukyns' book.

Of the many things that Daukyns had taught me over the years, the one that I cherished most was that he took the time to teach me to read. It opened worlds to me—insights and lore that I would not be able to learn elsewhere. We quickly discovered that during my childhood someone, presumably my mother, had taught me the basics of reading and I quickly learned to read as well as Daukyns. I pulled the book out of my pack and held it in my hands, rubbing the tree symbol engraved on the leather cover. Daukyns cherished this book more than anything and he could often be found, sitting outside the common hall, pouring over the contents and reading the words aloud to anyone who cared to stop and listen.

Books such as this were worth a fortune. Each was handcrafted and filled with the most beautiful handwritten words. I loved the feel of the soft leather binding and when I thumbed open the book, I marvelled at the thin paper that filled it. The paper was so smooth and white. The words on the pages were meticulously written and perfectly aligned row after row. On every page the blank border was filled in with the tiny scrawled notes Daukyns had entered with a lead pencil. He marked the passages that were of importance to him and I found that the book would fall open to those sections that he had frequently turned to. I had no idea where to start with a book like this and so I flipped through until I found that there were blank pages at the back filled in with Daukyns' own writing.

To my shock, I found that Daukyns had written about me. As I read the first passage, a numbness overtook me and I sat and read the passages hearing Daukyns' voice in my head. The first page was dated a month after I had first met him:

I have met the most interesting young man. He has introduced himself to me as Will; short for William, I imagine. When he cautiously walked into town, the first thing I noticed was that he walked with an air about him that belied his obviously impoverished state. His clothing was the remnants of scraps and rags. Craftily sewn together, but rags nonetheless. He is well mannered and speaks like someone with a bright upbringing. And yet he appears from the wilderness as if raised there and here lies the enigma. He has survived in the wild for years against all odds! I asked him about the wolves that hunted in the surrounding forests and he gave me such a peculiar look and merely said that he respected them. He showed me his herbs on that first meeting and asked my advice on whether there would be a market for them in town. On the Word, such herbs! He has such a natural talent when it comes to herbal lore that it staggers my mind. I spent years teaching myself how to work herbs and this twelve–year–old boy (if a day older) has discovered more than I have ever known. I felt such a high regard for this young man and such a curiosity that I soon found myself probing into his past and he replied by saying that he had little memory remaining of his childhood.

I talked to him about his herbs and suggested we could work together to help people. He agreed willingly enough. Through trial and error we established a laboratory of sorts in my room and through persistence, we have established a working pattern and agreement: I will provide him with tools and components and he will craft healing unguents for me to pass on to the deserving people in town. He will sell the extras. I must point out that he took to this arrangement with such a passion and such charity that I must admit he shames me. I feel that this young man will change me for the better.

His unguents are miraculous! They heal with such alacrity! It is causing some people to start whispering about the Church and I have to remind them of the Word and science. Such a dilemma!

Reading these words, I remembered my first meeting with Daukyns. The reek of wine off him was staggering in how sour it was and I wanted nothing more than to escape his attention. But he entranced me with his way of speaking, reminding me vaguely of my forgotten early days, and I soon found myself showing him my herbs. I had been forced into town to replace my worn out equipment. That same day, I fondly remembered, was the one I bought my tin cooking pot and my cherished tin teacup. I also remembered the sessions working out the formula for the making of unguents. Daukyns had tried to force me to follow the strictures in the Word and the success was not great. Alone one day, I let my own intuition guide me and the results were more than I could have hoped for. After that, all Daukyns cared to know was that I worked better alone and so he left me to it.

I did not know what to make of his comments about the wolves. I didn't recall the conversation. I knew from talking to people in town over the years that they were terribly afraid of the wolves and that they thought that there were hundreds of them. It was only a small pack of wolves; numbering usually around twenty, and that they preferred the woods well to the southeast of town where there were fewer hills and more rabbits to devour. They were afraid of people so that the townsfolk had nothing to fear.

The leader of the pack had once approached me. He stalked into my camp one night, walking a cautious but brave circle around the fire. He boldly sat next to me for a spell before chuffing and walking slowly out into the night. He howled a little later, and I heard a reply from his pack. He honoured me that evening, and I knew not why but we noted each other's passage with respect since that time. I knew instinctively that the townsfolk would not understand the wolves and so I am ashamed to admit to pretending to share their fear and spoke lies of keeping large fires at night to keep them at bay.

The next passage was dated mid last summer:

I have learned one thing about Will that I understand without hesitation: he is of both worlds. He walks into town and has the upbringing to make himself integrate and socialise like anyone else, but these times do not last long. After usually no more than three days, he will soon be almost running out the south gate and back to the wild. It is there in that world that he is at home. This might be the result of living most of his life on his own in the wild but I feel—no, I am certain—that it is in the wild he is most comfortable and that he was born to it. In my early years of schooling in the Word, my teacher mentioned a healing order dating back well before even the Church was created. I find myself wondering if people such as Will would have been drawn to that order and been part of it. He is drawn to helping people like no one else I know. Once, he mentioned that it is easier in the wild and that the animals know how to take care of themselves and I often wonder what he meant by that. There is so much more to Will than anyone suspects—even Will himself knows little. I find that I must keep his nature hidden from the townsfolk as much as I can. Already they believe that I am the creator of the unguents, aided by Will, my apprentice. So long as they keep their focus on me, the better. The Word must stay true and I must shelter Will from what they would likely fear and question.

Will raises many questions in me and I found myself approaching Bill Burstone for aid by asking him to allow me access to his unique library. He was surprised to know that I knew about it. I had sensed a love of books in Bill and one day, having seen him accept a large order of books (from a book merchant I once knew in Munsten), I was certain that Bill collected them. Bill agreed once I told him my reasons and I am excited about gaining access to his library; maybe some truth can be found there.

The second to last passage was dated a few months later:

I was shocked to discover that Bill Burstone is an extremely rich man. He could buy up this entire town or more! I chanced to see the contents of this chest of his and I was startled by the amount of coin he hid inside. I found myself overcome with the wealth and begged him to help the poor and he gave me such a look that I will not soon forget it. Such pain and horror! He told me to never ask him that again and to forget I even saw the money. We argued heatedly for a time, but it soon became clear that Bill Burstone would never help anyone but himself. He said that the only thing that could help the poor was the poor themselves and the look in his eyes drove fear into me. This man has a past that I do not want to know about and if I was not so dependent on his library I would have been done with him then and there. I hate myself for making this choice.

I have spent a considerable amount of time using Bill's library. His collection was extensive, but they hinted at books that he did not hold. I discretely asked Bill if he could help fill in the missing pieces. He seems equally eager to finish "our research" as he now calls it. And so, he has agreed to reach out to his sources for more information—if it can be found. I think the research has given him purpose. He is drinking less at the inn.

We were drawn to one of the acquired missing tomes where it discussed an Order called the Aretha Tacuinum Sanitatis and in the text we found a passage that seemed out of place by its singular, almost accidental mention of a training token used by the order to assist their initiates. The token was not described, and it failed to mention how it was used, but Bill became excited. For some reason, he was certain he could obtain one of these tokens through a friend that specialised in such oddities. When I asked for more detail, he only mentioned Munsten and ties to the Church and then said not to worry about it. The Church! Terror struck me and I begged him to stay quiet but he was determined to find the truth, he said. Truth was a large part of the Word and I hesitantly agreed but with trepidation. Our research has expanded outside our small town and I worry that we are opening doors best left closed.

The coin arrived some weeks later by special courier. The arrival startled the town and caused the captain to make inquiries. Bill told him to mind his own business and then brought me up to his library and excitedly showed me what had arrived. I was disappointed to see that it was merely a worn-out, gold coin; minted from decades before the revolution and bore a strange symbol on one side. Bill assured me that it was genuine—he had no doubt. He was certain of his source and that he held one of the rare training tokens. I wondered to what length he went to obtain it but Bill wouldn't say more. He seemed content that its very existence gave proof to what we were uncovering.

I had never heard of this order called Aretha Tacuinum Sanitatis. I was angry at Daukyns for digging into my past and trying to seek answers that I neither asked for nor wanted. I had made a promise to remain hidden and now I felt exposed and even betrayed. Daukyns and Burstone had pulled attention down on Jaipers and it resulted in the death of Burstone, the strange assassin, and maybe my death if I was to linger in the area. That scared me. The Reeve seemed to think any attention would be focused on him but I was tied to the death of the stranger through the coin and I knew that I could easily come under scrutiny as well.

I didn't understand why Bill Burstone would want to become involved in any of this. His wealth was curious and suspect to me. Bill had a past that was probably not good and was best left undiscovered. Daukyns should have stopped when he observed the contents of that chest and I wish he had—both Bill and Daukyns might be alive today if they hadn't started probing. Whatever the truth—it was my business and Daukyns should have consulted me first. I felt a stirring of anger toward Daukyns with that thought.

At least I now knew more about where the coin came from. I wondered who Bill's contact was in the capital city of Munsten. What was meant by a "training token"—training for what exactly? I pulled the coin out and looked closely at it. I couldn't see any writing. The symbol was simply three spirals connected in the middle and meant nothing to me.

I was probably more confused now than before I read these passages. There was more to read, and I turned my attention back to the writings of Daukyns, hopefully, to find some answers.

The last passage was dated only a couple of days before I returned to Jaipers. It was clear that Daukyns knew he was ill and that I would soon be in possession of the book and so he wrote directly to me. His voice became stronger in my head.

Dearest Will,

My health has been failing me for some time now and I fear that nothing in your basket of remedies can stop the ravages that time places on a man. If you are reading this, then I have lost my battle. The past couple of days have strained my body beyond what it can support and I fear that I will soon succumb. Know that I have lived a long and wonderful life and I now prepare myself to return to the stars and look forward to the next adventure that awaits me. That is the Word, and I have lived by the Word my entire life as best as I was able to and I have little fear; just a profound sadness, for I have enjoyed what life I have had and do not willingly give it up. This passion came in no small part from you entering my life and challenging all that I once held as truth in the Word.

The Word explains that all things can be explained through the teachings of the Word and Science. I have lived that credo in all things that I do. So certain was I of the truth that lies in the Word. You presented me with a shock to my beliefs. I could not explain the things that you do! I followed my teachings and developed hypothesis after hypothesis for the questions you raised in me but nothing stood up to the facts you present. You almost belong to the misguided faith teachings of the Church—and I know how shocking that must seem to you! Forgive my humour, for in truth I know that the Word, in time, will explain your abilities— they are just beyond my ken. Through you, I have found an even deeper appreciation of it. The Word teaches us that all things can be explained through Science: when Science permits such truths to be known and understood by modest men such as ourselves.

To that end, and as you have just read, I have been conducting an investigation into your past and more importantly, into trying to understand your abilities—I believe them to be linked. I apologise, Will, for doing so without your knowledge or consent and beg your forgiveness. But I have seen the affects you have on herbs and how they last much longer than herbs should once severed from their life-giving roots and the mystery drew me into its embrace. It defies the Word!

Some truth between you and I: you need to find your past to determine your future. Of that, I am convinced.

And so I can only point you down the road I started unbeknownst to you over the past year—a road I am sorry to say I could not follow to its end. I can only offer two facts to reaching your truth (if you are interested): Fact One, the Aretha Tacuinum Sanitatis which existed, it seems, before the Church, tantalisingly mentions members who could perform magic. The truth behind these magics remains hidden to me but surely some word or passage of this order must still exist in the library in Jergen, or, if you are willing to travel so far: in Munsten. Fact Two, I discovered (and kept hidden from Bill Burstone), notes translated from a special manuscript that should interest you. Tucked into the back of this book, *you will find three pages that I found in one of Bill's older and rarer books. They appear to be copied and translated from a document called the Draoi Manuscript. I cannot vouch for the authenticity of the pages but read them for yourself and seek the truth in the Word. These pages should entice you, I'm sure. There is a symbol drawn on the manuscript and it is identical to the one on the coin Bill obtained. It's meaning I cannot fathom. Perhaps this would be a good place to start your own investigation.*

Stay safe, stay hidden, and when you look at the stars, I hope you see me there.

Your friend,

R. Daukyns

Daukyns' notes changed everything and changed nothing. I never knew that Daukyns had hidden so much of his interest in me. I wish he had shared that curiosity with me so I could have saved him the time and stopped him. The mystery surrounding the coin and Bill Burstone's murder wasn't any clearer and nothing had been gained. All that I knew was that someone had traced that coin back to Bill Burstone and killed him to obtain it. The coin was the source of all this pain and I wondered if whoever had sent it had known the trouble it would cause.

I turned to the back inside cover of the book and found a folded paper sleeve glued inside. I pried open the end of the pocket and drew out the carefully folded pages I found. Altogether there were three pages within, yellowed with age but still strong. I slowly opened them to find them covered in rows of strange, spidery and cryptic symbols. Directly over the rows of symbols, someone had entered a translation. Oddly, the translated words were all pressed together and written with tiny letters, but Daukyns had placed tiny pencil strokes to separate the words and I could follow it without too much difficulty.

The first page was marked on the upper left corner with the same symbol embossed on my coin. Beside it was a title: *A Translation of the Draoi Manuscript*. I started to read the first page and realised with rising excitement that the page was discussing herbs, medicine and magic! The words also contained a warning:

Be warned that this content is lawful to that noblest of manuscripts, the Draoi

Manuscript, the discoveries contained therein which must remain hidden from common eyes through the most keenest methods of cypher so that the unlearned may not expose this knowledge for ill gain. The most learned man of Science, Averlino, drafted this lifelong work to capture his most remarkable findings so that others motan continue his fyne works on this Earth for the betterment of all mankind and in tribute to Gaea.

Contained within the tome are his most remarkable findings of the use of herbs and astrology in medicine and his discovery of sympathetic magics to support and enhance healing.

I quickly scanned through the translations on the remaining two pages and found a cursory explanation of a few plants and how to crop them for maximum use and how to preserve them through the use of potions and unguents. It was describing some of what I already practised, except excitingly, I read mention of herbs whose names and descriptions I was not in the least familiar with. I realised quickly that without corresponding drawings, the text was almost meaningless. It described new plants, such as basil, but failed to provide any more description than it was an aromatic with bright green leaves and that the flower was purple when in bloom. The pages also mentioned hyacinth and mandragora; their properties were so exciting and had such potential! Frustratingly, these pages of the manuscript did not describe the plants. I had to know more! The more knowledge I had the better I would be able to help others. My mind reeled with the possibilities and I felt giddy with delight.

These three pages must have been only a portion of a larger manuscript. Of that I was sure. There was also no more mention of this 'sympathetic magic' and I wondered if this was what I had used to destroy the motes. I knew that it must and I rolled the word 'magic' over my tongue to get a taste for it. The position of the Church was clear on magic and it described death for those that used it. It was one of the eight deadly sins they proclaimed and I shuddered despite myself. Few people believed in the Church these days, but their words still managed to circulate and some people still stubbornly believed in them despite a lack of any evidence to support their beliefs. Thank the Word that those days were long past. I could in no way describe my use of 'magic', if that was what I was using, as being a sin. My magic had healed dozens of people! It was no wonder Church believers barely existed today; no half intelligent person could believe such nonsense. I recognised the voice of Daukyns in my head when I thought this and smiled.

I turned the pages over and found some writing on the bottom of the last page. Two words: April and Munsten. This was translated in the month of April in Munsten, the capital city of the Realm, well north and on the east coast. I had no idea what year and even if the book still existed, but it was real and might still be there.

With this knowledge, my path was laid out in front of me. I was going to have to head to Munsten. I had to find and read the entire manuscript.

I spent the morning of the next day reading and re-reading Daukyns' notes and the three manuscript pages until I had them memorised. When I was finished, I hid the pages back inside Daukyns' book and tucked it safely into the bottom of my pack. For a time, I thought ahead to the journey I was contemplating. The thought of travelling to Munsten was daunting, to say the least. I only rudimentarily knew the way and I would need better directions and better supplies if I were to survive the distance. I knew the roads were patrolled but the highwaymen would know the patrol timings better than anyone and they would pose a constant threat. I could only hope that a solo traveller like me would not make for a tempting target. But the hard truth was that no one travelled the roads alone and lived to tell about it—except for one man that I knew: the Reeve. It was tempting to simply slip off into the night and attempt the journey by myself, but I knew that my chances would be slim. For a moment I considered staying to the woods and fields, but that would add months and months to my journey. The roads were the only sane route I could take and once I committed myself to that choice, I would need to seek the confidence of the Reeve. There was also the benefit of knowing someone at least knew where I was heading.

I found myself down at the stream and rinsed the grime from my face, savouring the cool feeling in the heat of midday. I tilted my head back and let the water run down my neck and back. I closed my eyes, listened to the sounds around me and drew strength from them. I thought ahead to the days I would be alone in the coming months of travel and realised that perhaps I had a way to ensure my relative safety. I eagerly pulled the coin from my pouch, closed my eyes, stroked its surface, and *reached* out to my campsite. Through my *vision,* I found that I could discretely survey my surroundings.

Encouraged, I swept my gaze around the area and marvelled at the lights from the animals that hid in the undergrowth and trees. They glowed like bright stars in the night sky, each standing out clearly to my mind. The trees, plants, flowers, grass and even the insects that burrowed in the ground and flew erratically in the air—they each gave off their own inner light. I never felt so aware of the nature that surrounded me and an intense sense of belonging and acceptance filled my body, threatening to overwhelm me. I *reached* out to embrace the nature in my area and I suddenly felt refreshed and renewed as if I had been dropped in a cool vat of water. I opened my eyes in shock at this unexpected boon. What was this gift I had? The sounds of life around me grew stronger and for a moment I could feel that the animals and insects around me were aware of me as well. There was a feeling of surprise surrounding me. Awareness grew and suddenly elation erupted, growing and spreading out farther and farther from where I stood. Suddenly, I was very afraid, and I clasped my hands to my head and willed, begged, for it to stop. With an almost audible snap, the connection broke. I was alone by the stream and sagged in relief. The surrounding sounds returned to normal, and I took a deep breath to steady myself.

What had just happened to me? What was this power that I had? What was that sense of elation? It was so strong! My thoughts leapt from one idea to another and my confusion grew. One thing was certain: I had to know more and the journey to Munsten would be the first step to coming closer to that goal. It would also mark a significant transition in my life. Once there, I would be able to research my gift and try to make sense of it.

My thoughts then turned to my mother, and I wondered for the first time if she was part of this secret society and if she had this gift. It might explain the sickle and my talent. I shook my head in frustration. They were linked; I was certain of that but knew not how. My memories were so incomplete.

My clearest memory of my mother was so vague now I doubted how real any of it truly was. The memory was a strange one. My mother's name was Belle Arbor, I had never forgotten that. In my memory, my mother and I were fleeing something I had no concept of at the time but knew now it had to do with the coup attempt in the capital ten years ago. I was six. She was frightened but was trying to hide it from me. Although she didn't realise it at the time, the fact that she was trying to hide it from me made it all the worse for me. I remember being frozen in fear most of the time and my mother dragging me by my upper arm. I could still feel the grip of her hand, so strong and so painful. I am sure she bruised me. We found refuge in the root cellar of one of the city homes. The musty smell of the root vegetables permeated the room. We waited just inside at the exit and it was one of the few times that we had stopped during our flight. I remember reaching for a potato in the basket near us and my mother slapping my hand away and muttering under her breath. She shushed me and closed her eyes.

I feel at times that I can remember her face and what she looked like. But if you were to ask me to describe it, I would be unable. I would know her if she came to me but her image is one of fancy now. Known but forgotten. It frustrates me and sometimes overwhelms me with anger or sometimes sorrow.

Soon I heard feet pounding on the cobblestones of the street outside followed by an angry yell and knew they were close to finding us. My mother slowly drew her hand up and with tenderness, gently covered my mouth. As I turned to question what she was doing, her hand clamped hard over my mouth, sealing my voice just as the root cellar door burst open. I screamed in fear into my mother's hand and my eyes large with fear shot to the opening. I kept trying to scream as the city guard who stood on the other side of the open door looked directly at where we lay crouched and huddled together. We were found! And then, miraculously, his eyes wandered away, and he looked about the small cellar. Clearly disappointed, as evidenced by the fierce scowl on his face, he slammed the door closed and I could hear him stride away on iron-shod boots, calling out to search the next home.

The urge to scream slowly subsided from me and my mother released her hand from my mouth. Before I could ask, my mother grabbed my upper arm in her rough grip, and with a whirl of memory we bolted out the cellar and ran silently down the cobblestones. To where—I remember not.

My next memory was watching my father's back as he walked away and abandoned us.

My last memory was finding myself alone in the wilderness knowing my mother was dead and having promised her to always stay hidden.

I shuddered as the memories came back so vividly. For the first time, I could remember the glimpse I had of my mother's face as I turned to stare in stark fear at the man in the doorway to the cellar. The look on her face was strangely peaceful and her eyes had remained closed throughout. Her serenity was such a wonder compared to the terror I had felt. I often wondered why I could remember the escape that night but not much else. I have desperately tried to recall anything that happened next and how I ended up, days later, alone in the woods with the small sickle grasped tightly in my hand and sobs wracking my entire body at the recent loss of my mother. There was nothing to connect the two events. What memories I had of what I did next were nothing but a blur of wandering the woods and fields and stuffing anything that looked edible into my mouth. In the end, I survived despite the odds and now I had the skills to let me survive on my own without much fear. I could forage for food just about anywhere. I knew how to watch for signs of predatory animals and avoid their territorial areas. I knew how to make an honest living off the land and keep myself in pleasant extras like flour and dried meats. I could find shelter and make a fire in almost any condition and I could find fresh water just by examining the lay of the land. I was proud of what I had learned on my own. Especially my herb lore—painfully gained over the years and hard earned.

I looked down at the three pages and book I held in my hands and knew that they confirmed that at least what I knew was real and more importantly that it was true and that there was so much more lore to gain out there.

And I had confirmed that I could at least survey my surroundings and discover anything that lurked nearby. I wasn't certain of the range I could achieve but it was sure to provide me a greater level of security. Knowing this, I started to feel an irresistible pull toward Munsten. I felt that the coin and the manuscript secrets would only be revealed there. My promise to my mother had been made when I was just a little boy and I must now set it aside and follow the path my life laid out before me. I had the mystery of my past to solve, my new abilities to explore, and a manuscript that tantalisingly provided clues that I needed to follow. Perhaps in finding those answers, I would find the truth of what happened to my mother and I so long ago. Perhaps. Of my father, I knew nothing and cared less to know. The image of his back turned to us was the only answer I needed from him.

For the first time in years, I spoke to the memory of my mother: *I'm sorry, mother. I can no longer keep my promise to you. I am a man now and I must seek the truth.*

I listened for a reply, unsure what I should expect. I waited but no feeling of acceptance came to me, no apparition of my mother appeared nodding her approval, and no shackles broke from my wrists and ankles to clatter to the ground. I merely stood there and waited and felt intensely more stupid the longer I stood there. I shook my head and laughed, breaking the spell.

I returned the translated pages into the book's back cover sleeve and tucked the book into my backpack as I looked around the clearing. The trees surrounding me swayed slightly in the light breeze and within them, the occasional cheerful chirp of a bird would fill the air. The buzzing of insects pulsed in intensity and reminded me of the beating of a heart. I closed my eyes and tentatively drank in the peace and solitude, wary of nature spiking in elation once again. All I sensed was tranquillity, and I sighed in gratitude but with some sadness. My past would remain, for now, a mystery. My promise to my mother was broken, but I was firmly taking charge of my future. It all seemed so anticlimactic.

Chuckling, I shouldered my backpack. By the height of the sun above the horizon, I had a few hours left to gather the herbs that Dempster had asked me for and still be able to make it into town before dusk. I owed the man one last haul of herbs and spices and looked forward to the gathering. I adjusted my backpack more snugly to my back and started upstream to a particularly good area for collecting herbs.

A little while later, I found the area I wanted and dropped my backpack to the ground. After carefully checking the area for observers and finding none, I pulled out my sickle and moved over to a rich patch of herbs. I crouched down beside them and closed my eyes. The rosemary plant in front of me filled my senses and I could feel the vibrant health of it. I could almost taste the roots reaching out for nutrients and water from the rich soil. This plant was content and reached strongly for the sun. The pleasant smell of the rosemary filled my nostrils, and I *reached* out to a branch covered in the spiky leaves. I caressed the branch and spoke to the plant, asking it to release the branch. I placed the sickle at the base and as always; I imagined I heard agreement from the plant. Gently, I drew the blade across the branch and it came free with an inaudible sigh. I soothed the plant and urged more nutrients toward its roots in return for the gift. I noted with some surprise that what I did was not too different from how I felt when using the coin and wondered at that. I was also surprised by how much easier this reaching out to the plant had been than before. It usually took me longer to accomplish this task. I opened my eyes to inspect the area where the branch had separated from the main plant and was happy to see that no marks were left behind. The plant was undamaged and content. The loss of a single branch meant nothing to it. I wished all things in life were so simple.

I spent the next couple of hours gathering the herbs for Dempster. I soon had rosemary, thyme and marjoram gathered in bundles and decided to reward Dempster by tying them with catkin ties and *reached* out to the bundles and halted their activity. The need for the branches to draw water and nutrients stopped, and they simply were. They would retain their water content if kept in a cool place. I knew no other way to describe what I did but knew through experience that these herbs would stay fresh for many, many weeks.

I packed the herbs, hoisted my backpack to my shoulders and started the walk toward Jaipers, squinting at the sun in my eyes. I paused at my old campsite and said farewell to the plants, animals and insects and I imagined their sad goodbye.

It was a little while later that I realised that I had unconsciously solved the problem of who deserved my healing gifts. It was so clear now and I wondered how I could have made the problem so complex. I didn't need any complicated set of rules to guide my actions. It was a simple matter: *everyone* deserved my healing gifts regardless of circumstance—with no exceptions. I knew at once that this was the correct choice and I felt an eagerness to put my new healing powers to practice.

I had a purpose and a goal in my life for the first time. I had gone from a wandering herb gatherer to a healer in only a short time. My mother had this gift—I knew that now. What images of her face I retained clearly showed the care that lay there. The amount of pleasure I gained knowing I could share in my mother's gift made my heart lift with joy and I felt lighter on my feet. I felt I could walk for miles and smiled at the road ahead of me.

N i n e

Jaipers, 900 A.C.

I ARRIVED IN Jaipers with about two hours of daylight remaining. My new boots were chewing up the miles, and I truly appreciated them. I no longer thought of them as the assassin's. They were well and truly mine now. As I entered the town, everyone was talking about the illness, the clean-up of the water in the well and the removal of the rats. I avoided these pockets of conversation and stayed to the quiet areas of town. Few noticed my passing and thankfully, no one knew of my involvement. The few people who did stop to speak to me simply said they were glad to see I had overcome the sickness too and passed on their best wishes. I was glad to know to the townsfolk I had merely fallen ill to the same sickness as everyone else; my secret was safe.

I stopped outside the common hall and struggled with my emotions. It was strange that I would not be entering that room with Daukyns and creating my unguents. I felt disconnected and a little lost. After a moment, I turned to the inn and hurried over to meet with Dempster. That would set things back to normal. I found him out back, fanning himself from the heat that hung oppressively in the early evening air.

"Back so soon?" he asked as he led the way into the kitchen. Once inside, I took a deep breath through my nose and savoured the wonderful smells of his cooking. I moved over to his prep table and placed my backpack on top.

"Yes, well, I've pretty much got all the herbs mapped out now. It's just a matter of getting around." I removed the herbs and placed them on the table. Dempster made cooing noises and reached out with eager hands to grab a bundle of savoury. He rubbed the buds between thumb and finger, breathed in the released aroma and closed his eyes.

"Ah," he sighed. "Beautiful." He fingered the cattail frond that bound the herbs but didn't remark that the bundles I laid out were tied up differently than normal.

I had wondered if he would notice the subtle change, but if he did, he said nothing. In time, he would notice that these herbs were lasting significantly longer than they should, but by then, I would be long gone and safe from questions I did not want to answer.

I had decided not to tell Dempster where I was headed, or that I was leaving, and felt guilty in not sharing that information with my friend. In truth, it was for the best and I thought perhaps I would get the Reeve to explain it all to him in a few weeks' time.

"Here," he said. "Let me give you something in exchange for these wonderful herbs." Dempster turned to his pantry.

"No, no! Please! I want for nothing! My backpack is already close to bursting."

Ignoring me, Dempster rummaged through his stores.

"Seriously, Dempster," I pleaded. "I've no room. I'll come back some other time, all right?"

This finally stopped him, and he looked dejected. "Ah, young Will," he said. "It hurts me not to give you something for all this." He waved his hand over the pile of herbs on the table. "Have you eaten today?"

"Yes," I said quickly and turned my face away from him, so he couldn't see the lie. I wasn't hungry. I was too excited and wanted to get away and start my journey. When I looked back at him, I could see that he hadn't bought my lie but nodded, anyway.

"You know," I said, eager to change the topic, "you could start a small garden outside the kitchen. You could grow your own plants. You have a perfect mix of shade and sun."

"Why would I do that?" he asked. "I have you and I have no desire to tend plants! Can you see me bending over pulling weeds?" Dempster laughed and patted his rather large stomach.

I had to admit he had a point, but I didn't want to see him do without after I was gone.

"You could get one of the kids in town to tend it for you," I argued. "You would always have access to the freshest plants! Think how wonderful that would be."

"Maybe," he said. "Maybe." But he didn't look convinced.

We talked for a time about plants and how to tend them but in time, Dempster sensed my need to leave. He followed my quick glances to the back door and smiled and clapped me on the back. "Off you go, Will. I see that you are eager to leave."

"Sorry," I mumbled, feeling ashamed. Dempster was always so good to me and this was perhaps the last time I would spend time with him.

Dempster laughed. "No worries, no worries. Tell me, though, before you leave, where are you staying? It's already late at night."

"I'm heading to see the Reeve and then heading back out." I looked to the door again. I had to lie one more time with him and I wasn't sure I was ready for it. "I... I... I don't know when I'll be back in town." I glanced quickly over to him and was relieved to see him examining his new plants.

"Hmm," he said. I wasn't sure he had heard me. "All right then." He turned back to me and handed over my backpack, making shooing motions with his hands. "Go, go! Off you go! Stop by when you get back."

Before I could blink I was outside his kitchen with a slab of cold roast beef in my hand. I stared at it in wonder. That was a neat trick. How had he...? I shook my head, laughed and took a bite as I walked over to the Reeve's office.

I entered the gaol building that was nothing more than a large single room with two empty gaol cells made from iron bars. A table was pushed up against the wall beside the entrance and it was covered with odds and ends. The only other things in the room were the desk and two chairs and it was behind this desk I found the Reeve. He looked up and smiled when I came in.

"Hi, Reeve," I said, slipping my backpack from my shoulders and taking a seat across from him. He was leaning back in his chair and trimming his fingernails with a knife.

"Hi, Will," he replied. "I saw you come through the gate and head over to the inn. How's Dempster?"

"Good. He's good." I looked around the sparse room. Nothing adorned the walls. No windows. No decorations. By the Word, it was dead in here.

"So," I began, my foot tapping on the floor. I had practised this conversation in my head during my walk into town. I had imagined the Reeve's responses and prepared replies. My arguments were all set and, in my mind, I had convinced the Reeve and he had supported me. Hopefully, this conversation would go as well. "I'm leaving."

"Okay. A bit late at night, but I'm sure the guards will let you pass."

Huh? I thought. *What?*

"No," I said. "I am leaving Jaipers."

The Reeve just stared at me and raised an eyebrow.

"I'm heading to Munsten," I said simply. *This is not starting as I expected.*

The Reeve sat up and glared at me. "You're what?" he asked.

"I'm heading to Munsten," I repeated a little louder.

"By the Word, why would you need to do that?"

I fumbled in my pack, pulled out the book and showed the Reeve the writings. He sat still for a while, flipping the pages back and forth, reading quietly. I sat watching him biting my lip. I needed his approval, but I wasn't sure why.

"You were heading out right now?" he finally asked.

I nodded, and he frowned at me.

"That's stupid," he said. "Come. You're staying with me tonight. We need to discuss this."

We made our way over to the Reeve's meagre house. It was provided by the town and was quite well maintained by the Reeve. He lived near the north gate which was odd seeing as the gaol was on the opposite side of town by the south gate. I asked him once about that and he told me he liked to separate his working life and his personal life. I smiled at the memory and remembered that I really didn't understand it at the time. I think I understood it a little more now.

As I walked in I looked around to situate myself and noticed a woman's shawl hanging on a hook by the door. The Reeve saw what I was staring at and muttered something under his breath as he propelled me deeper into his home. I smiled despite my best efforts not to and shrugged off my backpack.

He stowed my backpack in a small closet built under the stairs that led to the upper level and settled me in the dining area at his table. This house was remarkably similar to Bill Burstone's but then again, it was really only the second house I had ever been in and suspected all homes in this area were similar in design. From the table, I looked around as unobtrusively as I could and felt like I was seeing a side of the Reeve that few people ever did.

He kept a clean house—that was for certain. He had little in the way of furniture and mostly his walls were bare, except for a couple of paintings in the living area. The paintings I recognised from the artists who sold in the open market. His living room contained a massive couch, fat with straw stuffed upholstering, and it was pushed up against the far wall with blankets and a pillow stacked on it. There was not much else that I could see: it was an austere home. All-in-all the house seemed lived in, but lacked the feeling of comfort. I snorted at this thought. Here I was, a man with no home, criticising the home of the Reeve. I focused my attention back to the Reeve as he puttered about his small kitchen and lit the small pot-bellied stove.

We chatted about trivial matters while I watched him prepare a surprisingly pleasant meal. We talked about my herbs and what paired best with what foods and I found myself speaking with rising interest about the recipes Dempster shared with me. Candles were lit when darkness fell, and I helped clear the table and wash up. It was a wonderful meal, and I contributed by making a pot of tea using my best tea leaves. We settled back at the table and I quietly handed over the book to the Reeve and sat and sipped my tea. I watched as he studiously read the notes and the manuscript pages again.

The Reeve was a slow reader, and it was a little while before he closed the book, clutched it in his hand and shook it before tossing it on the table where it landed with a soft thud. It was startlingly loud in the silence and the flames of the candles twisted in anger at the disturbance.

"They opened up a hornet's nest," the Reeve said, finally meeting my eyes. "No doubt. That coin brought down a world of hurt on Bill." His brows furrowed, and he looked more intently at me. "And that hurt has spread to include you and Daukyns."

I had already come to that conclusion and waited for him to say more. The Reeve pushed Daukyns' book farther down the table in disgust and it narrowly missed the small tray of cheese that still lay between us. "There are too many questions," he said, exasperated. "It's too much to figure out for one man and one man alone and on his own. What do you seriously hope to accomplish travelling across the country on some wild chase for something that probably doesn't even exist?"

He was talking about the Draoi Manuscript. I had doubts about finding it, but I had expected this line of questioning and I shook my head. "No, it exists. I know it does." I paused when the Reeve scowled at me. "It does," I repeated with strength and I think I was believing it. "You know what I can do with that coin! You saw what it let me do. That alone confirms that the manuscript exists. The answer is in the Munsten library and I mean to go there to find it."

The Reeve shook his head and reached out and picked up his tea mug, forgotten while he was reading the book. He took a tentative sip of his tea, savoured the taste and nodded appreciatively to me. I smiled in return. He put down the mug and thought for a second before answering. "I know what you mean to do but you haven't thought it through all the way. It is a very long road and full of dangers. There's a reason the Protector's men guard the towns. There's a reason why traders hire men to guard their caravans on the road. The road is plagued with highwaymen—and worse!—and I can't see you alone walking the hundreds of miles to Munsten and surviving."

"I'll be fine," I said more than just a little stubbornly, angry that the Reeve had so little faith in my ability to survive on my own. "I've lived on my own in the woods for years –all my life, really! You know that. The walk to Munsten is just long—not impossible." I quickly snuck a hand out, snagged a piece of cheese and popped it into my mouth, savouring the rich, tangy taste.

"Humph. There's a world of difference in living in the woods south of Jaipers and surviving on the road to the other coast and all the way north to the capital. There's nobody south of Jaipers and everyone east of here. You've never been east of Jaipers, have you? Out to the other towns?"

I nodded my head and swallowed the cheese in my mouth. "Yes, I have. I've been out to Belger."

"But no further, right?" He glowered at me, no doubt trying to intimidate me. "I have, Will. I used to live up north before I came to Jaipers. It is tougher up north. *A lot* tougher. People are hard and wouldn't piss on you to douse the flames if you were on fire. Trust me on this."

I laughed despite the seriousness of the conversation. The image of a villager pissing on a fellow burning alive was a new one. I had never heard the expression before.

"I'm serious, Will!" he chastised. But I smiled back at him, refusing to be dissuaded. "That man I shot, remember him?" I nodded, and the sudden memory wiped the smile from my face. "You heard his accent; he was from Munsten if I don't miss my guess. Munsten! The very place you intend to go! It should be the last place you go! Head south, hide in the hills, no one could hope to find you there with your skills outdoors."

I was surprised to hear the pleading in his voice. "Hide? For how long? Reeve, I finally have a chance to find out more about who I am! I can't *not* go!"

"I understand that I truly do," said the Reeve more quietly. "One day you will need to go. But why right now? What's the rush? The answers, if there are any, will still be there next year or the year after that! Bide your time. Wait things out here first and see if anything else comes from this."

He had a point, and that stopped me. Why was I in such a rush? His suggestion was not unreasonable, yet I had to admit to myself that the pull to Munsten was strong. I couldn't ignore it. Even if I agreed to wait, I knew that it wouldn't be long before my feet found the road on their own. Everything that had happened to me so recently was screaming at me for answers. If I could have run all the way to Munsten, I would have. I knew that I would never be able to sit idly by now that I knew that I possessed magic and could really help people. If I was to use this gift and use it well—and wisely—I had to get answers. I shook my head, and the Reeve sighed.

"I need to go now," I said to the floor, not wanting to look him in the eye. "It will take me months to get there and what better time than now? I have to know."

"You realise that there is likely to be more men coming here looking for that coin, right?"

"Uh, yes," I said slowly but admitted to myself that I really hadn't thought too much about it. I think the Reeve sensed the lie because he snorted at me. I looked up at him. "And so what?" I said defiantly. "You said it would be you they would be after—not me. If I hide in the hills, they'd find me soon enough and I would have to come into town eventually and then they'd have me."

Just then a thought occurred to me and I spoke it out loud as the words formed in my head. "What if I left quietly, said I was heading to the hills but went east to Jergen instead? They'd be stuck here looking for me for months and by then I would be in Munsten, safe and sound." I slid my eyes sideways to look at the Reeve and saw his eyes widen in surprise.

This argument shut the Reeve up for a bit and he sipped his tea and considered it. I thought it through. I would need to plant the seeds of this deception. Spread it around town. But I really didn't need to do that at all. It's what I always did. I always headed south and back to the woods. It's what people expected of me. I said as much to the Reeve.

"That," started the Reeve slowly, "is not that bad of an idea." He looked at me and smiled at the expression on my face. "Yes, I am agreeing with you, Will!" And he chuckled. "But it has to be more than that. You'll be gone a lot longer than normal."

I didn't understand. He laughed and ran a hand through his hair. "Will, you are never gone from town for more than two months at a time. It has almost been routine. People plan around that, you know. I told you that before. People rely on you in this town. This time you'll be gone a lot longer. People will notice and start asking questions."

I stared at him, trying to figure out if he was making it up.

"Will, after two months the people in this town that rely on your herbs and unguents are going to notice that you haven't returned and yours truly," the Reeve stabbed a thumb at himself, "will be asked to go find you. They'll assume that something happened to you. And it's me they'll come see to look into it, mark my words."

I nodded in slow understanding. I couldn't quite grasp why the people of Jaipers cared about me enough to track my movements and I must have looked confused because the Reeve laughed and slapped the table.

"By the Word, you are dense, Will!" He laughed harder at my frown. "You have no idea what you do for these people. People rarely get sick these days and it's all because Daukyns spread your unguents throughout this town for the past two years. Now that Daukyns is gone, people are already talking about what that will mean to their health. Most people have tied the two of you together and it is only your continued presence that is keeping everyone calm."

"That's absurd, Reeve!" This was the only response I could come up with. Daukyns' death still sat heavy with me. Memories of handing pots of unguents over to a gleeful Daukyns came unbidden to my mind, and I wallowed in the bittersweet happiness they gave me. I knew Daukyns spread the pots around the neediest in the town, but little did I imagine the widespread effect of them. It seemed that I had broken my promise to my mother years ago without even realising it.

The Reeve grew silent and I think he regretted bringing up Daukyns' name. He waited a moment before continuing. "Will, you'll be missed. People will start to ask questions and you'll want to avoid that. A good cover story will help. Something that would explain an extended absence. Even if it only buys you a few months at best."

"What do I care?" I retorted, surprised at my sudden anger. "It's my business what I do! What would they do anyway? So, what if I don't reappear in two months, or three months' time! I'll be long gone by then!"

"They'll start to make inquiries, Will. They'll start to reach out to other towns asking about you. People will ask why they are looking for you and slowly word will get out. A strange young man who makes the most wonderful healing pots. A man who lives by himself in the woods and gathers the most potent herbs. Think about it, Will!"

I did, and my eyes widened as it sank in. Even though I found it extremely unlikely that people would care that much about me, eventually word would spread. The coin, the manuscript, Bill Burstone's murder and my herb lore were all connected somehow. Whoever was looking for the coin would follow any lead—no matter how slim—until it led directly to me. I looked up at the Reeve and nodded meekly. He grimaced in reply, seeing that I had finally figured out what he was saying.

"They'll hunt you down, Will," he said softly. "They'll hunt you down."

We grew silent for a while and savoured our tea and the cheese until they ran out.

"I understand, son," he said into the silence. "I understand why you need to pursue this. I won't stop you. But I will help you. I'll cover you from this end."

And with that, the decision was made. We slowly worked out a story that I would spread throughout the town, backed by the Reeve. The story would be that with Daukyns passed on, I was heading south, likely down to Port West and wouldn't be back for a year. People would be told that I was eager to expand my herb market and thought to check out the port town and perhaps beyond. It was simple, and the Reeve said that was best. Satisfied at last, the Reeve excused himself and headed upstairs where I could hear him rummaging around.

He came back down, stood beside me and dropped a leather scroll tube on the table, opened it and pulled out maps. I was stunned to see them. I had never seen maps; I knew about them, but I had never laid eyes on them before.

"These were mine from my early days. They're worth a fortune but priceless to me," he said smugly as he pulled his chair up next to mine and started to educate me on how to read them.

It took a little while, but once I figured out that I was looking down at the world as a bird might, I managed to understand them quite easily. I marvelled at the detail and traced roads and rivers with my fingers. When I pointed out how close Jergen was to Jaipers, he laughed and explained 'scale' to me. My heart sank when I realised just how far I had to travel to Jergen—it was going to be just over a hundred miles by road and with many more miles than that to Munsten. I would be on the road for months and months.

We talked well into the night and he offered me advice for the road and how I should divide my days. We talked about food and water and how to avoid others on the road. He convinced me that I should treat all people on the road as threats no matter how sincere they seemed. We considered that I take a barge downriver, but the Reeve felt it better that I shouldn't be trapped on the river and said that the road would offer me more escape routes should I need them. I agreed and didn't tell him that I wanted to stay close to the woods anyway—I needed to sleep on the ground at night. The Reeve pointed out areas where highwaymen were likely to be positioned and I noticed that strange marks inked on the map already near those same spots. When I asked the Reeve about them he quickly changed the topic.

When we realised that we were going over the same issues over and over, we glanced at the shortness of the candles and decided to pack it in for the night.

The Reeve leaned back in his chair and ran a hand down his tired face. "It's decided then." He paused before slowly continuing as if giving up something precious. "I've got a good friend who lives north of Jergen. He'll put you up for a spell if you need a break from the road. He has a family and a farm. Well, he has a wife and daughter—lots of farm hands, Word knows it's been years since I've set eyes on him—or her."

I knew nothing of the Reeve's previous life and I wondered what a friend of the Reeve would be like. I didn't understand the hesitancy I heard from the Reeve in talking about him. These two shared a history, and I wondered what that might be. I also sensed that I shouldn't pry.

"Just mention my name and he'll take care of you," he added quickly. "I'll give you some coin to give him, too. Tell him to buy his kid something nice with it. He'll understand." I nodded and looked at him. He had said nothing more about the wife but somehow, I knew he was thinking about her.

The Reeve showed me on the map where the farm lay and I memorised the details. He described a couple of landmarks to look for and, content that I knew where to go, he stopped and finally grinned at me. "His daughter is about your age. Her name escapes me though, 'C' something, long name..." He raised an eyebrow in thought. "My mate's a good man. Goes by the name Ben Rigby and probably still does, ha! We have a bit of history, he and I. Always did things together, and we were quite a team. Then he found a wife and started a family. And that was it. We parted ways."

The Reeve grew silent, and no doubt re-lived some memories in his head. I tried to imagine the Reeve as a young man with another life and failed. He could never be anyone other than the man he was today. *So proper. So, so...* I stared at him standing beside me and tried to grasp the essence of him and *reached*. A deep thrum sound filled the world. My eyes widened in shock. The Reeve still sat quietly brooding on his past. He had not heard or felt the sound. It resonated within me and made my back teeth feel loose in my mouth. The sound was startling, and I felt suddenly as if someone was watching me. I looked around feeling foolish. We were alone in the Reeve's house.

I turned my inner gaze to the Reeve and took a measure of him. I knew without a doubt that I could trust this man with my life. He had a rare quality about him that represented the best that people could offer. I wondered if all good men could be so easily read with my sight. Would I be able to tell friend from foe?

I must have been looking at him strangely, for when the Reeve glanced at my face, he scowled and smacked my shoulder. "What are you staring at me like that for?" he growled and then reached out for the map tube. "You'd best get some sleep. It'll be your last good sleep for weeks."

We rolled the maps back up and returned them to the scroll case. The maps would stay here but the Reeve had questioned me repeatedly until he was sure I had the route burned into my memory.

After that, he stood up and glanced down at me sitting morosely beside him in my chair. He grasped my shoulder and squeezed it. Then he stood, turned and went to his bedchamber and closed the door without saying a word.

It was a little while later, after spreading the blankets on the couch and settling in, when I realised that I had *reached* without the use of the coin.

Duilleog

Ten

Jaipers, 900 A.C.

THE NEXT DAY when I rose I found that the Reeve had already gone about his daily business. I was hoping he was going to see me off, but that didn't appear to be the case.

I ventured out of the Reeve's home and went searching for provisions for the road. I spent a half groat just on dried meat alone. It was lovely, well-preserved meat, and it was heavily spiced and mixed with berries and nuts. It would keep forever, so long as I kept it packed in its waxed cloth to keep it dry. One of the merchants I knew surprised me with a gift of dried beans, peas and lentils. He refused my money and explained that he still owed me from the last herbs I had sold him. I smiled and accepted the generosity. *Take it when you can*, my mother had once told me. That thought stopped me in my tracks. I didn't ever remember anything my mother said to me and I wondered where that memory had come from.

At one point, I realised with concern that my hand–sewn backpack would not likely survive the journey. I soon found myself over at the tanner's shop. He was the best tanner in town. He owned a shop with a proud sign stating Sheridan Leathers outside. We all called him by his first name and so he was known as Tanner Ross. I had often provided him with quality pieces of fur in exchange for leather pieces. I explained what I wanted, and he grinned and disappeared into his back room. I browsed through his display of belts and marvelled at the quality while I waited. A few moments later, the tanner emerged carrying a leather backpack. He laid it down on the counter and waved me over. I reached out to touch it and I was rewarded with the feel of soft, supple leather. The backpack was a rich brown and covered in many pockets with leather cinch ties. The straps were padded and could easily be adjusted. I fiddled with a strange belt at the bottom of the pack and the tanner explained that you used it to tie the pack around your waist.

"To stop it moving around on your back. Makes it easier to carry a load," he explained.

I tried the pack on and the tanner helped me adjust it. I was stunned at how good the pack felt on my back. It was a marvel of construction and I told him so. He beamed at the praise. I took it off and placed it on the table with regret. There was no way I could afford something so exquisite and I told him so.

"Son, that's fine praise from a young man who makes such wonderful things with your herbs!" And he chuckled at my surprised look. He looked around to make sure no one was looking and pulled up his shirt to reveal a livid purple scar that ran across his pudgy stomach. I could sense that it still caused the man some discomfort, but that it was cleanly healed and not infected. I glanced inquiringly at him.

"Sliced myself," he said simply as he laughed and held up a hand in mock protest at my frown. "No, seriously! It happened about three weeks ago. Did it to myself—a foolish thing to do. A little deeper and my guts would have spilt out. Good thing I'm a little thick around the middle, eh?" And he laughed again, lowered his shirt and patted his midriff.

"Daukyns helped sew me shut—with my own thread, mind!" He laughed deeper. "And then he gave me a pot of your unguent, young man!" He smiled as understanding dawned on my face.

"Ah! Good! I'm glad it helped you, Tanner Ross," I replied.

"Helped me?" he asked in a stunned tone. "*Helped* me? Son, it cured me! I would have been dead if not for that little pot!" He shook his head in remembrance. "I had a fever through the roof. The pain was something terrible! Daukyns spread that on the sutures and it felt like a cool breeze on a hot day. I almost fainted with the relief! Helped me?" And he shook his head in remembrance. "Son, I owe you my life!" With that, he grabbed the backpack and thrust it into my arms. I gawked at him.

"Take it," he said simply. "It would mean a lot to me. A way to make up for what I owe you."

"I–I can't take this!" I stammered and tried to give it back to him. This was too much for one little pot of unguent. This backpack was a work of art, lovingly made, and worth a fortune. I couldn't accept it but he refused to take it back. "It's far too much, sir!"

"Nonsense!" he said with feeling. "It's already yours. I didn't know it until you walked in here and asked about a backpack. It's almost as if it was here waiting for you! I hadn't even put it out for sale! It sat in the back room."

I stared at him wanting to say yes so badly but feeling guilty all the same.

He reached out and patted the backpack. "This is what I was working on when my knife slipped. The strangest thing, too. I never work a knife that way—too dangerous!" Tanner Ross chuckled again. This man liked to laugh, and his belly laughed with him. "Yours! Done and done!" And he clapped me on the back.

I remembered my mother's words and accepted the gift and thanked him profusely. Then I asked him if it was all right if I transferred my belongings over to it in his shop. He didn't mind and even helped me. When he loitered over a few bundles of my herbs, I left him with a few samples and some suggestions for their use. I pressed a jar of my unguent into his hands and wordlessly, he looked at it for a bit and then nodded once. That made me feel a little better. I hoisted the new backpack onto my shoulders and could feel the ease of the weight on my shoulders compared to my older pack. The tanner helped me adjust the straps more securely and tied the waist belt around me. I walked around the shop and loved the feel of it. It fit and balanced perfectly, and I felt I could walk for days and days with it on. Then I laughed when I remembered it would be months.

I thanked the tanner and was about to leave when he reached out and grabbed my arm to stop me. His face paled, and he stared at my boots and then looked up at me.

"W–where did you get those boots?" he asked hoarsely, his eyes white around the edges.

"My boots?" I replied, looking down at them, worried that he would figure out where I had obtained them.

"Yes, your boots!" he demanded and tightened his grip on my arm. "Tell me! What cordwainer made those?"

"I have no idea! The Reeve gave them to me!" I answered with truth. I did not want this man to know that they came from the man who had murdered Bill Burstone. The tanner searched my eyes and satisfied with the answer, he relaxed somewhat and released my arm.

"Take them off, please. Let me see them," he said with some authority in his voice. "There'll be a mark—a maker's mark—I need to see it to be sure."

Knowing there indeed was a mark, I shrugged off my pack and sat on the wood floor of the shop, untied my right boot and handed it up to him. The tanner eagerly took the boot and moved to the light coming through his front window. He pried back the leather of the boot and peered inside.

"Oh, my Word!" he muttered. "How can this be? Here in Jaipers of all places!" He turned to me and beckoned me over to join him at the window. He showed me the maker's mark and I nodded. I had noticed it before. "See this? This is the mark of the cordwainer in Munsten. A triangle with three lines passing through the points and intersecting in the middle" He looked at me for any sign of recognition, but I could only stare blankly back at him. The tanner grumbled and pointed at parts of the boot.

"See the sole? The triple stitching here and here? The triple stitching here? The unique way it is secured to the upper thigh? These are all the design of a unique man. And not just any cordwainer, son. This is from *the* cordwainer in Munsten. He makes the most marvellous boots and shoes in the entire land. It is a family business that goes back generations! Generations! It is the Cobbler family." And he looked at me as if I should know the name which I didn't, and he continued. "But they don't make these particular boots for just anyone. These are special. They are Trinity Boots. The triangle, three lines, and triple stitching throughout, yeah? The Trinity. Three, three, and three.

"The Cobblers make them for the Church. A special part of the Church and it's said they're the ones that do the dirty work for them." He looked at me for some kind of reaction. I could only stare back at him in surprise. The man who had murdered Bill Burstone had shoes that belonged to the Church? That seemed completely improbable. Unless he killed the previous owners; it seemed likely.

"The Reeve gave you these, hmm?" He seemed satisfied when I nodded. He handed me back the boot and watched as I tied them back on.

"Then you are a lucky young man. Those boots alone cost more than my entire store." He laughed when I gasped and stared at him for confirmation of what he said. "Yes, yes. Very expensive boots! Highest quality you can find. You'll find they will not wear out. Remarkable, no? Because of that, they are passed from owner to child and so on. Those are probably decades old."

"How can that be? They look brand new!" I replied, not really wanting to believe any of this as I stared at the boot on my foot and the one in my hands with alarm.

"I don't know. I really don't. The secret to making boots like that are only known to a few. It's guarded and protected by the families that know." He shook his head and grimaced. "Not my family! The best I can manage is that backpack you have there!" And he laughed anew at my look of guilt. "No, no, young man! No regrets! That is yours! Yours! Enjoy it—and you did admire the quality! Spread the word around town! Make sure everyone knows of Sheridan Leathers!"

I finished lacing up my last boot, stood and guiltily avoided promising him I would spread the word. Instead, I thanked him profusely for the gift and the knowledge and I turned to leave the store when he caused me to pause with a look.

"Something you should know about these boots..." he started to say then stopped, as if unsure of what he should be saying. "They, um... this is hard to say or believe! My Word!" He grimaced. "You may find that they leave little in the way of marks on the ground. You understand?"

I didn't but nodded. He seemed satisfied with that and he escorted me to the shop door.

I spread the falsehood that I was leaving Jaipers and heading west to expand my market for a year. He seemed to accept it easily enough and clasped my shoulder and wished me a safe journey. I turned, now anxious to leave, and started toward the exit.

"One last thing, young man," he said softly, and I looked inquiringly over to him. He looked so very serious. "I wouldn't flash those boots around too much. Not many would recognise the make except those that already have a pair. They run in families and your boots are perhaps, ah, not one of them, eh?" He smiled to soften the words and when I nodded in understanding his smile turned sad as I made my way out to the street. "If I were you, I would avoid wearing them in town or at least cover them while walking around, hide them with simple clothes. You understand, eh?"

I nodded again and quickly walked out the door, ducked in behind the building and shrugged off my backpack. I rummaged through it and found my old foot wraps. I looked from them to my new boots and felt a bit sad. My first real pair of boots and now I had to hide them. It only took a moment to tie my boots up in my old wraps. I stood and tested them, and they felt strange. I thought about perhaps taking the boots off altogether, but I had grown used to having my feet so snug and secure and opted instead to suffer the wraps while in town.

I emerged from behind the building and looked at the bustle of shopping activity. Cries from vendors filled the air with a sound I had come to be accustomed to. The smell from the food stalls filled my mouth with spit and hunger. *I love this town*, I realised with a pang. *I'm going to miss it more than I thought. Somehow, I have changed from a lone hermit of the woods to a man who finds comfort in towns.*

I reached out to the small flower box the leather worker's wife must've placed in front of the shop and I coaxed the flowers to brighten. They cheered me up and I pushed my way into the throng of people strolling by.

I spent the next couple of hours wandering around the open market, spreading my story of leaving for the south for an extended absence from the town to all the vendors I knew. Some took it very well and others expressed concern and urged me to return quickly. The honest concern of the town's people and their genuine feelings of good will toward me was a lovely feeling but it saddened me knowing I was being less than truthful.

Some gave me small tokens of thanks, such as pieces of leather, threads and two needles, cloth, and even a small pair of worn scissors that still worked. I tried to decline the scissors, but the owner insisted, and she pressed them firmly into my hand.

I hadn't truly realised how well liked I was in town. In fact, everywhere I had walked this morning people were nodding toward me, smiling and wishing me a good day. I found this to be very strange behaviour; normally I was not noticed by anyone except the few who dealt with me regularly. I wondered as I finished my shopping if this was an aftereffect of having healed so many of them. I too felt a connection to these people that had not been there before.

After a time, I tired of spreading my falsehood to the town folk. I completed my purchases by buying a second water skin for the road and headed to the town well to fill it. I knew water would be crucial to survival on the roads. Despite the Reeve's assurances that there were many sources of water on my route, I felt better knowing I would never be without if I could do something about it.

As I arrived at the well, the local children clambered around me and even raised a bucket of water for me and accepted a pence coin for thanks. I filled the skin and secured it to my pack next to my other, smaller one. Despite all the additions of weight, my new pack seemed less heavy on my back than my old one. It was certainly larger than my old pack and I had a large amount of food packed in there; I still had my hard cheese and all the supplies Dempster had provided me plus the added luxury of such wonderful items as beans, lentils and flour. The pack would grow lighter over the days and maybe one day I would be missing the extra weight. The children noticed my pack and commented on it; they even reached out to touch the soft leather and ooh-ed and ahh-ed over the feel.

I loitered at the well for a spell, hoping to see the Reeve one last time. I glanced repeatedly over at the Reeve's office and the adjoining gaol, but it was vacant and remained so. I could hear the garrison captain arguing with the quartermaster nearby at the barracks over some accounting discrepancy. I closed my eyes and listened to all the familiar sounds of the town that droned quietly in the background. It hit me then I would dearly miss the town of Jaipers. It had been my refuge and my tenuous link to civilisation over the past four years. And I had made good friends here. I glanced over at the common hall and felt a pang of grief at not being able to see the familiar figure of Daukyns sitting out front with his wine and stained robe. I could almost hear his ringing laugh in the air and my eyes stung with the threat of tears.

The corner of my eye caught Dempster coming out of the inn to stand in the doorway mopping his brow with a rag. The heat was already stifling, and the sun was only just a few hours over the horizon. Today would be a scorcher, I knew, and the road would be unforgiving. Dempster spied me, waved to me and I waved back and tried to smile. I would miss the large man and especially his food. I watched as he turned back inside and disappeared.

No matter. It was almost noon, and it was time to leave. I only wished that I could have said goodbye to the Reeve. I secured my pack, said farewell to the children and turned to the gate. This was it, I thought. The start of my life and my adventure. Who knew where the roads would take me? *All I can do*, I mused, *is place one foot in front of the other and see where it all leads.* Resigned and pulling my confidence up over my shoulders like a cloak, I started moving.

As I approached the south gate of Jaipers, two guards appeared from either side of the road and moved to stand between me and the gate. I recognised who they were: the new guards the quartermaster had been providing with gear just the other week. They stood staring at me in their new garrison leathers with the recruit look that came from white, untanned skin around their necks and on their skulls from freshly shorn heads. By the sallow cast of their skin, I knew they had likely also been one of the sick I had cured in town recently and they had lost weight. Thinking of the sickness, I remembered when they had noticed me when I paused for a drink at the well. And now they were showing more than a casual interest in me. No one was ever stopped leaving the town without reason. As I drew closer to them, a strange feeling overcame me and I slowed my approach to clear my head. Part of me was filled with the urge to run and I tried to hasten my way as I made to pass around them.

"Where are you going?" demanded the one on the right when I was only a few feet away. Beyond them, the gate beckoned with promised freedom.

Startled, I stopped in my tracks and stared at the man. It was none of his business where I was going and I could not believe he was questioning me. I must've looked the sight standing there with my mouth open. The strange feeling I had felt before doubled and became one of unease and a sudden urge to vomit started to overcome me as my knees grew weak. As I looked at these men, my new ability to sense people slipped off them in an odd way. The unsettled feeling was so sudden I could barely control it and I clamped my teeth shut and ordered my stomach to relent. They were staring at me so openly and then they glanced at one another. I could almost feel the anger that grew and passed between them.

The guard on the left moved closer to the other one, and he held my gaze with a look of loathing, directed squarely at me. His new leathers creaked as he adjusted his weight and I watched as his hand moved to grasp the pommel of his sword, my mouth open in shock.

"I said," hissed the guard on the right, "where. Are. You. Going?"

I watched in disbelief as his hand also moved to his sword. *This can't be happening!* His eyes pierced my own, and they were filled with a roiling anger and pure hate. The feeling of unease became so prevalent I had to swallow violently to keep from gagging. These men, they were not right with the world. *They*, and I searched for a word to describe them, *they were* wrong *inside.*

Then something unspoken passed between us like a heightened awareness. They were the enemy. Somehow, they knew what I was sensing from them. The anger and hatred in their eyes burned brighter. I knew without a doubt that they represented what my mother had made me promise to remain hidden from for all these years. I had promised to stay safe—to stay hidden—and yet here I was standing out in the open and exposed to them. Tension quickly filled the air, and I knew that something terrible was about to occur and I froze in fear.

I started to stammer out a response to buy more time while I tried to find a way out of this and I felt bile rising in my throat threatening to choke me. Then I saw their eyes lift from me to someone behind me. Their hands quickly came off their swords, and they straightened. I felt a weight come off me and I slowly turned, trying to keep the two guards in my sight, to see Captain Gendred rapidly approaching. A profound sense of relief overcame me and the foul, almost physical feeling of unease I felt coming off these two guards reduced when their focus left me.

The captain came right up to me, frowning first at the two guards who were so blatantly and oddly out of place standing in the middle of the street facing me, before clapping me fondly on the shoulder.

"The Reeve told me you were leaving, but I had to see it for my own two eyes. Off to new places, I hear."

The two guards exchanged a glance. The captain tore his gaze from his men to look at me.

"Port West, eh?" he continued. "I have a good friend down there. Runs the port authority. Make sure you stop by and see him when you arrive, all right?"

"Yes, sir. I will," I said, keeping my eye on the two guards. They were listening rather intently, and I recognised a chance to complete my misdirection. "What's his name, sir?"

"William! His name is William! How's that for an easy name to remember?" he said and laughed. "He's the harbour master and can help you reach out to the merchants in town. He knows them all, I dare say. Knows them all. If you don't mind me saying, I think you are making a good choice, young Will. About time you stretched your legs and escaped the life of the wild. It's respectable."

I nodded weakly, keeping my eyes on the guards.

"He'll be glad to take you in. He has a wife and two kids, but he has a spare room. Here, take this," and he pressed a folded piece of parchment into my hand. "It's a letter of introduction. He'll put you up until you get your feet on the ground. And that won't be long, I'd wager! Those pots of yours are worth their weight in gold crowns!"

I gripped the paper tightly in my hands. "Thank you, sir," I said. "I'll go to him directly."

My eyes remained on the two guards and while the captain nodded at my words, he sensed my interest in them and turned to look directly at the two men. They were oblivious that this was their captain standing in front of them and they were openly ignoring him and staring at me. It occurred to me that when the captain had first approached that they should have probably at least came to attention and saluted him as was befitting his rank and station. I sensed that the captain had just come to the same conclusion, and he fixed his gaze on the two of them, his jaw now clenched in anger.

"Ah–ten–shun!" he barked, and the men blinked in confusion at the unexpected noise and snapped their attention away from me over to the captain. Both of them failed to respond to the order and stood gawking at him.

The captain seemed to swell in size and he quickly forgot all about me and turned his full wrath to the two men. "I said, ah–ten–shun!" he thundered, his face now a livid red.

The men seemed confused on what to do and then sloppily started to move into the position of attention. They continued to glance over at me and this finally threw the captain into a fit. A drawn out, screaming, tirade burst out of the captain. The authority in his voice was unmistakable, and the men turned their full attention on him and finally seemed to forget about me.

I took the opportunity to flee, waved farewell to Captain Gendred, and walked briskly through the south gate. The guard on duty at the gate was peering at all the noise from around the corner of his post. I nodded at the guard at the gate who ignored me completely and suddenly I was free of the gate and the strange guards and I made my way quickly south down the road away from Jaipers. The feeling of unease faded away completely, and I filled my lungs with fresh air and thanked the Word for my escape.

Behind me, I could hear the captain's yelling fade into the distance and I had to smile to myself despite the fear that still lingered. *Those poor bastards*, I thought. *But it serves them right.* As my boots opened the distance from Jaipers, I fervently hoped that they believed my story and would soon forget about me.

I couldn't explain the illness I felt being near them. I was glad I hadn't used my powers to get a better feel; just being in their presence had been enough. I shuddered and felt a chill go through me. I lengthened my stride and opened the distance between myself and the gate. If I never saw those two men again, it would be too soon.

My promise to my mother was forefront in my thoughts. The urge to run deep into the woods and disappear was strong. I felt exposed and vulnerable. The assurances from the Reeve that I would not be a target were replaced with panic. As I debated simply hiding, I remembered the carefully laid deception. The people of Jaipers thought I was heading to Port West. The plan was still in place. I could still make my way east and find the truth about my abilities. With effort, I shrugged off my fears and pushed south as quickly as my feet could take me.

I walked just over two miles south of Jaipers before I abandoned the road and circled around the town to the east and then headed north until I connected with the road to Munsten. I pushed myself and travelled a good number of miles that afternoon. As I travelled my fears subsided, and I relaxed and stopped looking over my shoulder as frequently.

The road out of Jaipers paralleled the river but kept about a hundred yards of separation. Out on the river, I spied the occasional slow-moving barge running east with the current toward Lake Belger and the lakeside town named after it. On my side of the river, I saw two barges being slowly pulled upstream to Jaipers by labouring workhorses. The poor animals strained against the current and dug their hooves into the horse trail that hugged the bank. I imagined the barges moving upstream looked to the ones moving downstream with envious eyes. I felt for the horses, too—it was hard work.

Thankfully, no one shared the road with me and I blamed the heat of the day for the solitude. That heat coupled with a lack of wind soon drained half of the water from my skins. There were no streams along the way that I knew of and I refused to use the river water downstream from the town until I was well east of Jaipers. I would need to be careful about how much I drank. The Reeve had warned me about water intake and here I was drinking it with no thought to tomorrow. I wasn't worried though; I would refill my skins from the river. Daukyns had once taught me to boil the river water first, and I hadn't forgotten. With what I knew of the motes that had infected the people of Jaipers, I was understanding what the boiling did.

The surrounding area undulated in rolling, sun-browned scrub grass that slowly rose upwards to the hills in the south. It appeared as if the countryside mimicked the course the river now took, and I wondered how that was so. Throughout the scrubland, I could see the odd clump of trees that were randomly placed here and there breaking the scenery. The air was filled with the surprisingly loud and incessant buzzing of insects. Looking ahead, the road shimmered with the heat. As I walked along the side of the road, keeping to the grass, grasshoppers leapt away from me in all directions in panicked fright.

I was glad that my wanderings and life outside the town of Jaipers had kept me strong and fit. I seemed to have fully recovered from my convalescence in town and felt that my strength was good and hale. Despite the oppressive heat, I took in my new surroundings on a road I had only travelled once before, and I was thankful for every step that brought me that much closer to my goal while rewarding me with new sights and the promise of new wonders.

My pack fit snug to my back and at some point, early in my travel, I had found a sturdy and straight branch which I had whittled as I walked into a suitable walking stick and it now served me well to pace myself. I luxuriated in the feeling of my new boots on my feet and how they cushioned my steps. I no longer had to pay such close attention to where I placed my feet amongst the sharp stones, nettles and thistles that lay and grew along the roadside. Head held high, I strode along, gazing around me in comfort.

When the sun drew closer to the horizon, I knew I had to find a suitable spot to camp for the night. I spotted a copse about two hundred yards south of the road and made my way through thick, waist-high grass, trying to follow a deer trail that appeared and disappeared at random. Often only their spoor and hoof prints marked their passage. I saw no signs of anything threatening like a cougar or wolf—and I felt relieved. In the past, I had seldom had difficulty with predators. I had lived with wolves for a time and understood them. But I preferred to leave them alone, and I thought they felt the same way. The relief was real though: I didn't like to push my luck.

When the trail I was on veered sharply left, I headed right to a small copse of trees nearby. Sure enough, when I reached the trees I found a small clearing with the remains of a fire in a scorched ring of stones and a small pile of wood. The deer would swerve clear of what was clearly a common camp for travellers along the road and I counted my blessings it was deserted and based on the remains of the fire, it had not been used in many weeks.

I spent time foraging for fuelwood and returned with a large armful. I had spotted a few full raspberry bushes, enjoyed some of the tart fruit and marked them in my mind to return for them in the morning. I laid my wood down on the pile and finally dropped my pack down near the fire pit. Despite my earlier feelings of being fit, I could now feel my legs trembling with the day's efforts, and I fought the desire to plunk myself down and take a load off. Instead, I forced myself to tend to a small, smokeless fire. The wind was blowing off the river and would keep any smell of smoke from the road. Only after I had filled my small cooking pot with the remains of my water and brought it to a rolling boil, did I finally sit and prepare myself a tea to cure my aches and pains and replenish my energy. As the tea steeped, I *reached* into the brew and urged the nutrients to be stronger than normal. It was so easy to accomplish this simple act and I wondered how I could have survived before without it. The coin did not seem to be required by me anymore but having mulled this problem over during my entire walk and finding no answer forthcoming; I pushed the problem aside for now.

I transferred the tea to my tin cup and refilled the pot with the rest of my water, boiled it and added a handful of beans, lentils and some of my dried herbs for flavour. I carefully removed the pot from the flames, covered it with a piece of cloth to keep the flies out, and left it for the morning.

My mind was empty of thought. I could only think of sleep and dreaded the thought of a full day's travel in the morning. The sun disappeared below the horizon and the land was dark except for the small light my fire cast. I drank my tea, listened to insects chirping in the darkness and ate some of my dried meat, soaking it first in the tea to soften it. I sliced off slivers of my sharp, hard cheese until my hunger was sated and washed the remains down with my tea. Fatigue brought on by having food in my belly was quickly overcoming me and so I buried my small leather bag containing the sickle and coin and rolled my bedroll and wraps out over it. After relieving myself behind a nearby tree, I collapsed with a groan under my wraps. My last thoughts were that perhaps I should have found a more hidden location to sleep and then sleep took me and I was oblivious to any more thoughts of danger or threats.

I slept a dreamless sleep until morning.

The next morning, I woke with the sun and had to stretch out the muscles in my sore legs. I limped over to relieve myself behind the same tree and then foraged for the berries I had spotted the night before. I filled a small cloth with them and tied it closed at the corners—careful not to burst or damage the ripe fruit—and then hung it from my belt to enjoy as a snack during the morning walk. I checked my pot and verified that the beans and lentils had softened overnight and I had it for breakfast with a few added berries to sweeten the mixture. It was a pleasant meal and reminded me of the many solitary meals I had enjoyed over the years. Another mouthful of food always meant another day of survival and another day to take pride in my accomplishments. I mentally took stock of my food and was content I had enough to last me weeks, should the need arise.

Satisfied, I cleared up my camp, carefully stowed my leather pouch in my tunic, shouldered my backpack and made my way over to the river to wash out my pot and cup and refill my water skins. I returned a wave to a barge descending the river and started back down the road munching on the berries from my makeshift pouch. Soon the muscles in my legs stretched themselves out and my stride lengthened.

After a while, I realised that I was enjoying myself and I was filled with a strong feeling of contentment and purpose. For once I had a goal in my life and I was confidently heading toward it. The tart and sweet taste of the berries filled my mouth, and I chewed and swallowed as quickly as I could. A smile burst across my face.

I felt at that moment I could walk forever.

Duilleog

Part Two: Munsten

Duilleog

Eleven

Munsten, 900 A.C.

ARCHBISHOP REGINALD GREIGSEN of the Church of the New Order scowled at the missive on his desk where he had tossed it moments ago. It lay on top of the numerous religious writings he was studying to prepare for his next sermon. That sermon work could now wait. His anger threatened to consume him, and he tried to distance himself from the information it contained if only for a moment, so he could best decide what to do next. He wouldn't make smart choices if his anger continued to consume his thoughts.

He absently picked up a piece of the broken wax that had once sealed the missive and broke it into smaller pieces before tossing them unerringly into the fireplace behind his desk. The pieces landed deep in the flames and caught immediately, flaring brightly as they were consumed. He looked around what most people erringly considered a tailored insult to his position. His lowly office sat forgotten in the rear quadrant of the castle and was, as most people thought, in one of the worst locations and as far removed from the true workings of the castle as possible. It was a windowless room on the ground floor, with poor ventilation, and off the normal pedestrian wanderings in the castle corridors. Part of him still longed for the homage afforded him in the days when the Church ruled the country. His old office from decades ago was next to the castle's interior church. The Lord Protector now used the church as the council chambers.

This office was considered by most people in the castle as being more than he deserved and they rarely hid their contempt. The feeling of anger that washed over him had become such a well-known companion he barely recognised or acknowledged it anymore. It constantly burned through him. He walked the corridors and seethed inside while he gave the perfect expression of reverence and faith. He spat the word *faith* in his mind. *The heathens know nothing of faith. Nothing!*

Admittedly, compared to his old office this one was spartan, pallid, and beneath his station. The walls were bereft of ornamentation except for one tattered tapestry behind him in the corner wall and an icon of the image of God on the wall directly across from his desk. The floors were bare and exposed with the same rough stonework and poor mortar work that made up the walls. Two torches barely lit the dark room, and they sputtered and filled the room with an acrid smell that stayed with him throughout the day and tainted the taste of his food. The room was a carefully crafted insult to his stature forced upon him by the revolution so many years ago. His position as Archbishop was reviled by the heathens and only suffered by the graces of the Lord Protector, but only if he remained as unobtrusive as possible and didn't 'spew' the word of God everywhere he went, as the Protector had stated so elegantly one day long ago. Thankfully, he was rarely granted an audience with him and only when it seemed to suit the Protector's twisted sense of humour. The Archbishop hated the man with all his heart and soul but doubted the Protector even knew of it and if he did, he doubted he cared.

He kept his innermost emotions hidden from all those around him. He had mastered deception. He was considered quiet, reserved and pious. The Archbishop laughed to himself. *If they only knew*, he thought. *How that opinion would change.*

The looks the Archbishop received by people as he walked the castle halls were barely tolerable these days. And yet he suffered the exile as was befitting a man of his stature, regardless of how much he longed to reach out and strangle those who smirked behind loosely covered hands or worse: those who glanced at him with pity and disdain. He had tried for the throne once and had failed but like the mythical phoenix, he had risen from the ashes. This forgotten corner of the castle was his reward.

The Archbishop knew he would have the last laugh. He prayed for the days that would come when he could throw down those who mocked the Church and hid behind the Word and pretended to understand the blasphemy that the Word preached. Little did they know the horror they faced on their death when their refusal to accept God and the teachings of the Church would be proven to be their ultimate undoing. When they stood alone to face their Maker and be judged and tossed into the fiery pits of Hell to suffer relentlessly for all eternity. He smiled at this welcomed imagery, his imagination flooding with scenes of bodies burning and writhing in fire and sulphur. His Church, by God's will, would overcome the usurpers and he, Archbishop Greigsen, would wear the heavy mantle of the crown and rule the hearts and souls of the people of Belkin. He would guide them to the Promised Land. Forgiveness of their sins was the Lord's work and he would hasten them on to His righteous judgement. His work, he knew and accepted, was to return the country to its intended rule by God and God alone.

He looked around the small square office, finally forcing the words in the missive out of his mind. It was so small—barely twenty–five feet across. He couldn't host a dinner for the ten bishops and deans of the realm, should they all decide to visit. He remembered the days when he hosted hundreds of his senior flock in the castle seminary with the King seated beside him. Their dinner tables groaning with the weight of the feast laid out before God and King. In those days, his word made men tremble, and the King answered to God and only God. *The word of God as interpreted by myself*, he grinned.

Those days were gone. Today everyone openly scoffed his word. He heard castle staff chattering in the corners, speaking loud enough to be sure he could hear them, as they ridiculed the teachings of God and twisted their meanings to suit their weak arguments. *And they dared to call me delusional!* The Archbishop clenched his fists as anger rose to consume him. It was getting so hard to keep his face composed and calm in front of the internal inferno of rage that constantly threatened to overcome him.

How the Church has fallen, he thought, shaking his head. *All because of that incompetent asshole, Bishop Bengold.* As he often did, the Archbishop turned his memory to the images of Bengold doused in oils, being torched by the King himself. The sounds of that man screaming in agony were usually what let the Archbishop drift off to sleep at night with a smile spread across his face. *Bengold got off lightly*, he thought not for the first time. *Far too lightly for the crimes he committed.* He burned eternally now. His death had exposed him to the vast eternity he now faced in the deepest pits of Hell. *That was a comforting thought.*

His eyes returned to look upon the missive on his desk. His work was not yet done. The pursuit was not yet over. He thanked God that at least this one last thread had been revealed and he knew the Sect would soon complete the task he had laid upon them so many years before. The Sect had screwed it up, he knew, but all was not lost. It was salvageable, provided he gave the correct guidance and incentives.

The Archbishop cocked an ear at a barely heard sound behind him and knew with some surprise that the appointed time had come. Time flew by so swiftly now. The Archbishop reached out with a shaking hand and grabbed the cane that rested against the corner of his desk. Using the cane and the desk, he struggled to rise out of his chair. It was becoming harder to fight against the pain in his joints, but duty demanded he ignore them. He wasn't sure what was worse: the pain or the shaking. He finally managed to get mostly upright and leaned his weight on the cane. He glanced toward the door to his office and for once was thankful that the chamber was small so the door was not too far away. He methodically made his way over to the massive door and pushed a shoulder against it to force it closed. With well–oiled hinges, the door quietly shut. Only those with an eye for such things would have noticed that the door was well sealed to the frame. He slid the locking mechanism over and sighed, content that what transpired in this room could never be heard from any castle spies placed outside. He trusted no one.

After the revolution, the Lord Protector threw him out of the Church offices, claiming them for his own, and offered him any other chamber in the castle. In the end, it wasn't hard for him to decide upon this one from those available to him. The room was rather unique in the castle and only the Archbishop and the King knew its secrets. *The former King*, he corrected himself and frowned. These days he seemed to forget that the King was dead.

What no one knew or suspected, was that this room had a secret exit: an exit that led to a narrow corridor that snaked inside and around the castle's outer walls. In places it allowed him to see outside to the ocean and the surrounding city. In one place, it even led to a small area directly behind the throne in the Throne Room; the throne arrogantly and permanently held by the Lord Protector.

The secret corridor also led down to a chamber directly below the dungeon, a chamber that was accessible only from this room and from a hidden entrance from outside the castle deep within a sea cave accessible only at low tide. Originally, it had been used by the King as a place for clandestine activities and alternatively, should the need arise, as an escape route for the Monarchy and his family. The Archbishop knew clandestine activities were required to maintain the peace of the Kingdom by removing and interrogating malcontents. It had always been a necessary evil to keep the peace of the Kingdom intact.

After the revolution, all except for the Archbishop had forgotten the office and the lower chamber. When he had realised this, he seized the opportunity and took this office, claiming those secret areas for his own. And now it housed the secret society he had created within the Church—a secret society that was run by the very man who now waited outside in the secret corridor.

With the door to his office closed and secured, the Archbishop hurried as best he could over to the fireplace. He lifted a needlepoint image of religious icons that draped over the right corner of the mantelpiece to expose a well-worn button. Once, he knew, this stone button was built flush within the stonework of the mantel and had been undetectable to a common glance. Now, after years and years of use, the button was smoothed down and fit loosely in the worn hole that housed it. For that reason, it was now covered with a simple cloth. *Still*, thought the Archbishop, *you really have to know exactly where to look to discover it and even then you have to be standing to the right side of the fireplace near the wall.*

The Archbishop braced himself and pushed hard on the button. It was getting harder to activate it and his strength was not what it used to be. Sweat broke out on his brow, but he pushed harder still and with relief felt a click vibrate through his pressed thumb when the internal lock disengaged. Shaking with the effort, the Archbishop used his cane to rap once against the wall beside the fireplace. A few seconds later, he thought he could hear a slight scraping sound but knew he only imagined it. He knew the secret door had swung open completely silently behind the tapestry that hung on the wall.

The candles in the room sputtered and were pulled briefly toward the tapestry. If the Archbishop still retained the hearing of his youth, he might have heard the soft moaning from the wind that had been momentarily sucked under and around the heavy tapestry and into the opening beyond. As quickly as it had happened, the candles righted themselves and the Archbishop gazed expectantly toward the tapestry.

A moving bulge formed in the middle of the tapestry that grew and edged toward where the Archbishop stood. As it reached the edge, a hand was exposed. It grasped the edge of the tapestry and pushed it aside to allow the man behind the hand to emerge, blinking into the sudden brightness of the room. *That the man found this dark room bright speaks to the complete darkness inside the corridor*, thought the Archbishop with amusement. The man's eyes quickly adjusted and when he spied the Archbishop, he strode over quickly and sank down, kneeling while fervently reaching out to grasp the Archbishop's offered hand. He quickly kissed the Archbishop's ring of office and gave thanks to God. He waited until the Archbishop bade him to rise.

The Archbishop indicated the corner table in the room and they made their way over to sit in the two chairs that occupied it. The Archbishop beckoned to the golden wine urn that always rested on the table and the man grabbed it and carefully filled the gold goblet that lay beside it before pouring the fortified wine into a small wooden cup he produced from a pocket in his tunic. The man held his cup untouched and watched him. The Archbishop sighed and a ghost of a smile crossed his features. He took a small sip and the man eagerly started to drink his. *This old ritual,* he thought with a smile, *has become so common and yet so satisfying over the years.*

This man shared every secret the Archbishop held. He intimately knew what his goals were and to what length he would go to secure them. This man was the sword that God had provided to him to wreak his vengeance on the heathens that spewed forth the heresy of the Word. This man had already tortured and slain hundreds of the heathens on behalf of God, and now their goal was almost near completion. One loose thread remained that needed snipping and then they could begin in earnest to achieve the goal that so long awaited them.

The Archbishop waited until Seth Farlow had finished his first cup of wine and watched as he refilled it. The Archbishop could not stomach much wine any longer. It hit his stomach like burning embers and filled it with a pain that would persist for hours. Sometimes he would throw up blood after too much wine, so he kept its intake to a minimum and only during these meetings. One cup would be enough, and he moodily thought about the hours of pain that would follow as he took a small sip. *The pain is such a small price to pay for doing God's work,* he thought. He glanced over to Seth and smiled to himself as he sensed the devoted adoration that poured from his eyes toward him.

He was so blessed to have a man like Seth to deal with the darker and least understood needs of fulfilling God's plan. He cleansed the world of the evil that inhabited it and he was spectacularly good at his work. Only one person had escaped his reach, and that was a child of all things unholy. Seth still blamed himself for this failure and the Archbishop knew—and approved—of his daily flagellations. Soon, that failure would be cleared, and the Archbishop's goblet shook with the anger of how close they had come to finally reaching their goal only to fail due to the weakness of one man. Seth's chosen assassin had failed and died for it.

* * *

Seth relaxed as they sat in the comfortable silence. Seth was used to such silences and waited patiently for His Holiness to speak. He shuddered in ecstasy at the thought of hearing him. The voice of God was in his voice and he always longed to hear it. The fact that the voice of the Archbishop was unspectacular itself did not faze him—it was knowing that God spoke through this man that excited him. Years of training kept his face and hands calm and steady as desire rippled through his diminutive frame. He was now forty-five-years-old—fifteen years younger than the Archbishop, but he had aged well. A regimen of physical exercise and a strict diet had kept him vibrant and strong. His muscles were wiry and thickly roped but were hidden intentionally behind loose fitting clothes. His head and face were always kept smoothly shaved except for a small patch of beard he sported below his lower lip; this was his only vanity.

Seth had watched the Archbishop age and become stooped before his eyes over the years and knew the tests God gave him were the cause of his physical decline. The Archbishop bore the weight of the Church on his shoulders and fought daily for the rights and souls of those who still proclaimed their love of the Lord and it wore on him physically. Seth also was aware that he had an outlet for his rage while the Archbishop did not. The Archbishop kept his righteous anger locked up deep inside and knew it consumed him.

Many times, he had tried to convince the Archbishop to come down to his Chamber to assist in the purging and cleansing of the heathens, but he had always refused. He understood why; the Archbishop was answerable directly to God and could not soil himself with such menial tasks, but he knew this outlet would be therapeutic to him and felt sorrow for him. He wanted the Archbishop to witness his acts for God.

Now, as he sat savouring his weekly cups of wine, Seth tried to read the Archbishop's mood. He knew a missive had arrived—he always knew what was happening inside the Castle; rarely did anything escape his notice. Watching the small tell-tale signs from the Archbishop's face, Seth knew whatever it contained it had both upset and somehow sparked an excitement within him. Only someone as close as he was to the Archbishop could have recognised the burning anger that lay within him, but it wasn't his eyes that gave it away. It was found in the slight tightening of the skin around his eyes and a shallower and quicker breathing than normal. Signs that Seth could read instinctively, learnt through years and years of lovingly applying his skill to those heathens in the Chamber. Whatever was in the missive was important. Important enough that the Archbishop had summoned Seth to his office two days in advance of their normally scheduled meeting time.

Their meetings were always on a schedule. Nothing short of an emergency would alter that timing. When Seth had seen the indicator on the far wall of the Throne Room, he had hastened to wait outside the Archbishop's office. They always met at the same time every week if only to share a cup of wine. Sometimes they wouldn't even speak except for the words of absolution that Seth always requested at the end. They had agreed many years ago that nothing should alter that timing. It would not do for the secret door to swing open when someone from the Lord Protector's guard stood in the office.

The door could be opened from the inside as well as the outside, but Seth was under orders to never open the door from his side and to always wait for the faint tap from the wall near the fireplace. From inside the space between the walls, he could hear nothing from the adjacent room. The wall was the thinnest by the fireplace and it was here that Seth would wait for that faint tap in the complete darkness. Only then would he attempt to swing open the secret door by grasping the handle carved into the stone. He was always apprehensive about stepping clear of the tapestry. He was at his most vulnerable at this point—blinded by the sudden light and open to any form of attack.

For now, he sat and waited.

* * *

The Archbishop stared back at Seth, the man who was the head of the Church Sect and had been since the Revolution. The Archbishop had created the organisation out of the ashes of the King's spies when the King had been imprisoned. It had started innocently enough. The Archbishop used the network to communicate with the King in the Tower and to try to recover the Throne quietly in the background. The Archbishop's powers had been stripped, and he had almost perished in the riots. Seth had helped him survive. He had been sent by God, the Archbishop knew and had once expressed that to Seth, much to his chagrin. Seth's reaction to that had been disturbing, and the image of Seth writhing on the ground in ecstasy with the front of his trousers darkening with wetness was hard to clear from his mind. The Archbishop mentally shook his head to clear that image. The Archbishop smiled thinly and rested his hands on his lap. His goblet sat on the table, barely touched and now forgotten.

"Seth," he began and pretended not to notice the shiver that seemed to pass through him when he spoke. "A letter has arrived from Jaipers."

He watched Seth for any sign of emotion and saw only the calm, seemingly detached expression on his face He wondered how he managed that although he knew Seth had been waiting eagerly for this news for weeks.

"It is not good news, I'm afraid to say."

At this Seth reacted. A slight flinch crossed his face but just as quickly it was gone. The Archbishop knew no one would have caught that lapse except for someone waiting and looking for it.

The Archbishop beckoned over to the desk and the missive that clearly lay on top. "If you would...?"

Seth was at the desk in two strides and grabbed the missive before retreating back to his seat to read it. The Archbishop had it memorised and could see the writing in his mind. He recognised the writing right away. The pen strokes were hesitant from someone not used to writing and they were sloppy. The ink was spilt in spots and too much was used to write the letters. It was written in the Sect code but with practised years of reading it, the code could be quickly translated, and he and Seth could read from messages as easily as they read plain text. The words were clear and concise. There could be no mistake. They angered him deeply.

"Coin not retrieved. Knife killed by local Reeve. Coin in possession of the Target. Confirmed: Target found. Pursuing."

* * *

For Seth, reading the missive was a gift from God. The word 'target' swam in front of his eyes. *Could it be? Could the Target have been found after all these years?* A sense of wonder filled his thoughts and the potential for redemption leapt at him and ceased all remaining thoughts. *Yes! At long last, the Target is revealed! I had known he still lived, known it!*

The constant, welcoming ache of the lash marks on his back throbbed in a feeling that approached ecstasy. *God has revealed the last heathen! My work can be completed and free the Church to resume its rightful position as the power over this Realm.* His thoughts ran through his head in rapid sequence. They could be wrong about him being the Target, but that was highly unlikely and unimaginable. His agents knew better than to toy with that bit of news. No sect member was to ever mention the Target in missives unless they were absolutely certain they had found him. *The agents in Jaipers are young, that's true*, mused Seth, *but their devotion is strong and I had attached them to my best assassin; the man codenamed "Knife" for that very reason.*

Seth had briefed Dennis *'Knife'* Petard himself, along with Jeremy Lions, and Peter Custard down in the Chamber. Dennis was one of the original Church Sect members and could always be counted on to complete his mission goals. *And now he is dead—my top assassin!—killed by some local law enforcement commoner.* The chances of that happening were minute and yet, despite the odds, it had happened. That loss coupled with the loss of the novice coin was unacceptable.

Seth now understood the rage and joy that warred within the Archbishop. Seth's fury at losing the coin and his top assassin was enormous and he needed to lash out at something, anything to quell the rising storm in his blood. This emotion competed with the knowledge that the Target had been found. Ten years had passed since that eventful night when the Church had come so close to achieving its goals promised under God.

Seth himself had killed that bitch but had missed her whelp then he had lost him. It was as if the very earth had risen to hide him from his sight. He had relived that night every day of his life since. At the time, his mind had been clouded and confused by magic from the bitch, but inspired, he had targeted the centre of that confusion and had blindly fired his arrow. The scream from the bitch had been like a clarion of joy to his ears. The confusion had immediately lifted, and he spied her lying in her pooling blood, her life pouring into the ground she cared so much about. *The irony had been exquisite!* he remembered.

Of her son, nothing could be found. No sign, no marks on the ground, no anything to hint to his location. He had disappeared off the face of the earth. The powers that God gave him had not been enough to pierce the fog her evil magic had laid down to blind him to the boy. He still remembered that terrible agony in his soul when he had recognised that he failed the Lord so spectacularly. Not even the wet blood of the bitch in his hands could ease the wound to his soul. That night, after the Archbishop had failed to end his misery, he had started flagellating himself and he had not missed a night since.

But now he was FOUND! Seth found himself standing with the missive crushed in his grip and arms upraised and his face turned to the heavens in sheer bliss. The echo of his last thought came back to him and he realised he had screamed it out loud. Startled he looked over to the seated Archbishop and saw the flushed and furious look on his face. His vision spun as the horror and embarrassment of his outburst overwhelmed him and he fell to his knees in front of the Archbishop, hanging his head in shame.

"Forgive me, Your Holiness," he whispered. "God's Love fills me to overflowing, and I forgot my place."

Seth felt the Archbishop lay a trembling hand on his bald pate and he shuddered in ecstasy.

"Rise, my son. Sit."

Seth regained his seat and composed his face. He could see looking at the Archbishop he seethed inside. Using his gift from God Seth realised that the Archbishop was furious with him for placing his own agenda and past failures in front of those of the Church. Seth was ashamed.

"I recognise your joy, Seth, and I share it in truth," whispered the Archbishop. Seth felt the feeling of righteous anger that started to rise within the man. "But this is dire news! This loose coin was not retrieved and now it finds itself in the very hands of the person we most wanted not to have it!"

The Archbishop was not aware that his voice had risen but Seth heard it and felt the mounting anger behind it. Seth knew his own personal feelings regarding the Target had blinded him to the true issue at hand. The Target was a direct threat to the Church and he had to be stopped. His own failure was the cause of the Archbishop's anger. He knew. Oh yes, he knew. Seth sprawled on the floor and prostrated himself in shame. The Archbishop had risen to stand, towering over his prone form. He clutched his cane with whitened fingers. His arm shook with barely suppressed fury.

"This damned coin! It was tracked all the way to Jaipers by your best man! Your *best*!"

Seth heard the disdain and contempt in the Archbishop's use of the word 'best' and cringed inside.

"He failed, didn't he? Failed!"

The Archbishop was shouting now; his face was flushed a deep red but with splotched, bright white cheeks, his eyes flashed with hatred and the anger. With every word, the Archbishop struck Seth across the head with his cane.

"You. Let. The. Coin. Fall. Right. Into. His. Hands!"

The last word came out as a screech and Seth pulled himself into a ball on his side. Blood poured bright red and freely from his head where the cane had split open the skin. His ears rang and his vision swam and he nearly sobbed with shame, but not pain. The truth was: he had hardly felt the strikes. To Seth, each stroke of the cane had driven home his failures—his failure to His Holiness and his failure before God. The strokes had merely reinforced his shame. He deserved the punishment.

He lay in silence and watched his blood slowly pool on the stone floor around his head. He would not die anytime soon, he knew, for he was too versed in the knowledge of just how much it took to kill a man and knew his wounds were superficial at best. *And head wounds always bleed a lot.* He also knew that the Archbishop lacked the strength to do any real damage. Only the anger of the Archbishop had fuelled what strength he managed. *Still, that last stroke had been the worst,* he thought admiringly, *and it had been the hardest.* But sadly, it was also the last, and Seth knew he deserved more. The wounds on his head would heal, but his heart and soul had taken the blows directly. He had failed. He had failed his Eminence and God. He was tempted to heal himself but forbade it. This was his penance.

The Archbishop stood hovering over the still form of Seth, his breathing ragged and wheezing in his throat.

"You will correct this," he ordered softly, and Seth was surprised and pleased by how calm and clear he sounded when he spoke. "You will recover the coin. You will bring that evil spawn to the Chamber *alive*," he emphasised the last word with feeling. "And when you do, you will bring me to the Chamber to judge him before God and we will end this blight. Are we clear?"

Seth nodded once and nearly lost consciousness at the simple gesture of nodding. He had lost more blood than he thought and felt a weakness in his limbs, but a part of him latched onto the fact that the Archbishop had just said he would come down to the Chamber to judge the boy. Joy fluttered in his chest and the thought of showing His Eminence the glory of the Chamber brought a quavering smile to his face. *Such joy will be mine to show His Holiness his life's work in the celebration of God!*

Just then, the Archbishop drove the tip of his cane into the blood on the floor directly in front of Seth's eyes and he blinked despite himself, focusing on it with all thoughts of joy fleeing and forgotten. Seth felt the blood on the floor splash across his face and, inexplicably, it repelled him.

"Clean up this mess and see to it," snarled the Archbishop and slowly turned back to his desk.

Sometime later, after Seth had stumbled out of the room and away into the darkness of the corridor, the Archbishop sat quietly at his desk and considered recent events. Discovering that the coin had been found in the bitch's old room and then sent to the far-off west coast only to be found by the last of the heathen druids was almost too much to bear. For the past few months, he had waited to hear that Seth's assassin had recovered the coin and now so much more had happened. He felt a loss of control and pushed back the rage that accompanied it.

He glanced at the stone floor near his desk and could find no traces of the blood Seth had spilt. *That is good,* he thought, *for nothing must give away my secret workings for God.* He remembered the joy of beating Seth and how good it had felt to give in to the anger. He was reminded of the sexual desire it used to bring to him and he smiled in fond memory of those nights spent in private in his bedchamber. *God has been good to me*, he thought and mentally gave thanks.

Beating Seth had been energising. He remembered how the edges of his vision had tinged with red and the anger he had let loose threatened to overwhelm him and control his actions. He had felt his heart pounding painfully through his rib cage and had thought for a moment that at his age he feared it would soon stop forever, but at the moment, he had felt so very much alive!

The Archbishop had so wanted to crush this man lying in front of him, and he had gripped his cane in eager anticipation. But he could not. Seth was his finest weapon. And so he had stopped himself but the caning had been over far too quickly for his likes. Every part of his very being had urged him to raise the stick to continue. Slowly he had willed himself to remain still and with a momentous effort, he had pushed his anger back inside where it belonged— small and tight within his chest. He had stood there for several minutes, watching the blood slowly congeal around the head of Seth.

The Archbishop reached out with a trembling hand and took the missive in his fingers, bringing it close to his face to scan the words once more. They were easily committed to memory, and he lazily swivelled in his chair and let the parchment slip from his hand to fall into the small fire in the fireplace. It caught immediately and blazed fiercely for a mere moment before vanishing into white ashes.

If only I could wipe these druids clear from the earth as easily as I can burn this parchment, he thought tiredly. *My life's work all but ruined by these druids— or draoi as they liked to call themselves.* The word of God had been smeared and thrown down to the lowest of lows within the Kingdom. It had been replaced by the Word and science. *The shame is mine*, he thought. *I had allowed it to happen all those years ago when I watched helplessly as the King destroyed whatever hope the Church had of recovering from the foul acts and treasonous words of Bishop Bengold. I have endured through it all*, he mused not for the first time as he rubbed the aching joints of his hands. *I thought the demons gone and now look what has happened.*

When Seth had returned from killing that demon's spawn and reported that he allowed her son to escape, the Archbishop had been beyond rage. He wanted her spawn killed before her eyes. He wanted her spawn ripped open before her to expose the evil that lay within. He wanted her to witness the last hope of her kind being slowly destroyed until all taint of the druids was washed clean from the earth. It was to be his gift to God and proof of his faith and unfailing worship. All of that had been denied to him. *Denied.*

He thought back to that day ten years ago in the Lord Protector's chambers when he had come so close to regaining the Church's authority in the land after months of detailed planning. His Sect had come so close to killing the Lord Protector and then that bitch interfered. She was one of the two-person Word contingent that advised the Lord Protector. She had stumbled on to the assassination effort and stopped it. She had used and exposed her magic to the Lord Protector and himself. The horror of seeing such evil loosed upon the world had struck deep within the Archbishop's core. It brought back the horror of the revolution when he had lost the Church and witnessed the use of magic for the first time.

She had revealed her foul powers to the Protector and to all. The Archbishop could recall in vivid detail the image of her looming over the Sect assassin she had just killed, a horrible grimace on her face as she gloated. God had intervened then, he knew. He had intervened and told him what to do and what to say. The Archbishop chuckled as he remembered turning to her and accusing her of the very acts he had just been attempting. The Lord Protector had hidden behind him then, seeking solace behind the robes of his Papal office. She stood there accused and exposed and looked up at them and fled. She escaped the castle with her son helped by her husband, an officer in the Protector's Guard.

Later, he knew he should have killed the Protector himself. He had the opportunity and could have laid the blame on the bitch. He had failed to find the courage or strength; he couldn't be blamed for that. His was the power of faith. Killing was the purview of those God chose to act for him.

From then it had been easy to find the other druids. The Lord Protector had encouraged the hunt and financed it. The Church Sect knew what to look for and they crusaded across the realm rounding up druids in every village and hamlet. At times, people rose up to help them or keep them hidden. All were culled. For a time every tree from Munsten to Bergen held the swaying corpses of druids and sympathisers. His Church had eradicated them until just the boy survived. A boy with the potential to grow into something that had to be stopped. For ten years, they searched and hunted and now he was found and on the run.

The Archbishop thought then of Seth and was satisfied that he had allowed him one last attempt to recover from his one failing. So many little mistakes had built up over the years. Like the coin which had escaped detection all these years only to be found in the old chamber, the bitch had lived in. That angered him greatly. His people had let him down, but he blamed the evil that lay in the land. An evil his Church continued to work against and would never tyre from.

Deep in the Chamber, he had a small locked chest full of the evil coins. All efforts to destroy them had failed. They could not be melted for their gold and so they were locked up and placed on a sanctified alter deep in the Chamber. It was guarded night and day by members of the Sect. One guard at each Bishop point—two looking in and two looking out.

It was through the tireless efforts of the Sect that they had determined how many of the coins existed. They had hunted them down and then counted them carefully. Satisfied that they had found them all, they were locked up. Now it was discovered that one coin had eluded them for all these years and they doubted that this last coin was even the last. *Perhaps details revealed through torture are not always accurate*, he hissed to himself. But that was past and now this one coin was found and it had been tracked all the way to Jaipers. There, against all odds, they found Bill Redgrave and the spawn boy. Evil worked in mysterious ways, and the Archbishop did not doubt that great evil was at work, conspiring against the Church. But God was guiding them in this effort, he was certain of that.

The Archbishop's hands started to tremble again. The shaking episodes were coming more often now and getting harder to hide. He pressed his hands against his desk to quell them as best he could and waited until the moment passed. Afterwards, exhausted, he leaned back in his chair in relief.

He looked up at the icon of his God on the far wall and pleaded with it. "Forgive me, my Lord," the Archbishop cried in prayer. "My sin was pride. Let nothing stop me from demonstrating that magics are the evil that works through Man! Let its existence serve as proof of your magnificence and allow you to resume your rightful place in the minds and hearts of all who live in the Realm! Through your Glory, will the Church resume its rightful place and rule the hearts of Man! Through your blessing, I will humbly remain thy most trusted and willing servant!"

The icon of God on the other side of the room suddenly exploded into light, blinding the Archbishop. He blinked furiously to see again and stared in awe as a blurred form stepped forward, bathed in the light to tower over him at his desk.

Duilleog

And then the word of God filled his ears and Archbishop Reginald Greigsen laughed loudly in rapture—the sound distorted in the empty stone room.

Twelve

Munsten, 900 A.C.

KNIGHT GENERAL FREDERICK Bairstow strode purposefully down the hall that led from the audience chamber with the orders of the Lord Protector John Healy still clear and loud in his burning ears. Dressed as he always was in full regalia, he made for an imposing figure. His armour clinked loudly as he made his way down the wide corridor back to his office. The grimace on his face was permanently etched in the wrinkles on his aged skin. Without his helm, the grey in his hair could be clearly seen in the stubble of his shaved head, but his physical fitness kept the appearance of his fifty years of age at bay. Furious, he clenched his gauntlets in his right hand and unconsciously smacked them hard against his thigh as he walked. With practised ease, he held the pommel of his sword in his left hand to stop it from swinging wildly with his gait. As he made his way down the long entranceway, his eyes no longer noticed the years of history of the Realm that resided in the numerous ornaments, tapestries, and display cases that decorated the hallway. The audience chamber behind him lay central in the castle and accessible only by this contained hallway. Outside the walls lay gardens that filled the empty spaces between the central and main castle areas that surrounded the chamber. Inside the hallway, afternoon sunlight streamed through the openings cut into the arched roof above him, and years of dust glittered in the air and swirled in eddies behind him.

His mind had already started methodically examining options to fulfil his latest orders and pushed aside the irritation he felt regarding the level of minutia in the Protector's interest in the security of the region. His brother, General Brent Bairstow, was in charge of the Protector's Guard, and he would be even more annoyed by the orders. The orders defied reason and anger swelled in his breast.

He mentally spat and swore out loud as he flew past the first pair of saluting sentries in the hallway. He failed to notice their eyes tracking him with surprise and a smattering of sympathy. In an instant he was past them, his boots ringing and echoing off the polished marble floor. If he had noticed the movement of their eyes—despite his urgency to escape the hall as quickly as possible—he would have stopped and loudly reprimanded them for failing to remain impassive and immovable in their assigned duty. They were his brother's men, but that didn't mean he couldn't berate them for failing their duty. Bairstow was a stickler for protocol and allowed no lapses by his men or in himself. He knew his men respected that, and that they knew with certainty exactly what was expected of them. The military thrived on order and discipline and he provided both with an almost religious passion. He lived to serve and nothing gave him more satisfaction than the call his country placed on him. He imagined he looked calm and official, but internally he seethed at the Protector's lack of trust in him and his brother.

The discipline of his men was far from his thoughts as Bairstow stormed out of the audience chamber and he replayed the events of his latest audience with the Protector. Bairstow could still see the smug smirk on the Protector's face as he peered down at him from the high throne at the rear of the audience chamber. The position of the chair made full use of the acoustics in the massive room and the Protector's voice easily carried to the corners for all surrounding seated members of the House of Representatives to hear. The Protector always made it perfectly clear to any who observed their interactions he regarded him with little respect.

As always, when he was granted an audience, Bairstow was painfully aware of the hundreds of eyes of the members of the House of Representatives that sat in rising rows of rich mahogany chairs and desks on either side of the long chamber. This is where the council adjudicated with the Lord Protector when they weren't bickering in their own council chambers. They were oblivious to the beauty that surrounded them. The entire throne room was made from the purest marble, cut from the quarries in the northern region. Its domed ceiling rose over fifty feet above his head and was covered with large stained glass windows that splashed every imaginable colour across the room. The white marble was thickly veined with bright silver and gold and it blended beautifully with the tall carved and gilded statues of former kings that lined the back wall on either side of the throne. High, and emerging from the walls, flew white marble angels, brandishing shields and swords of fire. Mixed within the angels cowered fat, intricately carved cherubs surrounded by vines with bunches of grapes bursting with juice. The throne room reminded every one of the days when the Church dominated the governance of the populace. It reminded Bairstow of the Church's avarice and apathy. *It is beautiful*, he thought. *If only they could see it.*

Despite the majesty of the room, Bairstow knew the truth that few would admit. It was from this room that the land was ruled by the corrupted iron grip of the Protector. Behind him, crouched in their seats, the members of the House of Representatives sat in two broad tiered arcs divided by a broad passage through their centre that led directly to where the Protector sat perched like a vulture on his throne. All the council members knew they were nothing but figureheads; each of them was methodically placed by the Protector, all their decisions carefully orchestrated and in line with the wishes of the Protector. All a guise of the republic democracy the Revolution paid for in blood thirty years ago. The Protector had long ago given up sitting in the small chair placed below and to the right of the throne. Now he sat high up on the throne, lazily reclining from the vast height.

As always, as Bairstow stood in the chamber gazing up at the Protector, he could feel the combined heated eyes of hatred from the council on his back. He was despised by them for all that he represented and for their falsely perceived notion of largess on his part with the Protector. They felt he had some degree of autonomy and envied and craved it for their own. It still surprised him how little they knew about just how little authority he actually held. It grated him as the senior military officer in the Realm—presiding over the Army of the Realm and the Navy of the Realm—that his actions and decisions were carefully orchestrated and controlled by the Protector. He was nothing more than a puppet. Just like the rest of them. And yet, they chose hatred instead of empathy. They rejoiced when the Protector openly exposed his lack of respect for the Knight. And the Protector lorded it over him every chance he had these days.

His only friend in this chamber, if he could be trusted, was the Dean of the Word and Advisor to the Lord Protector, Robert Hargreaves. He sat in that same abandoned chair beside the throne in its long shadow. To Bairstow, Robert looked particularly distressed at the moment and he knew this did not bode well for him. Robert clenched his hands together, the knuckles white with the effort, and refused to look toward Bairstow and looked instead to the rear of the chamber as if something interesting there had caught his eye.

Despite the lack of respect from the Protector, Bairstow knew his men did not share that same lack of respect and he wrapped that security and trust around him like a blanket. These thoughts kept him grounded and safe from exploding in anger during his audiences with the Protector. The last audience—the one he had just been dismissed from—had been particularly insulting and he barely managed to remain civil and keep his tongue in check. Sometimes he would entertain the image of thrusting his sword deep into the belly of the Protector and slowly twisting it, revelling in the sounds of his screams. As always, his sword was surrendered at the entrance to the chamber and it was held guarded by his brother's men, a good hundred feet away.

So he stood with his back straight, his sword and the badge of office it represented absent from his side, and listened to the Protector as he started to find yet more fault in how he managed the security of the country. The soft chuckles and whispers from the council were amplified and loud in the amazing acoustics of the large chamber. Robert flicked his eyes once to Bairstow and winced in sympathy. Bairstow glared back at him and tried to send his thoughts to him. *Fuck off, Robert*, he thought with real feeling as he turned his eyes back to the Protector.

"My dear Bairstow," the Protector started, and as usual, he intentionally left out his honorary title and rank. Bairstow gritted his teeth and steeled himself to survive the carefully pointed insults the Protector would no doubt start stabbing him with. "I'm so glad you found time to answer your summons to the House of Representatives. I and my colleagues have spent the time ruminating at what could have possibly delayed your appearance, hmm?"

Bairstow knew better than to answer a rhetorical question and chose instead to stare straight ahead at the leather boots worn by the Protector. His boots were always polished to a high shine by one of the guards assigned directly to the Protector by his brother. Bairstow spotted a fresh scuff on the right toe and began to muse on what could have caused the mark. The Protector carried on speaking more to the amusement of the House of Representatives than Bairstow directly. Bairstow knew eventually he would tire of the game and that he would get around to stating the business he had been summoned to address. He just had to suffer this fool for a short time and he could be back in his office dealing with military matters and the security of the country.

"We decided that you were most likely delayed by some urgent military matter. Would you not agree? Is that why you have made this honoured council wait in speculation and rising ire for a mere member of the military to respond to an urgent summons? Hmm? Bairstow? What say you?"

Bairstow raised his eyes to look directly into the face of the Protector. The petty amusement etched there by years of passing scorn and insults to better men was plain for all to see. This man held all the power in this country and ruled as a monarch, despite the cost it had taken to place him there. Bairstow and his men were answerable directly to this dishonourable man. The House of Representatives had no authority over the military while martial law still ruled—a martial law enacted by the Protector that provided his position with direct control over the military. *A law that should have been repealed years and years ago by the House*, he thought with disgust. But the Protector would never allow that vote to happen and he retained all the powers afforded a Lord Protector when the realm was in a state of war. It was surreal how all reason seemed to flee in this chamber. No one could honestly believe that any war remained in this land, yet his powers remained unchallenged.

Bairstow pondered how best to respond to the question of the Protector. The truth—that he received the summons and had opted to finish a set of orders of no real importance to spite the man—could obviously not be voiced. A simple grovelling response often worked well with the Protector, but as Bairstow gazed at the vengeful delight in the Protector's eyes and saw out of the corner of his eye that the Adviser was now wringing his hands, he knew perhaps he should have come at once rather than delay by the hour it had taken him to pen the meaningless orders. Grovelling would not be enough. Still, he mused, he had felt some measure of delight in being able to keep the Protector waiting for him for once, but realised that perhaps he had overstepped himself this time.

"Nay, my Lord Protector. I have no excuse. I beg the House's pardon in keeping them from the urgent business of the land. I was delayed by paperwork and the time escaped me. My age has sped the sands in the glass more and more these days, My Lord."

The Protector's eyes gleamed and Bairstow tried to think fast on what he had said to make the Protector happy, but before he could even finish going over his words in his head, the Protector spat at his feet and barely missed his own equally shined boots. It shocked Bairstow to his core, and he stared at the phlegm that lay on the marble floor and looked up in horror at the expression on the face of the Protector.

"Your age?" spewed the Protector with revulsion. "Your *age*? Are you admitting that you are now too old to hold your post, Bairstow? To fulfil your duty to the country? Ah, yes, I can see the marks of time on your body. Everyone here can!" With this, the Protector opened his arms wide to encompass the House. "Your uniform is ill-fitting around a body that has already shrunk and grown weak with age."

Several soft chuckles could be heard from the House along with a couple of 'hear, hear!' cries. Like the actors on a stage, the council members knew their role well and played it to perfection. The Knight grimaced, despite his resolve to show no emotion. He had made an error in word choice; he would pay dearly for this in time. The Protector had once hinted that his age would one day remove him and now he worried that perhaps he had just given the bastard the ammunition for his bow and that he had pointed the arrow at his own heart. The irony here was not lost on him that the Protector was at least ten years older than Bairstow. Admittedly, it was true that his uniform was a little looser these days than in the past. It was so hard to keep up his muscle mass without working daily at keeping up his strength. He had already felt the boney fingers of age working their cold methodical way into his mind and body. He worked that much harder at staying fit, but it required so much of his time that he could little afford to these days. He had briefly pondered retirement but tossed the thought away—his duty to his country would remain firmly on his shoulders until the day he died, proudly wearing this same uniform. He would be buried in this uniform, he knew, and then fought to keep a smile from his face when he realised he was wearing his own funeral clothes.

"Are you now too old, Bairstow? Is that why you smile? You welcome the grave after so many years of less than stellar service to your country?" The scorn in the Protector's voice was clear to all and more hoots from the House followed. The Protector was warmed to the subject now as he placed his hands on the armrests of the throne, pushing him forward. "I ask you here to this esteemed House to speak to issues at hand and you blame your delay to my official summons on age. For how much longer should I continue to support you in front of this House? You should know the House calls for your removal daily, but I alone resist and stand in their way. You owe your position and fealty to me, Bairstow. I alone hold your future in my hands and you should be wary of insulting this office and this House."

The Protector's initial soft voice had risen and could no longer mask the vitriol in it and the catcalls from the House faded to silence. The council members knew the deer was blooded, and the wolf was closing in for the kill. Their instincts now kept them quiet and hidden in the forest of the council chairs.

"When I demand your presence in the House, you will answer without delay and with all due haste. Do I make myself clear?" The last few words came out as almost a shout from the Protector. Bairstow glared at the gob of glistening spit that lay at his feet and let the words wash over him. He was repulsed not by nearly being spat on, but by the act itself in this hallowed chamber that should represent the best that men of office could offer. These puppets were the worst the land could offer. He was surrounded by corruption and vanities. He longed to lash out and smite these men. He would crush them and replace them with men of honour. But his own power was an illusion. He too was pulled by the strings of the Protector and he had already done questionable actions when he had thought he was doing good for the better of the land. Little by little, the Protector had corrupted his own honour and one day, he had discovered to his horror that all those little acts for the greater good had not made a right. He struggled daily with his shame. He could not forget, though, that he alone provided the sole buffer between the Protector and his men. That was what kept him fighting to remain in his position more than anything else—to protect his men from this madness. Let the shame be his and keep his men free of the stain. And so he fought against his rising anger and stood silently, taking the berating he knew he did not deserve. He seethed inside with the knowledge that he had made them wait for a mere moment in time. *You would have thought a war had been fought and lost in that time*, he thought.

With the silence drawing on, Bairstow realised he owed the Protector an answer and so he raised his eyes momentarily to the Protector's and answered in a loud, clear parade ground voice. "Yes, Lord Protector. You have made yourself clear." His voice reverberated around the chamber, the sound of authority and command rich in the tones.

The Protector glared at the sound and considered the words. Bairstow knew he had skirted the actual question, but he also knew the Protector could not draw that out without losing face himself. He heard the Protector suck in air through his teeth and waited.

A few moments passed and Bairstow took the opportunity to distract himself with some logistical issues that had risen lately with a new influx of recruits into the military. Some of his senior men had voiced concerns regarding the quality of the new men and surprisingly, this had made it all the way to his desk. Those issues bore some attention on his part. Something was not being said, and he had to find a way to read what was being said between the lines. The problem had been sitting in his head for days now without resolution. So far, he had only found that the new recruits were not typically coming from local recruitment drives. Recruiting officers had reported that the new recruits were not known by the locals in the regions they were being picked up from. *It bears attention, yes indeed,* thought Bairstow. *The smallest of details is often what ends up biting you in the ass the hardest when the sky falls.*

"Look at me," hissed the Protector and Bairstow calmly raised his eyes to the hatred that was returned. "You will very well remember that promise or I'll have you hung by your balls from the castle walls."

Bairstow simply nodded in return with an impassive face.

"And now," droned the Protector as he settled back into the throne. "The reason I summoned you..."

General Brent Bairstow, head of the Lord Protector's Guard and younger brother to Frederick, headed through the Waiting Room outside the Protector's audience chamber. His brother was still in attendance inside that lofty chamber and Brent was concerned. He had been trying to see the Protector for the last couple of weeks and he had been denied. *It did not bode well.*

The petitioners waiting and sitting patiently along the walls on both sides of the chamber rose quickly to their feet at his passing, bowing their heads in respect. He nodded in return and exited the room for the back hallways that led to the military offices. The two guards standing at attention at the exit saluted as he passed by, snapping their pikes upright and loudly slapping them with their left arms straight across their bodies parallel to the ground. He ordered them at ease without pause and carried on quickly past them toward his brother's office.

From years of striding the same path, he made his way down the twisting corridors to Frederick's office with little thought. He nodded to the two guards posted outside the office, entered and flopped down in the chair positioned before the ornate desk. He didn't have to wait long before his brother entered the room, grunting in surprise at finding his brother already inside and seated in front of his desk with both feet propped upon it. Brent watched as he purposefully looked around his office ignoring the impropriety of a general lounging with such disrespect.

"Hello, brother," Brent said.

Frederick continued to ignore him and stepped quickly back out into the adjoining antechamber where his visitors normally would wait. Brent heard him thank and dismiss the guards stationed at his door and asked them to return in a half hour. Brent heard their salute and listened to them stride down the corridor until the sound of their footsteps faded. Frederick returned inside and shut the door.

He made a show of removing his sword and hanging it on a wooden peg behind his desk where it would always be within easy reach. He slapped his gauntlets onto the desk corner and collapsed into his chair with a loud, explosive exhale of breath. He glared across his desk at Brent, who was now fully reclined and doing his best to plaster a cheeky grin on his face.

"Brother," spoke Brent with a laugh. "You look like shit!"

Bairstow glowered through his bushy, white eyebrows at his younger brother looking like he was trying hard to think of a witty response but failing. "Fuck off, Brent. That was truly horrible."

Brent, the younger of the two by a scant four years, nodded sagely and found no offence in the language; he'd used worse himself. He knew what political troubles his brother faced and the delicate balance he maintained in his working relationship with the Protector. It was a heavy mantle that his brother wore and one he could personally relate to by being the General in charge of the Lord Protector's Guard. Which also meant that he was also next in line for his brother's position, should his brother resign himself to retire or—should the unthinkable happen—he be unwillingly removed from office. Still, that didn't mean that he couldn't find opportunities to poke the bear—the nickname his brother was known by throughout the Army and Guard. Brent was known as the Fox and secretly relished the name but suspected his brother had already figured that part out. And the title Fox gave him a certain 'air' that he was always more than happy to embellish, given the opportunity.

The difference in the two men was startling enough you would never guess they were brothers from the same parents. Bairstow's hair, now mostly gone from wearing a helmet all these years and what now remained at the sides was speckled heavily with white, was once a rich brown while Brent's was reddish–blond, hence the nickname. The older brother sported hazel eyes and Brent had eyes a blue so deep they often won him the favours of many of the less chaste women in the castle—both married and single. Brent also looked much the younger of the two even though Brent was now forty–five. Neither man was married, both having chosen a simple and solitary marriage to the demands of military life instead.

Their father had been a military officer, and both sons had eagerly followed him in the profession, but, having seen the strain the life had placed on their mother, decided to never subject a woman to that same loneliness. Their father had been wounded and nearly killed supporting the Revolution and their parents were forced to raise the boys on the meagre stipend the Lord Protector's government had provided in recognition for supporting the cause. Their father died a few years after the Protector had declared martial law to complications from his wounds. His kidneys had failed, and he died in agony, yellowed and thrashing. By the time he finally died, his boys had already moved up in rank within the officers' core and had begun to make names for themselves. They buried their father with all the pomp and circumstance he deserved and watched, amused more than anything, as their mother then blossomed and found happiness.

Now duty and honour replaced any prolonged interest in women and they permitted themselves only the occasional dalliance; Brent much more so than Bairstow. It helped that the bachelor life suited them well, and they had only felt minor regret over the years. When their mother quietly passed away two years ago, she had expressed a dying wish that they have children of their own to continue the family line and they told her they would, knowing they lied, but wishing simply to comfort her in her last days. Brent had suggested to his brother afterwards it was entirely possible they actually did have children somewhere, and that they hadn't lied—they just had no knowledge of them. Bairstow hadn't found that particularly humorous. They buried their mother beside their father and plunged themselves into their careers.

Today, Bairstow was the Marshall of the Army of the Realm and Brent was the General of the Lord Protector's Guard. The Protector's Guard was filled by men of the army selected through acts of honour and prowess from the Army ranks. The Guard was the elite of the military and acted like it. Bairstow ruled over both the army and navy. Both brothers answered directly to the Protector and not to each other. Outside the castle, the Guard had no authority unless Bairstow or the Protector permitted it. Those lines had been drawn from centuries of law back when the Guard protected the King.

They knew within their hearts that their father would be immensely proud of them, but they were saddened at the lengths they had to go to keep the peace in the Realm and in the castle. The Lord Protector hated them both. It was only the insulation of the devotion their men placed in them that kept them solidly in their positions. They had earned the men's respect over the years through hard work, blood, and sweat. They were the 'two brothers'—the Bear and the Fox and the Army and the Guard loved them both.

Brent looked wonderingly at his brother and smiled to lessen the look. He wondered what latest news would have him so angry this time. Anger from his brother was normal, but this was a whole new level of anger, judging by the bright flares of red high on his brother's cheeks, and he had no doubt his latest summons to the Lord Protector had not gone well. They seldom did. Brent knew the Protector harboured a deeper dislike for Bairstow due to the ease at which his brother had earned and been provided the immense respect from his men. He had a natural leadership style that resulted in intense loyalty and respect from the military as a whole. Despite his strong army background, his brother had also gained the respect of the Navy of the Realm and the current Admiral of the Fleet was now a close friend of the two brothers. His brother didn't even know he had it—whatever 'it' was. You just knew, looking at him that he would do anything for you and you wanted to impress him and live up to his impossible standards of duty and honour. The Protector was his exact opposite in so many ways, but it took years to see that for truth and you had to be close to him to catch the faint and sour smell of incompetence. Years more to recognise that the Protector was an expert in manipulating people and hiding it. A talent he had proven as he had methodically worked his charms on the brothers in those early days so long ago. Too late, they found themselves trapped by his machinations.

Brent's smile faded a little as he remembered the days of the Revolution but he shrugged it off as best he could and admitted, not for the last time, that it was getting harder and harder to do that. He fixed his smile, dropped his feet from the desk, and extended his middle finger with practised ease and leaned forward with a gleam in his eye.

"Right back at you, sir!" He laughed and thrust his finger forward for emphasis. The lines etched around in his brother's eyes lessened a little and Brent took that as a good sign. The day his brother failed to find some mirth in the daily grind would be the day he packed up both their gear and fled for the fabled eastern lands of milk and honey.

"Ah, Brent," Bairstow said with a smile. "You have a way with words. And such reverence."

"For you always, you old codger. You appreciate me and my loose ways."

"Pfft. It's getting more difficult these days to remain positive. Any hope we have that the Protector will drop dead of heart failure is fading fast as the years go by and the Protector seems to grow stronger while mine fades with age. I fear I have opened up a new line of attack for the arse with an accidental comment about my age." Bairstow sucked air through his teeth. "Nothing to be done now about it now. I'll tighten my defences and prepare for the shit storm that surely will follow."

Brent furrowed his eyebrows for a moment. The spite and anger the Protector threw at them both was now open for all to see and the illusion of working as a team with either of them was all but shattered. "What was your audience about?"

His brother looked down at his hands spread open across his desk. "Brent," he said at last. "The Protector has a new task for you and it includes men of your Guard and my Army."

Brent raised an eyebrow at this but remained silent. His brother's authority did not extend to include any authority over the Guard. The Guard answered only to the Protector and to all matters that directly related to the safety of the Protector. Lately, it was not becoming uncommon for Brent to hear things from his brother rather than directly from the Protector. It bothered him immensely, but he took painstaking effort to keep it hidden, but his brother knew. They often discussed it.

"The Protector has ordered me to send my men to retrieve the belongings of a known traitor to the realm, long thought dead, in the far off town of Jaipers—a town I barely recalled until I remembered seeing it once on a map. It lays in the southern Turgany Barony." Brent leaned forward in his chair, intent on the words from his brother. *This can't be*, he thought as his brother continued. "Being ordered to use the regular military as simple errand boys grates me—that's what the Realm Guards are for. Surely to Word, the Captain of the garrison in Jaipers could arrange transport and cover for mere belongings? But no, the Lord Protector disagreed and now I'm forced to provide my own men to the task."

Bairstow started rummaging through his desk until he found what he was looking for. He drew forth a rough map of the realm and opened it on his desk and peered at it squinting. After a moment he speared the map with a finger.

"Here, they'll have to travel all the way to Jaipers and then back again—a journey of at least three months by the looks of it." Bairstow looked up at his brother. "That's not all, I'm afraid to say. If that was not enough that my men have to attend to this, the Lord Protector dropped the other glove and informed me that men from your Protector's Guard would also be going and that they would be in Command." Bairstow grated his teeth before continuing.

"The Army does not take orders from the Guard unless it deals directly with the security of the Protector. It just doesn't happen. So I told him that."

Brent found his voice. "You did? What did he say to that?"

"He got that gleam in his eyes, you know the one?" Brent nodded. "He said *'Not done?'* and by the Word, if he didn't hiss with glee and smile down at me. The evil was there for all to see. I'm a bloody fool! I opened the door for him. He then insisted that the General of the Protector's Guard would accompany them to ensure success in the mission and then laughed with his head thrown back high on his perch on the throne."

Brent blinked for a moment and digested what his brother had just said. "Me?"

Bairstow nodded, his mouth set in a grim line. "Yes, you. The head of the Protector's Guard, my own brother, is being sent to gather a traitor's belongings!"

"Me?"

"Yes, you. Nothing of this makes sense. It seems too calculated. Why would he risk such insult to the Guard? I stood there, Brent, stupefied in front of the Protector, with the laughter echoing off the walls, repeating the orders in my head and looking for an out and knowing I wouldn't find one. The Protector had planned the entire audience and knew he could manipulate me into whatever response he wanted to hear. The intelligence and manipulative nature of that man are astonishing! In the end, I just nodded, and he dismissed me with a flip of his hand. I felt like a dog with its tail between its legs as I left the audience. I kept my head up though. The gleeful eyes of the council followed me out the door like rats in the corner."

"Did he name the traitor?" asked Brent, already certain of the answer. *He knew there was only one person in Jaipers who could be labelled a traitor.*

"Bill Redgrave, if you can believe it. The Protector has informed me that the belongings of the traitor are to be gathered up in Jaipers and escorted back to the capital. It is to be a combined Army and Guard contingent led by the Protector's Guard." Bairstow's eyes opened in shock as he noticed the look on his brother's face. Brent could no longer hide the pain he was feeling. "What, Brent? I knew you would be pissed at the news but you look horrified! I haven't even told you the worst part!"

"Bill Redgrave, you say?" said Brent quietly and looked around the room, turning his head to confirm the door to the room was still closed.

"Aye, the traitor himself! All this time we thought him burned in that house fire that destroyed his family and there he was, alive and well in Jaipers. He's dead now. Killed some weeks ago. He went by the name of Burstone down there—he kept the name Bill. Hiding in plain sight all this time."

Brent stayed quiet for a while and kept his face immobile so Bairstow couldn't read his emotions. Bairstow knew something was upsetting him but couldn't possibly be able to fathom what it could be. *He will be wondering why I'm so shocked at the news. He'll figure it out shortly. He'll know I already knew he wasn't dead all these years.*

"You knew him, didn't you? You knew that traitor! You knew he was alive!"

Brent looked up to his brother and saw the astonishment there. Bairstow's eyes grew wide when he didn't correct him. Brent just nodded once curtly, and grimaced against the guilt that flooded him, and lowered his head. He heard his brother rock back in his chair and felt his eyes boring into the top of his head.

When Brent looked up briefly, his eyes were red-rimmed with grief. Bairstow cried out.

"You–you're mourning this traitor? Brent? How can you? The man was vile! A traitor to the Realm. Tell me!"

Brent stayed silent for a long time and then spoke to the floor. "It's true. I knew him. I knew he was alive. But brother, believe me when I say this: Bill was no traitor to the Realm. His family was murdered in front of him and he was tossed into his burning house alive to die beside their still warm corpses. I was there and watched it happen. I watched as the Protector himself ordered their execution and then stood and watched the house burn to the ground. It was a horrible sight to see. Horrible!"

Brent knew his brother would find the truth impossible to accept. All Bairstow knew was that he had been involved with the execution of the traitor. Brent had never spoken of it and Bairstow, he had assumed, had simply thought the memories too painful to ask about it. The military often had to do things they would rather not talk about and likely the events at Redgrave's home had simply been one of those times.

Brent waited a moment, sorting out his thoughts before he resumed his tale. "That was, what, twelve years ago?" Brent shook his head to himself. "It still seems like yesterday. After the house burned, the Protector directly ordered me to stay and sift through the structure with two of my men to see what we might find. I wore only a captain's bars back then and was full of piss and vinegar. I took to the task with all my will and energy. It wasn't until later that I realised he had simply left me there to ensure I was not with him on the journey back to the city. He learned to hate me back then."

Brent laughed once—a cold, hard laugh—and resumed his tale. "We had to wait for two days for the remains of the house to cool enough to allow us to enter the ruins. It was filthy work, Bairstow. Filthy! We covered our faces with cloths to keep the soot out of our lungs but it still got in. Overnight we would cough up black phlegm. It was all we could taste. Soot and more soot. Horrible, it was. So, after two days of digging through the soot and charred remains of the house, I took pity on my men and ordered them to take a break and rest in a nearby common inn. We stunk and were black from head to foot with that soot by then. They were glad to go. The men had a hard time getting the innkeeper to let them in! Ha! I remember that I coughed up the black snot for weeks after that. Weeks! Anyway, I stayed there at the house while my men happily rode off to wash and bed down wenches. An officer's lot, eh? And so I did my duty and remained to watch over the remains of the house and to keep pillagers away." Bairstow nodded in understanding.

"I wandered the ruins and poked into corners for hours. There was little I could do by myself. Thankfully, the remains of Redgrave's family were completely incinerated. Just some charred bones and we buried them with some dignity. I ensured that though the men complained. They were a traitor's family and deserved it, they said. I didn't agree that the family deserved it and made them dig a proper grave. I said some words, from the Church, you know how I am."

Brent looked up to his brother to gauge his reaction. Bairstow followed the Word but Brent was still a follower of the Church, albeit in secret. There were many like him: still religious despite the Revolution and the Great Debate. Bairstow nodded again and Brent continued.

"That house had burned so hot for so long! I don't think I could have remained by myself had we not buried them. The sight of those children being slaughtered haunts me enough. It was then I found the trapdoor at the rear of the house nearest the river. Based on the remains of the cast-iron stove it was where the kitchen had been. The door had been covered over and hidden by the fallen charred support beams and whatnot. It was a mess. I wouldn't have noticed it except for a glint of sun off the steel ring that remained to open it. A chance beam of sunlight.

"I remember being excited at the find. I knew what it was at once: a root cellar. But it was so unusual that a root cellar was accessible from inside the main building and I imagined treasures. Rumours had it that Redgrave had stolen gold and for a bit there I imagined it all buried in the cellar." Brent chuckled, but it was forced.

"Redgrave had been wealthy, you know. I thought if I returned to the capital with gold the Protector would think highly of me. And so I used my horse and with ropes dragged the debris clear of the opening and lifted the door only to find it full of what you would expect: a room lined with wooden shelves and a cupboard containing nought but carrots, potatoes and bottled preserves. Most had burst with the heat of the fire above.

"But imagine my surprise on discovering an opening in the cupboard. Behind it was a low tunnel passage that led from that cellar clear down to the riverbank. A metal grate had been pushed aside, and I got down on my hands and knees and crawled the length. I was twenty feet in when I started to smell the nearby river. Then I smelt him. Lying at the end of that tunnel was none other than Bill Redgrave. At first, I thought him dead, but I soon discovered that he lived!"

Brent clenched his hands together and looked quickly up at his brother to see his reaction. Bairstow was simply staring at him and cocked his head to get him to continue. Brent took a deep breath. "Against all odds, Redgrave had made his way through his burning house, past the burning remains of his wife and children, and escaped that inferno. But his lungs were now filled with liquid and he could barely breathe. I knew at once that he was drowning from within as I had seen it before from people who'd survived house fires. It's the smoke, you see. It burns the lungs and like a burn on the skin, it blisters and fills with water. They die soon after if they've inhaled too much smoke."

He paused to look at his brother to see if he knew what he meant and when he nodded, he took another deep breath and continued.

"I made a decision then that if any man could survive that inferno from Hell then I would do what I could to ease his passage into death. I thought for sure that he would die. He was burned badly. Infection was sure to set in. He was not long for the earth, but he clung so hard to life. After a time, and to be truthful, I realised that I had to know what could drive a man to conduct such acts of treason after a lifetime of heroic acts. I was beginning to understand that the Protector was not what we thought him to be. I think that even then I was looking to the future and perhaps saw that this man was my future too." Brent paused and gathered his thoughts as if unsure where to continue the story.

"I had been the one to escort him from gaol to his manse, you knew that. My major at the time and our men had carted him down that road for days. That was a horrible journey. The major insisted that we treat him poorly, and I protested only once and had been disciplined down by orders of the Protector. That was when he started to hate me, I think. But all along that journey I listened to Redgrave weep and plead for mercy, for the simple luxury of water. And it wrenched my heart. The man I had idolised had fallen so far!"

Brent stopped and relived the moment in his head and remembered far too vividly how his honour had been stripped bare at the time.

"I had looked only once into that covered cage and I was shocked to see what had remained of the Marshal of the Realm, the hero of the Revolution, the man you and I had admired for so long. I ordered the men to provide water to him but the major stepped in and ordered it stopped. I argued once—my honour demanded I try—and the look the major gave me stopped any further discussion on the subject. The Protector had ordered me to the rear of the train where I could ride in the dust of our passage.

"Ashamedly, I followed those orders, knowing they were wrong. It had been the first of the small cuts to my honour, Bairstow. Over the years, you and I have suffered longer and deeper cuts and now I wonder what honour remains to me. As General of the Lord Protector's Guard, I have accepted and carried out far too many orders that I should have disobeyed. I'm not alone in this. You've suffered too! We find ways to justify it with false arguments about the greater good, and so we carry on doing the best we can, eh? Despite the growing shame that lingers in our hearts."

He could see how his brother started at these words. He was putting to words the shame they both carried and surely it pained him to hear it. He could hear his own grief in his voice. *The words are pouring out of me like pus from a wound.* Brent shook his head to clear his thoughts. *Best to just press on.*

"Anyway. I lay at the end of that tunnel and stared at the traitor, as he lay before me, a mere shell of a man and so close to death. I made to finish him but something stayed my hand. I felt the Realm owed him at least some small comfort and so I tended his wounds, all the while thinking that he would soon pass to the afterlife. A return surely to the pits of Hell that he had only just escaped. When my men returned, I said nothing of him and I kept him hidden by leaving him in that tunnel and keeping them clear from the river entrance, lest he cry out and expose himself. I had covered over the trapdoor with debris and told my men that I had cleared that area. If they suspected anything they gave no sign.

"At night, during my watches, I would quietly return to Redgrave through the brambles by the river and force water and soaked oats down his throat. I could do little else but I did clean him up and tend the burns on his back, hands and arms but mostly, I just left him lying on one side, propped up against the wall of the tunnel and covered with a spare horse blanket. Thankfully, he remained unconscious the entire time and his breathing was so shallow that he often seemed but a corpse to me. Many a time I thought to best end it quickly, and I was ready to provide him mercy but something always stayed my hand. I think now that perhaps it was remembering his cries as he was thrown into the house to burn with his dead wife and children. His were not the cries of a man desperate to claim innocence at any cost—they were the cries of a man wrongfully accused and knowing he had failed in some significant regard. The anger, the despair and the helplessness in that cry still haunt me to this day."

Brent looked up at the disbelief etched on his brother's face and he raised a hand and patted the air to reassure him.

"Aye, I know how it sounds, but hear me out. I was not wrong as it turned out." Bairstow leaned back in his chair and tried to relax his pose but Brent could see he was as taut as a tent rope. Brent mimicked his posture but then raised his eyes to the ceiling and closed them as he continued.

"He lived despite the odds. Imagine that. I suppose his anger fuelled his recovery. But now I had a man who would clearly live when I had expected him to die and be done with it. I knew not what to do. My first duty was clearly to the Protector but, Bairstow, believe me, I had to know what had caused such anger in the Protector that he would kill this man's wife and children and then burn him alive with their bodies.

"You heard the tale of his treason. Hearing it and seeing the man accused of it and you could immediately sense the wrongness of it. Think, brother. You and I had discussed the Protector between us in private back then. We know now what a horrible, evil man he is. We started to see the cracks in the facade. Those discussions came from what I discovered in that tunnel. You know the Protector for what he is, correct?" Brent watched as his brother considered his words and then nodded once and he continued. He paused, sorting the scenes in his memory before he continued.

"And so I waited by that river, dividing my time between overseeing my men and examining the ruins and escaping for a few hours each night to see if he still lived. I was exhausted at that point, I remember. All day we would struggle to lift heavy beams and clear what remained of the upper floors. I staggered around like a drunkard. My men were finding it harder and harder to shake me for my watches. They tried to get me to sleep through a night but I forbade it. They're good men, those two. My closest sergeants. You know them?"

Bairstow murmured yes.

"Bill had been given a title, lands and wealth as a reward for his actions during the Revolution and so his house had been more a mansion than anything else. It used to be Archbishop Greigsen's, ha! Two stories and all solid brickwork. Solid. But it had burned like kindling in mere hours. The Archbishop was so irate when he heard that his beloved manse had been burned to the ground. He had always hated Redgrave for moving in." Brent chuckled.

"The examination of the ruins was extensive, but it kept us in place at any reckon and gave me time to care for Bill until he recovered enough to speak to me. My night watches were when I would sneak down to the river and tend to him. It shames me to this day that I left my men unguarded by that house, the air foul with that horrible reek of oily smoke—so thick it was! All to care for this man—this known traitor. And my lies to them as well. That shames me, too."

Brent looked at his brother for a moment to see his reaction but only saw a crafted, blank expression.

"Don't judge me yet, brother!" he implored and pushed forward with his tale. "When he finally gained consciousness after about five days, he wept. He wept for a long, long time and nothing I could say could console him. I sat in silence, watching him cough and when he was not coughing he wept. Finally, he was able to speak. His first words were to ask me why he still lived and when I told him he cursed me and told me he wished for nothing more than to join his wife and children in the afterlife and that he could not remain in this world where all he would have was the memory of his pain and suffering at their loss. This talk of an afterlife surprised me, as I had not thought him a man of the Church, but I was wrong. He did not follow the Word, mind you, but he had an odd belief in God—I'll share it with you one day if you want but that is not for today. Anyway, after a time, he calmed down, and we spoke."

Brent paused here and considered something.

"It was a strange thing for him to do, you know. To curse me for saving him. He had been the one who clawed his way through a burning house and struggled down that tunnel to fresh air. Afterwards, he told me he had no memory of that and I believed him. I think he had lost a significant amount of who he was in that house. He was broken—shattered. His mind shards of what it once was."

Brent grew quiet and lowered his head, opening his eyes to stare at Bairstow.

"Brother, I am thinking that perhaps, maybe... yes, maybe first you should tell me what you know of this man? It would be easier, I think. You'll be surprised at what he told me but I want to be certain you heard the common tale of the treason Bill Redgrave committed. It will be important when I explain what really happened. You'll see the twists and lies that much clearer. What say you?"

Bairstow seemed surprised at this request and sat in silence while clearly pondering a response. Brent could see the simmering glare of anger from his brother. *Or was it disappointment? I can't blame him. Not really. Surely he feels some measure of rage at me. A rage that I could sit there so calmly and admit to my compliance in the crimes of the traitor Redgrave by keeping him alive.* Brent knew his brother was an honourable man and until the full tale was exposed he would keep his mouth firmly shut when all he probably wanted to do was scream in his face.

Everyone thought they knew the tale. It had happened some twelve years ago while both of them were still junior officers. But the tale had spread quickly from the men in the barracks and from fellow officers, many who bragged on having been there in hopes of claiming some glory in Redgrave's defeat.

It was the tale of the rise of a hero and the sudden fall from grace. It had all the makings of a fairy tale, only one with a foul ending. And it was often used as a tale to warn others of the price to pay for treason. His brother had likely known little of Redgrave at the time, only that he had been the Marshall and had been above familiarity or common gossip. They had often seen him in the Officer's Sword Room during social events but they had never spoken and they had never once been noticed in return as both of them were lowly and with Bairstow recently promoted to major.

His one clear memory of Redgrave when he was the Marshall was seeing him with an elbow raised and resting on the corner of the bar with the senior Army officers surrounding him and hearing him laugh in that easily recognisable laugh of his: a loud clear laugh that would bring a smile to anyone who heard it. When word came out of his acts of treason, the Army suffered the loss more than anyone. One of their own, a hero of the Realm and their leader, had been a traitor. Today, at all formal mess dinners, a plate of food is laid out for Redgrave. At the end of the meal, the plate is lifted by the youngest officer in the room and then ceremoniously tossed into the fireplace to burn with his memory. Lest they all forget.

Brent waited patiently for Bairstow to sort out what version of the tale to tell. There were a few, to be certain, but they all ended the same way. *And now I would head south to pick up Redgrave's belongings and learn of his final end.* There was some level of closure there but Brent couldn't figure out what it was. *God's will, I suppose.* A thought occurred to him then. The Protector knew he had been at the manse and now Redgrave turns up alive. *Had he put it all together? Was that why he was heading south?*

Bairstow stretched his legs out under his desk and leaned back in his chair, closing his hands over the flat of his stomach. That didn't seem to suit him and Bairstow shifted again in his seat, crossing his legs and finally settling himself.

"Redgrave. You know the tale but I will humour you, Brent. I had been up-country when the events happened and missed witnessing them myself. Afterwards, there were many closed sessions with the Protector that resulted in harsher laws and then the brutal enforcement of those laws across the country. It was a terrible time, you'll remember," Bairstow grimaced as the memories of the more terrible events returned to him. "Those events called into question our integrity and honour and the guilt of those times, well, they haunt me still,"

Bairstow paused to glance briefly at his brother, who merely looked back at him and he continued, haltingly.

"Redgrave had been stealing. Stealing money from the Realm for years. Ever since the Revolution, it was said afterwards. He had contrived with the Senior Accountant—I forget his name now, but no matter—and even had what, two, three of his own men involved? You'd know better. It was the Guard's mess to clean up here in the castle." Bairstow looked up, trying to remember more details. "Marshall Ran Pawley had been the one to expose him, he was his second at the time, the General of the North. Pawley discovered that Redgrave and the accountant had been skimming money from the treasury accounts, sneaking it away to some other account. Later he had his own run-in and met a bad end.

"When Redgrave suspected he had been found out he had the accountant arrested and then murdered in cold blood in the gaol. To cover it up, he killed his own men and framed them for the murder of the accountant. The horror of it all was that he didn't stop there. Afraid they knew too much he killed the families of the men. He killed the wives and children and even the new born of one of his men by burning their houses to the ground. That was the true horror of his acts. And hence his own manner of death.

"Ran Pawley exposed it all and was promoted to Marshall the same day. They hauled Redgrave off to his house, executed his family and burned him alive. Harsh punishment, but the Realm needed to see that treason would not be tolerated. Especially not after such heinous crimes. It was all almost too much to believe."

Brent nodded at the words. "Yes, you have the tale correct. That was the story that was spread to the Realm by the Protector. Remember how it swept the Realm? The hero of the Revolution, the man who had arrested the King on that horrible day? Then exposed as a thief and a murderer. But the truth is a much more evil tale than that. I've proven what Redgrave told me. God, Himself knows it took me many months to unravel the truth of his tale and I had to be so very careful. Redgrave taught me that. Trust no one, he told me. He made me swear to never share this tale with anyone. I swore it on my honour and have regretted that decision ever since. With Redgrave dead, I am free to discuss it now. Listen, here's what truly happened..."

Thirteen

Munsten, 888 A.C.

MARSHALL BILL REDGRAVE entered his office and dismissed his guards as he strode through the doorway. He quickly sat and opened the right drawer and pulled out two glasses scratched with age and a heavy crystal decanter, depositing them unceremoniously on his desk. He grabbed the stopper off the decanter and tossed it onto his desk then poured a healthy amount of the amber liquid into one of the glasses. As he lifted it, he was chagrined to see his hand was shaking. He brought the glass to his lips and drained half in one swallow, suppressing a shudder when the liquor hit his throat and burned on its way down to his empty stomach. As he went to swallow the last of the amber liquid, he heard a knock on his door frame and looked up to see General Ran Pawley standing morosely in the doorway, gauntlets twisting in his hands.

"Get in here," he ordered gruffly. "And shut the door." He grabbed the decanter and filled the second glass and refilled his own. He cursed as some precious liquid sloshed over the rim of his glass and onto the paperwork strewn across his desk.

The General shut the door and stood just inside watching the Marshall as if unsure of what to do. After a moment, Redgrave looked up, frowned and jutted his chin at the empty chair across his desk. He took another large swallow of whiskey and watched over his glass as the General eased his large frame into the chair and sat with a straight back.

"Oh, relax, for fuck's sake, Ran! And take your drink like a man."

General Ran Pawley was Redgrave's second in command of the Army of the Realm and had been with him ever since the Revolution. Ran had been the first one to join him when he overthrew the King so many years ago and he was the only man he trusted in the entire Realm. *But he can be a self-righteous prig sometimes*, he thought to himself. As if proving his thoughts, he watched Ran eye the glass with some disdain and noted he failed to take the drink. "Don't be such an ass, Ran," he growled. "You'll need this drink. Believe me, duty or not. Now drink, that's an order!"

Ran reached out and took the offered glass but held it with only a thumb and one finger as if it might burn him with the sacrilege of drinking while on duty. Ran looked once at Redgrave and seeing his accusing eyes on him, lifted the glass and pretended to take a small sip and faked a shudder. Not fooled, Redgrave growled and then looked at his own glass in some surprise to see it already empty. He refilled it and set the glass down. He knew northern Cala whiskey was a rare and expensive treat and should be slowly drunk in order to enjoy it all the more. *Lord knows, the peat it is made from is hard to find in the northern territory*, he thought. *At least I drink it neat like my father taught me. Keeping myself supplied in the stuff is turning out to be an expensive habit, even for a man of my wealth.*

Redgrave was not only the highest-ranking officer in the Realm; he was also a Knight of the Realm and had been bequeathed a large tract of land just outside the city of Munsten. A knighthood also came with a rather large salary that paid for the upkeep of his manse, servants and lands. Archbishop Greigsen once owned his manse and not a day went by that the Archbishop didn't make his displeasure known. It used to make Redgrave laugh but now it only angered him. *That man,* he thought, *holds onto grudges stronger than a mastiff in heat.* His Knighthood had been his gift from the Lord Protector for siding with him during the Revolution. Many believed he wore the title with honour, but those that knew him truly knew he wore it with no little amount of shame, for it reminded him of his role in the Revolution. A role that was pivotal to the success of the whole war. He often wondered what his life would be like had he not overheard that simple conversation between the former King and Archbishop Greigsen. *Probably not much better*, he admitted to himself. *Not much better at all.*

Redgrave watched while Ran took another faked sip of his whiskey. He thought over what he had called Ran to his office for. He needed to bounce this off him; he had to hear the words out loud and gauge Ran's reaction before he took any steps. Ran wasn't truly a friend. He was more a colleague, but he was a damn good tactician and he would find holes in his own logic when and where he failed to see them. Together over the years, they had forged an efficient and effective military following the chaos of the Revolution and without Ran, he would never have succeeded. A hero, they called him after all that pain. 'Friend of the Revolution' was another title they threw on him. He could only grin and accept the accolades while gritting his teeth and swallowing the shame he carried with him daily. He had broken his vow to the King. He had turned on him in the worst possible way and handed the Realm over to a House of Representatives that was made up of spineless bastards and then watched as they elevated that asshole Healy to that of Lord Protector. Redgrave picked up his glass and swirled the liquid inside with precision, watching as the whiskey just missed spilling over the rim. *Ah, he was a talented man*, he thought and took a large swallow.

Redgrave's arm, seemingly of its own, grasped the bottle and poured another stiff drink from the rapidly emptying decanter. He knew he had a drinking problem. His wife berated him all the time about it. And that made him want to drink more. Redgrave glanced at the look of disapproval on Ran's face and ignored it. *Fuck him. He hasn't the worries I have.*

"I have a confidence to share with you, Ran," he said, giving his glass another swirl in his hand.

In reply, Ran merely raised an eyebrow and waited for Redgrave to speak.

"It seems to be my lot in life to overhear what I don't wish to hear," he started slowly and set his glass down on his desk. "There's no easy way to start this so here it is: I overheard two members of the House discussing their latest scheme outside the Protector's chambers yesterday. It seems they had just come out of discussions with our illustrious leader and they had come to strike a deal that would earn them both a sizeable reward." He paused and looked at Ran, who merely continued to stare at him.

Redgrave slapped his hand on his desk loud enough to startle Ran. The decanter stopper bounced and hit the bottle with a clink.

"With the Protector, dammit it all to Hell!" growled Redgrave. "They mentioned a construction contract up north, with a small firm called Windthrop Construction. Heard of it?"

Ran shook his head in response.

"Well neither had I and so I looked into it. Seems this small firm has been awarded several sizeable contracts with the House and all of it has to do with road maintenance in the Northern Province, my good General of the North!" Redgrave pointed a thick finger at Ran to emphasise his words. Ran was the General of the North and being the General of the North meant that he was also second in command of the Army of the Realm. But being responsible for a region didn't mean he would necessarily know such minor issues as who had been awarded the contract for road repair. It was a trivial activity.

"It took me all day yesterday to look into it without raising suspicion, but it was worth it." Redgrave grew quiet and toyed with the decanter stopper before gently placing it back onto the bottle. Ran followed the stopper with his eyes.

"And why is the Marshall looking into common contract deals?" asked Ran into the silence. It was Redgrave's turn to look quizzically at Ran.

"Because, as you should know, the patrols we send out routinely have been reporting serious issues with the state of the northern roads. The reports cross your desk before mine. So, here we have a firm repairing roads in the north, all at the blessing of our Lord Protector and all his lackeys in the House. And coincidentally, we have reports from our own trusted men stating the roads have been sorely neglected. It didn't add up, Ran. I would never have known except for hearing the excitement in those two fools' voices. When they saw me they shut up and hurried away like children caught in the castle pantry. That caught my attention. Then I remembered the road reports and so I paid a visit down to Accounts. You know the man who works there? That small insular man called Barges?"

Ran shook his head and seeing this; Redgrave frowned but continued.

"He's an ass. Surprised you haven't had to deal with him. He holds onto coins like they were his own. Bookish fellow, no meat on his scrawny carcass, couldn't hold up a sword if his very life depended on it, hands soft like a girl's." As he spoke, Redgrave played with the stopper in his hands. He stopped and stared at it in surprise, not remembering having removed it from the decanter, and put it down on his desk. He looked at his own rough and calloused hands and laughed. "I asked him to show me the accounts for the firm and he refused me. Refused me! I was dumbfounded. I could only stare at him and watch that smug look on his face. I might have overreacted at that point." And Redgrave smiled in memory. "I might have reached across his desk and brought his face a little closer to mine. Ha! Anyway, he 'obliged' me in the end. Then I had to have the prick explain what the files contained. It took a while, but I finally understood what I was reading."

Redgrave poured more whiskey into his glass and took a gulp. "Windthrop Construction is a firm created by those two House fools. The firm is under contract to provide all major road repairs from the city out to the northern port. They are provided with a monthly account to draw from that comes directly out of the realm treasury. It all looks up and up at first glance and I forced that gadfly of an accountant to painstaking lengths to explain the official rules that govern the payments. I swear my eyes glazed over more than once! Anyway..." Redgrave grew quiet again. He ran a finger over his upper gums and was dismayed to find that he could not feel them.

"Anyway?" questioned Ran. "What's this leading to, Bill?"

Redgrave glanced up at Ran and grimaced.

"Those two assholes are taking money right out of the Treasury, Ran! But that's not the worst of it! It took a while to sort it all out, but in the end, the trail is clear. The money leaves the treasury and is provided to those two men to provide to the firm. Except there is no record of the money being transferred from them to the firm. To get to the truth, it cost me some of my markers, but the details, let me tell you! You'd be surprised how hard it is to look into the financial records of House members. But there it was. The money was being funnelled to another account. An account called 'Windthrop' which at first glance seems legit, but once you scratch the surface, you can see that 'Windthrop' in this case is not this false construction firm.

"And that got me looking for more. It wasn't hard once I started. I had Barges hauled off to gaol and ordered a couple of my most trusted officers to start searching for more like it. It's everywhere—rampant! Almost all the house representatives are taking money out of the treasury and funnelling it to Windthrop. Thousands of coins! And it's been going on for years. It's a den of thieves!"

A cold glint shone in Ran's eyes that Redgrave assumed was a reflection of his own anger. He watched Ran look pensive and stroke his goatee in thought. "Years, you say? But what is this 'Windthrop' account, Bill?"

"That's the real problem. 'Windthrop' is none other than our Lord Protector." The words hit the air like a thunderclap. Ran froze in his seat and blinked at what had just been revealed.

"The Lord Protector? Are you sure?" he asked in a hiss, showing the first real emotion since he had come into the room. A cold calculating look came over Ran's features.

"Positive. I had my men go back through ten years of records before I stopped them, for I'd seen enough. Barges is in cells. He knew, and it showed in his eyes. And of course, he knew! He controlled all the accounts. All of them! He created them. Moved the money around. I can still hear all his arguments, his attempts to distract me, pleading to leave it to him, all efforts to stop my investigation. It was all there to see. Which is why I sequestered the bastard and brought my own men in. Good men, too. Trustworthy, no ties to the Protector."

"But how can you be sure, Bill? What details led to the Protector? Tell me what you know. All of it."

"Humph," grunted Redgrave, glad to hear the interest in Ran. "It was the name 'Windthrop'. I'd heard the name before during the early stages of the Revolution. Shortly after I had taken the King to the tower, remember that?"

"How could I forget?" murmured Ran.

"It was something the Protector had said to no one in particular back then, amid all the chaos. I don't think he knew I stood just near him at the time. He had whispered, 'This day will live in infamy and this time the Windthrops will get their due'."

"He said that? Windthrop?" asked Ran quietly.

"Yes, it struck me as odd at the time but I had tucked it away in my head and forgot about it until yesterday morning when I heard the name again. Windthrop. At first, I thought it would lead to the Windthrops in Turgany, but it didn't seem right since Barons are not allowed to invest in other provinces. So hearing it yesterday and thinking back to the whisper from the Protector, I thought: what a strange name for Healy to state at the time. With nothing linking Baron Windthrop to anything, I thought to examine the lineage book in the library. And surprise, it turns out that Windthrop was the Protector's grandmother's maiden name! Linked to Baron Windthrop of course, down in Turgany, but by name only. The Baron is his cousin, a few times removed—I can never figure family shit out. Three times removed? Bah, no matter. And Baron Windthrop and the Protector hate each other, don't they?"

Ran nodded. It was a well-known hatred in the Realm. Turgany suffered for it and saw little in the way of political favours out of the House. The Turgany province representatives were typically absent from the House. No one missed them.

"What do you plan to do, Bill?" asked Ran.

"I've no fucking idea, Ran! Why the fuck do you think I called you in here? You're the tactical genius! You tell me!" shouted Redgrave. The drunken slur that had started in his voice was becoming more pronounced. Redgrave raised a shaking hand to wipe his face to clear his thoughts. He felt oddly numb all over. He ran his tongue over his teeth.

Ran rose from his seat and grabbed the bottle of whiskey, emptied what little remained into Bill's glass and sat back down. Bill mumbled his thanks and drained his glass in one gulp. As he went to place the glass on his desk, he lost control of the glass and it dropped from his hand to shatter on the stone floor. Bill squinted down at what he had done and observed the fine shards of glass that lay strewn across his floor.

"Whoops..." He laughed.

Ran remained seated. He didn't have to wait long and watched as Bill's head hit his desk with a surprisingly heavy thud. Ran sighed and rose from his seat, opened the door and beckoned to the two men who waited outside wearing the uniforms of the Lord Protector's Guard. They quietly came around the desk and took Marshall Bill Redgrave, a hero of the Realm, under each arm and hoisted him unceremoniously out of his seat and carried him, feet dragging across the floor, and out of his office.

Redgrave woke up in near darkness and feeling cold hard stone under him, knew immediately that he wasn't lying in his own bed. He tried to stretch out his legs and encountered a wall with his knees still bent. Confusion filled his thoughts until the strong smell of rotting hay overwhelmed his nostrils and combined with the sharp pounding in his head threatened to make him violently ill and he concentrated on that. He swallowed against the urge to vomit, but he failed, and he felt saliva aggressively squirt into the back of his throat before he quickly rolled over and forcefully emptied his stomach onto the stone. His vision shot full of internal bright lights and his head threatened to explode with the increased stabbing pain that came with the effort. He felt his stomach seemingly clench hard against his backbone and this was quickly followed by yet another violent spew onto the floor. He spent the next thirty minutes dry heaving again and again until all the muscles in his stomach were torn.

Fully spent and emptied, he rolled over onto his back, knees in the air. Sweat coated his body sour and slick and he waited in vain for the pain to subside. His thoughts were addled. He had no idea where he was or why. He simply wanted relief from the pain.

The smell of his acrid puke stopped all wonderings of where he lay and he was once again consumed with trying to void an already empty stomach. After a time, he could smell bile and the unmistakable coppery smell of blood and he knew he had torn something in his stomach. He flopped back onto his back and mercifully succumbed to the pain in his head and fell unconscious.

When he woke much later, the pain in his head was still pounding with an unearthly intensity, but he could think past it now. He raised a hand, unknowingly covered in his own vomit and with pieces of hay matted onto it, to wipe his brow and then wiped his hand in disgust on his tunic. The feel of the rough loomed tunic surprised him and he realised he was no longer wearing his finery. He cracked his eyes and in the thankfully dim light, he realised he was in a windowless gaol cell deep in his own dungeon in the castle. Panic set in and he thought quickly about how he could have ended up here and struggled to remember recent events. He had met with Ran and then... and then... nothing.

With sudden clarity, he then knew that Ran had drugged him with his own whiskey. He had been set up and betrayed by his closest colleague: Ran Pawley. A stalwart, humourless man with more honour than brains. Now a traitor. Ran Pawley, the General of the North. Of course, he was complicit in the embezzlement. He saw the reports. He knew the roads weren't being worked on. Of course, he knew.

I am such a fucking idiot, he thought and a weariness overtook him until he suddenly remembered his wife and children and he found himself at the cell door banging on the thick, locked, wooden door until his fists bled, yelling for someone, anyone, to attend to him. He had to save his family! Warn them!

Silence was his only answer to his cries and yet he kept screaming and pounding on the door for hours.

Without sunlight to mark the days and nights, Redgrave's days became one long blur until he no longer knew just how long he had been locked up with any certainty. Three of those initial days were how long it had taken before the effects of the drug had worn off and left his head clear of pain. Food was brought to him once a day in a small bucket pushed through the small opening at the base of the door. Whoever delivered it said nothing and did not respond to his cries and pleas. He had long ago stopped the effort.

He had been given a bucket of the slop forty–three times thus far and he pretended they counted the days. But he understood the practice. Prisoners were fed at odd times to help break them of a sense of time and to disorient them. He felt it had probably been only thirty days since he had been locked up.

The food was always the same: a miserable kind of thin, cold broth containing little in the way of meat or vegetables, and with a small solitary piece of bread floating near the top of the swill. But Redgrave ate it all, nonetheless. His hunger and thirst had become a constant, unwelcome companion to him and he found that he now waited on the buckets with an eagerness that shamed him. A short-lived joy had been returning the buckets full of his piss and shit but that had stopped when his food was placed back in the same unwashed buckets.

His cell was square and was too small to let him stretch out to his full length on the floor. He could touch either wall with his arms barely stretched out. He could stand to stretch, but the fatigue that filled his body yearned for him to lie down and stretch out full on the floor. The gaol cells were designed that way for a purpose, he knew, to torment the occupants. That he was unable to lay flat and stretch out completely would sometimes fill him with such distress that he could barely get himself back in control. His uncontrollable whimpering often forced him to bang his head against the door until he stopped.

It was a door that mocked him. It was only three inches thick at most. A small opening in the bottom that allowed his small bucket of food to be passed through but that was all. A small, barred window lay just above his eyes if he stood on his tiptoes and robbed him of any ability to look out into the corridor beyond. Little light came through that opening and by the flickering; it was a simple torch farther down the hall. He had barely enough light to be able to see his own physical decline. He knew he had been placed deep in the dungeon. In the same area he himself had used to break hardened criminals in the past. No one shared a nearby cell. No one answered his cries.

Redgrave could no longer yell or scream. His throat was torn beyond making any more noise louder than a rasping whisper. He had broken his small finger in his right hand by banging it on the door and something was wrong with his left hand that wouldn't let him straighten the fingers. The pain from them kept him from sleeping. Not that he could sleep without exhausting himself first. He thought constantly of his wife and children and sobbed most times uncontrollably while imagining the worst.

He had moved past hate and anger and only sorrow remained. Thoughts of seeking vengeance on Ran and his betrayal had long faded. He cursed himself for the fool that he was. He should have known better. He should have stayed clear of it all. He should have ignored what little of his honour remained, and had demanded of him, and walked away from the "Windthrop" issue. But he hadn't. And now his family would pay the price. His despair was complete. He thought vainly for a way to warn his family. He tried to convince himself that someone would warn them after realising what had happened to him. He tried talking to the silent ghosts that served his bucket of slop but no one ever answered. He knew he lied to himself. No one cared and no one would come to save him. He was doomed.

Redgrave spent his time imagining his execution and rise back to power and redemption. More often than nought he imagined that a simple gallows lay before him, its noose beckoning to stretch his neck with a rough caress on his skin. He would be standing in front of a crowd of jeering people, eyes thirsty for blood and death, and he would proclaim his innocence and point an accusing finger at the Protector. He would convince them with strong words and they would rise in anger and throw down the evil bastard and he would triumph. He would turn and see his wife and children looking up at him with admiration in their eyes. And then reality would return. His fantasies always left him sobbing in the corner of his cell.

He kept his back pressed up against the wall with his legs extended out straight. It was the only position that afforded him any comfort. He thought often of killing himself and how to best achieve it. In the end, he knew he was a coward and would not be able to follow through. And despite everything, he harboured some glimmer of hope and his desire to live always won out in the end.

And time passed painfully slow.

Fourteen

Munsten, 888 A.C.

WHEN THEY FINALLY came for him he welcomed it with profound relief. Redgrave's food bucket count had risen to fifty–eight, but he was no longer sure of the correct number. But something new was happening, and that was better than the nothing world he was mired in. As the two guards opened the door, he struggled to rise, but he was surprised to find that he could no longer stand on his own. They had to prop him up on either side and carry him out the door and down the long corridor with his legs dragging uselessly behind him. The light from the torches blinded him and he closed his eyes and cried out against the intensity. He could not make out who carried him except he knew with a certainty, born of years of working with them, that these were men from the Protector's Guard. Neither spoke to him.

He thought he was to be brought in front of the Protector to answer to him directly but he soon realised he was wrong. He knew right away he was being dragged out the back entrance of the dungeon and he was dumped into a cage on the back of a single horse-drawn cart with the driver sitting tall and observant up front on the box. The feel of the cool, clean night air was a relief to him. Redgrave could see that the nearby torches were extinguished, and he realised that the almost complete darkness of the night was intentional to hide the actions of the guards.

Two horses stood quietly nearby in full tack with bulging riding bags. He was ordered gruffly to keep quiet or be run through and the cage door was quickly closed, locked with a large padlock, and given three sharp tugs to ensure it was securely locked. The men covered the cage with a large waxed tarpaulin and he was engulfed in total darkness. He could hear the men mount up on the waiting horses and a murmured order to the man driving the wagon had them moving with a sudden lurch and he grabbed one of the bars before he remembered his injuries and he cried out in pain. The driver banged the cage and ordered him to shut up.

Fear tightened his stomach. Redgrave knew now with a certainty that there would be no trial. No opportunity for justice. Despite the fear, and with nothing else to do, he curled up in the cage and felt the cart jerk as the horses took it under strain and then heard and felt the cart rattle on the cobblestones as it made its way through the empty city streets—cleared in advance; he was sure, by the Guard. Slowly, he rolled over onto his back and realised with a wonder he could stretch out to his full length and soon found himself crying quietly with relief as his extended himself out fully on the bottom of the cage. Sleep quickly took him.

When he awoke, there was enough daylight making its way through the cracks in the wax of the tarpaulin to make out the inside. A little straw lay across the boards and nothing else. He examined his hands, and he was appalled to see how twisted and damaged they were. His tunic was thickly covered in filth. Redgrave was alarmed at how thin he was. His muscle mass was gone. *No wonder I feel so weak*, he thought. *There is nothing left of me.* He could see through the gaps in the boards to the stone road below. The cart ride had smoothed and he could tell they were now outside the city on one of the King's Roads—still called that despite the Revolution. The heat was stifling under the cloth and he croaked more than once for water but none of the guards cared to hear or answer him. He suffered his thirst, which became almost unbearable, and he found his vision spinning. He closed his eyes and lay still.

After what seemed like an eternity, they stopped the cart which woke a surprised Redgrave from a deep slumber. He didn't remember falling asleep and yet he clearly had. Watching the light through the cloth growing dim, he knew the night was approaching. He had suffered in the cart the entire day with no water. *Surely they don't want to kill me this way? No, that would make no sense*, he thought as he waited.

Earlier in the day, he had counted the sounds of the horses and he knew with some certainty that at least twelve men now guarded him. Two of them were officers by the sound of the orders they gave; the rest were probably all enlisted men. And all of them, he was certain, were from the Lord Protector's Guard.

He heard the familiar sounds of a soldier's camp being put together and shook his head as the men argued over simple tasks. His own men, he knew with pride, would put a camp together blindfolded and with much less noise and confusion. These lackeys couldn't even dig a shit hole, by the sounds of it. One of the officers soon took charge and organised his men. Despite his predicament, Redgrave admired the authority in the man's voice and by the manner in which he managed to get his men to respond so quickly. He hadn't even yelled, he merely spoke with clear authority in his voice and with a practised ease few officers possessed. But Redgrave could still hear the youth in his voice and placed him as likely a young captain. *I wish I had taken the time to get to know the Guard officers,* he berated himself. *Then I might talk my way out of this.* He almost laughed at this thought but the swelling in his throat from being parched too long threatened to close it completely and he leaned against the bars for support.

He croaked out for attention and waited. He heard an order given and soon the cloth covering the back of the cage was lifted with the tip of a sword and Redgrave found himself looking out to a young Captain of the Guard sitting on his horse. *So this is the young man*, he thought. *He bears himself professionally at least.*

"Water," he rasped. "Please..." He could barely make out what he said and looked pleadingly at the officer, hoping he understood.

The man just stared at him with either disgust or disinterest on his face. Redgrave couldn't tell. He wondered what he had been told, what lies he had been fed, or whether he knew the truth and didn't care. Before he could ask, the cloth was dropped and Redgrave heard the horse move away. He heard the captain order water for the prisoner and soon after, a skin full of water was pushed through the bars to land beside him. His thirst had him swallowing mouthfuls of the water before he realised that the guards had pissed in it. He kept swallowing, listening to the snickering laughter outside the cloth. His thirst was too great to care. A man could stay alive drinking his own piss, he knew, but he still had to fight the revulsion that threatened to spew the liquid out of his mouth. He closed his eyes and shut the world away.

Redgrave stopped himself from drinking before he became too sick but then, despite his effort not to, he threw it all up. He settled into the corner of the cage farthest from the door and closed his eyes. Exhaustion made his head feel light, and he felt close to fainting. He had no idea where they were going but a stab of fear kept pushing at his thoughts. He knew what road they were on. He had travelled it countless times himself. They hadn't crossed any bridges that he knew. There was one specific bridge that lay between the city and his manse and if they crossed that bridge in two days, he would be certain of the destination. *But why would they be bringing me home?* It made no sense and dread filled his thoughts when he thought of his wife and their two young children.

A sudden sharp pain struck his belly, and he doubled over in agony as he clutched his stomach. A spasm hit hard in his intestines and in his weakened state, he could not stop what happened next and he voided his bowels into the cart. The acrid stink of black diarrhoea immediately filled the air, and he wept in shame and moved away from the quickly spreading pool. The pants of his prison garb clung to his ass. Nothing could humiliate him further and he knew he had sunk as far as he possibly could.

The major swung by at the men's laughter and he looked in the cage and spied the empty water skin. He then yelled loudly for Captain Bairstow to come front and centre and then berated him in front of the men for providing sustenance to the prisoner. It was a disgraceful tirade and Redgrave felt sorry of the young officer. The major was a man of little honour.

One of the guards, a little later, while delivering his food for the night, took one whiff of the stench and threw the bread and meat into the cage in disgust. It landed in his waste. Redgrave, his hunger allowing nothing else, knew then while he swallowed the food, that perhaps he could sink farther as he tried to ignore the taste of his own shit.

The next day, the captain ordered buckets of water to be tossed through the bars to wash out the stink. The men quickly obeyed. They threw off the tarpaulin and with loud laughter, dumped bucket after bucket of river water in on him. Redgrave welcomed it but hid his joy, lest they stop. The water cleansed him and refreshed him as he watched the shit drain through the cracks in the floorboards. The men made a sport of it, trying to hit him with the most of the water from the bucket at once. He managed to catch mouthfuls of the water and swallowed it fitfully. Finally, it was over and the cover was thrown back over the cage.

But Redgrave had seen enough to know his count of the men had been correct and that they were heading to his manse. Dread filled and consumed him. One major, one captain and ten men of the Lord Protector's Guard were escorting him home.

He found that he had regained some of his voice and he tried to call out to the captain. Hearing nothing, he grabbed two bars as best he could, pushed his face closer to the cloth and started to explain out loud what had happened when suddenly and explosively, the cover was ripped off and he found himself staring at the flint-hard eyes of the major seated on his horse. He held his sword unwaveringly between Redgrave's eyes.

"You will be silent!" hissed the major. "Silent or I will cut that tongue from your mouth! Understood?"

Redgrave saw the determination in the major's eyes and he nodded once in reply.

The major lowered the sword, leaned in closer and lowered his voice until only the two of them could hear what he said. "Disobey me, say one word, and I will follow through on that. It is not a threat. It is a promise, Redgrave." And he wheeled his horse away.

For the first time in a long time, he felt the flicker of anger starting deep within him. He welcomed it and covered it as a man might with that initial flame whilst lighting a fire in the wind. He took stock of his appearance and grimaced at the site of his hands. His small finger of his right hand stuck out straight; the bone had fused the wrong way. His left hand was curled up and almost useless with all the little bones in the back broken and not correctly set. He gave his body a once over and grimaced at the multitude of bug bites that covered him. His head was full of lice—he knew that already—and he had spent many hours in his cell amusing himself by finding nits and crushing them. He had sunk so low. From the most senior military man in the Realm, the hero of the Revolution, to a man in a cage being slowly eaten by insects. His anger flared inside him and brought with it some modicum of dignity. It was such a welcomed feeling, and it gave him brief focus.

Determined, Redgrave grasped the small finger and found where the break had been and snapped it again. The pain hit him like the buckets of cold water. It woke him fully out of his stupor and he muffled his scream by jamming the fist of his other hand into his mouth. The pain washed through him and he embraced it. He tore the hem from his prison garb with his teeth, made small strips and tied the broken finger to the next one to brace it. He then looked at his left hand and grimaced. He tried to force the hand to straighten, but it was locked. There was nothing he could do about that and he sat back in the cage, revelling in the feel of his beating heart.

Redgrave glanced out the bars and recognised a passing copse of trees. At this rate, he would be home early in the morning in two days. Two more days and he would be dead. *Fuck this hand*, he thought and stoked the anger within him.

The horse pulled the cart and cage along the arced driveway that passed in front of the veranda and the main entrance. There was a small barrack tent erected in front of the house that bore the mark of the Guard. The cart was stopped directly in front of the manse's large double door. The dust settled, and everyone remained stationary. The tent looked like it had been here for a few days. Redgrave looked around, desperate for any sign of his wife and children.

Suddenly, the front doors banged open and Redgrave watched in horror as first his wife Rebecca, and then his two young children John and Amanda were thrown out the door to land mere feet from the cage. He reached through the bars to try to help them and cried out their names. His children slowly and painfully picked themselves up, and it was clear that they had both been severely beaten. Their faces were black and blue, and their eyes were almost swollen shut. They started toward their mother, calling out to her, but she continued to lie unmoving at the bottom of the stairs.

"Leave her!" barked a recognisable voice, and the children cowered in fear and stopped moving. Redgrave looked over to see Lord Protector Healy standing at the top of the three stairs that led up to the entrance. He was flanked by four senior officers of the Guard. Redgrave knew them all, and they had their heads so firmly up the Protector's ass that they shared his bowel movements.

Healy looked over at the major who had escorted Redgrave.

The major dismounted and strode over to the Protector and saluted crisply.

"The traitor is delivered as per your orders, Lord Protector!"

Healy looked over at Redgrave and sneered. "Well done, Major Reid. Any problems on the road?"

"No sir, we kept him hidden as you ordered. Bairstow gave him water at one point but I handled it, sir."

"Very good, major. Move your men out and wait for further orders. I want you and your men to cover the approaches. Move out."

Major Reid acknowledged the order and bellowed at his men to follow and they all watched as they wound down the driveway and exited the grounds.

Redgrave ignored it all. He continued to call out his wife's name and was rewarded with a small movement of her head. Her dress was torn and barely covered her. Her skin was mottled and bruised. Blood ran down her legs and he knew that she had been beaten and raped repeatedly. She struggled to lift her head at his cries and finally managed to look up at him. His children whimpered and cried for their mother and Redgrave could only look on in horror at the state of his family. The pain and anguish in his wife's eyes were straight from the pits of Hell. He screamed her name and his children's cries became wails. She locked eyes with him and he saw in her eyes loathing and hatred and he realised with horror that she blamed him.

"Silence them," ordered the Protector.

One of the Colonels marched down the stairs with a smirk and drew his dagger. Redgrave cried out for mercy. His children looked at him on hearing his cries and seemed bewildered, not understanding this new fear. They did not know what they had done, and he heard the oldest, no more than ten, cry out 'daddy' before the knife slit his throat from behind. The blood fountained into the bright daylight and hit the cage and Redgrave. The youngest, his daughter of eight, turned to her brother just as the knife ended her life in a similar manner.

Whatever remained of Redgrave snapped and he went berserk. He dimly remembered the cries of his wife. He watched, almost remotely, as her life was drained beside their children and he tried to reach through the bars in vain, hands grasping the air. He didn't notice when he crushed his own cheekbone in an attempt to push through the opening.

He watched, screaming as his children and wife were dragged and then picked up and thrown into the house.

He watched as the Lord Protector grabbed a torch placed near the doorway and casually throw it deep inside the open door. A large roar answered and flames immediately sprung to life in the fuel soaked house. Smoke billowed out the doorway and the Protector faked a cough, smiled and moved closer to the cage just out of reach of Redgrave.

"You should have left your nose out of my affairs, Redgrave," and he walked around the cage to watch from the other side. He nodded to his men and one of them approached the cage and unlocked it. Redgrave dragged himself through the opening, desperately trying to reach the Protector, but he was struck down from behind and he fell out of the cart to the driveway. Two of the men stepped forward and starting dragging Redgrave toward the house by his feet, his face down into the dirt. When he struggled, they kicked his head, and he slumped, stunned and unmoving. Together they hoisted Redgrave by his arms and legs and climbed the stairs to stand at the burning entrance to the manse. They swung him between them and on the count of three tossed Redgrave across the flames, deep into the burning house.

As the flames and heat touched Redgrave, he was instantly revived, and he struggled to stand but his atrophied legs would not support him. He rose to his knees and stared out the open door to see the Protector looking in from across the lawn, laughing at him.

His impotent rage boiled up through him. The sight of his family's murder remained seared in his eyes and burned them red. His hatred for this man threatened to overwhelm his remaining senses. Despite his wrecked throat, his voice boomed loud and clear.

"HEALY! HEALY! I'll make you pay for this, you fucking bastard! HEALY! You killed my family! I will fucking kill you, you evil bastard!"

As if in response, flames shot up higher in the entranceway, obscuring any sight of the men outside and his last vision of Healy was watching him turn away, still laughing. Redgrave tried to move to the entrance, but the flames stopped him. Redgrave turned and coughed against the smoke as he struggled to move clear of the flames. His hand struck the bodies of his family and he wept and tried to wrap them in his arms. The flames shot higher and burning debris landed on his back. He screamed in agony and writhed onto his back to extinguish the flames. He batted frantically at the flames that had erupted on his clothes and fought desperately to extinguish the searing pain. Screams tore from his throat.

Redgrave managed to extinguish the flames on his clothes and dragged his way clear of the front hall. The walls, doused in fuel, burned freely but the wooden floors were still free of flames and he quickly slid his way over to the hall that led to the kitchen. He took one last look at his family to find that they were now engulfed in flames. He sobbed and begged their forgiveness and disappeared around the corner into the hallway. He started to whisper the Lord's Prayer to himself between bouts of coughing.

Thick smoke filled the room above his head and he saw he was crawling under a thick, roiling cloud. The sounds of the flames were loud around him, almost deafening. The smoke burned his lungs and yet he continued to crawl forward and pushed open the kitchen door. Flames shot out above his head as the air of the kitchen turned to fire. The heat was so intense he thought at any moment that his skin would simply burst into flame. Somehow, he reached the trapdoor to the root cellar.

He took one look at the back door that led to the outside. It was only a few feet away and was free of flame. But that path, he knew, would only lead to a quick death by a sword stroke from observant guards. Instead, he struggled with the small ring that opened the cellar door and pulled it open enough to be able to drag his body down and through. He slid down the wooden stairs and heard the door slam shut behind him. The air was fresh and cool and thankfully clear of smoke. He could breathe between coughs that wracked his frame. He slowly crawled his way on his belly down the hidden tunnel to the river's end.

His grief and despair had broken him completely. The man he had been was gone. The betrayal, the meaningless and horrific murder of his family, and even his fall from grace had completely shattered him. As he lay just inside the tunnel entrance by the river, trying to draw air into his smoke-filled lungs, a realisation struck him and he cried out in horror. He had made a terrible mistake. He started to turn himself around, determined to go back inside the inferno to die beside his family, when the world rose up, spun around, and he lost consciousness.

Duilleog

Fifteen

Munsten, 900 A.C.

B RENT FINISHED THE tale and leaned back in his seat, drained. For years he had wanted to tell this tale to his brother, but as always, his oath to Redgrave stopped him. Nothing good could have come from it, he knew. But now, with Redgrave dead and perhaps now finally at peace with his family, he could expose the truth. First, he had to determine how his brother would react and what he would do with the information. He would doubt him; he already knew the arguments he would hear. He had used them himself on Redgrave all those years ago.

His own investigation had revealed the truth of the tale and exposed Redgrave for what he truly was in the end: a victim. So many people had died to protect the actions of Lord Protector John Healy. So many. Brent had done what he could for the families that remained but the Protector was thorough back then. He had wiped out everyone who could have remotely had the knowledge, even the two House representatives. He had replaced the Accountant with another well-paid lackey and access to the books was now completely forbidden by all except for specific members of the House. Members who were already part of the grand conspiracy. All in the name of protecting the Realm from future traitors such as Bill Redgrave.

The Protector had laid all those deaths at the feet of Redgrave: Traitor to the Realm. The man who had helped secure his own authority and position had been tossed aside like so much discarded garbage. And the horrors he had inflicted upon his wife and his children; all so innocent and trusting. The injustice of it all rose up again within and threatened to choke him.

Not a day went by when Brent didn't try to rationalise why a man with the power of the Lord Protector would covet something as simple as coin. But yet he did. He coveted gold from the Treasury with a dark and fierce desire and then hid it away like a magpie. All that Brent understood was that the Protector was a truly evil man. So evil that Brent had turned to the Church for answers. And it was here that he found peace. He carried a small bible on his person and consulted it daily. He hid this from everyone fearing the Archbishop as much as the Protector. The Church was tainted in the Realm. No one could trust it since the Great Debate and the fall of the King.

His investigation into Redgrave and the Protector took many months, but Brent had been persistent. He took each small step with the fear of a rabbit in an open field with hawks circling high above. The results had been revealing. The reach of the Lord Protector was an amazing thing to behold. His influence was everywhere; tendrils reached out into every major household in the Realm. The House of Representatives was completely under his control and with the Realm under martial law, they were living in a country ruled by a dictator. Some of those under his yoke knew not that their neighbour suffered similar pressures. But people weren't complete fools. Most knew but were loath to admit it.

When the Great Debate ended, and the King reduced to madness, John Healy had been prepared and he had positioned himself with a speed and an accuracy that boggled the mind. Healy had snapped up all the power in the Realm and left Redgrave to dispose of the King. When people thought of the Revolution, they remembered the King's insanity and the military coup that had seized power and handed it over to the newly formed House of Representatives. No one looked to Healy for blame. Redgrave was the symbol of the Revolution.

The coup attempt against Healy, years later, had merely solidified his position and ensured that martial law would remain in place for years. The security of the Realm trumped all reason. The executive powers of Healy equalled those of the King that came before him. Nothing could change that.

Brent sighed and forced his mind back to the present. It was time his brother knew all the truth. He already mistrusted the Protector, but he didn't know why he should hate him. The truth was painful and ate at him. Perhaps now sharing the tale with his brother would ease the load.

"What say you, brother?" he asked and looked closely at Bairstow. Brent saw that he was visibly struggling with the information. He knew by the expression on his face that he looked for flaws, some evidence that he lied. And sure enough, his brother's first words reinforced that.

"What proof have you, Brent?" he asked bluntly with a challenge in his eyes.

"Plenty, brother. It's all there. Before you say more, I recognise that you will need proof; I've been there myself. All I had at first was the word of Redgrave. I chose to trust him then and arranged for him to recover and make his way clear of the Northern Province down south. It was only after I returned here that I was able to slowly uncover the truth. It took me months and the patience of a saint, but Redgrave's fate proved to me that I needed to be careful. I trusted no one. No one at all. The role of Ran Pawley reinforced that."

Bairstow nodded slowly and Brent was relieved. He knew Bairstow trusted him like no one other but he also knew he would have to see the proof for himself if he was to believe. That had to come first, then he could let him decide what to do with it. It seemed his brother was trusting him now.

"Show me then, brother. Show me, damn your hide! I thought this day couldn't possibly get worse! Show me before you tramp off to the south."

Brent nodded. He knew what the Protector wanted. He would send him with his own selected men and recover the gold Redgrave stole all those years ago. He doubted he would be expected to return alive.

"The Protector is sending me to my death," he said simply. He watched emotions play across his brother's face and then settle into grim acceptance.

"Yes," he said. "Though I cannot understand his logic. The head of the Protector's Guard does not tramp off across the country and get killed. People will gossip. Questions will be asked."

"Humph," snorted Brent. "Truth is, I'm being sent there to find out what happened to the gold Redgrave stole from right under Healy's nose years ago. Either it's sitting right in Redgrave's house in Jaipers, or failing that, there'll be clues to where he hid it."

His brother merely gaped at him. Brent smirked at the look. No one knew that the secret treasury of the Protector had been stolen by Redgrave after he had recovered from his wounds. *Healy must be beside himself wanting it returned. Healy had always suspected me of being involved but could never prove it. And proving it would be admitting that it had existed.* Brent smiled around his growing smirk.

"Bairstow, follow me," he said. "I've something to show you."

Hours later, Bairstow looked up from the documents strewn across the desk in a secured office deep in the bowels of the castle to gaze into his brother's blue eyes. "Fuck."

"Yes, 'fuck' indeed," Brent replied with a grim smile. "All this while we knew something was, well, not right in the Realm, yes? And it was all there for someone who knew what to look for, brother. Most of those statements you read there were painstakingly and patiently gathered by me over a long period. Bill told me where to start and what to look for. After that, it was a simple matter of taking it slow and cautious. I hasten to add that there are many who know about this, or parts of it at least, and the people involved demanded to remain nameless, and I promised them that. They live under fear of discovery."

"Hmm," was his brother's reply as he read over one such statement, noting the lack of a signature on it. "Can't say I blame them, really. By the Word, this is all enough to bring the Protector down! But without witnesses, these writings are without worth. We can't do anything with this!"

"Patience, brother. Patience." Brent and laid a hand on Bairstow's arm. Bairstow dropped the parchment he was reading on the pile and looked down at a large amount of testimony his brother had gathered. Of those he had confirmed he had placed a small mark and now almost all the documents bore this mark. His brother had been thorough and somehow had kept all this hidden from the Protector and his men. The Protector had hundreds of men and women under his thumb and held them silent either through bribery or extortion. Too many to silence. Brent had compiled lists of people under two simple headings: those under the control of the Protector and those who still managed to keep their honour and integrity.

"You name these people," he indicated a small journal where Brent listed names. "as worthy of our trust. But can you be sure? Our lives and their lives are dependent on that."

Brent nodded, picked up his journal and opened it to peer at the neat rows of names he had inked in it. He had coded the names, and he shared the cypher with his brother. He had picked the name they had given the small dog their family owned when they were still children living at home. It was their mother's dog and one of those breeds picked by wealthy women to carry around with them during the day. Both of them had hated that small yappy dog. Officially it was called Ruby, secretly they had called it Ratface, for it had had the appearance of a rat. Now it hid the true names of the people who hated the

Protector almost as much as the two brothers.

In the same journal, he had compiled the list of those people who sided strongly with the Protector. They were to be avoided at all costs. Brent was certain that his investigation had been secretive but these latest orders gave him some concern and he had expressed this concern with his brother who had, of course, agreed. It made no sense that Brent, the General of the Protector's Guard, would leave the city to gather up the belongings of a man, even someone as infamous as Bill Redgrave. No, the Protector suspected something and was removing Brent from the city. The men assigned to the task were suspect as well. It did not bode well but Brent was forewarned and the best trap to walk into was the one you knew about.

"Yes, I trust them. But only so far as I can throw them. Once I'm gone, you will need to continue this. There is still so much that is unknown. The Archbishop, for example—I have no idea of what his role was in all this. He was extremely close to the King, all agreed to that. I find it curious that he remains in the castle, close to the Protector, yet seems to do nothing than preach the Faith to an empty church. He's laughed at by the people who know him. An old fool, they call him. It saddens me, somewhat. I've only ever known him as the ousted religious icon. I wonder how he feels about it, eh?"

Bairstow thought about it only for a moment. "He's nothing. Holed up in that privy of an office of his all day long. He has nothing to do with anything political. The Protector keeps him alive only as a pawn of the Realm. There's still enough religious folk out there that he needs to use the Archbishop to his own ends."

Brent winced slightly at the comment. He was one of the religious folk. He often wished he could meet with the Archbishop to discuss his faith but, truth be told, he despised the man. And yet he was the voice of the Church. It still surprised him how low the Church had fallen. Some of his men followed the Church and the faith usually carried through families. The Word was fine with him. It had a cold logic to it, but the Church gave him the peace he sought. He prayed when he could, always in private. Believing in the Church was now a very private thing. People were often shunned for being of the Faith.

Bairstow was still speaking and Brent dropped his thoughts.

"He buggered all the young men in the castle despite his vow of chastity. But other than that, you can see how much it pains him to even walk about these days, despite that emotionless expression he carries on him all the time. I'm surprised he hasn't keeled over at his age. No, the Archbishop is not involved. He's too sallow."

Brent nodded with a small motion, agreeing with the Archbishop being useless but not that he was sallow. Brent had seen something behind the eyes of the Archbishop. It made him a little afraid at times if he admitted it to himself.

"I suppose you are right. The Advisor had not much to say about his Holiness when I inquired once—what, two years ago?" He shook his head to disregard the thought. "He is never granted an audience with the Protector, not anymore at least. It is rumoured that after the coup attempt the Archbishop spent a considerable amount of time going in and out of the Protector's suites. It was a strange rumour, but when I looked into it, I couldn't find anything of interest in it. No one knew anything about it. Just rumours. The castle's full of them."

Bairstow nodded and picked up another statement from the pile and scanned it. "I'd heard the same rumours, brother. In this case, it's true. In the first days after the coup, the Archbishop spent a considerable amount of time with the Protector. Then nothing. But the end result was the Archbishop was pretty much left to his own devices. Allowed to continue preaching and all that other nonsense. Word knows that the Church has hardly any influence in the city. There are what? Three bishops and a few deans in the city?"

Brent nodded. They were all that remained to represent the Provinces. Except it was one bishop and one dean per Province. It was all the Barons were allowed. Now that all the cities and towns in the Realm were converted over to the Word, only a smattering of churches remained. He supposed if he gathered up those people in Munsten that staunchly retained their Faith he could fill one church. Maybe. First, they would need to admit to it. The outlying Provinces were a different matter. Many of the merchants remained with the Church. Their caravans filled with grain and goods were what filled the granaries and fed the cities. It was their business that kept the Archbishop living in the castle. Mouths had to be fed and the easiest way to do that was to keep the merchants happy. And the Archbishop was instrumental in that. The Protector would not throw away a useful tool.

"He's seen everything, though, hasn't he?" mused Bairstow. "He started the Great Debate thirty years ago and was there to stop the coup ten years after that!"

Brent laughed. "Maybe he had something to do with it!" And Bairstow joined him in laughing at the thought, which seemed to bring an end to their talk. They stood in silence and shuffled papers on the table.

"So what is the gold you mention? Was it true, then? Did Redgrave really steal from the Treasury?"

Brent grinned at the questions. And he nodded.

"Yes, it's true, but that was after. After he healed from the fire. I brought him back to Munsten. He insisted. He wanted revenge on the Protector. He stayed in my loft in my house. He was not recognisable from the man who had been carted down to the gaol. Far from it. He wore beggar's robes and snuck about the city looking for any way to get into the castle and assassinate the Protector." Brent paused for a moment and gathered his thoughts.

"You need to understand, Bairstow. I kept my distance from Redgrave even then. I had just started investigating his claims. I only cared that he not get caught with me or in my home. I was young and reckless back then. Immortal. Stupid and naïve, yes. Lots of that, I suppose.

"Anyway, Redgrave had found a way into the Treasury. He never explained it to me. Over many nights he snuck in repeatedly and stole gold from right under the Protector's nose. He left a clue that it was him, he said. Something the Protector would recognise. He filled a large chest with the gold. He showed what he had to me once. He cracked the lid, and all I saw was more wealth than anyone can imagine. I came home the next day, and he was gone, chest and all. Later, much later, he contacted me and I knew where he had run: Jaipers."

Bairstow just stared at his brother, doubt clearly etched on his face. "Right. He broke into the treasury not once but many times and stole an entire chest of gold. Then left the city with it."

Brent nodded and smiled a crooked smile. "Yes, and the Protector knows, and he is sending me to fetch it back. Just wait and see. I'll see the Protector before I go and he will mention it to me. Mark my words."

Bairstow rubbed his face to force the tiredness away. Brent glanced over at the nearby candle to see the mark and was surprised to see how low it had burned. He jutted his chin at it. Bairstow glanced at it and his eyes opened in surprise.

"Brent, you'd best be about your preparations for the road."

Brent grunted. "Dammit," he said. "No rest for the wicked, eh? I have to see that major of yours first, then I have to run."

"Brother," said Bairstow, his voice thick with emotion.

Brent turned toward him at the tone and raised his eyebrows when his brother gripped him in a quick embrace. "What's this, Bairstow? An emotional farewell?"

Bairstow pounded Brent on the back once and hard. "Take care of yourself, Brent," he whispered into his ear. He let him go and strode quickly out of the room before his brother could reply.

Not for the first time, Brent wondered what his life would be like if the Revolution hadn't occurred. The Revolution had caused such anguish, death and turmoil. It was hard to believe the realm had once flourished under a monarchy led by a King who owed his rule to the Church. Brent had spent many hours reading what he could of the times. Of the King, the Archbishop, Marshall Bill Redgrave, Bishop Bengold and Advisor Benjamin Erwin. The hero and villains of the Revolution. It was distant enough to now be a matter of history and yet recent enough to still feel the vibration of fear of further chaos. The new recruits had only known the new world order from after the Revolution. They knew nought of the times when they were ruled by a King.

He licked his thumb and forefinger, snuffed out the candle and strode out into the corridor to find the Army major. Brent secured the room behind him and quietly made his way through the castle. The sun would be rising in a couple of hours and he had much to do before he would be on the road. He was exhausted and his eyes felt gritty but he knew he could sleep in the saddle. He had done that often enough and his horse seemed to know when he did and helped keep him upright. He laughed to himself and then found his thoughts turning back to the Archbishop and times past.

The Archbishop had once provided religious guidance to the King and he, in turn, led the Realm with divine authority. Surprisingly, Brent learned that was only how it appeared on the surface. In Munsten, certainly, at the seat of the King and the Archbishop that was true. The people back then had all believed in God and followed the strictures of the Church.

Outside the cities, it was a different story. The Word was strong in all the small villages and homesteads. The Word taught that science and nature were the strengths of the world. They taught much the same values of morality and ethics, but the Word attributed such values as being human in nature and not divinely ordained as the Church believed.

Brent believed in the Church. He felt the calling of God and aspired to humble himself before Him. He had to be careful though, for saying you believed in God led to shunning and ridicule. The Protector would remove him as head of the Protector's Guard in a heartbeat if he knew. Within the military, religion was strictly forbidden and you would be dismissed immediately. Your honour stripped from you in a public ceremony. The realm feared the return of religion. They felt that religion clouded actions and religion was to blame for violence. Not so with the Word—the Word was immune from religious zealotry. Or so they said. Brent doubted that.

He believed any following could be corrupted, bent and twisted by the hearts of man. Not so with the Church, he knew. The Church provided moral and ethical guidance. He knew without religion man had nothing to guide his actions by. The promise of heaven kept Brent grounded. But the law of the land was clear, and so Brent hid his beliefs. And it made him angry, if truth be told, if the Revolution had not occurred he could be open with his beliefs and he dreamed of that in private. In his chambers he read from his bible and sought solace in the word of God. He knew his faith was strong and could not be shattered. But it was so hard, he admitted to himself. So very hard at times.

One day he had come home to find a small notebook wrapped in plain brown paper lying on his doorstep. When he had opened it he was surprised to find it contained the memoirs of Advisor Benjamin Erwin. It covered the events of the Great Debate and Brent verified the handwriting as being the Advisors. The Church named him the *Defiler*, the man who had debated against the Church and corrupted Bishop Bengold. It was a rare document and only those with access to the Church library could have accessed it. He tried to determine who had left it for him but failed.

Brent shook his head remembering reading Benjamin's account of the horror of that day. Surprisingly, Brent read the man's own account that he had been dismayed that the Church had not won the debate. The death that came afterwards was too horrific. Unbelievably, he had even written that before the final debate; he and the Bishop had agreed to allow the Church to win. None knew that today. Certainly, it wasn't something the village Wordsmiths spoke of. They stuck to the Book of the Word and rarely discussed the Revolution. Now, the memoirs lay hidden in his basement secured in waxed linens to preserve them.

Brent wished not for the last time that he could have met Bishop Bengold and asked him all the questions he had now. He wanted to tell him it was not his fault. He wanted to forgive the man. His death had been beyond imagining and Brent shuddered. He would have liked to talk with Benjamin, too. Had he seen a flaw in his own argument that would justify the Church? *It will never be known, I guess.* Unfortunately, shortly before his memoirs had been found, Benjamin disappeared.

They searched far and wide for him, for adulation had descended on the man. They scoured the land and cried out his name. His was the name heard whilst torching a church or slitting the throat of a clergyman. But no trace of the man could be found. He had vanished into the night and some whispered that the Church had been behind his disappearance, but Brent thought that was foolish.

Today the Wordsmiths still gave homage to him even though there had been so much death and destruction in his name. They simply acknowledged his mind and his ability to reason. Brent suspected that Benjamin would not have approved. The anguish in his writings was a terrible thing to digest. He mourned for his friend the Bishop; he mourned for his Realm and he mourned the loss of humanity that came about when he had unwillingly won the Great Debate.

As soon as the Protector had been hastily voted in to rule the realm, he had reached out and with Redgrave at the head of the Army; they quelled the rioting. They arrested those they could and executed the worst offenders. No trials. No testimony. Just judgement. Instantaneous and irrevocable. It had been called the Cleansing. Bairstow was one of those in charge of the cleansing as a young lieutenant in the Army. Once he had been in the King's Guard, the oath sworn and standing proud in his livery, and suddenly he was one of the Revolutionaries. His captain gave orders, and he followed them as any good soldier would. It still bothered his brother today and would likely always do so. He sought solace in the Word but Brent knew the Word was cold and calculating and that his brother would find relief there.

Brent sighed and began the climb up the back stairs to his chambers. Inside, he would find some refreshment left by his squires. Right now he only wished for water to slake his thirst. He paused on the stairs and pinched the bridge of his nose to quell the sharp pain that lingered behind his eyes. *My squires will need to stay behind*, he thought suddenly. *I won't risk them.*

Brent wondered what Bishop Bengold would have to say, had he lived. He had been the strongest theist the Church had ever known, and yet— suddenly—he had surrendered the Debate to Benjamin. The Word spoke in awe about that moment. The words of the Bishop had been heard throughout the city. Magic, most said. Evil, others said. *Preposterous,* Brent thought. The questions he had gnawed at him though and he needed to know the truth of that day. It was a critical point—it wasn't that the Word won the debate; it was that the Church had surrendered to the Word. It was a fine distinction to be sure, but one that the Church still grasped to like a drowning man clings to a piece of driftwood. Church writings were clear that they were about to win the debate. Benjamin Erwin's writing confirmed that, and yet the Bishop surrendered to the Word. *Unbelievable*, thought Brent.

Brent reached his chambers, grabbed a goblet and splashed wine from the ewer into it and finished it in three strong gulps. He gasped for air, went to the washbasin, rinsed his face and neck and wet his hair. Looking into the mirror above the basin, he wiped his hands down his face to draw out the tiredness. His eyes were dark hollows, and he needed a shave. He looked like shit. His mind was full of cobwebs and he was spending too much time dwelling on the past. He had a task to do and not much time remained to sort out the logistics of the road.

What a long journey this will be, he thought and cursed to himself. He hated leaving his brother behind. It seemed to him they were being separated, and it was probably exactly that. The Protector was a conniving son of a bitch; Brent would need to remain vigilant the entire time. For months. He sighed, not relishing the prospect. He would need to find men within the troop heading south he could trust.

The major was going to be a problem. He was one of the men that had his hands deep in the Protector's pockets. The major should have been tracking him down to go over orders. That he hadn't meant that he felt he was in charge of this particular mission. No doubt the Protector had already spoken to him. *This does not bode well*, Brent thought. He turned and entered the squires' room and kicked the two of them awake and started shouting orders.

Duilleog

Sixteen

Munsten, 878 A.C.

THE KING'S ADVISOR Benjamin Erwin located Bishop Arnold Bengold sitting in his usual place in the back corner of the library, where he was reading with the light of a single candle. His attending priests had removed themselves out of earshot from his presence but loitered to attend to his needs, should he want for anything. The Bishop looked up at his approach, gave him a tight smile and nodded in greeting.

When they had last spoken in private, Benjamin saw the haunted look in the Bishop's eyes and realised that the man had at last recognised the truth. They ended the session, and the Bishop had quickly retreated back to his faith to look for comfort and answers. *Answers he would not find in the false words of an imaginary god*, mused Benjamin.

Benjamin truly liked and admired the Bishop. He had a kindred spirit, and the Bishop was an intelligent man. The only problem was that he suffered from a lifetime of forced theology that excluded all rational thought. Children in the Church were pressed into their false beliefs at an age when anything an adult told them was to be believed unreservedly. They were told of the horrors of hell and fell asleep with nightmares of falling into the pits of Hell. *Simply horrendous*, thought Benjamin. The Church was manmade and was created to serve the lust for power that men craved over others. There was no greater power than ruling the souls of men and holding them in fear.

Throughout the Realm, believers in the Church suffered from those same forced beliefs and rarely did Benjamin find someone thinking outside the box or willing to listen to reason and logic. At least that was mostly true in the cities. Outside the cities, Benjamin knew that the beliefs of the people were far different. The people in the villages and those who worked the land believed in the power of nature and pursued a balance in the world. There, far from the cities, the people planted the seed and tended the plants and grew life. Through them, the great balance of the world was maintained. *More or less*, thought Benjamin. *It is far from perfect, but it is enough.*

Benjamin was the Freamhaigh, or head druid, of the Aretha Tacuinum Sanitatis. Theirs was an ancient, secret order of druids sometimes referred to by the other druids more lovingly as *The Tree*. For the people in the land, they simply knew their teachings as *The Word*. For most people in the Realm, particularly those who lived outside the harsh, lifeless cities knew it for *Truth*. The Word was not a religion. The Word was the knowledge of how nature worked and how people, animals, plants and insects all lived in balance in the Realm. His order lived and moved through the Realm and worked diligently to educate the people and reassure them through the teachings of the Word. These druids, called Stocs, maintained the balance as best they could. The people outside the cities, being closer to nature, were seldom religious people. They lived simply by the Word and all was well. Where there were not enough druids the order employed Wordsmiths; simple but learned men and women trained in the Word and science and Truth. The Wordsmiths were numerous, and they taught the children and adults to respect nature and look at the world with logic, reason and compassion. The order had produced the Book of the Word and distributed it to the Wordsmiths. It had been this way for centuries and the balance it preserved was wondrous to behold.

As head of the order, Benjamin placed himself where he could most influence the politics of the land. He dearly missed the feel of grass and soil beneath his feet. He communed often with Cill Darae Analise Bracewell. She was the High Priestess of the Tree and together they maintained the balance. Always when the Freamhaigh was a man, the Cill Darae was a woman. The balance demanded it. Benjamin snorted and thought to himself: *More accurately, Gaea demands it.*

Benjamin was troubled at the moment. Analise had been quite upset with him and he struggled to understand. She was deeply troubled with him and yet she was unable to discuss what her concerns were. She said that Gaea had forbidden it and that troubled Benjamin. Friction between them was unheard of. Usually, the Freamhaigh and Cill Darae connected at a level that begged no misunderstandings between them. Their bond with Gaea allowed it. He had seen the fright in her eyes. She told him to trust Gaea. He could see that she yearned to explain the problem to him but could not and so he had relented in the end. His urgings had caused her considerable distress, and it had pained him as well. The Great Debate was surely the root of the problem. It was why he was here in the library. It was why he needed to talk to the Bishop and convince him to accept a solution he was sure he would not like.

Fortunately, the Bishop was a man who thought outside the strict tenets of his orthodoxy. He was an expert theologian, and yet open to new ideas for change. But he hid it well under layers and layers of dogmatic theology. And thus, he was hiding in plain sight right in front of the Archbishop and the other senior clergy of the Church. It delighted Benjamin, who could see it so plainly now that he knew what to look for. The Bishop hid his true nature so well he had been personally selected by the Archbishop to represent the Church in the Great Debate. Benjamin worried for him, for he knew that the Church could not tolerate free thinkers. Freethinkers, they knew, would tear down the foundations of a belief system that was built on lies, circular arguments and fabricated stories.

Hypocrisy cannot stand the light of truth and reason, he thought. *Arnold needs to listen to me this time. Perhaps I need to make a demonstration?* But Benjamin immediately thrust that thought aside and forced a smile upon his face. He nodded politely to the two priests sitting quietly some distance from where the Bishop sat and increased his pace to something more energetic and positive.

He approached the table where the Bishop slouched with little dignity, his rotund belly was pressed up against the lower wood and threatened to lift the table off the ground. Books were towered all around him, and papers were strewn every which way. The bright flame of the candle on the table lit up the disturbed motes of dust and they danced thick in the air currents like smoke. The candle was scented and a pleasant lavender scent filled the air. On the table, Benjamin could see the familiar large inkpot with several pens stacked beside it sitting precariously near the edge closest to him. Trails of splashed ink led from the ink pot to papers recently scribbled on in haste by the Bishop. Books and papers covered the remainder of the table except where an untouched plate of food lay pushed by the spread of books over to the far edge of the table. Placed on top of books, on the table nearest where Benjamin's chair lay waiting, was a small bowl of fruit. A silver tray had been placed on a small stool next to the Bishop that held two tumblers and a small pitcher of wine. *It is a chaotic sight but a familiar one and it balances the tidy and brilliant intellect of the Bishop himself*, thought Benjamin with amusement.

As if hearing his name in thought, the Bishop looked up to Benjamin and gestured with ink-stained fingers to the chair beside him. Benjamin smiled in a friendly way, serendipitously pushed the inkwell away from the edge of the table, and sat down quickly in a mirrored slouch to the Bishop. He crossed his legs in a pose of nonchalance and started bobbing his extended foot up and down. He immediately spied an orange in the bowl next to him and feigned surprise to see it there. He reached out and snagged it with a viper's strike. Rolling it in his hands, he reached to Gaea and breathed some life back into the fruit that had probably been picked a couple of months ago. He then reached out to the orange with his gift and pushed a tiny amount of his own life force into the fruit to freshen it and then asked the orange to separate its peel. He placed the two halves of the peel on the table and sectioned the orange into two piles on the table.

The Bishop watched all this in silence. This was a ritual of sorts between the two of them. Benjamin knew that the Bishop had yet to determine how he managed it. He knew that he thought he must swap the orange in some sleight of hand, but had yet failed to detect the swap and it frustrated him. He knew it made his mouth water in anticipation of the rapid swallowing that always followed the sectioning of the oranges. He had learned that the Bishop had even queried the kitchen staff at length about Benjamin's source of the oranges only to be met with strange looks from the staff.

With the two piles of orange segments complete on the table, Benjamin waved magnanimously at the pile closest to the Bishop. He then waited respectively a moment while the Bishop spoke a few words of thanks to his god before popping one from his pile into his mouth. The Bishop took his time selecting one and then after placing it in his mouth, closed his eyes in pleasure, chewed and swallowed.

Benjamin watched as the emotion of guilt flashed on the Bishop's face and he sighed and simply enjoyed his own fruit in quiet contemplation. *These poor religious types*, he thought, *so many self-imposed issues. Life is meant to be enjoyed, not feared. Certainly not full of guilt over the simple pleasures in life. Perhaps, if I could remove the guilt from their religion, then this Great Debate could be worth it*, he thought, *but I doubt it. Nothing good is coming out of it.* He cursed himself for even thinking it. *It is, after all, my own stupid idea. Well, not the way it is now*, he admonished himself, *but what it has grown into*. He had tossed out the idea to quell an argument and now here he was. Deep in the shit.

The Bishop finished his orange segments with a satisfied sigh and fulfilled his part of the ritual by filling the goblets with the fine wine he had brought in from the southern region he had grown up in. Benjamin savoured the wine above all others and rightly so. The southern sun sweetened the grapes to perfection and the wines the vineyard produced were highly sought after. The Bishop had several cases hidden in the wine cellar. They clinked rims together and sipped their wine in quiet contemplation.

Benjamin and the Bishop had been meeting in the library for months now. What had started as a quiet conversation at a Provincial dinner had grown into this friendship between the two. They came from opposite beliefs and opposite backgrounds but shared a common love for debate. To the Bishop. Benjamin was simply the King's advisor and a non–religious type. Perhaps he saw Benjamin as a conquest to be had, a man to convert over to the teachings of the Church. Benjamin had no idea but suspected the Bishop simply enjoyed being able to openly discuss his Faith with another who could provide an intelligent response and counter-argument. Perhaps it was a way for the Bishop to convince himself that his Faith was strong.

Benjamin sensed that the opposite was true. The Bishop was getting closer to the Truth, and he sensed a growing sadness in him. The Bishop was not winning their debate. He had already stopped defending himself with the argument that the Book was the word of his God. Well, mostly—he still occasionally fell back on that particular argument when pressed to defend a position and was losing badly. Benjamin was tired of hearing about his *Book*. The contradictions and blatantly wrong details in it proved it could not have been written by his god. Clearly, it was a book written by man. Men who wanted to own slaves and place women behind them in subservience. The god in that book was not a nice god; he was cruel and violent. Benjamin tackled their arguments by speaking to the logical and highly intelligent mind of the Bishop. He stayed calm and asked probing questions based on fact and truth and not rumour and conjecture. The hardest part had been working around the concept of Faith. Faith is a panacea for religion. If it fails to make sense or is illogical, then have Faith. Faith answers those doubts. Set aside your troubled mind and seek solace in Faith. Faith is a drug and yet it has failed to cure or solve any known illness since its creation.

As a druid, I have cured many illnesses of man, beast, and plant, thought

Benjamin. *Gaea provides that power through me and urges the draoi to heal the land where she requires it. This is the work and calling of the Stocs. The Bishop, if he possessed the ability to work magic, would have made a great druid. Instead, he found another calling, and he has been sucked into the impossible theology of the Church—but with such passion. Sadly a great man has been lost,* he thought. *What was it that one of the long passed druids said a long time ago? Oh yes*, he remembered, *'Clearly the person who accepts the Church as an infallible guide will believe whatever the Church teaches'.*

Benjamin found his thoughts pulled back to the start of the Great Debate.

The Great Debate was sparked when a chance conversation was overheard by the Archbishop and King Harold Hietower as they passed a quiet alcove the Bishop and I shared. The King did not think fondly of the Word and with me as his advisor. He often spoke out strongly against it and my teachings and this had not gone unnoticed by the people who lived outside the cities. The King owed his reign to the Church. The Church granted him his powers and right to rule through god. Unquestionably, this was a terrible way to convey authority—with an imaginary deity giving the nod to a single man and then ordaining that this man rule over the people without question or face the wrath of that same imaginary god. And then there was the Archbishop. Supposedly, he spoke to God. Regularly. And yet God wouldn't tell him when something terrible was going to happen. Or where a lost boy could be found before he starved to death. Not a very nice god. Not very loving if he couldn't even tell his right-hand man when a house was going to burn down.

And so when the King and the Archbishop had overheard the Bishop and I arguing a single point of theology—Great Gaea, I can't even remember now what it had been about—it had been enough for the King to stop and listen in and then insist that a formal debate occur to settle the age-old question of who was right: the Word or the Church. Gaea knows I had tried to stop it from happening. I argued against it with solid logic, but the Archbishop got a taste for it and declared that his god thought it was a brilliant idea. It was settled. By the gleam in the King's eye, I could tell that he saw this as a chance to gain more authority in the Realm. The Archbishop saw it as some kind of divine intervention. It was all so sad and no good could come of it, Benjamin knew.

The debate wasn't initially the Great Debate. At first, it was merely the two of them arguing some minor point of disagreement while the King and Archbishop sat and listened in, occasionally adding to the conversation on some trivial point or two. In those early beginnings, it had appeared that the

Bishop was winning the arguments. *Well, it had looked that way to the Archbishop and the King*, thought Benjamin sardonically. He had been merely patiently setting the Bishop up by getting him to take firm positions on some particularly important point—like admitting that in his belief that the Book was, without question, written by their god and not by man. Seeing these points being driven home by the Bishop was enough for the King and Archbishop to sense blood and declare the debate to be the Great Debate and opened it to the public.

Gaea had noticed that, thought Benjamin, chewing his lip in sullen remembrance. *Nothing good ever comes out of Gaea noticing the people that lived on her. Humans are little more than parasites to her,* he knew. *Tolerated parasites*, he admitted grudgingly.

So every week the Bishop and the King's Advisor met in the grand nave of the Church in the castle. They positioned themselves up front under the apse where their voices could clearly travel the length of the building and they debated openly. The seats, at first, were sparsely filled but as word spread, more and more of the people of Munsten filled the pews until they were forced to stand along the outer walls and press themselves tightly inside the buttresses. The King and the Archbishop sat regally at the transept and listened in reverently, sometimes applauding when the Bishop seemed to make a strong argument. The crowd would join in the applause and Benjamin would need to wait for the noise to die down before making his rebuttal. *No one clapped for my points*, he thought childishly and grinned despite himself. Lately, he couldn't help but notice that the number of people clapping like harbour seals was quickly diminishing. And with the loss, the King was becoming more and more vexed.

More infuriating to the King was that despite his immense stupidity about the Word, he was starting to understand that Benjamin was arguing the long game. Like chess moves, Benjamin had been slowly but surely positioning his arguments and counter-arguments well in advance and was starting to close in for checkmate. The King was a stupid man, but he was politically savvy. He sensed that his Advisor was close to a fatal strike on the Bishop. The entire audience could sense it now. More worrisome to Benjamin was that he could sense the attention of Gaea on the debate. Nothing good ever came from Gaea's direct attention. *Perhaps this is what worries the Cill Darae*, mused Benjamin.

Benjamin was now concerned about what would happen when he won. The rules of the Great Debate were simple: they would continue until one of them conceded the contest. That was the one rule the King insisted on, back when he still smelled blood. Benjamin had tried to argue just how stupid a rule that was by saying that neither of them was ever likely to abandon a lifelong belief in the Word or the Church. The Archbishop had smiled then, thinking Benjamin was worried about losing and not recognising the truth of his words and evoked his *'I'm best friends with God'* trick and convinced everyone that his god thought the rule perfect. Benjamin had felt the satisfaction of Gaea at that announcement and a cold shiver of foreboding passed through his body.

Benjamin knew what the King wanted. He wanted to strengthen his authority over the provinces where the Word was so strongly followed by the people. He saw their beliefs as being contrary to his own and more importantly, to his power base. Benjamin had spent countless fruitless hours with the King on behalf of the Word, arguing that there was no conflict. His people were his people despite their beliefs. He merely had to govern them well. They paid their taxes. Grew the wheat that filled the royal granaries. Raised and slaughtered the livestock that put meat on their tables. All for the King and the Realm. The King was never convinced and instead saw conspiracy everywhere.

Harold Hietower was not supposed to be the King—his older brother was. But he had been killed in a riding accident while the younger brother watched and in an instant, the Realm had been changed. The older prince had been carefully and lovingly groomed for the role of King. Meanwhile, the younger prince had lived a life of carnal desires. Flitting from one brothel to the next, he drank, smoked strange hallucinating weeds, fornicated and committed acts of debauchery and violence. Nothing seemed to placate him. He did everything his older brother couldn't—and wouldn't—and bragged about it. The King kept him at a distance and barely acknowledged he was his own flesh and blood. And this incited the younger brother even more until his behaviour could not be kept hidden. The people knew and thanked the Word or god for the older brother.

Then suddenly, unexpectedly, the older prince was dead and Prince Harold was next in line to be King. As soon as the mourning period was over, he came under the full attention of his father. He was dragged, half-naked, drunk and smelling like cheap perfume, in front of his father and the provincial lords. He was scrubbed with soap and cold water until he stood shivering and naked in humility, his head hanging in anger and shame, his arms straight beside his body with fingers clenched in a rage. The Queen, had she still been alive, might have put a stop to it. Everyone knew she had favoured and spoiled her younger child. But she was gone and so he had stood alone in that cold room. His father openly declared that his whoring days were over and dismissed him. Two guards were tasked to shadow him everywhere he went, and they reported directly to the King. If he strayed even marginally from the straight and narrow path his father ordered, he was dragged in front of his father and scrubbed again. Outwardly, he appeared to change, but whatever his father had intended to do, failed.

One day, the King was found dead in his bed with all evidence looking like it was by a massive heart attack. But rumours of poison started circulating at once and soon everyone believed the son had killed the father. Regicide. It was a horror that no one dared investigate. Soon after the two chambermaids that had scrubbed Harold naked in front of his father disappeared only to have their bodies found days later in a field. They had been scrubbed so hard that their skin had been sloughed off. Everyone knew that their future King had arranged the murders, but no one dared accuse him. The head of the King's Guard, forced by his duty, questioned the Crown Prince, which only drew a smirk in response. His coronation was held days later, and it was only attended by those that had no choice but to attend and offer fealty. The land mourned for their former King and mourned for their new King.

All this was not lost on the King. He openly spoke of how he knew his people didn't love him and wanted him gone. The Great Debate was his way, he had proudly stated one day, of striking back at those same people who swore their fealty to him but didn't mean it.

Benjamin dismissed the intruding thoughts of the past as he sat in the library and tried to enjoy his wine. It was such a pleasant red colour. Fruity, rich, and gentle and not strong in alcohol. A perfect wine and aged to perfection. The Bishop was looking thoughtfully at him over the rim of his cup. There was a sense of camaraderie between the two of them that Benjamin thoroughly enjoyed. He had no other equal in the castle and the city. No one with whom he could discuss the more interesting aspects of life, like science and nature. No one who challenged him with an equal intellect, with a similar mind, and take him down paths he would never have considered or seen had Arnold not opened those doors first. Today they only debated religion and only because the King and Archbishop had tasked them to do so. Normally, they discussed much more interesting topics and intentionally left religion out of it.

No longer. Now, due to the royal edict, they were forced to meet in order to prepare their public debates. Despite the King's sole rule regarding the debate, they had quickly recognised that they had to form a set of rules for the debate and their conduct. They had even worked out the questions they would debate together. To the King and audience, their weekly debate over the past months must seem impressive. They laboured to make it structured and honourably conducted. They had no referee. And so they took pains to never raise their voices or speak out of turn. They never interrupted each other, and they kept their rebuttals polite and within a set amount of time. Small sand timers, hidden behind books, let them know how long they should speak to a topic. They followed their own rules to the letter. To their surprise, it was all so wonderfully academic and structured that they enjoyed the debates and the stimulus it provided their minds. But they had both sensed the change in the King and the audience as the debate went on. It could hardly be missed. The Archbishop seemed oblivious to it all, secure in his faith. The others though, they sensed the end and could follow the logic of the debate. The Church was losing. It was only a matter of time.

The companionable silence stretched for a little while longer before the Bishop placed his goblet on the table and started to refill it from the pitcher. He motioned for Benjamin to extend his cup and poured a healthy measure.

As he placed the pitcher back on the tray, he cleared his throat and looked over to Benjamin, who was now stretched out fully in his chair, with his legs extended and ankles crossed. His wine cup held by both hands and perched on his chest just inches below his chin. It took very little effort for Benjamin to tilt the goblet and take a sip.

"Benjamin, this debate is proving to be a problem. Do you not agree?"

Benjamin simply nodded and glanced over at the nearby priests out of habit. They picked this spot in the library because the acoustics didn't allow their voices to escape from the corner. They had tested the acoustics long ago to see if the priests nearby would react to their words but always the priests failed to pick up their conversation, so long as they spoke in normal tones. They sat with their heads together, whispering who knew what. *Religious babble most likely*, thought Benjamin. Benjamin took his time finding a response to Arnold while wondering where this conversation would lead. He feared this conversation and was not surprised that his friend picked this time to discuss it.

"I fear where we are headed, my friend," continued the Bishop when Benjamin stayed quiet. Benjamin sat up a little straighter in his chair at this admission. He looked closely at his friend and saw the deep lines of worry that etched his face. His hair, once jet-black around the dome of his bald skull, was now heavily tinged with grey and his heavy sideburns, reaching down to his chin line was pure white.

The proverbial privy bucket that sat in the middle of the room that no one wished to speak about was now ripe and starting to fill the room with its stink *I am very close to winning the debate,* Benjamin thought, *and know in fact that I could easily wrap it up in short order. But I have held off for fear of not knowing what would happen next. The Bishop knows it, too. It's a strange thing*, thought Benjamin, *that he and I both know that he has lost his faith in his god but won't acknowledge it. The Bishop remains stuck to his rituals, to the little things his faith demand he do to overcome his doubts, but subconsciously, it is already over.* This quiet session right now would pave the way for what would happen next. Something significant and probably not good, he knew.

Their last public debate had been a quiet one. They followed their script to the letter. When they had finished, the silence in the Church had been deafening. Not one soul spoke in the entire audience. Over a thousand people had sat in rapt attention and when they finished, they merely stayed seated. They were waiting for something. Some subliminal call had them focused on their words. Then over half the audience had raised their left hand, with three fingers spread, thumb holding the little finger down, and palm forward. It was the sign of the Word. The members of the clergy in attendance had cried out at that and the room had erupted in angry shouts. The Bishop and Benjamin had exchanged looks and then quietly left the crowd to the guards and exited the Church. As soon as they left, they could hear the shouts grow angrier behind them and the ring of steel as swords were drawn by the guards. Two people had been nearly killed in the skirmish that had followed. The King had been furious.

That was last week, and rumours had already started circulating. Benjamin had spoken to the Cill Darae, but she refused to acknowledge what he already knew: the Bishop was losing the debate. Everyone could sense that. The King had left in the middle of the last session dragging a confused Archbishop behind him. That caused a stir and for once, the two of them had left the script and ended the session early.

His meetings with the Cill Darae were worrisome. The Cill Darae could always commune with Gaea and according to her Gaea was well pleased. The Cill Darae, also known as the High Priestess, or the Elevated Druid, was hand chosen by Gaea herself for just such communication. The Cill Darae was pleased as well, he could see that, and that did not sit well with Benjamin. It made his role as Freamhaigh that much harder when he was in disagreement with the Cill Darae and Gaea. The Tree was in turmoil. They were trying to deal with the increase in tribute to Gaea throughout the Realm and remain hidden from the people. It was proving harder to do so and Benjamin feared for his people. Their use of magic would never be accepted by humans. It was far too abnormal for them to accept. History had proved that time and time again.

"The Archbishop spoke to me this morning," said the Bishop, pulling Benjamin from his thoughts.

They speak all the time but this time I am sure it was different, thought Benjamin. *Maybe it was the way the Bishop had just announced it.* He remained silent but sat up in his seat and leaned forward to close the gap between them.

"He had some choice words for me about you. You might call them threatening if you believed in them. Something about your eternal damnation in the fires of Hell. You know—the place for all heathens such as yourself? Seems he wants to hasten that event, had he the power." The Bishop laughed at the raised eyebrows of his friend.

"Heathen? Me?"

"Yes, you!" The Bishop smiled with the words to soften them. "You know of God and yet you refuse to believe in Him. That makes you a heathen of the worst kind! I'm sure God has a special place put aside for you down there. A real hotspot!"

Benjamin chuckled, reached out and briefly grasped the top of the Bishop's hand. "My dear Bishop. Let me enlighten you to the real truth in the world! Let me be the first to introduce you to the one and only true God. The god that is hidden behind the clouds! He is, in fact, a lovely pitcher of red wine that looks very much like this one before us. Sadly, now half empty. But I digress! What is important is that I have now told you of him and I suspect you do not believe me. That makes you a heathen of..." and Benjamin lowered his voice ominously, "*Ewer God*! And now, sir, you will suffer for all eternity in the wine–less wasteland of some truly horrible place. So on and so forth..." He waved his hands majestically. The Bishop was gaping at the horrible pun.

"Ewer God? Your God? Terrible pun, sir! But pshaw! I say! My God trumps Ewer God—a false god I might add and getting lower in volume, and so I still get to go to heaven! The Book tells me so!"

"The same book that can't get right simple animal classification, or the anatomy of insects?"

The Bishop spluttered in his wine.

"You know, written by the very same guy that actually created said animals and insects?"

"Yes, yes, Benjamin. We argued that particular point months ago. I successfully defended that."

"Defended? You just changed how you counted the legs!" Benjamin slapped his leg and sat at the edge of his seat. "Hmm. Honestly, how can anyone believe your book was written by God?"

"Yes, yes, enough!" demanded the Bishop. "That's not what we need to speak about."

Benjamin laughed and sat back in his chair. *Ewer God*, he thought. *That's brilliant.* They sat for a moment in silence before Arnold looked up intently at Benjamin. *Here it comes*, thought Benjamin, *this is when he tells me that he has lost the debate but then asks me not to win.*

"I think I need to win this debate, Benjamin," he said quietly.

Benjamin glanced at the Bishop. "You do, do you?" he asked, though he knew the answer.

The Bishop grew quiet for a moment and looked at Benjamin for a long while before responding. "Yes, I do. I suspect you already know why that must happen, though, don't you, Benjamin?"

Benjamin looked away for a moment and then nodded. Tears stung his eyes for a moment and it surprised him. He glanced at the books next to the Bishop as if seeing them for the first time and was startled to spot the symbol of druids prominently displayed on the spine of one of the uppermost books. It was the symbol of his order represented by three twisted spirals and it was called the triskelion. It was on a book easily recognisable to him as the Draoi Manuscript, a secret book of his order. The book was often times simply called the Tree. There were only five copies of it in existence. His vow to Gaea could not allow others to know the extent of what his order could do. It was impossible that the Bishop possessed one—they were all accounted for and carefully guarded. He would have known if one had been lost.

Nothing about this made sense. If the Bishop had read it, he would have to take measures to ensure that that knowledge did not leave with him. The Bishop did not miss the look at the book and leaned back in his seat.

"Relax, my friend. I have not read it—well, mostly. I read the warning and a little more. But not much more."

Benjamin stared at the Bishop in disbelief and felt anger starting to well within him. He felt betrayal flood him, hard and hot. Someone within his order had allowed the book to escape. That was inconceivable. And now he would need to clean the mess up and would need to take measures with his friend. Benjamin struggled with options. The Bishop reached up, took the book off the pile and passed it over to Benjamin. Benjamin took it in his hands and drew it protectively to his chest.

"You've not read it and yet here it lays here on your pile. How am I to believe that?"

"Because I am here now handing it to you in private," said the Bishop softly. "That is how you are to believe me."

Benjamin regarded his friend for a moment and then, seeing the honesty reflected back to him, he forced himself to relax and try to think this through sanely. He settled back in his seat and placed the book on his lap, caressing the cover. As soon as his hand passed over the symbol of his order, he knew it was a copy and he glanced at it in surprise. The symbol on the cover, the triskelion, was embossed on all five copies of the tome. But he could feel that this one was engraved. He looked up at the Bishop and saw him smiling back at him.

"Yes," he said. "It's a copy, that much is clear. I don't know how accurate it is as a copy—you will need to be the judge of that, I'm afraid," The Bishop leaned back in his seat and clasped his hands over his ample stomach. "I found the book deep in the Church archives in the section reserved for heretical publications. The listing for the book simply stated that it had been copied some decades ago from an original. It did not say who or how I'm afraid."

Benjamin gathered his wits for a moment. He willed his anger to subside. Not his fault then. It hadn't happened during his watch. It had been copied decades ago, the Bishop had said, and he believed him for he could hear the sincere truth in his voice. The Tree was a closely guarded secret in the realm; only those with druidic powers knew of its existence. The book revealed far too much of his order. It explained their powers, their weaknesses, and their strengths. He was dumbfounded that a copy had sat in the Church archives for decades and yet the Church had done nothing about it.

"I don't understand," he finally said, and he really didn't. "You found this in the archives and you knew what it was and now you freely hand it to me, unread. You need to explain this to me."

"*Mostly* unread!" corrected the Bishop with a smile. "It is a simple matter, Benjamin. Do not worry yourself. Let me explain," he said quickly. "During my research for our debate, I decided to peruse the more disturbing books that I could in desperation. I was stumbling about looking for anything to support my Faith. It was an easy matter to gain access to the section. Nothing is off limits to me at this point in the Debate. Anyway, the section is normally under heavy lock and key. The books in that section are evil, you have my word on that. Horrible books." The Bishop shivered despite the warmth of the library. "But I digress. I found that book almost at once. I opened it and I read the warning."

The Bishop looked at Benjamin for a moment at these words but Benjamin merely glared back at him.

"Benjamin, I ignored the warning at first and started to read it. Once I understood what it was and what the implications were, I stopped at once, I assure you."

Benjamin thought for a moment and then nodded once. The Bishop chuckled. "I know about your order, Benjamin. You are the head druid of the Aretha Tacuinum Sanitatis, no? The Tree?"

Benjamin rocked back in his seat. This man now knew what people had been unable to discover over many centuries. He was at a complete loss for words and could only stare back at this man of the Church who now threatened all that the druids took painstaking care to hide from the world. All the other druids, the full Stocs, the journeymen Craobhs and even the fledgling Duilleogs were spread all across the land tending to their tasks and now completely at risk of discovery as druids with magic powers. The balance was in jeopardy. Benjamin's ears began to ring loudly in shock.

"And?" he said, seeing no reason to lie about the order at this point. He was certain that this learned man had read some of the words and then simply put the pieces together, no matter how slight, over his many years of secular study to conclude what his order was. The Bishop was a very intelligent man.

"Hmm. How to best answer that?" The Bishop looked at the vaulted ceiling in their quiet corner for a moment and then glanced at the priests to make sure they were still out of earshot. "I think I always suspected something grander was at work within the Realm. It was not a simple matter. It was just a few tantalising bits here and there. Words from priests returning from the villages and towns. Strange happenings that many attempted to credit to the work of the Lord. But I knew better—these were not the miracles the Lord typically conducted in the Realm. And so, after many years, the tapestry was built for me, as it were." The Bishop smiled, looked over at his wine cup and took it into his grasp. "A scant word here and there in books—you could find them if you knew what to look for. I won't pretend it was easy and I doubt anyone else could have put it all together. It took me years." The Bishop gave a small smile and took a sip of his wine.

Benjamin regarded his friend with some fondness. Only this man could have figured it out, he knew. He took pleasure in such pursuits and that he admitted that it took him so many years was a comfort to him. It meant that the Tree was still secure and still safe. He relaxed, thumbed open the book and looked at the contents. A passable copy. Clearly, a forgery since no life magic emanated from it. Whoever had created the copy had to have had an original in their hands and for long enough to painstakingly copy each image and word. The five books were held in their most sacred groves and hidden from all eyes except those of the order. He would need to study this copy and find clues to its maker. He had to discover whether anyone else knew about them.

"I haven't been able to determine its maker, Benjamin," answered the Bishop to his unspoken question. Benjamin sighed at the powers of this man's mind. He would have made a great druid had the Earth Mother granted him her powers. "Perhaps you can, hmm?"

"Perhaps, perhaps," murmured the druid, and he closed the book and set it on the table beside him. He raised his own mug and tapped the rim to the Bishop's. "A toast then, to integrity and honesty."

The Bishop smiled and visibly relaxed at the words as he drained the last of his wine in one swallow. He bowed his head in reflection.

A long moment of silence passed between them, each lost in his own thoughts. Benjamin calmly stared at the top of the Bishop's head until finally, he looked up.

"You need to win the debate, you said?" he asked, reminding the Bishop of his earlier statement.

"Yes, I'm afraid. You must concede. The realm is poised for a terrible time should the Church lose the debate. You must know this."

"Yes, I'm afraid I do. I would like nothing better than to concede to you, but I fear that I may be unable to without seeming to be purposely throwing the debate." Benjamin looked sad. "I've word from the towns and villages. They have always been strong to the Word—you know that. Well, it seems that the city is being quickly converted over. Fights have broken out all over the city in the past few weeks. Church fighting the Word and the Word fighting the Church. And it's only getting worse."

The Bishop nodded. "I've been getting reports on the increased violence particularly right after our debate sessions. Word of the results is now spreading like wildfire. But what concerns me the most is the King. His temper, already terrible as you know, it's becoming increasingly erratic. The Archbishop does nothing to help. He's withdrawn from the public eye as much as possible and this, I'm afraid, is only fuelling the anger in the streets." The Bishop wrung his hands. "He's no longer meeting with me to discuss strategies and options. He has closed himself off from all save his personal attendant, a friend and priest from his childhood."

Benjamin sipped his wine. He had the same reports. He had also seen the same anger in the eyes of the King. And for good reason, his power was tied to the grace of the Church. This debate was becoming a true threat to the balance. He had spent hours discussing strategies with the Cill Darae. Little had come from those sessions; she seemed distracted, distant and upset about the whole issue. She had claimed that Gaea had a plan. Nothing more. *It was so frustrating!*

The Bishop reached out and touched Benjamin's hand and drew him out of his thoughts. "My friend, should the Word win the debate, chaos and anarchy will descend throughout the Realm. The only solution is for the Church to win. Sanity will return in time. It will secure the King's power and provide stability to the masses."

"I've had similar reports. And with the King unbalanced, he needs something to stabilise the politics..."

"Hmm. It's far worse than you may know. The Church has come under direct attack in the villages to the North. Buildings have been burned. People killed."

"I'm afraid the balance of the Realm is upset. The pendulum has swung too far away from the Church. I think we both know what needs to be done..." Benjamin grew quiet.

He would direct the Tree to restore the balance. And not a moment too soon. *First, I would need to concede the debate.* At that thought, Benjamin felt the presence of the Earth Mother turn her attention directly on the library. Stillness filled the world. It was as if a thousand eyes all turned to stare at you and Benjamin felt infinitesimally unimportant and small. A faint smell of loam and flowers caught his nose, and he looked around in alarm. Only someone with Gaea's powers could sense her unless you were very sensitive. Animals and insects always felt her. It was people that seemed almost numb to nature and Gaea. Sweat formed under his collar and he pulled it away from his neck.

"Yes, you were saying?" asked the Bishop, looking at his friend in surprise and unaware of the focus filling the room. He swivelled his head around to try to catch what Benjamin was looking for. Just then a chill filled the room, and the Bishop rubbed his arms for warmth. He could see the two priests nearby look up in confusion and peer around the room with frowns.

Benjamin suddenly felt as if every hair on his body stood up on end. His teeth rattled in his mouth and he was unable to speak as waves of power flowed through the library and his body. Each pulse of power reverberated in his skull and stole his breath away. Motes of dust seemed to freeze in the air and glinted in the candlelight. Time seemed to slow and then stop.

FREAMHAIGH. YOU MUST NOT CONCEDE. OBEY.

The voice was a roar in his head and he blinked against the enormity of it.

The Bishop sat, oblivious across from him with concern starting to etch into his face. As quickly as the words and the presence of power came, they were gone. Benjamin felt as if he was dropped from a great height and he reached out to the desk to steady himself, lest he fall out of his chair. Sweat poured down his face. With an effort he forced himself to draw in a breath.

"My friend," said the Bishop, leaning forward to grasp the hand on the desk corner. "You've gone white as bone. Are you alright?"

"Y–yes," he said slowly, his tongue feeling too large for his mouth. "Just give me a moment." Internally, Benjamin was reeling. The Earth Mother had only spoken once to him before and that was at his inauguration as Freamhaigh. Gaea had simply and quietly said to him "Obey me in all things" and then she had gone silent. He had felt her presence almost daily in small ways but never words and never with such intensity. Gaea simply did not interact with the world in that way—she *was* the world—and he and this entire realm were just one tiny part of her. Suddenly, the Freamhaigh was very afraid. Something terrible would be sure to follow. Gaea did nothing in half measures. She also knew nothing of pain and death. It was all about balance, regardless of the cost to individuals.

It was the purpose of the Tree to maintain that balance and protect humanity from Gaea.

"I'm sorry, Bishop," he said quickly and rose and steadied himself once more with a hand to the table when his head swam. "I have to go. We will talk about this soon, I promise."

Without waiting for a response, he grabbed the Draoi manuscript copy and hurried out of the library. He felt unsteady on his feet but pushed himself to move quickly. The two priests rose in alarm and reached out to help him but he pushed them away. He had to find the Cill Darae. The High Priestess of the Tree would need to commune with him and try to determine what was happening. Then his wife, a wonderful Stoc and his daughter Belle, a new Duilleog with great promise, would need to leave the city and head to the woods and the nearby commune. That, perhaps, would be the hardest thing to manage. They would not want to leave him behind.

As Benjamin rushed out of the library, he failed to notice a thin man emerge from the deep shadows of the massive library bookcases. The man's eyes were locked on the book Benjamin carried under his arm. The man was covered in a thin sheen of sweat and all the hairs on his body were standing on end and he rubbed a hand down each arm to calm them.

He had felt the presence of God in the room only a moment ago and he was still lost in the joy that it had brought him. He had heard the word of God. The ecstasy of the moment remained strong within him still. He felt a new energy within him and he could sense the world around him much clearer than before.

He had listened in to everything the Bishop and the Advisor had spoken of. Each week he eavesdropped in on their strange conversations and reported back to the Archbishop. The Tree, they had said. This was new and might explain what had been happening during the Great Debate. He had to learn more, and he needed to get his hands on that book.

Seth Farlow grinned to himself. This was something he was uniquely talented at doing. The Archbishop would be pleased.

Duilleog

Seventeen

Munsten, 879 A.C.

B ENJAMIN WAS NERVOUS. He noticed the Bishop smiling down at him as he shuffled his speaking notes high up on the podium and he smiled back at the Bishop. Benjamin looked out over the massive audience that filled the Church. Attendance was high once the word had spread that today was likely to be the end of the debate.

Today the Freamhaigh of the Tree was going to concede to the Church. And for this reason, he was worried about Gaea. She would not take this lightly, and that, more than anything, scared him deeply. Never in the history of the Tree had a druid disobeyed Gaea; their allegiance was vital to the safety of humanity. He fought a constant battle against his own best instincts. The Cill Darae had been vexed. He had never seen her so angry. She had vowed to flee the capital and take his wife and daughter with her. His wife had cried and pleaded with him to reconsider, but he knew he could not. He could not understand why they could not see the chaos that would occur, should he not concede to the Church. The balance was almost shattered. The last words to him from the Cill Darae were not kind. Benjamin was living in a dreamlike state now. He felt like a leaf caught in the wind and never finding purchase.

The Great Debate had stirred the people far and wide in the Realm. The people of the cities and larger villages were now joining the farmers and workers—those who believed most strongly in the Word and laughed in secret at the Church. It was happening too fast and Benjamin feared what the results would be. Should the Word win the day, the King would strike out into the heart of the people. Civil war at best. Death for many was certain. His Army would decimate entire villages to quell unrest. Benjamin could not allow that to happen. Even if Gaea was displeased. His conscience could not stomach anything less from him. He looked out at the people gathered here in the Church and knew he would do everything he could to spare them their lives.

Bishop Arnold and he had discussed the proceedings of today at length and they had mapped out a logical argument to present to the populace. They would act out a scripted circular argument that would eventually focus in on the power of Faith and how in the Church it could overcome all doubt and obstacles. Only through Faith could salvation and eternal life be granted in heaven and earth. It was a weak argument. But it would suffice.

Benjamin had deflected any and all discussion regarding Faith during the debates. It was a rather touchy subject and far too ethereal for his tastes. Faith was nothing more than religious delusion, but on a far grander scale than normal. You could back a zealot up into a corner but they would remain defiantly professing their Faith and that was enough for them to close their ears to logic and reason.

And so he would lose the debate. Any other option would ensure that nothing healthy could grow from it. The land would suffer. *Surely Gaea understood that?* Thankfully, the Bishop understood and agreed. The deception bothered them both but the greater good demanded their solution. They were united in that.

Benjamin was saddened for his friend. The Bishop had lost his faith some time ago, and he was greatly diminished by it. Not that his faith had been his strength, but his character and personality he had nurtured for all his years was now reduced by its absence. He was struggling for direction and a purpose in his life. He hoped to remain in a purely secular life following the debate today. He would find peace in seclusion and read and study. Benjamin had promised to stay in close touch with him and they had embraced briefly as only true friends could.

Benjamin looked over to the King, who was seated nearby, speaking to his aide in quiet tones. *At least we will be able to avoid the King's reaction to losing the seat of his power.* He grinned despite the severity of the thought. *That would be a nightmare of biblical proportions.*

Arnold caught the grin and beamed at him, confidence seemed to flow from him and Benjamin tried to relax and prepare himself mentally for the role he was to play.

A short time later, the debate was well underway, and they were building to their carefully orchestrated finale. Benjamin was hanging his head and giving off the body language of a man defeated. He could sense the reaction of the audience. Many were not happy, and he smiled to himself. *Wait until they hear the conclusion,* he thought. *Better their disappointment than their death.*

He stole glances at the King and was happy to see him sitting tall and straight and smiling. Even the King could sense the direction the debate was going, even though Benjamin knew he could barely follow the details. His years of whoring, drinking and drugs had permanently damaged him.

It wouldn't be long now before he could end this and be done with the farce. Soon he could bring his family back to the city and repair his relationship with the Cill Darae and Gaea. He had to merely be patient. He and the Bishop exchanged a look and Benjamin nodded imperceptibly. Here it comes: his act of defiance against the wishes of Gaea. *She will understand in time.*

Just then Benjamin felt the focus of Gaea shift entirely to this chamber. A hush fell on the room and many looked about, trying to discover where the feeling of being watched was coming from. The Bishop stopped speaking mid-sentence and an unearthly silence filled the air. A deep, resonant hum filled the chamber, and it throbbed with intensity, growing stronger with every heartbeat.

Benjamin reeled inside with the horror of what he was sensing. Gaea, the Earth Mother, had placed her *entire* focus on this one small region of the earth. Benjamin shuddered to think what chaos was happening worldwide. He felt so infinitesimally small and insignificant—his very being cried out for release from the scrutiny. Suddenly he understood his folly. *How could I have gone against her wishes? How could I have failed her?* He grovelled inside to her. He mentally begged for forgiveness. Tears flowed freely from his eyes. Benjamin saw others prostrate themselves on the ground in the Church. Some cried out to God and others merely wept. Some were full of joy and rapture.

Elsewhere in the capital, people stopped what they were doing and gazed about at each other. No one knew what was happening, only that they could sense a presence nearby.

All cries and shouting from the people broke off at once by some unheard command that they all obeyed without question and a great silence filled the air, shocking in the abruptness of it.

Benjamin whispered a silent *no* to Gaea and pleaded with her. He sensed a wry humour from Gaea at his plea and he knew with certainty that he had been played by her. She had orchestrated all this for this moment in time and he cried in shame. She had selected him to be Freamhaigh not because of his abilities as a druid, rather it was his ability to make a case against the Church. To win the debate on her behalf. He was nothing more than an actor on a stage. He felt her sympathy for him for a brief moment, but as quick as it came, her attention shifted.

Suddenly, a great cry erupted from the Bishop and many people cried out in shock at hearing it. The Bishop turned his head to look at Benjamin and Benjamin recoiled in horror as he saw Gaea looking out from behind those eyes. She possessed him and looking into those eyes was like looking into your own being and losing yourself completely. A sense of falling overcame him and with it fear. He was nothing to her. He was nothing on this earth. With a blink, the eyes released him and Benjamin nearly collapsed in relief. Gaea turned to face the crowd.

In a thunderous voice that could be heard in all recesses of the castle, Gaea spoke to the crowd with the arms of the Bishop raised high. Later those who were asked said that they had heard the voice in all areas of the city—but those witnesses were not truly believed. All admitted to the power in the voice and the pain felt in the airs with each spoken syllable. Those in proximity fell to the ground and covered their ears against the volume. They recognised the authority and felt the truth of it down to their bones. Each word came singly and with a slight pause between them as if each word carried a great weight.

"I concede," Gaea said. "The Church surrenders to the Word. There is only Truth in the Word. Through the Word lies balance."

There was stunned silence following this proclamation. Then the room erupted. People started yelling and screaming. Fights broke out throughout the Church. Benjamin stared in shock at the still form of the Bishop and then without knowing why started to move toward him. On the other side of the podium, another figure ran toward the Bishop, his face twisted with anger.

The figure reached the Bishop first and Benjamin cried out. The Bishop turned to face the threat just as the figure leapt to tackle him to the ground but when he struck him, he hit him like hitting a tree and he crumpled to the ground at the Bishop's feet, stunned senseless. Benjamin looked down and saw that tendrils of thick roots had grown up through the stonework and had wrapped themselves up and around the form of the Bishop. The figure at his feet groaned and clutched his forehead, blood pouring between his fingers.

Benjamin reached the Bishop and grasped his arm. He was solid as a tree. Gaea, Benjamin knew, still possessed the Bishop. She turned her face to him, sorrow etched in the features of the Bishop.

"You disappoint me, Freamhaigh," she said in the Bishop's voice and he shuddered. "You willingly disobeyed me. Beware. A great unbalancing will now occur and it must occur so that true balance can be achieved. The Tree has not achieved what it promised so long ago."

"Unbalance?" asked Benjamin in disbelief. "*You* caused this unbalance. The Tree has maintained the balance you demanded for centuries! What you have done will cause untold death across this land!"

"Careful," she hissed and her eyes lit with anger. "I know far more than you, and I can see the path that humans would follow and where that will lead. The balance was lost and harmony all but destroyed. That path has been followed before and I did nothing almost to my own end. I will not let that happen again. The Tree has failed and is broken."

"No!" cried Benjamin in horror. "You can't! We have done all that you have asked! We restore the balance as you will!"

Gaea gazed out at him with sadness. "Keep your daughter safe. She is the seed I would now see grow strong. The Cill Darae understands. Ask her," she replied and then she turned her face to stare down at the man still dazed at her feet. She reached down and a bright white light engulfed him. The man looked up with confused, blood-filled eyes, blinked and fell unconscious. The light faded.

At that moment, someone fired a crossbow bolt, and it struck the Bishop's forehead and shattered. Gaea slowly turned her head to stare at the source of the intrusion and watched as a priest was wrestled to the ground by one of the audience. In a moment both were swallowed by the chaos in the room. She turned her attention back to Benjamin.

"You are dismissed, Freamhaigh," she said and then she was gone. The roots wrapped around the Bishop retreated back into the ground like serpents and the Bishop staggered and grabbed the podium. Benjamin steadied him.

The Bishop blinked repeatedly at Benjamin. "Wh–wha," he stammered in confusion. "What happened?" He looked around the chamber and gasped at the mayhem happening all around him. He watched in horror as the King struck down a kneeling woman who screeched out for mercy before the King's sword lopped her head from her body.

Benjamin blinked and finally took in what was happening all around him. *This can't be happening.* Gaea and the Tree had worked together for centuries ensuring the balance of nature was not disrupted by human interference. It was painful work, kept in secret from people, tasked to those few who could feel Gaea and make use of her strength and power.

How could the Tree be broken? It makes no sense. I have to speak to the Cill Darae as Gaea instructed. And at once. My daughter is a seed? What was that about? The lives of all the druids in the Realm are at risk and so many lives are ignorant to the true threat. I have to warn them.

The chaos was already spreading far beyond the Church. He watched as the King strode through the room, his guard in tow, striking at anyone who stood before him. Blood flew through the air like rain. An endless rain of red. People clawed at each other. Guards wrestled with men and women. It was madness. Anarchy. Everything Benjamin had feared.

Benjamin took one look at the Bishop, apologised and ran to find the Cill Darae. He needed answers. He had to fix this.

The image and words of God were still reeling in Seth Farlow's mind as he lay on the ground where the Bishop still stood crying out for Benjamin to return. God had just spoken to him in his mind and he repeated the words to himself so that he would never forget them.

I see you. You seek those who possess that which you do not understand so you may strike them down. These 'magics'. You who profess to know your God's justice. So be it. The Tree is broken. Your justice will be my cleansing.

Seth was confused by the words. Surely God was telling him he approved? Of course, he did. He understood God's justice. He enforced it daily with the Archbishop's blessings. He was God's instrument. The Archbishop had told him many times, and he did not doubt it. Now God had spoken to him and reaffirmed that knowledge. It was all he could ever hope it could be. And God had gifted him!

His contact with God in the library had awakened powers within him and Seth could feel it coursing through his body. He could sense all those around him as if he was physically touching them. They were all the same. Sheep in the field. God's will was clear. He would carry out God's justice with his power. He watched as around him the sheep scurried about and were slaughtered by the King and his guard. Yes, they were all sheep.

Except. *Except for that one.* And he turned and watched the retreating figure of Benjamin as he ran from the Church. *That one is different*, he knew without knowing how. *He possesses magic. He requires justice.*

Seth struggled to stand up but knew at once that his collarbone was shattered on his right side. He grimaced at it, then concentrated and reached for his powers and groaned in pleasure as the sharp bones moved inside his body and sent ripples of pain through him. He pushed the bones together, found the slivers and fused them back to the main and repaired the torn veins and blood paths in his shoulder. He closed the gash on his forehead with a mere thought. It took only a few moments.

He grinned, stood and took a deep breath. God's power was great. The Bishop looked at him in surprise.

"Sir, pray, tell me," he asked him. "What happened here? How is this happening?"

"God's justice," replied Seth and turned and walked confidently out of the Church.

Duilleog

Eighteen

Munsten, 879 A.C.

S EATED BEHIND HIS office desk, Archbishop Greigsen—now Archbishop for a mere two years—looked up in anticipation as his personal assistant and long-time friend, the young priest Ronald, pushed open the double doors and entered without permission. He was Greigsen's friend and lover, and he knew he would want to hear the news of the debate directly from him. As he drew a breath to ask for the results, he realised that the young man was flushed and tears streamed down his face. Then he heard some strange far-off sounds that he couldn't quite understand.

"Your Eminence! Terrible news! Terrible!" The words repeated themselves over and over from his friend and he collapsed at the foot of the desk on the area rug. The sounds of his sobbing echoed loudly in the large room.

Dismayed, the Archbishop rose quickly and rushed around the massive desk to comfort his friend. As much as he loved him, he knew he was terribly emotional, and he had to be handled with a firm hand or else you couldn't get a word out of him. He knew he had to act quickly or he would only get more emotional.

"Ronald! Whatever is the matter? Calm down and stop crying! What news?" As he reached him he grasped him by the shoulders and roughly turned him in order to face him. The man's face was blotchy, and the Archbishop watched in disgust as tears and snot ran freely down the man's face. *No matter the problem*, he thought, *you need to keep up appearances. This man is not fit for anything other than reading prayers in solitude.* He shook the man in desperation to get him to stop sobbing and start answering his questions.

"Speak, Ronald! Speak! There's no time for this nonsense!" Outside the Archbishop could hear that the sounds, whatever they were, were getting louder and closer. He looked quickly at his open doors and thought briefly about rising to secure them. Ronald squealed a little then, and he turned his attention back to the priest.

Ronald was drawing in deep, shuddering breaths, and his eyes were wide and wild. The Archbishop heard a scream somewhere far down the corridors. *The King can't be in danger or the bells would have sounded. Whatever is happening? The debate? Surely not.*

"Ronald! Speak! Answer me!"

"The unthinkable has happened and word is spreading like a sickness throughout the castle!" he sputtered, his voice rising quickly in volume and pitch. "It's too late to contain it. Too late to do anything! The King was there; he's gone mad! He'll come here! What will–"

Smack!

Ronald raised a trembling hand to his cheek where the Archbishop had just struck him. Then he quickly raised his other hand to ward off another slap. Reason seemed to return and Ronald's eyes focused in on the Archbishop.

"My Eminence, I beg forgiveness!" he stammered. "The news, it's all over the castle! The Bishop! He... he... admitted defeat to the heathen! The Bishop, he... he abandoned his Faith! In front of all to see! We all heard his voice! It was like God Himself spoke through him!"

The Archbishop collapsed onto his behind on the rug and released Ronald. His strength drained from him and without knowing, a small whine of fear escaped his lips. The roaring of blood in his ears drowned out whatever Ronald said next. His mind whirled in an attempt to understand what was happening and he started speaking out loud. "This is impossible! The Bishop could not have abandoned his Faith. It's unthinkable. Inconceivable! No, no, you're wrong. I selected Bishop Bengold *myself* after a long prayer session communing with God. He's our brightest academic in theology. Bengold suggested the Great Debate, didn't he?"

Outside in the corridor, a large crash was heard with a scream—loud enough to be heard over the sound of his own heartbeat in his ears—and he stole a glance at his door. Whatever was happening outside was coming closer and distantly the Archbishop knew he should be paying attention instead of sitting on the floor of his office.

"This is Bengold's fault, not mine. Ronald? Right? He assured me that he could disprove the ludicrous concept of there being no God. We spent weeks preparing arguments and counter-arguments. They were solid arguments! The Debate was a simple matter. A chance to finally throw down those heathen representatives of the Word! I *prayed*!"

As the roaring in the ears of the Archbishop subsided, he heard cries and shouts echoing down the Church hallway outside his office. He then heard the unmistakable metallic sound of a sword on sword but dismissed it. *Surely not,* he thought. *Not here in the Church that is not allowed; swords are not permitted past the sacred entrance.*

He heard muffled voices and cries growing louder and then he heard the voice of the King. With a roar his King strode into his office and stopped, standing just inside the entrance looking around for the occupant. The Archbishop looked up at his King and then over to Ronald. They must look the pair lying on the carpet in front of his desk. *I should stand for my liege.*

"What in God's name are you doing sitting on your ass?" yelled the King.

The Archbishop just gawked. He now noticed that the King was clutching his sword tightly in his hand and blood ran down its length to drip to the stone under his feet.

"Your Eminence!" barked the King. "Get up!" The King strode forward with wild eyes and reached out to grab the Archbishop.

Ronald cried out and pitched himself forward to place himself between the Archbishop and the King.

Instinctively, the King impaled the man through his stomach and drove the sword up into his chest. He grabbed the priest's frock by the collar and held him for a moment, growling. Ron twisted his head to look to the Archbishop, and the Archbishop watched as the look of pain and horror in his lover's eyes dulled to nothingness. The King spilled the priest off his sword.

The Archbishop followed the priest's graceless fall to the floor and sat staring transfixed at the dead eyes of the young man lying beside him. *That can't be right,* he thought. *Ronald's okay, he just isn't moving,* was his next thought. *He was just alive. You can't be dead that quick.* He looked searchingly to his King for answers and was shocked to see the insane face that glared back at him.

"Oh, for God's sake! On your feet, man! You're needed!"

"Wh–wha?" stammered the Archbishop. He looked over at Ronald but he still hadn't moved. He had to help him. But he couldn't seem to move his own feet. *My love is dead? That isn't possible. He was just alive. I had been speaking with him.* "Ronald?"

The King reached down and hauled the startled Archbishop to his feet and only let go when he seemed to be able to support his own weight. "Your man, Bengold, he's a traitor to the Church and the Realm! Follow me. We need to put this down at once!" He strode to the door and stopped and looked back at the Archbishop. "Now, your Eminence. We must be decisive!"

What followed next was a blur of events. When they emerged into the gathering chamber of the Church, the Archbishop was startled to find that people from all over the castle had gathered there for guidance. They cried out to him for guidance but he ignored them. He could see bodies everywhere. *Heads were missing from some! Surely this is some jest? Nobody just cuts off people's heads. That's not right.* He thought then of Ronald and pushed aside the notion that he was dead. *He can't be*, he thought with conviction. *Ronald? No.*

The passage here was a nightmare. The King had burst out of the Archbishop's office, trailed closely by his personal guard. His sword was crimson red with blood, leaving a trail along the stone floor. When they entered the hall, the nearby women started screaming in terror and scrambled to move away from the King. A panic almost set in then but the King screamed orders to his men and dozens of guards flooded in from the corridors outside the church and herded the occupants away and restored order amid the crying and screaming. The more unruly were struck down with little thought. *Why were they killing some of them? They're only scared, not a threat...*

The Archbishop gazed around in numb shock. His eyes strayed to the bodies on the floor and he recognised some of them. *The guards are killing people. They are killing people!* He watched as someone moved toward the King only to be struck down by a guard. *That looked too easy. The man had been alive. The sword had gone inside him, but only for a moment. A short moment. Too short to kill him, surely?* But the man cried out and fell and moved no more. *Like Ronald*, he thought. He had to stop this madness! But he didn't know how and he stumbled blindly after the back of the rapidly moving King. The Archbishop could see now that he was surrounded by guards and they herded him into the corridors racing somewhere with the King. Flashes of faces, torches bright in the early evening, guards fighting guards, the crushing sound of voices screaming in anger and pain overwhelmed him and he very nearly lost control of his bladder.

Throughout the chaos, little bits of truth slowly pieced themselves together. Bengold had declared the heathen the victor in the Debate and had removed his robes of office before all who stood witness. The castle had erupted into violence. People supporting the heathens were openly fighting those who retained their Faith. It had spread into Munsten. Hatred for Bengold rose swiftly in the Archbishop and the implications of what was happening continued to be revealed. The King, who ruled and was granted his authority by virtue of God's graces and the Church, was now being threatened from within. The King fought for his crown.

A period later, and he knew not how much time had passed, he stood in the large open courtyard of the castle beside the King. There, kneeling in front of the King, was Bishop Bengold. His clothes were torn on his body and he had been beaten. He was covered in filth and someone had cut his hair and beard from him in anger leaving deep cuts that still bled freely. His head was bowed but there was no mistaking him. The courtyard was filled with yelling and jeering people. They clustered in as close as they could and even sat up on the battlements and roofs of the buildings that surrounded the area. They were screaming for the blood of Bengold.

The Archbishop looked around in wonder. These were his most devout flock in the Church. And now they surrounded him with such anger; thankfully not directed at him. There was fear there, too. He could taste it and smell it. It filled his senses and wiped clear his thoughts. There was a sense that something significant was about to happen and an anticipation filled the air and squeezed out the fear. Perhaps it was a sense of more violence yet to come that was unstoppable, almost destined to occur.

He struggled to understand what he was feeling and seeing. The horror built within him to a point of breaking. He had lost his love. Ronald was gone. His Church was in ruin and it had happened while he was Archbishop. History would record him as the Archbishop who failed the Church. He who had failed God and his King. The weight of this realisation threatened to choke the life from him. He could see no escape. Panic devoured him. The taste of fear and horror of witnessing the senseless deaths narrowed his vision to a small tunnel of light. He fought to free his mind. He shook uncontrollably, and he clutched his head in a silent scream. The pressure built unbearably. *God! Answer me! I need your guidance!* Suddenly, like the breaking of a soap bubble, his thoughts cleared and a profound sense of detachment filled him.

He felt the presence of God all around him. God Himself was watching what was happening in this very Courtyard. *Of course, He was!* All this was meant to be and God's wrath would be swift and violent. That was God's way! He met evil with death! He slew his enemies and blessed those that remained. Death was the doorway to Heaven and the afterlife! The Archbishop looked around at the sheep that surrounded the disgraced Bishop and knew that should God command it, he would righteously strike them all down and find redemption in their blood. An ecstasy splashed through the Archbishop like a cooling breeze and stole his breath away. Such rapture! Everything around him was nothing! Only God mattered! He would strike down all that stood in his way. He would raze the very earth to fulfil God's desire. A loud ringing filled his ears, the hairs all over his body stood up, and an unmistakable erection pushed painfully hard against his underclothes. He was being filled with God's love! Lust and hunger filled him and he arched his back with the intensity of it. He wanted it to last forever. And then, with an almost audible snap, the feeling was gone, and he staggered at the loss.

Despite the loud ringing in his ears, the Archbishop heard a sharp intake of breath near him and glanced over to the source of the sound and spied the heathen Benjamin Erwin standing only a few people away from him. Benjamin was staring at him in alarm. This heathen was the worst kind of evil; he would soon die at his hands. Seth had explained what this man truly was. The secret of the druids. This was God's plan. His purpose was to seek them all out and eradicate them from the earth. To rip the Tree from the earth, roots and all. The Archbishop imagined how he would take this man's life and his excitement returned and he moaned as he ejaculated into his underclothes. The Archbishop wanted this moment to last forever, and he thanked God. Ronald and Benjamin were forgotten, and the Archbishop turned his attention back to the King and the kneeling figure of the Bishop.

Benjamin stared in horror at the Archbishop. He had felt and heard his connection to the earth snap. The man that remained was no longer the man he was before and Benjamin knew what he had become. All creatures on earth were attached to Gaea. *By the Word, all creatures on the earth are Gaea!* And yet the man who was Archbishop had just had that tie severed by Gaea. He was now adrift in the world—separated and no longer protected by her presence. He was *aos'si*, one of the *sluagh sidhe.* He had read of them in the manuscript. Nothing grounded the Archbishop to the earth and Benjamin knew fear. All around him he could sense the people. They were born of Gaea and received sustenance from Gaea. Without that tie, life should not be able to continue. The Archbishop was no longer physically there. Years of sensing everything around him at all times warred with what his eyes were telling him.

He expected the Archbishop to drop lifeless to the ground, but he remained standing with a face flushed red with clearly orgasmic delight. Why Gaea would sever this man from her was beyond his understanding. He sensed only satisfaction from her. His attempts to find the Cill Darae had failed. She had left with his wife and daughter just as she said she would. *No worry*, he thought, *I know where they went. I'll re-join them soon enough.*

The events of the last few hours were muddled. He could look back at the events and see how Gaea had served him up to his role, and he had performed it perfectly well without knowing it. Now he worried for his friend and grieved for the poor man. There was nothing he could do. The mob tasted blood, and they felt that killing the Bishop would correct what had happened.

He could sense the intent of the King and knew nothing could sway the desires of the hundreds of people that now bore witness and craved the outcome. These were the deniers. The last remnants of the Church. Those who refused to believe the words Gaea had spoken through the Bishop. Benjamin could not use his powers to help here. They didn't work that way. His powers were for maintaining the balance. It was also forbidden and sworn in his vow to Gaea. He also knew that Gaea would deny him any attempt to intervene. All the events of the last few hours had pushed him here—to this Courtyard—so that he could bear witness in silence and sorrow. His impotence filled him with shame. The Bishop was a good man. He had an intelligence that was rare these days. And he was doomed. He only hoped his death would be swift and painless.

The King strutted around the poor figure of the Bishop and repeatedly pointed at him with his bloodied sword as he spoke to the crowd. Words of hatred. Accusations of betrayal to the crown and the Realm. All words to stir up the crowd. Benjamin could sense the anger in the King and how much he enjoyed playing to the crowd. Through his ties to Gaea, he could also feel just how much more the King felt. Anger, yes, but deeper than that was a profound fear. A fear that drove the King to commit whatever he felt was necessary to protect his Faith and safeguard his rule of the Kingdom. He saw the Bishop as nothing more than an immediate threat and a means to an end he had not clearly thought through. He would remove that threat and hope to use it to solidify his position. And he would remove it in a way that no one would ever forget. He would make an example out of this man.

The King cried out and demanded oil. The Bishop jerked his head up upon hearing the word and looked around in panic. The King must have told someone of his needs before this assembly, for a gallon barrel of oil, appeared almost immediately. The King grabbed the small wooden keg and brutally slashed at the top, barely missing his own hand. The power of his anger shattered the wood top, and the King hoisted the barrel up in the air and poured the contents over the head of the Bishop. Thick oil poured down the Bishop and Benjamin watched as he tried to wipe the oil off himself. He pleaded directly with the King. His voice was high–pitched and verging on hysterical. He screamed for mercy from the crowd. The crowd roared in approval and the King smiled at the praise.

The King stepped in front of the Bishop and stood with his arms and sword outstretched, turning slowly until he had captured the gaze of the entire audience. The crowd grew quiet and some near the back pushed back to escape. The crowd was now starting to understand that their King had lost his mind. The reality of what was about to happen was too much for most of them.

The King called out and a burning torch was handed to him. A small burning ember dislodged from the torch with the movement and drifted down toward the oil that pooled under the Bishop. The Bishop tried to squirm away from the small ember but the oil caused him to slip and his cries renewed. All who noted its fall watched and a collective exhale occurred when it touched the oil and went out.

The King had missed this minor drama and continued to speak to the audience. Eyes turned to stare at the sight of the King. Few understood his words. They were now the words of a madman. The King had lost his senses and some of the people began to move away from him in fear. Benjamin clearly heard what the King declared: he had just sentenced the Bishop to death for the crime of abandoning his Faith and the Church.

Benjamin was frozen in place watching the insanity of the scene play out in front of him and he thought furiously. The King had struck down and killed his own subjects with abandon. And now he stood there holding the bloody sword and a torch he meant to use to burn a Bishop of the Church to death. He had ordered his own guard to kill his own subjects. The only crimes committed here today were those of the King and select members of his guard.

Thinking of the guard, he glanced over to spy Major Bill Redgrave standing near his senior officers. Bill was one of the few honest members of the King's Guard and by the clench of his jaw, he did not approve of what was happening here and now. *How does one stand up to your sworn King in front of his subjects? Subjects he knows are in a near frenzy?* Benjamin didn't know the answer to that, but he knew suddenly that Bill Redgrave might soon figure something out.

Benjamin watched as the King turned to the recoiling figure soaked in oil in front of him. The Bishop fell to his back and held up his hands in front of him, pleading. Benjamin watched as if from a great distance as the King tossed the torch onto the Bishop. It seemed to fall so slowly, but as surely as a stone falls to the ground when released, the torch fell to land at the feet of the Bishop. It lay sputtering in the oil for a mere second and then with a soft whoosh of sound, the oil ignited and rapidly spread up the prone form of the Bishop and across the puddle of oil on the ground that surrounded him.

The King stepped quickly away from the oil and checked the stone pavement around him for oil that might reach him. The Bishop was screaming in fervour now and beating at the flames. Benjamin could sense that the pain of the fire had not yet touched him. His screams were primal fear alone, and it tore at his heart. The Bishop batted vainly at the flames and ended up spreading them more quickly. It was clear when the first touch of burning pain hit the Bishop. In an instant the Bishop was transformed into a screaming banshee although his scream lasted only for a moment—his voice was torn from him. All watched in horror as the Bishop inhaled to scream again and the flames filled his lungs.

Benjamin could no longer stand apart from the scene. His power called out to him to aid this poor man. He moved quickly and weaved past the guard that protected the perimeter that surrounded the Bishop and King. He had to reach his friend and end his pain.

The Archbishop could not believe what he was seeing. Unabashedly, he stared in fascination as his Bishop was consumed in the flames. If anyone had chanced to turn from the macabre scene to observe the Archbishop, they would have been shocked to see an almost feral and hungry look consuming him. The Archbishop watched in fascination and glee as the man's hair disappeared in a burst of flame and his face erupted red with bursting blisters like pork fat in a fire. God rewarded his witness of the events with strong feelings of orgasmic bliss and he almost fell to his knees in prayer of gratitude. A movement out of the corner of his eyes pulled his vision to watch amazed as Benjamin pushed past the guards that ringed the scene to run to the side of the burning Bishop. The vision of what occurred next would remain forever burned in the eyes of the Archbishop.

The heretic Benjamin strode with purpose through the inferno. All that watched swore later that the flames had not touched him. A few observers thought that it might be that the flames simply needed more than a few seconds to reach him or that he moved too fast. These thoughts also passed through the mind of the Archbishop but he had a unique vantage and could also see that where the heretic placed his feet that the flames were immediately extinguished. It was so visible that the lack of flames marked his passage like dark wet footprints on an oil-covered stone floor. On reaching the Bishop, the heretic bent down and reached through the flames to grasp his shoulder and arm, holding firm to the writhing figure. The Bishop arched his back once more and then fell limp, his cries abandoned as he lay still. It was if the heretic had stolen his life from him.

Still engulfed in the inferno, the heretic remained where he was for a moment and then smoothly rose to stand next to the deceased man. Flames roared all around him and some people screamed in terror. He was the very image of a demon from hell. He lifted his gaze to look around at the mob who surrounded them and locked eyes with the Archbishop. In that instant, the Archbishop was pierced by the combined look of horror and disgust that lay behind those eyes and for a second, he felt his soul exposed as unclean and oily. He squirmed internally to break that stare but could not tear his eyes free—he was trapped and a whimper threatened to break free of his throat and he fought it. The image of the heretic standing in the flames untouched and glaring defiantly at him tore at his fear. He struggled to find his Faith and felt it slip from his grasp. This demon stood there defiantly goading him and he was helpless and afraid. Just as suddenly, the heretic looked away, releasing the Archbishop. He sobbed and fell back a step in relief.

With a cry from Benjamin, the flames roared to a massive height, and the crowd screamed, the Archbishop included, and they turned away in fear. Just as quickly the flames were gone, snuffed out as if they never existed except for the remains of the Bishop that smoked within a puddle of melted body fat and grease. Benjamin turned and strode directly into the crowd. The people hastened to move out of his way and they parted before him like a wave and then closed behind his retreating form. A profound silence filled the courtyard.

After a moment, the King shook his head as if removing a spell and then screamed in a rage. He reached out and grabbed the nearest guard and screaming ordered him to track down Benjamin and then tried to throw him after his Advisor. The scream seemed extraordinarily loud in the silence of the courtyard and many flinched and recoiled. The thrown guard stumbled and fell onto the remains of the Bishop and screaming, rolled off quickly in horror. A couple of guards leapt forward to help drag him clear.

"Leave him!" screamed the King. The Archbishop could see that madness filled his visage and so could the guards nearest him and they stepped back in fright. The King was beyond noticing the reaction of his men and continued shouting orders. "Grab that man! Grab Benjamin! Kill him!"

No one moved; a fear rooted them. The King slashed his sword at the Captain of the King's Guard nearest him and the edge bit deep into his side. Blood sprayed, and the man cried out and collapsed, grabbing at his wounded side. The Archbishop grinned at the sight of more blood.

"Move! Now!" yelled the King once more, swinging his sword and spraying the blood that covered it on all that stood near him. The spell was broken and the senior guard officers started yelling out orders. Many cried out and wiped at the blood that came off the King's sword.

The crowd was starting to look ashamed at one another and avoided eye contact. Their frenzy had been quenched with the flames and now they stood naked for all to see the depravity that lay within them.

The Archbishop watched the men and women scramble to clear the courtyard and several ran off in the direction Benjamin had gone. A couple of men raced to the side of the captain, one of them, the Archbishop noted, was Major Bill Redgrave.

"Archbishop," said the King, and he turned his head to look at him standing there with his sword dripping blood to the stonework. "I am going to clear the land of all heathens. I will not suffer their presence in my Kingdom and under the eyes of God. I will slaughter them all. Men, women and children."

The King, clearly mad, turned and started hacking at the bubbling remains of the Bishop.

Redgrave knelt beside the captain and knew he would not survive the wound. Already the pumping blood slowed and then stopped altogether. Redgrave could stand it no longer. He had watched the Kingdom collapse into complete anarchy over the past few hours—all over the loss of faith of one man. He knew intuitively that it was much more than that—but how could it have led to so much horror?

The memory of seeing the slaughter of so many innocents numbed him. And now a man had just been burned alive in front of a hungry mob. The chaos was wide and spreading with a madness that knew no bounds and it needed to be quelled quickly in order to minimise the loss of life. Hearing the words of the King to the Archbishop had frozen the blood in his veins. He knew, watching the King continue to poke and hack at the corpse of the Bishop, that through the King there remained only madness and more death.

His thoughts returned to a quick conversation he had with Baron John Healy only an hour ago. The Baron recommended a course of action that had appalled him at the time and he had almost arrested the man for treason. But the Baron had always been his friend, supportive of him and his family. They had spoken of this course of action many times in the past but always hypothetically and without real intent.

Now, watching his King hack at a man who had done nothing to deserve his plight, his thoughts turned to the course of action the Baron had recommended. Could he do what needed to be done? Could he rise to the challenge and prove his worth to the Kingdom? More importantly, could he break his oath and then live with himself?

He would need his own men to support him in this and he had spoken to his most trusted men over the past couple of years. He looked around the courtyard and realised with a start that it was his own men, strongly loyal to him, who remained by his side now. Redgrave looked directly into the eyes of his captain, Ran Pawley, and then looked with a purpose at the King and back again. The captain tightened his lips in a line and then nodded once. It was decided. They would act now. He was startled by how quickly the decision had been made and queasiness flooded his belly and a sour taste filled his mouth.

The ringing from the King's sword striking the stone beneath the corpse filled the silence of the almost empty courtyard and it sounded like a death knell to Bill Redgrave. He moved slowly to the King's side and circled him until he was sure he was in the King's line of sight. He did not want to be hit in error with the King's sword.

"Your Highness," he began and placed his hand on the pommel of his sword. His voice caught, and he cleared his throat. He waited until his men moved to surround them both. Bill glanced nervously at the Archbishop who still remained but he did not appear to be interested or following what was happening. The Archbishop was continuing to stare in the direction that Benjamin had wandered off. Bill tore his eyes from the Archbishop and focused on his King.

"Your Highness, please!" he started again and watched with horror as the King looked quickly at him and then away to the shattered corpse at his feet. The King drove his sword into the head of the Bishop and twisted it. Steam rose from the inside as the brain was exposed. Not sure what was causing it—either the look in the King's eyes or the smell rising off the dead man—but Bill had to fight the urge to vomit and swallowed bitter acid. He stood straighter and drew his sword. The steel of the sword rasping inside the scabbard as he drew it caused the King to pause and look over at Bill with a puzzled expression.

"Your Highness," Bill stated with some authority in his voice he did not feel. "I place you under arrest for crimes against your Kingdom."

The King merely stared back at Bill. Bill wasn't certain that he had heard. As he drew a breath to repeat himself, the King screamed and launched himself against him. Bill deflected the King's sword thrust and quickly rapped him on the skull with the pommel of his sword. The King collapsed at his feet. Bill stared at his sword in disbelief—as if it had somehow turned on him. His men stood in their circle unmoving. Bill looked to his captain.

"Ran, take him to the apartment at the top of the tower. See to his comfort. He is still our King. Post two guards. See to it yourself and then gather the King's Guard in the courtyard," he ordered.

Ran nodded once. "And you?" he asked.

"I need to find Baron Healey," he replied after a small hesitation. He was making this up as he went along. "We have a Kingdom to secure and he's the man to lead it."

The captain nodded again and looked down at his King in disgust. "Too bad his older brother died all those years ago. Now he would have been a great King." The captain looked up at his men and started barking orders.

Bill turned to stare at the Archbishop. The Archbishop had seen what happened and did nothing. Bill could not be certain what the Archbishop would do next, so he stood there with his sword in his hand, uncertain what to do. The Archbishop flicked a glance at the guards as they lifted the King to transport him to the tower. The Archbishop looked back at the sword in his hand and seemed to make a decision.

"Baron Healey, you say?" inquired the Archbishop with raised eyebrows.

Bill nodded his reply.

"Then might I accompany you, major?"

Duilleog

Nineteen

Outside Munsten South Gate, 900 A.C.

BRENT WAITED OUTSIDE the southern gate seated high on his horse and watched the men under his command muster beside the road under the vigilant eye of Major Sean Gillespie, his second for the mission. He was Army, and therefore not one of his own. Looking to his left he could see that the King's Road turned from dirt to cobblestones after a mere hundred feet leading up to the gate beside him to the right. This part of the road rose to the wide stone bridge that crossed the river. This river split further upstream and surrounded and made an island out of the city. Beside him rose the massive stone wall that surrounded and defended the city. It stood at least twelve men in height and was complete with parapets and towers placed strategically along the wall to give an unobstructed view of the terrain surrounding the city. All arcs of attack were covered and an assault on the castle would be unimaginably costly for an attacker. A siege could last years and never be truly effective. It was simply the best-defended city in the Realm and home to the Lord Protector and his government of puppets.

The stonework of the wall was thick and well maintained. It was kept clear of any vines or mosses and no tall trees or bushes grew within one hundred feet of the base. The Realm Tax—a more reasonable version of the King's tax from before the Revolution—paid for the city upkeep. The city engineers reported to him on a regular basis on any possible areas or breaches where a significant repair was required. Brent knew it was solid.

Major Gillespie had insisted that they muster here outside the wall instead of outside the barracks and seeing no reason to object, Brent conceded and allowed it. And so it was here on the north side of the bridge between the river and the wall that the men laid out their gear in the shaded, grassy area by the tree line. Late in the day, this whole area would be completely shaded by the high southern wall but it was now only late morning and the entire road leading to the gate was baking in an unforgiving sun. Brent regretted his allowance to muster here. The heat was stifling.

Brent also didn't like the exposure. The south gate was one of the more populated areas leading into the city and today was no exception. People thronged the area, and the noise was deafening. The road was full of laden carts and wagons, horses, sheep, goats and hundreds of people—both rich and poor—all in line and waiting impatiently to be passed through the checkpoints and gain access to the profitable markets and stores. There was an equally busy line of merchants and travellers leaving by the same gate and entry and exit was slowed by the chokepoint. It was slow going and the majority of these people, Brent knew, had all arrived at the gate before the dawn.

Guards were positioned at the bridge and at the gate, all of whom were made up of Army regulars, and they were being absolutely thorough with their duty. Brent caught the glances toward him from the guards and chuckled to himself. The guards were being extra thorough today due to him standing watch over the area. That wasn't completely fair. His brother would never allow contraband to pass into his city and so the guards at the bridge routinely were very thorough in checking the contents of carts and wagons and would only allow one cart at a time over the bridge, in both directions. His brother was known to try to slip a cart or two through the gates to test security. The people in line, with the heat of the day starting to wear thin their patience, and being unable to argue with the guards, took to arguing amongst themselves and the heat and noise of so many raised voices was starting to give Brent a terrible headache. He pinched the bridge of his nose to ease the pain. It didn't help.

Brent looked past his own carts lined up on the side of the road to his men that were assigned to the mission. They were now standing in front of the carts in three straight ranks, more or less at attention, and they were being reminded of their orders and responsibilities for the long road ahead of them. The major spoke in sharp clear tones and it was one of those voices that could pierce the noise that filled the air outside the main gate. He had his captains beside him and the two sergeants were positioned in front of the ranks of men. Civilians passing by the men would shout out jeers and japes and laugh when they were ignored except for the occasional glower by the major.

A troop of young boys was gathered off behind the men and were mimicking the events before them. They were lined up in three rows and one of them was gesticulating to the words of the major. It was quite farcical and was generating quite a bit of attention from the people lined up on the walls of the castle looking down. Another boy of maybe eight years was cheekily throwing small stones at the feet of one of his men and every time he hit a boot it would elicit cheers from those that watched. He was soon joined by another boy who had found the courage once he saw that the men couldn't move from their positions. They took turns tossing the stones and their combined laughter was just more noise in the chaos outside the gate.

The major finished his speech, and he dismissed the men for a kit muster and beckoned the captain over for a quiet word. As the men were dismissed, the two boys throwing rocks ran off squealing in delight, one shouting loudly that he was the winner of whatever contest they had arranged between them. The men turned to gather their kit in the small grassy area behind the carts and as they reached it they started placing their weapons and gear out in precise order on their bedrolls for inspection.

The captain and the sergeants started moving through the men and their horses to examine their gear and tackle, occasionally berating a man for a speck of rust found on their armour or weapons. They studiously ignored the men's leather backpacks, which all bulged oddly beside the gear. Brent smiled, knowing that it would not help for the sergeants to discover the flasks of hard liquor that were likely tucked away inside the packs. Looks of relief passed quickly over the men as they realised they could keep their alcohol. What concerned the sergeants was not alcohol but badly maintained weapons and armour. That could mean life or death for the party and that bore serious scrutiny. The same was true for the horses, and they too were examined, teeth to hooves. The inspection would continue for at least another half an hour and so Brent took the time to examine the area and think about the long road ahead of them.

Brent eyed the small band of beggars that clustered near the bridge but far enough away from the nearby guards to be ignored. The beggars would approach the carts as they slowly paraded toward the city and ask for coin with plaintive voices, each of them providing imaginative reasons for why they were so impoverished and needing the charity. Brent hated them and pitied them at the same time. He could not tell the real beggars from the fakes and there was nothing he could do to help those that truly needed charity. But they were docile enough and clearly knew where the line was drawn between begging and being a nuisance. As he looked them over, nothing stood out to alarm him. Thankfully his men were being intentionally ignored by them and even avoided. He suspected it was the abnormal presence of the men of the Protector's Guard outside the castle, and himself. It was not every day that the General of the Guard was seen on horseback outside the castle. Eyes would flick to him and quickly look away. Their open curiosity was plain to see when they stared too long and secretly shared their wonder; the General of the Guard and his men joined with Army soldiers and travelling south. How strange! Rumours would already be spinning all through the city by now. Brent chuckled. He should start a few rumours himself. Even his own men were looking sideways at him and he knew that they too wondered why he of all people was being tasked to run this errand.

His men now all knew that Redgrave had been found in Jaipers. Whatever the men thought of him being in charge of the mission, they were likely rationalising it as only military men can. Still, he thought, it's never much fun when the big boss is around. This would not be a trip they would enjoy, but Brent truly did not care. He had been there and done that, and now it was their turn. In any event, discipline would be his major's problem and he would keep an intentional distance between himself and the men. Major Gillespie would be the face and voice to the mission; Brent would tell Gillespie what he wanted in private.

It would take them a few months to reach Jaipers and by the time they arrived they would immediately turn around to return by the same long road— provided the gold was indeed there. If not he would need to figure out where it had gone—that could prove impossible. But right now it was already early in the month of Luil, which meant they would likely be returning just before Yule, barring any delays. Over half a year would be gone from his life, and all for a minor errand. Brent grimaced, wondering again why the General of the Guard was being tasked with such a shitty mission. It grated him. And so he growled at no one in particular just to feel better.

As soon as he left his brother's office last night he had hurriedly found Major Gillespie and issued his orders. The major had not been surprised at the orders and Brent fought the desire to interrogate the major on how he knew so much of the mission before the head of the Guard did. But he resisted the impulse, gritted his teeth and simply left the major to deal with all the logistics for the journey. After that, he had seen to his own gear and horses and then found that the entire night had already passed.

He went to his brother one last time and had him grudgingly admit to the authenticity of his claims. Brent would not soon forget the haunted look that had passed over his brother's features. He had years to become used to the revelations, but for his brother, it had all come as a sudden shock. Admiringly, once he accepted the evidence, his brother had quickly become resolved and together they tried to determine a suitable path forward on what to do next and they tried to formulate some kind of crude plan. In the end, they failed. There simply wasn't enough time to deal with it and so they agreed to keep everything quiet for now and wait for Brent to return from the south. They clasped hands and embraced and Brent hurried off to prepare himself to lead his mission to the south and to finalise the details in following the Protector's orders.

Earlier this morning, he went to the Protector's spacious offices and chambers to request an audience in order to discuss the finer details of the mission, but to his feigned surprise, he had been stopped by the Protector's own secretary and deferred to seek the Advisor instead. He expressed his displeasure at the slight, making sure to be heard, stating loudly that a man of his position, as head of the Lord Protector's Guard, had unobstructed access to the Protector, and more importantly he should never be tasked with something so trivial. He hoped he fooled whoever was listening. The smirks from the secretary and later from the Advisor all led him to believe they bought his act of displeasure. Of course, he knew the truth of it all, the game to keep the Protector's involvement at arm's length and to continue his efforts to discredit the Bairstow brothers. And so, he played his part and frowned when required, acted surprised when expected, and when the Advisor finally revealed to him what the true nature of the mission actually was, he gasped in shock and eagerly agreed to be sworn to absolute secrecy. Interestingly, the Advisor confirmed that the gold had been found. The turnaround should be quick and he would be home before Yule. He left the Protector's spacious offices laughing in private.

Brent's horse took that moment to shuffle sideways a step and attempted to lower its head to graze on the grass that grew thick beside the road and Brent quickly jerked the reins back. The horse chuffed and gave up its sly attempt and then, cheekily, turned its head to look back at its rider. Brent ignored his horse. *It has far too much character*, he thought. Then to spite himself he patted the strong neck, and the horse looked away. Brent turned his head to look at the parapet above the gate and quickly spied the unmistakable form of his brother gazing down at him from the heights. There was no need to acknowledge him and he turned to look far down the road. The heat of the day was already rising, and he felt sweat trickle down his back inside his leathers and chain. He, like his men, was dressed simply for the road, but they wore their armour and adornments that marked them as men of the Lord Protector's Guard and the Army of the Realm. There was little chance that they would meet with hostiles on the road, but they were prepared nonetheless. His brother had routine patrols that kept the peace in the Realm and the King's Roads were safe, especially for military men.

Brent reserved some concern about how the two groups of men would get along. Already he could hear the men passing insults between each other and jostling for position within their ranks. The men of the Army were pissed at the task they felt beneath them and the Guardsmen were angry at having to leave the comfort of the castle. This was unheard of, after all, for Guard and Army to mix like this and Brent knew it would be challenging to keep the peace. These men fought each other routinely in pubs. He did not know Major Gillespie, and when his brother had expressed his concern about his nature on hearing his name, Brent knew he was being set up further by the Protector. Gillespie was not one of his brother's trusted men in the Army and the Marshall had intentionally halted any possibility of Gillespie being further promoted on account of acts of misconduct and insubordination.

Brent sighed internally. His own men were not to be trusted either, he knew. The selection of the men had been left to the major, and they were all of a similar ilk. Changing the men at such short notice would expose that he knew far too much and so he had accepted them all without fuss, other than a few simple 'tut-tuts' to the Advisor to express his concern when he had been shown the list of men. He knew this was part of the Protector's design to rush this quickly and place men the Protector trusted into the group. Brent watched as the sergeant from the Army berated a guardsman, questioning whether he knew the front end of a horse from the rear end. Brent eyed the head of his horse and was thankful that his brother had insisted over the years he maintain his horsemanship skills. The Guardsmen would soon be suffering, much to the Army men's humour—and his own, he had to admit.

The men in the Lord Protector's Guard were not equal to the men of the Army. It was like comparing two kinds of fruit. In some ways, the Guard was better than the Army. They were highly trained men specific to a variety of close in weapons and hand-to-hand combat. They were skirmishers trained to fight in narrow corridors and rooms—to protect the Lord Protector even at the expense of their own lives if required. They were sworn to that. What they were not was horsemen, or cavalry, or archers or any of the other skill sets so common to the men in the Army. His men could ride horses—anyone could. No, the problem was fighting on them. That took years of training and his men simply didn't have it. Training to fight on horses was the purview of the Army. The Army men were soldiers first, trained to fight in lines on the field or high on horseback, all while maintaining the discipline of the line of offence or defence. The common saying was that the Guard was water and the Army stone. *An apt analogy*, thought Brent. His job would be to find a way to get them to work together.

And so, after consulting with Gillespie, Brent had ordered the Guard to cart duty. Some would ride but be rotated through on the carts throughout the journey. There would be grumbling from the Army. The cart detail was deemed the sweet spot on the road. It allowed for riding in comfort and was much preferred over sitting on horseback for hours. After a time he would change that rotation, but only after the Guard grew more familiar with working with the horses. Even camp detail would be harsh and foreign to the Guard, except for what they remembered from their earlier days in the Army. All Guardsmen came from the Army ranks. Typically they were the best the Army had to offer—or sometimes the worst, but they were quickly turned out. And the Army regulars hated them for it. Elitist prigs, they called them, or worse. *And there is truth to that*, Brent admitted to himself.

Now it was the Army's chance to shine. Life on the road was a common task for them and they would enjoy watching the discomfort of the Guard. Brent had already warned Gillespie that he would not tolerate any dissension in the ranks. Punishment would be swift and harsh. They had to get along. They had to be as quick as they could on this mission. Their orders were clear—they were to return before the New Year—at all costs.

In truth, he knew there was no need to rush to Jaipers. The garrison in Jaipers was led, his brother told him, by a good and trustworthy man. The coins would be safe until his arrival and Brent should have been afforded the time to properly organise and prepare for this journey. But his orders were made all too clear: he was to be on the move before noon. The major, surprisingly, had them all ready to move well in advance of noon and if the men were angry at the short notice they hid it well, too well in fact. They seemed the opposite, almost eager to get moving. That too did not bode well. Brent felt almost like an outsider to his group. The men in the Guard were not well known to him. They were men from the fringes of the Guard. Not the aggressive kind vying for notice and promotion. *Which is not the norm*, thought Brent. *Guardsmen are all alphas and fighting their way out of the Army to the elite Guard and then fighting their way upward in the ranks was the norm*. These men were different. They kept to themselves and Brent simply didn't trust them. The deck was stacked against him and he knew it.

A shrill whistle blew through the fingers of the major followed by sharp orders to mount up and the men quickly responded, loading their gear into the three carts and mounting their horses. Two guardsmen per cart climbed up onto the bench seats and waited patiently for the order to start the journey. One of the carts, he knew, contained all their rations for the journey to Jaipers. Once there, they would restock and probably clean the town out. One more cart contained their extra equipment, weapons and armour. Blacksmiths in small towns knew nothing of smithing weapons and armour and so they carried their own replacements.

The last cart was for Redgrave's belongings and carried a large, heavy strong box for which only Brent carried the key; a key handed to him by the Advisor in private. With the key came the orders that none knew but himself: Redgrave was suspected to have a significant amount of coin on him and Brent was to oversee its covert and safe return to the castle and hand it over directly to the Accountant. The Advisor informed him it was the money that Redgrave had stolen all those years ago from the Treasury during his acts of treason. Brent feigned a suitably shocked and awed response. The tale was not far from the truth, but the timing was wrong.

Redgrave stole from the Treasury months after the so-called treasonous acts. A strange revenge in hindsight, Brent often thought, but one that obviously meant something to Redgrave. A slow smile crept up on Brent's face. Without that theft, he would never have risen to General of the Guard. Marshall Ran Pawley had disappeared the same time Redgrave was stealing the Treasury. The rage of the Protector had been a sight to see. They had scoured the entire castle and Munsten looking for evidence but all efforts to find Redgrave and the gold had failed. No one thought to look in Brent's residence. If they had, they would have found Redgrave sitting cosily and smugly in his loft with a rather large chest of gold coins beside him.

With Ran gone and the Protector devoid of coin to bribe his people, both Brent and his brother had advanced quickly in their careers. They owed their current rank and positions in the Army and Guard to Redgrave. Redgrave had gloated and admitted to having killed Ran. He described it in excruciating detail that turned Brent's stomach. Ran Pawley had not died well. Bill had also tried to reach the Protector but was forced to abandon the effort. He said he had been too tightly guarded and that he could not kill those who did not deserve to die—and certainly not innocent Guardsmen doing their duty. So the Protector had lived, much to Redgrave's visible dismay.

Redgrave had shown Brent the inside of the chest. It took him hours to remove it from the Protector but when pressed, Redgrave would not explain how he had achieved it.

"This," Redgrave had said, waving an arm over the chest. "Was only a tiny portion of the Protector's stolen wealth. A sizeable portion," he chortled gleefully, "was safely hidden deep within the castle itself."

When pressed, all that Redgrave would say was that he would take this small portion with him, spreading the coins across the land to distract the hunt. Redgrave would keep the Protector searching for years for his gold, never knowing the bulk of it lay beneath his very feet. Seeing Redgrave with a smile on his face was so out of the ordinary that Brent could easily recall it without effort. He smiled at the memory.

Remembering he stood out in the open with eyes on him, Brent wiped the smile from his face. After all, it wouldn't do to be seen grinning like a fool when he was supposed to be pissed off. He adjusted his open-faced helmet and checked that his sword was secured to the saddle in easy reach and waited, looking around again in feigned angry boredom.

Over the years, Brent had almost forgotten Redgrave until unexpectedly, he had received a letter from him with a simple request. He had been looking for a coin with a strange marking on it. Coincidentally, just the day before, one of his officer's presented him with that exact same coin; found when he had taken residence in one of the better chambers in the castle. One owned and left vacant when that Arbor woman had fled the castle following the coup. His man found it lodged in a crack in the mortar in the corner of the room. He thought it peculiar and had given it to Brent out of curiosity. Brent had given him a gold piece in exchange and asked him to keep it quiet. It was a man he could trust, he was certain of that, and he was sure he would keep it quiet. Brent was the godfather to his oldest child after all. He had thought it strange at the time that Redgrave would be searching for the coin so soon after its discovery, but he thought nothing of it at the time and he had simply sent the coin immediately to Redgrave by courier and hadn't thought of it until recent events. He was now starting to wonder if somehow his death was linked to the coin and whether or not his officer had spoken to anyone about it. A second shrill whistle from his major interrupted his thoughts. *Lord, that is annoying*, he thought. *You whistle to dogs and horses, not men.*

Brent watched the major take a quick trot on horseback along the line of men, looking sharply for any last second faults, and finding none, stopped next to next to him and saluted sharply. Brent returned the salute.

"Ready, major?" he asked.

"Sir, aye," was the simple reply from an emotionless face.

"Let's be about it," he ordered, and Brent took one last look over his shoulder at Munsten, and at the castle that loomed high in its centre and wondered if the Protector looked out now. He nodded to his brother, still high on the wall, and then turned and spurred his horse to a slow walk down the road. A sharp order to move out came from the major and behind him his men followed in his wake and he heard the creak and rattle of the carts as the horses took the strain. A tethered train of replacement horses took up the rear. Shouts from his men beside him cleared the people off the road as it spread out before them.

Earlier that morning, shortly after Bairstow had left his outer office in a temper, the Lord Protector John Healy had received Major Gillespie into his inner office and bade him sit. He was settled in behind his desk and looked the man over. He was only one of his many spies in the Army, but he had not truly used him with sensitive issues in the past. Certainly, he had never invited him into his inner office before. But this was a critical matter and would require some direct involvement with the man to make certain he understood the mission.

The major sat confidently and quietly under his gaze. That was a good sign.

"You understand what is at stake here, major?" he asked after a moment.

"Sir," he replied sharply. "Yes, sir."

"Good," he said simply. "Do not disappoint me. Bairstow does not return. I'll have you transferred to the Guard on your return. I suspect a man of your talents will rise quickly in the Guard."

Gillespie nodded and fought to keep the corners of his mouth from turning up into a smile.

"Ensure that none tell the tale of this adventure. Am I understood, major?"

The major openly grinned at the Lord Protector. "Yes, sir," he said. "No witnesses."

An hour after Brent's troop had disappeared over the horizon, a rider hunched over on the back of a piebald horse made his way carefully past the southern gate and was unopposed by the guards. The rider was cloaked despite the heat of the day and nothing about him was exceptional other than it seemed that the various people lined up along the road, waiting to gain entry into the city, failed to notice him as he passed. Their eyes would slide off him without seeing him. If asked, few of the people would have remembered spying him even seconds after his passage. And those that noted his passage kept it to themselves and shuddered, but without knowing why they did so. The only thing people remembered or noticed was that for a moment the air grew chiller despite the heat of the day.

Once the traveller had cleared the gate and the number of travellers on the road had dwindled to nothing, the rider pulled back the cowl of his cloak and stopped his casting, and suddenly appeared with his horse in the bright light of the day. A crow beside the road, pulling with its beak at the rotted meat of a long-deceased rabbit, took flight, cawing loudly in startled fright. The horse shuddered underneath him as the powers that had hidden them both dissipated back into the earth. The rider grinned despite the weariness that now flooded over him and thanked God for his gift. He sat up straighter in his saddle and pulled off his cloak to allow the breeze to dry the sweat that soaked and covered him. He wiped the sweat that beaded his face and looked down the long, empty road. He didn't need to cloak himself so heavily for his power to work but he felt safer knowing should his power fail, he would not be recognisable.

He fumbled for his waterskin tied to his saddle and took a deep draught to quench his thirst. The shaking in his hands would pass as his energy returned to him. Using his powers did not come easily. It caused an indescribable pain to flood him. It always felt like something was tearing deeply inside his body. Pain was something he knew well. It was the cost of doing God's work. Shivering in delight, the rider looked up and down the King's road and satisfied that he had left the city unnoticed, heeled the ribs of his horse with his soft-soled, black boots and the horse responded by breaking into a swift canter.

Seth Farlow rose in the stirrups and let the horse move gently beneath him, quickly putting miles between Munsten and himself as he followed behind General Brent Bairstow.

Duilleog

Epilogue

On the Road to Belger 900 A.C.

I FOUND THAT having a fixed destination in front of me was making my trip that much more enjoyable. In all the years before I had wandered more or less where I wanted never giving too much thought to anything more than where to go the next day or the day after that. I was free to travel from one interesting copse of trees to a particularly engaging outcropping of rocks. Whatever caught my fancy at the time and moment. Truth be told, more often than nought, it was the herbs that pulled me from one place to the next. Now, as I placed one foot in front of the other and slowly paced out and reduced the distance to my goal, I found that each step was eagerly placed before the last. Slowly and surely, the distance behind me stretched and the distance before me dwindled. The journey was exciting to me and this strong sense of purpose drove me like no other time in my past.

After a week on the road, I was approaching the town of Belger. The town was much smaller than Jaipers, its trade focused almost solely on salts brought south from the small mining town of Finnow. Belger was the closest town to Finnow on the river and shamelessly benefitted from it. I had only been in Belger once before and that had been many, many months ago in early winter.

This comforted me knowing it was unlikely anyone would know or remember me after all this time. Keeping my obscurity gave me no small comfort. *It was also true*, I realised, *that they would also remember me passing through.* Not many strangers would or could pass completely unnoticed through small towns; I knew that much of village life. If anyone was looking for me, as Reeve Comlin of Jaipers believed, then I would need to make myself seem as small and as unrecognisable as possible.

But not right now though; the majestic lake before me drew my immediate attention. I had been watching the lake grow in size as I grew closer to Belger. It was a massive lake and I could barely make out the shoreline on the other side. All morning I had been thinking about jumping into that cool water and washing off the dust of the road. As the edge of the lake grew closer, I found myself running toward it in eager anticipation. I only stopped by the edge of the rocky shore in order to drop my backpack, sit on it, and unlace my black boots and tear them off, thankful that I had stopped hiding them under wraps and the gain in time I now enjoyed. Two quick steps and a jump and I was splashing into the water, then wading out deeper until I could lie back with just my head and shoulders floating clear.

The coolness of the water flushed the heat of the noonday from my skin and invigorated me. I whooped in glee before ducking my head under the surface and scrubbing my scalp and hair. Breathless, I stood and tore my clinging clothes off my body and tossed them over to the shore before diving back into the lake and swimming briefly underwater out to the deeper and cooler waters before surfacing with a cry of joy. I rolled over on my back and floated for a time; legs and arms spread and gazed serenely up at the passing wispy clouds high above me.

With a thought, I *reached* out with my powers to take in the nature of the lake. I gently touched the life that swam everywhere I sensed. The lake absolutely teemed with life: fish, insects, and plants swam, lived, and thrived. It was such a rich segment of nature compared to the land and I was amazed at the diversity and complexity of the life that surrounded me. I could *sense* both the fragility of it and the strength. It was a careful balance, and I found that sensing that harmony provided me with extreme satisfaction. I smiled, closed my eyes and revelled in the feeling of harmony. Balance was not what nature was about. It was about this harmony. All life depended on other life and the sustenance the air, water and soil provided. A profound sense of belonging and peace filled me, quickly followed with a joy that filled my heart almost to bursting. My awareness grew, and then with a shock, I realised the life in the lake was growing increasingly aware of me.

It was the fish I noticed which were the more interested in my presence. What small intelligence they possessed became focused on me and the sensation was frightening, to say the least. One moment the fish were all milling about searching for food and trying to survive and then all that no longer mattered. Now nothing mattered but me. As one, they all turned and swam eagerly toward me. At first, I felt fear, but then I sensed that it was their curiosity that drove them toward me and not a wish to do me harm. Just as I started to relax and think not too much about it one of the fish closest to me started brushing up against my body. The slimy feel of a fish rubbing up against you is a disturbing feeling, and I rubbed at where the fish had brushed me. I started treading water and almost panicked at that moment as first another and then many fish started bumping into me harder and harder. As others joined in the surrounding water boiled and I felt myself sinking deeper into the water until I had my head tilted back to keep my mouth and nose clear to breathe. They were starting to impede my swimming, making it impossible to move my arms and legs and stay above water.

"Stop it!" I gargled against the water splashing into my mouth.

I could sense that huge numbers of more fish were swimming eagerly toward me and I struggled to figure out how to stop them. At that moment, a particularly large trout drove into my stomach, bending me over and forcing my face into the water and then I was submerged. Panic threatened to win over reason. I was under the water, with the fish pressed up against me and impeding my attempts to swim upwards. The water churned with silver darting shapes. I thrashed and only barely managed to keep sane by focusing in on my senses that told me that they weren't trying to kill me—they were merely completely focused on me. *That doesn't help me any though, does it?* I thought as I struggled to win my way back to the surface. I tried to step on the fish and use them as a ladder but that did nothing. *I am going to drown here unless I stop this.* I had only been underwater for mere moments, but I felt my lungs already starting to burn. *Help!*

The presence I had felt time and again over the past few weeks returned, and I sensed the surrounding fish react to it. Many of the fish broke away and swam from me and my arms and legs were able to move a little less obstructed but still not enough to let me make my way to the surface and the air I now truly needed. The presence seemed disappointed in me and that made me angry. I focused and with a start I realised that I was the one calling out to the fish. I was doing two things: I was sensing the fish, and I was calling them to me. I could almost visualise my power reaching out like the tendrils of a vine and pulling the fish to my side. My heart was pounding in my chest and my lungs burned for air. I tried to ignore the pain and struggled mentally to control what I was doing. *It wasn't difficult. I just need to focus.* And with that thought, I knew what to do. I severed my call but maintained my awareness, and as I did the fish surrounding me quickly darted away and started searching once more for food as if nothing had happened. I stroked for the surface and the glimmer of sunlight above me and as I burst through, I gasped in huge breaths of air.

I treaded water for a time and enjoyed the ability to breathe unimpeded. "That was stupid, Will Arbor," I said out loud. "You're lucky you didn't just drown yourself."

The presence was gone, and the surrounding harmony continued as if nothing had happened. I was tired now, and I swam for shore and scrambled over the rocks and onto the sunlit grass. I flopped onto my back and waited for the bright sun to dry me off. I dozed for a moment and woke feeling much stronger. I propped myself up on my elbows and looked down at my body and laughed to see myself covered in fish scales stuck to my skin. They glinted with colour in the sun.

"Will you look at that," I said to myself and started laughing.

I jumped back into the lake and scrubbed the scales off my skin and out of my hair until I was reasonably sure and hopeful I had removed them all. I waded ashore and dried myself in the afternoon sun. I looked about and recognised that my location beside the lake was an ideal place to camp for the night. *Belger will still be there on the morrow.* My near drowning and the twist of hunger in my belly convinced me to stay put and relax my journey for a bit.

I rose and scrubbed the sweat out of my clothes and laid them out on rocks to dry. I pulled out another set of clothes from my backpack and soon I was feeling clean and refreshed and rather peaceful. I looked out over the lake and felt a strong desire to have fish for dinner and laughed at the irony. *Justice?* I thought and laughed out loud. I was tempted to call a fish and thought about it but as soon as the idea entered my mind my laughter was cut off and I was overcome by a repulsive horror that staggered me to my knees. I pushed aside the thought, and the horror vanished as quickly as it had arrived. *What in world was that?* Sweat beaded my brow, and I wiped it away.

I got up and sat on a nearby rock and leaned forward, elbows hanging on my knees and head drooped, to calm myself. Okay, that was weird. No using powers that way. For the past week, I had been experimenting with my abilities. Sensing nature and trying to draw strength from the land and trees. It was becoming much easier but until now I had assumed that it was my power to use as I willed. *There were limits, it seemed. Limits I had best start learning. I almost drowned out in that lake and now I almost made myself throw up.* The need to get my hands on the Draoi Manuscript was all too real and fresh now on my mind.

"Soon," I said out loud. "For now a meal of fish—fairly caught!—and a quiet night. Okay?" I wasn't sure who I was speaking to but receiving no answer I turned my attention to my camp and my stomach. I stood and was grateful I felt whole and hale.

I rummaged through my backpack before remembering that my new pack had all those wonderful pockets on the outside and I had stored my fishing line and hook in a small tin in one of those same pockets. I retrieved it and dug up a few worms and found a sturdy branch on the ground. I tied the line to the end of the stick, attached the hook and baited it with a worm and laid myself down on a large boulder that hung out over the water. I dropped my hook into the shaded water where the reeds were, and I was soon rewarded by a twitch on the line and I jerked the hook up. Fish on! I pulled hard on the stick, set the hook, and with practised ease and twitch of the stick, I lofted a shining trout clear of the water and onto the ground behind me. I raced over and scrambled to grab hold of the flopping rather large trout. I yelled in joy as I grabbed hold of it and keeping my senses away from the fish I struck its head on a sharp boulder and killed it. I cleaned and gutted it in the water at the edge of the lake and tossed the entrails out into the lake for the other fish to enjoy. I then built a small, smokeless fire and spit roasted the fish over it.

The last few nights I finally tried making some of the camp cakes that Dempster, my friend and cook from *The Woven Bail Inn* in Jaipers, had taught me. It didn't take long and soon I was savouring my fish, tea, and fluffy pancakes as I lay back and enjoyed the sounds coming off the lake, the occasionally mournful call of the loon sounding longingly over the water.

I spent the rest of the early evening exploring the use of my gift. I reached out to sense the nature around me and was pleasantly surprised to find that very little effort was required. However, the farther out I tried to sense, the less clear it became. I found that I could focus my attention on something specific and I could reach much further that way. I looked up and spotted a duck flying out over the lake and I kept it within the focus of my senses, following it well out over the lake. I found I could continue to sense it well beyond the reach of my vision, although it grew fainter and fainter with my senses until I lost it altogether in the noise of the life that was everywhere. I thought of the Reeve in Jaipers then and tried to sense him but felt nothing in return. So there were limits, I realised, pleased with my efforts. *Limits I needed to better understand.*

Inspired I *reached* out to a robin I sensed hidden high in a nearby tree. It appeared the more complex the life the brighter it seemed to everything around it and to my senses. In Jaipers I had seen the bright myriad of colours that surrounded people. People had stood out like torches in the night: bright and loud and easily noticeable. The rats in the well—I shuddered as I recalled them and the sickness that had plagued Jaipers—were not so bright as people but I could easily see them back then, as opposed to insects and even the motes that had infected people.

The robin in the tree was a semi-bright flare of yellow and green. She stood out from the more muted yellow glow from the tree. All plants were a faded yellow in colour and almost uniform wherever I looked. I called to the bird and watched amazed at how quickly it responded to me and flew down to land on an outstretched finger. I held my hand up and stared in wonder at this wild bird that stood strongly grasping my finger with its talons. She trembled with fright and wanted to fly fast and away, but she had answered my call nonetheless, and amazingly she trusted me. She did not fear me but feared what she did not understand. My call had been irresistible to her, and I felt a small measure of guilt at coercing the poor bird. She cocked first one eye then the other to peer at me and I sensed her growing curiosity. I felt I had to give her some rational explanation for disturbing her and so I took a small piece of my cooked fish and offered it to the bird and watched amused as she eagerly devoured it. Her colours sparked with green.

I sensed all the emotions that went with her eating the morsel. First, she felt curiosity at what I held, and then joy as she recognised it as food, and a spark of hunger followed. I sensed her joy at successfully capturing the food in her beak and the happiness of swallowing it. There was brief contentment quickly replaced with a strong desire for more of the same. All of this I sensed in an instant.

I could see a small amount of intelligence in the eyes of this bird. I felt that I could almost communicate with this bird if I wanted to but knew it would be extremely limited. Perhaps a simple request or direction, but nothing too complex and it would have to be in a way that the bird could understand. In comparison to the fish, the bird was much smarter, but it still wasn't a lot to work with. Her conscious thought was all about food and safety. Finding food and eating it while staying safe. They competed within her and let her take risks but always she fought the instincts. She led such a simple life, and I almost envied her.

Satisfied, I released my call, and she stood on my finger for a moment longer, looking at me with both eyes with a quick twist of her head, before she leapt up and flew off across the lake and toward the setting sun. She fled, no longer remembering the reason but followed the demand of instinct, her small heart beating fast in fright. Instinctively, I reached out and calmed the bird and she slowed at once and spread her wings and turned back to shore and the nest she had built in the nearby tree. I followed her with my eyes and senses and felt her settle in for the night, eyes bright and alert for threats.

I knew then I had to explore this ability more.

The next day, I approached the town of Belger in the late morning. I had slept so peacefully the night before and had continued to sleep even after the sun rose well into the morning sky. By the time I had cleaned up my camp, the morning was fast fading. Belger appeared as I rounded a bend and walked up a small rise in the road. From my vantage point about a half mile out, the town was spread out in front of me and I was pleased that it remained the same as I had remembered it.

The town was nestled on both sides of the river beside the lake. Barges and warehouses littered the shoreline of the town. Boats worked out in the lake, fishing or simply enjoying the water. Belger was much smaller than Jaipers and boasted no walls and hence could not legally hold a garrison from the Baron of Turgany County. With no gates or guards, I simply strode into town. I reached out with my senses and searched for signs of the sickness that had struck Jaipers and I was relieved to find it absent here. I hadn't realised until that moment, but part of me had been concerned that the sickness had escaped Jaipers to spread throughout the country. That didn't seem to be the case and my step felt lighter as I strode through the town. I was struck by how similar Belger was to Jaipers despite the smaller size. The buildings were constructed much the same, and the people looked and talked with the same manner of speech.

I soon found myself standing in the market over by the docks and browsed only with mild curiosity. I had all I required but you never know when something will catch your eye and so I wandered from stall to stall. I watched to see if anyone would remember me, but I was ignored almost completely by the villagers. Only the merchants showed an interest but for nothing more than to make a trade or sell their wares. I was pleased and glad to find that once again the Reeve Comlin had been correct. He had predicted that none would truly notice me or remember me.

I was startled to see an armed and armoured man clink past me and recognised the minnow symbol for Finnow Mines on his breast. The minnow design was unmistakable, I carried a small bag of Life Salt from the mines in my backpack and it bore the same mark. No sooner had I spied the fellow then I noticed more of them milling about the market and streets. I chastised myself for not seeing them right away. I need to be smarter than that. I watched them for a time and saw they were merely shopping like me. With Finnow so close they must frequent Belger. *Finnow Mines must take an interest in the security of the town*, I thought to myself.

At that moment, I spied a large outlet store for Finnow Mines standing proudly at the main corner of the market nearest the docks. The quality of the store was unmistakable. Finnow Mines had money, and they hadn't squandered it on their store in Belger. Their artisan mark stood proudly on the sign outside the shop door and it flashed gold in the sun. Below the sign, in the shade of the veranda stood a guard, alert and eyeing the people who strolled by. Another guard strolled by and nodded to the guard at the door. He disappeared into the building attached to their store and I recognised it as a small barracks that housed probably a dozen guards. Finnow Mines was sparing no expense safeguarding their wares.

I couldn't help myself and made my way over to the store. I had to see inside a shop of this quality. The guard at the door surprised me as I approached by smoothly moving to block my path to the door with a raised arm. He took a long look at me, running his eyes down my frame and cocking an eyebrow as he did so. The slight was intentional, and I grew angry and was about to say something when I saw that the guard had stopped his appraisal and was looking pointedly at my boots. Both eyebrows shot up together this time, and he lowered his arm to let me through as he mumbled an apology.

I murmured quick thanks and stepped up through the door, past the guard, who was now looking at me strangely and entered the shop. At this point, I was no longer certain about my actions and thought of simply walking away, but now I had gained access I was determined to at least enter and quickly look around and then leave. I was also now worried about my boots. The tanner in Jaipers had warned me about exposing them and now I had done just that with someone who clearly recognised them. *Too late now*, I thought and chastised myself.

It was dim in the store and I paused to let my eyes adjust. I heard a rustling behind the counter and watched as the proprietor rose from his seat. He was extremely tall and thin with a large hooked nose. He wore the dark robes of the merchants' guild and the tall pointed hat that went with it. I had only seen a member of that guild once before in Jaipers and that had been a merchant merely passing through from Port West. The guild members usually did not stray from the major cities and his presence here meant that Finnow Mines took this store seriously. He looked down his nose at me with open disdain. *Proprietors in Jaipers would never take that stance with a customer,* I thought and instantly disliked the man.

"May I help you, young man?" he intoned with a surprisingly high voice and I wasn't certain, but I thought I heard a condescending tone that matched the look.

My eyes were now fully adjusted to the light, and I stepped over to the counter and looked closer at him. He had his head tilted back and with his height, he was clearly looking down his nose at me. I felt heat flood my face and became tongue-tied. I didn't know how to respond to this man. I didn't handle confrontations well and so I opted to not answer and looked down to study the counter. The counter was made with a glass top framed expertly in fine woods. The glass was so pure it was like looking through water. Beneath the glass, large slabs of salt nestled in beds of the finest silks. I drew in a breath as I realised the amount of wealth that was displayed beneath my gaze. The price of the counter alone was equal to the cost of a home in Jaipers. But, by the Word, the salt under the glass comprised more wealth than the entire town of Jaipers. My breath and thoughts escaped me.

I was about to turn and leave when I spied the slab of Life Salt. It was a brick that had to weigh about three pounds. I used my sight and examined it and its vibrant golden aura. It pulsed and swam with energy. I couldn't tear my eyes away from it. I heard the proprietor clear his throat.

"I-I..." I stammered, still staring. "That's Life Salt, isn't it?"

"Yes," he replied unimpressed with my deduction.

"M-might I enquire to how much this piece would cost?" I asked quietly.

A silence filled the air and after a second or two I looked up to see the proprietor looking past me to the guard at the door. I glanced over in time to catch the guard pointing at his own boots. I looked back to the proprietor to see him now leaning over to look down at my black boots and I watched as his eyes grew round in surprise.

An expression I did not recognise passed over his features. Just as quickly it was gone, and he wrung his hands in front of him. The change in his demeanour was startling, and I wondered how and why my boots would elicit such a reaction. The warning from the maker of my backpack returned and I felt a stab of fear.

"Sir," he said, "my apologies, I did not recognise you."

My mind whirled at that. *Recognise me? I had never met this man in my life.* I simply stared back at him, completely unsure of what to say. I felt an urge to bolt from the store and keep running until the store and the town were far behind me.

"You wish to inquire as to the price of the Life Salt, yes?" His voice had gone silky and grovelling. The change was startling. At my continued silence, he spoke again. "Normally, the price of Life Salt, especially a piece as pure as this one, would go for the modest sum of twenty crowns per ounce. Precisely measured, of course, using the finest and most accurate scale south of the capital." He paused, and he seemed to be looking more closely at me. His voice was now thick with honey. "The entire block you see here is worth a modest six hundred crowns."

I couldn't help myself and I gasped out loud—the sound harsh in the quiet of the shop. The price was surreal. Dempster, the cook in Jaipers had given me at least one ounce, probably closer to two ounces, of crushed Life Salt. It had been a rare and expensive gift and I hadn't known its value. He had gladly given it to me and I had no way to return that gift. I had used up over half of the salt in my potions in Jaipers. *Those are expensive potions I carry.* My mind reeled, and guilt descended on me. I gripped the counter for support.

"Sir?" he enquired when I did not respond. "Can I interest you in some of the Life Salt? I am sure we can accommodate someone of your position quite handsomely."

I looked up sharply at the man. *Someone of my position?* I thought. *What in the Word was he talking about?* And then it hit me: my boots. They saw only the boots. They knew what the boots represented. *Did they now think me an assassin? Is that what they thought? How is that possible that a man of my stature could be mistaken for a trained assassin?* Nothing made sense.

"Accommodate me?" I repeated with a weak voice, not sure what else to say.

The man looked alarmed, and he looked back to the man at the door and back to me and then wrung his hands more quickly. "Sir, my apologies. No, no, not accommodate. A bad choice of words! I would be pleased, yes, pleased, to provide a donation, a tithe, to you as a token of Finnow Mines' continued respect."

This whole scene was beyond my ken. I had no idea what this man was talking about. His change in demeanour, his way of speaking to me, all rang alarm bells in my head. I reached out with my senses and immediately felt the fear that poured out of the man and the guard behind me. It was so thick I could choke on it. But the fear was not directed at me precisely—that much I could tell. They were afraid of something they felt I represented. These black boots were anathema to these people. *Did they fear some sort of assassins' guild?* I found myself wishing I could know what these men knew. I felt blindfolded. Like I was stumbling around in the dark.

"A donation..." I echoed and wondered what I was being offered. I really wanted to just escape this shop but saw no way out that wouldn't alarm these two men. I was determined to leave here without incident.

The man's eyes lit up with hope and he held up a finger. "Just one moment, kind sir. I'll return in just a moment." And he turned and disappeared through a curtained doorway behind him.

I looked over at the guard and he was now completely blocking the door but still facing me. My first thought was that he was blocking my exit but as he nodded respectably to me I realised that he was blocking anyone from coming in. I heard a murmuring behind the curtain and the sounds of drawers being quickly opened and closed. I reached out with my sight and saw the proprietor with another man standing together in the back room whispering urgently to one another. I didn't know anyone else was in the shop and berated myself for not using my senses to check the entire building. I did so now and felt no one else in the building.

Behind the curtain, I could *sense* that the large drawers that lined the back wall contained large slabs of quarried salt rock. A large machine stood in a corner that presumably was used to crush the salt. My vision was drawn to the large table lay dominant in the centre of the room. It held a large elaborate brass scale with a tray of weights beside it. On one side of the scale were fine black velvet bags. Large glass containers lined the table and contained many hues of fine to roughly crushed salt. The two men leaned their heads together and whispered to one another. The proprietor held the other's upper arm. I *reached* to hear what they were saying.

"I don't understand, Gearold, this is most unexpected!" said the proprietor. He released the man and moved over to one of the glass jars on the table and lifted a small silver measuring cup. He held it up to the light and squinted at it and then blew on it to remove some small contaminant.

"Yes, most unexpected," agreed Gearold. He was clearly the older of the two and carried a slouched posture. I could see that it pained him and I reached and eased his pain somewhat and he seemed to stand a little straighter. I could sense that his spine was bent and twisted, and I felt for him. He rolled his shoulders and reached a hand up to massage his neck with a slight expression of surprise on his face. I smiled to myself. "We already gave our tithe. Just last week, remember Abram? Most unsettling, most unsettling." He sucked air through his teeth and picked up a weight and squinted at it before gently placing it on the scale. He repeated this again and watched the scale pan sink downward.

The proprietor, Abram, scooped a measure of crushed salt from his jar and stepped to the scale. A small black velvet cloth had been placed on the other raised pan and the proprietor moved to empty his measure on to it.

"Careful now, pour carefully!" whispered Gearold, and I watched as Abram gently poured what I could see was Life Salt onto the pan. Light burst and sparked from the falling grains and the salt on the pan shimmered with all the colours of the rainbow. It was beautiful, but I realised with sadness that these poor men had no *sight* like mine and were blind to the beauty. For them, it was a simple mundane task.

"Yes, yes! I know! Now hush, I must concentrate," he replied. As he continued to pour the crushed salt, the scale pan slowly lowered until it matched the level of the pan on the left that carried small weights. Abram stopped pouring and returned the scoop and salt to the jar. Gearold crouched down to squint at the scale and then rose and carefully dipped a pen in ink and wrote in a large ledger on the table.

"Do you think that is enough?" whispered Abram looking from pan to ledger.

"Hmm. Yes, I should think so. More than the last time. That should please them." Gearold placed the pen on the table and lifted a small velvet bag from the table.

Abram nodded and lifted the piece of cloth that the measured salt lay on. Gearold held the small pouch open and Abram carefully poured the Life Salt into it. I watched fascinated again as the aura of the salt sparkled and burst out into the air. It was like watching the embers of a fire burst free into the night; only hundreds erupted up into the air as I watched. The tiny specks of the salt escaped with the air currents and floated upwards, free to light up the air with such beauty that I was mesmerised. Finished, the proprietor cinched the bag shut with the silk drawstrings and knotted it carefully closed. They looked at each other and nodded.

"He appears new to the organisation. Young. Unsure of himself. I don't recognise him." He paused a moment. "Gearold, I'm sorry. I treated him like any other urchin. That worries me. You know how volatile they can be," whispered Abram.

Gearold nodded and placed a hand over Abram's and squeezed. "Yes, we do, don't we." With a shock, I knew his back problem was no accident. *Someone had beaten him. Who could do that to a simple merchant?* "Be nice. Let him know we appreciate their protection. It will be all right."

Abram nodded and moved back to the storefront. I released my sight. The proprietor came through the curtain and hurried with poise to the counter opposite me. He laid the pouch gently on the glass counter and opened his hands on either side of it, presenting it to me. He smiled beneficially. "Sir, I am pleased to offer this generous donation. Please accept on behalf of Finnow Mines." And with that, he stood quietly but continued to smile at me. Fear tugged at the corners of that smile as he fought to maintain it.

I was uncomfortable and felt sick to my stomach. I knew not what to do and so, with few options, I reached out and picked up the pouch and expected him to cry out 'Thief!', but he did nothing. He just continued to smile at me— that strange painful smile. *This man was handing me a pouch full of Life Salt just because I wore these black boots?* This was disturbing. I held the pouch in my hand and hefted it for weight.

"Sir, if I may," he said, "that is six ounces of our finest Life Salt, equal in purity to the prized piece you see here." He gestured to the slab of salt under the glass.

Six ounces, he said. Did I hear that correctly? I held one hundred and twenty crowns worth of Life Salt and he was just giving it to me. The fear was still strong in the room and I could almost now smell it but mixed within it I could now sense a spark of hope. It came from this man and Gearold, now hidden close behind the curtain listening in. *They had hope that I would take the salt and leave them in peace.* They wanted that more than anything and I realised with a sinking feeling that I would have to do just that. And so I nodded once and quickly drew off my backpack and stuffed the pouch on top of my belongings. It felt wrong to treat the salt so roughly, but I had to get out quickly. I felt sick to my stomach. I felt very much a thief at that moment and guilt struck me in waves. I struggled internally to find justification for taking the salt. I thought of Daukyns and with a sudden insight, I promised myself to make potions from the salt and hand them over to the first man of the Word I found. That promise invigorated me and I hoisted the backpack onto my shoulders.

"Thank you," I said simply and nodded once and started toward the door. The guard moved quickly out of my way and I almost bolted right then at his sudden movement. I forced myself to stop at the door and looked back. Beads of sweat dripped from the brow of the proprietor and still, that same smile remained frozen on his face. He licked his dry lips.

"Sir, please pass on our deepest respect to His Holiness," he said and bowed deeply.

I hid my astonishment, nodded again and quickly left the shop and emerged out into the bright sunlight of the morning day. *His Holiness?* Bile rose in my throat. The black shoes and the assassin were linked to the Church? The need to run almost overtook my common sense. I looked around frantically and expected to see all eyes turned toward me. Of course, no one even so much as glanced at me. I breathed out a deep breath when I saw that the guards that roamed the market took no notice of me and with an effort I walked out of the market and left town as quickly as I could, looking behind me as often as I could to see if I was being followed. The sensation of eyes on me grew stronger and my fear kept me moving quickly.

Once clear of the town, I ran down the road as fast as I could and then turned off to hide in the bushes under a large group of trees. I expanded my senses and searched for anyone following me out of the town. I ripped the boots off my feet and stared at them with new insight. These belonged to very bad people. They marked them as belonging to the Church of the New Order. Men that extorted merchants, punished them and even killed for the church. I felt exposed and vulnerable. My quest to reach Jergen seemed that much more important to me.

One thing is certain, I need to be more careful and more invisible. I wrapped my feet in rags and grimaced at the old feeling. I had grown so used to having boots and the feel and speed they gave me over the ground. I would need to buy boots in Laketown, the next town downriver. I could afford them and had herbs to sell. As I held the boots in my hands I was certain that I could never wear them again. I tucked them into the bottom of my backpack and tried not to think of them.

I remained stationary and hidden and *reached* out with my senses to try to discover if I was being followed. After an hour of sensing nothing, I finally composed myself and returned to the road. Laketown was a few days away, but I felt I could reach it sometime the day after tomorrow if I pushed hard and I was determined to do just that. I had to get Belger and the salt shop behind me.

The fear of being watched was still strong and the urge to run kept trying to push me from behind. I tried to rationalise the involvement of the Church in all this and failed. It made no sense to me. I had never encountered the Church of the New Order. The little I knew of the Church was their loss at the Great Debate and that the Archbishop resided in Munsten. They had no presence out west in Turgany, but Daukyns had told me they were experiencing a surge in popularity. He had word that small churches were appearing in the larger towns and small cities across Belkin. The Word had little interest in the Church but I could sense that Daukyns had been alarmed for some reason. It was all beyond my ken. *Certainly, nothing that should concern me,* I thought.

I determined that I would need to send a note to Reeve Comlin in Jaipers. He had to know that the Church was behind the murder of Bill Burstone. Perhaps he could make sense of it. A warning was the least I could do.

End of Volume One

Duilleog

The New Druids Series continues with:

Craobh: A New Druids Novel (Volume Two)

By Donald D. Allan

Duilleog

Acknowledgements

Washington, DC, June 2015

WHEN I WAS in the fourth grade, at the General Vanier Public School in Ottawa, Canada, my teacher sent me home with a note for my mother. In it, she complained that I was spending too much time in the library reading. My mother laughed and ignored it. I know why the teacher complained. The problem was that I used to sneak off to the library ALL the time. At the expense of everything else. Nothing else mattered.

Today, I still prefer the written word over pretty much every other kind of entertainment or media source. It is my escape from the harsh realities of life and reading lets me explore all the worlds that can be imagined. I'm proud to say my children read and love it almost as much as I do. If I have a legacy to leave behind, it is this: my children love to read. That puts a smile on my face.

I've been trying to write a novel since fourth grade. Or I should say I've wanted to write a novel. It's hard. It's hard because there is so much more to a story than just the story you've just read. I've had to build an entire world in my head and then tell a story from it. In doing so, I've accidentally written two other stories. They come next.

So, my acknowledgements:

I must first acknowledge my family. My wife, Marilyn, my son, James and my daughter, Katherine. They supported me like no one else during all my writing attempts. My life is so positive and filled with joy because of their love. I do my best to be a husband and loving father—it's not easy and I am probably not doing it well, but I try so very hard all the time. It's all I have to offer you in return: my love and my effort.

I also must acknowledge my mom and dad, Senga and Hector, who immigrated to Canada from Scotland in the early 60s. My mom passed away just recently, and I had so wanted her to see this work. I missed that opportunity, and that saddens me. I miss my mother.

On writing this book I was assisted by many people. They took the time to read it, provide feedback, and correct my many errors. Special thanks go out to my wife Marilyn, my sister Heather, my best friend Gord, and my "Aunt" Emmy for providing constructive criticism and praise when I needed it most.

Ottawa, Canada, April 2019

Duilleog is now in its fourth edition. With the help of beta readers for later novels I have corrected a great many typos from the first edition. Recently, I hired JD&J Book Cover Designs to redo the cover for the novel and I am very pleased with the results. I want to thank the readers of my series for staying with my little world and supporting my art. This is a work of love. I hope you enjoy the New Druids series.

World Details

Ranks and Hierarchies

Draoi (Druid) Ranks:
Freamhaigh (Root) – Head Druid
Cill Dara(e) – Druid Priest/Priestess (The Elevated Druid)
Stoc (Trunk) or informally just Draoi – Full Druid
Craobh (Branch) – Journeyman Druid
Duilleog (Leaf) – Apprentice Druid

The Church of the New Order Ranks:
King (in abeyance since Revolution)
Archbishop (acting head of the Church)
Bishop
Dean
Vicar

Army of the Realm Ranks:
Officers:
> Knight General (former rank from before the Revolution)
> General
> Brigadier
> Colonel
> Lieutenant Colonel
> Major
> Captain
> Lieutenant
> Second Lieutenant

Enlisted:
> Warrant Officer
> Staff Sergeant
> Sergeant
> Corporal
> Lance Corporal (appointment, not a rank)
> Private
> Recruit

Lord Protector's Guard Ranks:
The highest-ranking officer is General. Because the Lord Protector's Guard is a speciality occupation, the members come from the Army of the Realm, and occasionally from the Navy of the Realm. They share the same rank structure except that the lowest

officer rank is Captain and the lowest enlisted rank is Corporal; those being the earliest rank you can be selected or request service in the Lord Protector's Guard.

Navy of the Realm Ranks:
Officers:

    Fleet Admiral

    Admiral

    Commodore

    Captain (Navy)

    Commander

    Lieutenant-Commander

    Lieutenant (Navy)

    Ensign

    Midshipman

Enlisted:

    Chief Petty Officer

    Petty Officer

    Master Seaman

    Leading Seaman

    Able Seaman

    Ordinary Seaman

It should be noted that the General of the Realm is the head of the Army, the Navy, and the Lord Protector's Guard. The Lord Protector's Guard recruits from the Army of the Realm, and rarely, from the Navy. The Navy's top rank, the Fleet Admiral, is not equal to the General. In this world, the Navy is not the senior service.

Calendar and Seasons

The calendar is in the background of the world and not specifically referenced except where it occurs accidentally. We don't dwell on the calendar and neither do the folks in Turgany. In this world, the Celtic names for things have slipped and are rarely used. The common language is English.

Seasons:

Winter (Geimhreadh) – December, January, February (Nollaig, Eanair, Feabhra)

Spring (Earrach) – March, April, May (Marta, Aibrean, Bealtaine)

Summer (Samhraidh) – June, July, August (Meitheamh, Luil, Lunasa)

Autumn (Fomhar) – September, October, November (Mean Fomhair, Deirreadh Fomhair, Samhain)

Time Frames:

Day – dia

Night – nocht
Week – 8 days and nights—deug
Fortnight – 15 days and nights – cola-deug
Month – mios

Days of the Week:
Sunday – Domhnaich
Monday—Luain
Tuesday—Mairt
Wednesday—Ciadain
Pluday (Extra)—Durdaoin
Thursday—Ardaoin
Friday—Aoine
Saturday—Sathurna

Breakdown of a Year:
365 days in a calendar year for which only 360 are provided actual dates. The extra five days per year (see Solstices/Equinoxes) are used as celebration days and are known by their title rather than as a calendar date. It works like this: there is a December 24th, followed by Yule, which is then followed by December 25th.
24 fortnights (24x15 days) per year
45 weeks per year
3 weeks and 6 days per month (totalling 30 days per month)

Solstices (longest/shortest day of the year)/Equinoxes:
Vernal Equinox is the day after March 19th (or Marta 19) and is celebrated for 1 day as Ostara Day (non-calendar day).
Estival Solstice (summer) is the day after June 20th (or Meitheamh 20) and is celebrated for 1 day as Litha Day (non-calendar day)
Autumnal Equinox is the day after September 21st (or Mean Fomhair 21) and is celebrated for 2 days as First Mabon Day (harvest) and Last Mabon Day (feast) (non-calendar days).
Hibernal Solstice (winter) is the day after December 20 (or Nollaig 20) and is celebrated for 1 day as Yule (non-calendar day).

Holidays:
Samhain. Nov 7 (Samhain 7). The midpoint between Autumn Equinox and Winter Solstice. Celebrates the last harvest, the cycle of life and gifts for passing spirits. Preparation to survive winter, confront the possibility of death. Colours: black, brown, reds, oranges. Opposite to Bealtaine.
Yule is the day after December 20 (Nollaig 20) and is a non-calendar day. Shortest day and longest night of the year. Celebrates the end of darkness, the return of light to the

Duilleog

earth. Herbs are at their least potent. Colours: green, red, white, silver, gold.

Imbolc. Feb 1 (Feabhra 1). The midpoint between Winter Solstice and Spring Equinox. Celebrates the quickening of spring, the end of winter, time of planning and hopes. Colours: red, orange, white.

Ostara Day is the day after March 19 (Marta 19) and is a non-calendar day. The first day of spring, the night and day stand equal. Celebrates the birth of spring, rebirth. Time of planting. Colours: red and yellow.

Bealtaine. May 6 (Bealtaine 6). The midpoint between Spring Equinox and Summer Solstice. Time of rebirth. Colours: blue, pink, yellow, green. Opposite to Samhain.

Litha Day is the day after June 20 (Meitheamh 20) and is a non-calendar day. Summer solstice, the first day of summer, longest day of the year. Celebrates the light and the sun without there would be no life. Time of strengths and accomplishments. Gather herbs as "herb night" is when they are at their most potent. Colours: blue, yellow, green.

Lammas. Aug 1 (Lunasa 1). The midpoint between Summer Solstice and the Autumn Equinox. First harvest festival. Celebrates the beginning of harvest season, the decline of summer to winter. Time to dismiss regrets, farewells, preparation for winter. Ceremonies involve bread, grains and corn dolls. Colours: oranges, greens, browns.

Mabon Days are the two days after September 21st (Mean Fomhair 21) and they are non-calendar days. Referred to as *First Mabon* and *Last Mabon*. Autumn Equinox, the first day of autumn. Celebrates harvest. First Mabon is harvesting time and Last Mabon is the feast. Time for thanks and learning, repairing all things. Colours: dark reds, yellows, browns.

Important Calendar Dates Summary:
February 1 (Feabhra 1)—Imbolc
March (Marta)—Ostara Day (Vernal Equinox) is the day after March 19th
May 6 (Bealtaine 6)—Bealtaine
June (Meitheamh)—Litha Day (Estival Solstice (summer)) is the day after June 20th
August 1 (Lunasa 1)—Lammas
September (Mean Fomhair)—First/Last Mabon Days (Autumnal Equinox) is the two days after September 21st
November 7 (Samhain 7)—Samhain
December (Nollaig)—Yule (Hibernal Solstice (winter)) is the day after December 20th

Currency

1 crown (large round gold coin) = 36 groats = 144 pence
1 half-crown (large round gold coin with a centre hole) = 18 groats = 72 pence
1 mark (small gold coin) = 9 groats = 36 pence
1 groat (silver rectangular coin) = 4 pence
1 tuppence (a small silver coin or large copper coin) = 2 pence
1 pence (copper coin) = 1 pence
1 half-pence (copper coin with a centre hole) = 1/2 pence

1 farthing (small rectangular copper coin) = 1/4 pence

Coins are measured by known weights under the Turgany Weights and Measures Act. For example, a full crown must weigh one royal ounce (28 gramme). A half-crown weighs a half ounce (14 gramme). And a mark weighs a quarter ounce (7 gramme) which means it is heavier than a Canadian quarter (25 cent piece) but sized about the same. A groat weighs the same as a mark (but is larger), and a tuppence weighs half that of a groat (hence if it is made of copper it will be larger). Typically, wealthy merchants will carry coin scales to verify that they are not being cheated with counterfeit coins. The habit of biting a gold coin was to prove that it was indeed gold—which is soft—and not some impostor.

Seven Tenets of Morality

1. Strive to act with compassion and empathy toward all creatures in accordance with reason.
2. The struggle for justice is an ongoing and necessary pursuit that should prevail over laws and institutions.
3. One's body is inviolable, subject to one's own will alone.
4. The freedoms of others should be respected, including the freedom to offend. To wilfully and unjustly encroach upon the freedoms of another is to forgo your own.
5. Beliefs should conform to our best scientific understanding of the world. We should take care never to distort scientific facts to fit our beliefs.
6. People are fallible. If we make a mistake, we should do our best to rectify it and resolve any harm that may have been caused.
7. Every tenet is a guiding principle designed to inspire nobility in action and thought. The spirit of compassion, wisdom, and justice should always prevail over the written or spoken word.

Duilleog

About the Author

DONALD D. ALLAN is a Canadian author of fantasy and science fiction and a retired senior Royal Canadian Navy officer.

He is the GOLD medal winner of the Dan Poynter's Global eBook Awards 2016 for the category Fantasy/Other Worlds for his debut novel Duilleog, the first novel in his New Druids series. The second novel, Craobh, won the BRONZE medal in the same category in 2017 and Stoc won GOLD in 2018.

Donald lives with his wife Marilyn, son James, daughter Katherine, and dog Woody, in Ottawa, Canada.

Connect with Donald D. Allan:

BLOG: http://donalddallan.com
FACEBOOK: https://www.facebook.com/donalddallan
TWITTER: https://twitter.com/donalddallan/
EMAIL: donalddallan@gmail.com